A DEEPER
LOVE INSIDE

Also by Sister Souljah

The Coldest Winter Ever

Life After Death: The Coldest Winter Ever II

Midnight: A Gangster Love Story

Midnight and The Meaning of Love

A Moment of Silence: Midnight III

No Disrespect

A DEEPER LOVE INSIDE

THE PORSCHE SANTIAGA STORY

SISTER SOULJAH

EMILY BESTLER BOOKS

———

ATRIA

New York   London   Toronto   Sydney   New Delhi

EMILY
BESTLER
BOOKS

ATRIA

An Imprint of Simon & Schuster, Inc.
1230 Avenue of the Americas
New York, NY 10020

First Emily Bestler Books / Atria Paperback edition February 2014

EMILY BESTLER BOOKS/ATRIA PAPERBACK and colophon are trademarks of Simon & Schuster, Inc.

For information about special discounts for bulk purchases, please contact Simon & Schuster Special Sales at 1-866-506-1949 or business@simonandschuster.com.

Book cover photographer: **Mike Lay-Low**, contact mikestrongandtrue@gmail.com
Book cover model: **Sandra Segura**, contact spsegura13@yahoo.com
Dress design by Arlinda M of Sofistafunk, The Skirt Company, contact arlinda.mcintosh@gmail.com
All Sandra Segura photography is by Mike Lay-Low, sneakers by Converse, courtesy of Nike.
Interior model is **Jada Brielle Demerey**. Photographer: **Mike Rich**, contact mikerich100@gmail.com

Manufactured in the United States of America

25   27   29   30   28   26

The Library of Congress has cataloged the hardcover edition as follows:

Souljah, Sister.
A deeper love inside / by Sister Souljah. —1st Emily Bestler Books/Atria Books hardcover ed.
p.   cm.
1. African American women—New York (State)—New York—Fiction.   2. Inner cities—New York (State)—New York—Fiction.   3. Brooklyn (New York, N.Y.)—Fiction.   I. Title.
PS3569.O7374D44   2012
813'.54—dc23   2012029222

ISBN 978-1-4391-6531-7
ISBN 978-1-4391-6532-4 (pbk)
ISBN 978-1-4391-6534-8 (ebook)

DEDICATION

To all of the children and young ones who feel unloved, unprotected, without guidance, or who have been abandoned. If no adult has ever apologized to you, please allow me to be the first.

To all of the real-life "Winters" who believed in something false and the real-life Porsches', Lexus', and Mercedes' snatched up by social services and trapped in group homes or foster care or who have become parts of families with whom they share no blood relation.

I apologize not out of pity for you, but out of pure love—the ingredients that each of you needed in the first place.

Remember that whatever your circumstances, you are still responsible for yourself and your choices. You may be young, but you are not powerless. Speak up, speak out, read, study, learn, build, and resist injustice.

Above all of the hurt, pain, and corruption there is still a MAKER of your soul to whom you can direct your prayers and seek guidance. No matter what others may do, make sure you do what is right and true. Have faith! All of your faithful efforts, discipline, and hard work will be rewarded.

Chapter 1

Not every bitch is a queen. Most chicks are just regular. Most of them know it and accept it, as long as nobody points it out. A queen is authentic, not because she says so, just because she is. A queen doesn't have to say nothing. Everybody can see it, and feel it, too.

A bunch of bootleg girls been try'na come up. That's what they supposed to try and do. But their borrowed, stolen style sucks cause it's borrowed and stolen. A queen knows who she is, inside and out. She wouldn't imitate anybody else. In fact, she creates original styles, waits for the bootleg bitches to catch on and copy, then switches, making their heads spin, eyes roll, and their short money pile disappear.

I'ma tell you what I hate first. Then Im'ma tell you what I love. Every word that I say is straight, cause I don't have no time to play with you. The majority of my time is spent stacking my status and plotting to get back my stuff.

I hate conceited girls. They're played out. You may think that I'm one of them, but there's a difference between conceit and quality, or should I say conceit and truth. Matter of fact, some of the ugliest females I know are conceited. We living at a point where this shit is all mixed up on purpose. The ugly ones pretend they look good, when everything they got is cheap and fake, including their personalities. The pretty ones play themselves down, cause jealousy is more realer than the air we suck in and blow back out. I, Porsche L. Santiaga, am a real, *real pretty bitch*. I try my best to stay in my lane and mind my own business, to keep all the envious ones from talking shit, mobbing up and jumping me.

It isn't easy being the sister of a queen. Naturally, I look up to her.

But still, I gotta be me. Imitation gets no respect. I would never live my life trying to look like or be someone else. Regarding my sister, Winter Santiaga, every day for eight years I had my big brown eyes trained on her. She's a queen, not because she's beautiful, which is automatic, not because she's a badass, with endless styles and personality, not because she's my older sister, my mother's best friend, and my father's most loved jewel. None of those are the reasons.

Ricky Santiaga has four daughters. His firstborn, Winter, seemed to have occupied his whole heart. My handsome father was not to blame. Everyone loved her. When she was in a crowded room, everyone was looking her way or trying to stand or sit right beside her. Even in our home she soaked up all the love, as though she were the only child. But she wasn't the only child.

Me, I'm the "middle daughter." Maybe you know a little something about how that goes. Everyone's eyes were either on the oldest daughter, because her young figure was ripe and ready, her eyes so mischievous, and her face so feminine and perfect that they were all scared she might get pregnant. Or, their eyes would be on the youngest, because they are the babies and they might get hurt.

The middle girl is too young to be fucking and too old to be falling down. So everyone forgets where she is and what she's doing. I got mixed feelings about being invisible. There are benefits. I can't lie. But sometimes, quietly, I was yearning for Poppa and Momma to pay more attention to me simply because their love for me was as true and as strong as my love for each of them. I didn't want to have to beg them for love. I didn't like the idea of having to be annoying to get attention or having to make a dramatic or phony scene. I hate pretense.

Winter was a queen in my younger eyes because she didn't have to ask for love, but she was always receiving it. When she did receive it, no one cared if she returned it. They loved her whether she loved them or not. She didn't seek attention. She commanded it. Winter had the best of everything without working or obeying. Her friends, who were coming and calling constantly, surrounded my sister. Even my young friends wanted to grow up to be Winter. My old aunties wish they could be young again only to try to look and live like Winter.

More than that, in my younger eyes, Winter was above pain and punishment and mostly no one else in the world can claim that. In the chaos of any crisis she walked in looking good, stylish, clean, and untouched. She'd shift her pretty eyes right and then to the left and come up with the swiftest plan, which only she knew the details of.

I was home when they arrested my father. Winter wasn't. I was left at home when they arrested my mother. Winter wasn't. I was home when the kidnappers, "social services," snatched up me, Lexy, and Mercedes. Winter wasn't. We three sisters were separated and trapped in the system. Winter wasn't.

In fact, Winter and Momma came to check me one time at a "state-supervised visit," where I was being held and watched over by the kidnappers. When they walked in, my beautiful momma's head was shaved bald. Shocked for some seconds, I still wanted to hug her and have her hug me back tight enough to signal to me silently that she knew that this shit was all wrong. That she would take me back home with her.

Momma's eyes were filled with rage and sorrow. Winter looked rich. She was sparkling and free, like she had a thousand little light-bulbs outlining her entire body. Her caramel-colored skin was glowing. Her hair was fresh, soft, long, and second only to her pretty face. She looked unbreakable, untouched, and unaffected. Then it was confirmed in my eyes on that exact day, that Winter was straight royalty, above everyone else who suffered on a regular, including now my momma and me. That so-called visit was the first time I saw my mother and sister after being tooken, and the last time I saw both of them together ever again.

I miss Momma so much I ache, like when you have vomited to the end and there's nothing else to throw up. Only a thick yellow fluid comes out, that one nurse said is called *bile*. Have you ever been in the emergency room strapped to a bed, screaming out "Momma" 156 times, "Poppa" seventy-seven times, and "I want to go home" thirty-three times?

As for Poppa, six one, light-skinned, strong, and suave with not even a teaspoon of bitch in him, no man on earth is better than him. Momma is like a cup of hot chocolate on a freezing morning. Poppa is like a cup of black tea with a whole lot of heavy cream mixed in. Dark and light, they complemented one another.

Winter was the best parts of both of them, all in one. I love her, and fuck anybody else who doesn't, no matter his or her reason.

Listen when I tell you, I am 100 percent loyalty. If you can count, you'd know that there's nothing left over from that.

Unique, I know I'm different from her, but we sisters. We're full blood related. So I'm royal. I inherited these looks. Like Winter and Momma, my beauty is undeniable, captivating, and offensive to many. No, I'm not light-skinned. Stop that silly shit, as if there is only one shade to be deeply admired. I'm honey-brown like an expensive Godiva that can only be purchased in a specialty shop. My brown-gold eyes are outlined with a thin black line that circles around the pupil, like an exotic bird. When people first notice them, they pause and look again.

Every day I fight. Not because of anything I did, just because of who I am naturally. I fight young angry bitches cause they wish they had these same eyes and can't get comfortable until they poke mines out. My skin is flawless like satin, or an unaffordable diamond. I'm a dancer, not a stuck-up ballerina or a fucking stripper. Back on our Bedford-Stuyvesant, Brooklyn, block I had an all-girls dance crew. We used to rock. We even won first place at our block party over some girls that was older than us. People were amazed at how our young bodies could bend and move, flow, bounce, and shake like we knew shit we couldn't possibly have known, and experienced shit that none of us had experienced yet. We tore it up, moving to a Rob Base throw-back titled "It Takes Two." That night, Momma placed her hands on my hips and said I would grow up to be her "moneymaker." I liked the feeling that I was doing something that made Momma look my way for more than a few moments, and believe in me.

My hair is black. It grew from my own scalp and lays on my back. Momma says it's long because I'm loved. She says, "Other bitches don't know or don't want to keep their daughter's hair clean, oiled, combed, conditioned, and clipped." Back then Momma would say, "If you see a bald bitch she's unloved. Or, she cut her hair off because she don't want to be loved. Or, she cut it off because she ran up on some rotten love."

Me, I know mine is real nice, but I don't worship my hair. I keep it neat and never throw it in nobody's face. Apparently that ain't enough.

In a two-year stretch, I had seventeen fights. Nine of them were brawls *over hair*, with half-bald bitches with homemade weapons. I fought a conceited ugly girl named Cha-Cha four out of the nine hair fights. In arts 'n crafts class, I grabbed the one pair of scissors shared by twenty girls and chained to the desktop, and cut off my hair and gave it to her, so she could stop fucking sweating me. She wore my hair braided into single box braids on her head the next day.

I didn't say anything to her. I had gotten comfortable with my short cut overnight. Then she got mad cause I wasn't mad. So she fought me again. The authorities, that's what we call them, they locked me up in isolation for fighting. *Every time* they act like they don't know what the fight is all about. *Every time* they act like we fifty/fifty involved in the fight when they know damn well that chick hates herself and is gonna fight till somebody kills her and puts her out of misery.

Even with my wrists locked and my ankles chained, headed to isolation, I don't react. They release me into that little space butt-naked. Then I dance. Repetition makes my legs beautiful, strong, and tight. I don't eat, so I don't have no body fat. I taught myself to accept hunger, cause people try to use it against you when they think they got something you really need, even if it's only a sandwich. I dance until I'm drenched. The music plays in my head, sounding crisp like it did back in Brooklyn. I stop when I collapse. Then, I wake up in another wing with a tube in my arm and a bad-breath nurse faking concern and whispering something like, "You could've died last night." I close my eyes and wish I had enough fluids in my mouth to spit on her, just to clear my throat.

When they would bring me back into the population mix with the rest of the bitches, 522 of them to be exact, I'd see most of the girls from my section gasp like they seen a ghost. I know certain ones of them won't be happy until they slit my perfect skin open, or at least put a permanent stamp on it. That's why I plot.

In one of the monthly head sessions they make us have, one of my enemies told the therapist that she fights me because I think I'm better. I told her she fights me because *she thinks I'm better*. These regular bitches don't get it. It's not my hair or eyes or legs or none of that bullshit that makes me who I am, plain and simple. It's that

I'm Porsche L. Santiaga, born rich. My daddy was rich. My momma was rich. My sisters were rich. I'm not gonna act like a regular bitch when I was born royal. They never had nothing, so they don't know no better. They got nothing to miss. I had a queen-sized bed when I was seven years old. Even before then, back in Brooklyn at my sister's sixteenth birthday celebration at Moe's, in the dead of the winter season, my whole family was styling. I rocked a three-quarter mink, and mink earmuffs, and a mink muffler instead of gloves.

I have a mother who taught me the difference between everything cheap and high quality. I had three sisters, all dimes living swolled in a beautiful Long Island palace. The last thing my poppa promised me was a pony so I could trot around our property. It's the police who are the criminals, kidnappers, and thieves. The authorities know the deal, they all in it together.

That's why I jammed the sharpened number two pencil in my caseworker's neck as she was driving me in her state-owned vehicle. She tried to say something slick about my family, about Winter in particular. I don't play that shit. "Family sticks together."

If a bitch believed she could say something rude about a Santiaga out loud and in my face, I obviously wasn't on my J.O.B.

Now I don't know if I was trying to kill her. I just wanted the bitch to pay attention to what I had been telling her for many months. I am Porsche L. Santiaga, sister to Winter Santiaga, the twins, Lexus and Mercedes Santiaga. Brooklyn-born, we chill now in a Long Island mansion. Stop driving me around and dropping me off to the broke, broken, perverted, ugly-ass, foster-care providers and introducing me to strangers who wanna pretend to be my parents. I don't pretend at nothing. I don't like fake shit. Take me home. I have a house and a family. I told her clearly in a respectful tone. I recited to her my exact Long Island address.

"You shouldn't look up to a girl like Winter, even though she is your real sister," the bitch said one autumn morning when I was seated and trapped in the back seat of her state vehicle, where I had been seated and trapped many times. She must of felt good and big about herself with her files filled up with dirty talk about my real life, and her folded newspaper that must have reported some lies that she decided to believe. So, she started saying something foul.

"Winter," my caseworker said, referring to my well-loved sister. . . .

My caseworker is paralyzed now. So she got a lot of time to sit still and think about all the lies she been telling little kids, about taking them to live in a better place, in better circumstances. She knew what the fuck was up. She'd say and do anything, no matter how evil it was as long as they paid her to do it. She'd drop me off anywhere, including hell, and leave me with anyone including the motherfucking devil, even if she knew for sure I was in serious danger. As long as that was the address printed on her paper, she'd leave me without looking back. So they got me locked up in juvy. It's better than playing house. Everything is clear in here, the way I prefer things to be. No one is pretending to love me, or the rest of us. We damn sure ain't pretending to love them or each other either. In here, there's only friends and enemies, no in-between.

Chapter 2

I overheard my poppa, Ricky Santiaga, say, "A good hustle starts with a tight team." I got mine. We call ourselves the Gutter Girls, cause one of our teachers said we act like we come from the gutter. I didn't feel fucked up about the gutter thing. I figured if a rich bitch dropped a diamond in the sewer, even if it got covered with shit and slime, and trampled on by mice and rats, if some one discovered it ten years later, they'd easily clean it off and it would still be worth major paper, probably even more than it was back when it first got dropped. I turned that gutter shit around, made it pop; two upside down lower case interlocking *g*'s. When we got our shit together we would capitalize it, turn it right side up, like Gucci.

When I first formed the little seven-chick clique, I took the leftover, looked over, overlooked chicks from the C-section and gave them a do-over. My first recruit was a fat, stinky girl. Her friends called her Greedy Gail. Her enemies called her Pig. I checked how she got a lot of letters and even a box of goodies from home once a month and seemed to have a big budget at the commissary. While everyone else took the time to tease her, I approached her to strike a deal. I disregarded her funk and went right into it. I called her by her true name, Gail, and kept it polite on purpose. "Do you like music?" I asked her. She looked like she wasn't used to nobody being nice. After a pause she said, "A little bit."

"You wanna dance with me on the yard?" I asked her. "We can do a dance workout together. It will make you feel good and look good, too," I said.

I could tell she was thinking about it. So I pressed her some more.

"You have a pretty face. You might as well match it all up," I said. She seemed to like the way I put it, taking the edge off.

"Not on the yard, cause everybody be staring," Gail said.

"Okay, then we'll do it in the dorm at night in our section, starting tonight," I compromised for her. Then I eased her into purchasing a Department of Corrections radio and cassette player for $39.99. "We gotta control the beat," I told her. "I help you, you help me?"

"How could I help you?" She said like it wasn't possible, like she thought I was already perfect.

"Just put in the work for the first two weeks. We'll do you first, then me," I said. She agreed.

I put up with her farting every time she lifted her fat legs and even when she bent over to try and touch her toes. In a short time, in addition to the workout, I put her on a diet. Convincing her that I was helping her resist temptation, I took over her care box and her commissary, selling and trading her goods and candies on the low for half the price the authorities charged. It was easy for me, cause I didn't pay for nothing in the first place. My hustle was so sweet that it tipped off the Sugar Wars in the young section-C dormitory, where we was locked. I made a name for myself. The more sugar schemes I invented, the more rules the authorities invented. The more they punished and stressed us young girls, the more the demand for my discount sugars increased. The more sugar everybody ate, the more tempers flared and fists began flying.

I wanted to be known for making money and moves, not for brawling. Fighting was an interruption to my business. But the better my business, the more the fighting came along with it.

Truthfully speaking, we didn't have no Grants or Benjamins on lockup. I made paper money in arts 'n crafts, and I made my section believe in it, work for it, trade and pay for things that we all should've had anyway, but that the authorities didn't provide, charging us for it instead. They knew that shit was fucked up for girls like me who didn't receive no letters or visits, and had no one placing even one piece of copper on my commissary.

As Gail dropped the pounds, she grew more confident. I taught her to stop munching up the product and to work out even harder. She liked me. I didn't just talk shit, I worked out beside her and never let her see me laugh at her flaws. When she wanted to skip a night of working out, I refused. I held her feet down for sit ups and cheered her on when she made the smallest improvement.

Music is influence. We picked up four more chicks from our section, all strange but drawn in by the music and dance workout, as well as the results of seeing Gail's recovery. When she got down to an attractive size, and her face that had been buried under layers of fat got revealed, she became ruthless and loyal. If I got in a fight, she'd handle the business while I was trapped down in isolation.

Now she fought on my side along with five other girls I recruited. Now that Gail looked decent, I liked her for true. Big, sloppy, stinky girls can't get no respect cause, more than anybody else with a problem, theirs is the first thing you'll see and smell. So, everybody uses it against them.

Chapter 3

She's a white girl. I don't look up to her because of that. But I don't look down on her either. I already told you, I don't play the skin-color game. "Riot," she said, introducing herself to me in the "slop house," which is what I call the cafeteria at juvy lockdown.

"Riot?" I repeated.

"Yeah, like when shit is so fucked up and you can't take it no more, so you start brawling, setting shit on fire, blowing shit up." She gave a Jolly Rancher green-eyed stare into my eyes. Her lips were watermelon red. I didn't crack a smile.

There was a pause. Looking away and up towards the ceiling, she continued.

"The authorities hate my name, but it's the name my parents named me. It's on my birth certificate. It's official."

"What do you want?" I asked her as I was checking her out. I could tell from her hairstyle she had at least one ghetto chick for a friend. Her hair was black. It was one thick and pretty cornrow that started at the center of her head and swirled around in circles until it finally dropped down and dangled over her right shoulder. It was frizzy like she had gotten it braided three days back. I could tell that unbraided her hair was crazy long. She was smart to rock it like that, laying tight on her scalp, cause if she were fighting someone younger like me, a furious lightweight who wasn't naturally a fighter and needed a way to protect myself, I would take long loose hair and choke her with it, the same way the young ones tried to do me when I first got locked.

"You look hungry," Riot said. She was right. But she looked hungry, too. Her face was lean like a supermodel. Her teeth, the tops and bottom were not crooked or buck or bent. They were all white and lined up in a perfect row.

"What do you eat? You gotta eat something to stay alive, right?" She asked me as though she were my real-life big sister.

"What do *you* eat?" I threw the question right back at her, didn't like to be questioned.

She smiled. "Apples, oranges, bananas. If I'm lucky, a few nuts and raisins. I got a girl who works in the kitchen and a girl who does a shift at the commissary. So I get mine," Riot said confidently, not bragging, but more like she was try'na offer me something. That's how it goes up in here. You gotta watch and listen for the slightest twist of the tongue so none of these slickass girls could front like you agreed to something you didn't agree to or accept.

I couldn't and wouldn't front. I was surviving on sugar and trained myself to be satisfied for hours off of the flavor from a Lifesaver. Dinner would be something big like Twizzlers or Cheez Doodles. Beneath my red "juvy jumper" there was zero body fat.

Before I could ignore or answer her questions, my belly started churning and a noise came out. Our eyes locked, then we both broke out and laughed. I marked that down in my mind. It was my first true smile since getting tooken, a smile that led to real laughter. After that, the feeling between us loosened up some. She started telling me her dope-ass story. That's how me and her met, got tight, and got ganged up.

Riot's parents owned a marijuana farm in upstate New York. I don't know how big an acre is, but she said she had a fifty-acre property. Riot got here on lockdown before me. She said she murdered a man. That made me feel closer to her because I figured she was strong, or at least that she would defend herself, and I liked that. No one believed more than me that there are some who definitely deserve it. She said she tagged me because she noticed I wasn't eating the shit they served, which meant I was smart and unlike the "robots," which is what she called most of the other young inmates. Riot said she knows how to grow real food. Her family had apple trees, cornfields, tomato and lettuce patches, and an herb garden. She claimed she even knew how to make maple syrup from a tree.

My mind envisioned a stack of silver dollar pancakes dripping in syrup.

"I live not too far from here, two hours to the west in 'quiet country.'" That's how she described her place. "So quiet you could hear mosquitoes, bees, crickets, and snake bellies sliding through the tall grass, or even the wind pushing around, depending on the season."

I pictured a serpent in my head.

"I'm not afraid of snakes," Riot said. "I used to lie in the grass right beside them and swim in the lake with the water moccasins." She used her hand and motioned a snake movement. It looked like she was remembering something that felt good to her.

"I was lying in the long grass on my back late summer when I saw those 'hell-copters.'" That's what she called them. Then she pointed to the sky. "I didn't panic. I just counted and watched them flutter in."

"Our farm field workers dropped down and laid low like locusts," she said, gesturing dramatically.

"That was *their* first time also, seeing hell-copters over my parents' place. They were still flat on their bellies after the copters had flown for half an hour before fluttering out." Riot paused like she was remembering it too clearly and waiting with her workers.

"Some workers didn't show back up the next day. The workers who did show, my dad paid 'em double. He believed in 'profit sharing,' worked the land the same as if he wasn't the owner, when he was. He hated the word *boss*, didn't answer anyone who used it. He said workers united are more powerful than any boss, any state or any authority. My mom wasn't the agreeing type, but she agreed with my Dad. My mom hated the words *boss, authority, state,* and *government.*"

The murder Riot committed, and the weed farm she came from, caught my attention. When she would talk some sentences I didn't understand or give a fuck about, I'd just listen to the feeling of her storytelling, and watch the intense and swift way she switched her face gestures. Oddly, it felt like her words were filling my belly with a real meal, temporarily at least. And they were flooding my mind with movie pictures. I thought about how I had not seen even one film since I was seven.

Riot said her parents drove a lavender station wagon with huge yellow daisies painted on. I thought to myself, "Who would buy that shit if they were getting gwop?"

Riot said her parents were caked up but didn't care about fashion and money. "Mom and Dad were in love with freedom, the land, the soil, the animals, and people."

She said her whole family was all vegetarians. Yet, they had four pet pigs who wasn't locked up or fenced in, and roamed around a big area freely.

"I could tell each one of 'em from the other, and they each had names—Weed, Seed, Smoke, and Puff," she said, pulling a finger as she counted em out. "We treated them like people." She smiled, remembering. "Seriously, they each had different personalities, and I hope you know for sure that I'm not making none of this up."

"You like animals?" she asked me. I smiled, remembering myself.

"Something like that," I said, snatching my smile back. I didn't want anyone in here to know my likes and dislikes. I knew they would use that shit against me. But I had obviously already given that one fact away by mistake.

"Then you would love Ganjah, my colt. He's incredible," Riot said.

"How fast is he?" I asked curiously.

"He could outrun the bullets fired from the tower," Riot answered, referring to the rumored guards who, everyone said, stood watch from way up high over the lock-up facility for violent juvenile girls, where we are both prisoners. The sky guards were the threat, make one wrong move and they would riddle our little bodies with bullets. None of us saw them, though. At least I didn't. But I didn't doubt that they were up there lurking.

"Ganjah's faster than my brother's horse, Sensimillia," Riot added.

I pictured pretty ponies galloping in my mind. I liked the way Riot put her words, like she wasn't afraid of shit. I liked that she was rich—even if her people didn't know how to spend or wear it right. At least they had a family, and the pictures in my mind said they was happy.

"Have you ever seen a diamond needle?" she asked out of nowhere.

I had seen plenty of diamonds. Winter had fifty princess-cut diamonds in her tennis bracelet and 125 in the matching necklace. I counted them secretly, since I wasn't allowed to touch her jewelry or

Momma's and wasn't scheduled to get my own diamond set until I turned sixteen. I shined Winter's diamonds after I tried them on and before I placed them back on the black velvet and placed them exactly where they were hidden in her room before I found them.

"Diamond needles are insects with beautiful wings," Riot said. "They look like a mix between a dragonfly and a honeybee. That's what the hell-copters looked like the second time they showed way up in the sky, a swarm of diamond needles dancing behind swollen clouds on a rainless, gray day. Our fieldworkers scattered like ants in all directions. I crawled into my hiding place like my parents told me and my brother to do if the copters ever returned," she said, and I felt in my gut that something real bad was about to happen in Riot's story.

"Unlike the previous time, the copters cut their way through the clouds and actually landed on our land." Her fingers were fluttering in the jumpy motion of the helicopters landing.

I glanced at the guards. In here if any of us keep using our fingers, they swear we gang signaling. As Riot described the raid on her property, pictures and sounds of the Nassau County Police, geared up and guns drawn, flashed through my mind from the night they swooped down and barged in on my family. They smirked smiles as they cut open our leather sofas and love chairs, broke vases and dishes, jerked down pictures from walls and pulled furs and fashions out of our closets. Capturing and cuffing my handsome and fashionable father, who was dressed in a thick black suede v-neck leisure suit and sporting black Gucci loafers wasn't enough for them. They seemed to want to destroy his success and lessen him some in our eyes.

"Jealous motherfuckers," I whispered under my breath before I tuned back in to the story Riot was still telling.

"Ragweed and gunpowder, that's all I could smell. I didn't move. I was frozen by the sounds of war," Riot said and struck a frozen frightened pose.

"I knew my dad and mom were firing back. After all, *the Feds were the intruders*. The fifty acres and all of our animals were our private property, brought and paid for in full by my parents."

A slop house guard patrolled by our table. He knew it was unusual for an older girl to be sitting with a young one. Besides I was in my red jumper, so he would've been watching closely anyway. Red jumper meant violence. Riot glanced at him.

"You know a shootout is nothing like what you see on television. The speakers in your TV set can't capture the deafening noise or the thickening of the air or the scent of flesh ripped open and guts and blood bursting and pouring out, till there's nothing left except for dark stains."

Riot described the murder of her parents, who were killed defending their freedom, their property, family, and hard work. "They went out the right way. That's what they would say. 'Fuck a government that wants to tell you what you can grow on your property and still charge you property taxes for property you already paid for,'" she said, imitating what I guessed was either her mother's or father's words.

"Live free or die fighting. That's our thing." She put up two fingers like a peace sign, but then put her fingers to her lips pretending like she was smoking a cigarette but she wasn't. There's no smoking allowed in juvy lockdown. None of us are over sixteen.

Riot and her brother stayed still for days in an underground bunker their father had built long ago. "We had books, blankets, a toolbox and candles, two flashlights, a limited supply of water, a fruit basket, a first-aid kit, flares, emergency items and canned beans, dry snacks and, of course, our guns."

"When the intruders, cars, trucks, sirens, and voices had ceased for more than forty-eight hours, we climbed out," she said.

It wasn't long before their head count confirmed what "our hearts couldn't handle," but that they had already suspected. Not only their parents' bloodied bodies had been removed, but their animals had been seized also. They had heard their cries, their feet and their voices from the underground. "It sounded so sick I forced myself to forget it. Otherwise it would've kept replaying in my head. We felt helpless, like cowards. My brother and I both fought and held one another back from coming out of the bunker like our parents told us not to do." Riot's face revealed her regrets.

"My collie named Clyde had been taken and his wife, Bonnie. We loved our dogs. We were all family." Riot spoke as though dogs could actually be married. I wanted to laugh at that, but from her look, she was dead serious and still hurting. So I didn't.

Her and her brother scrubbed up spilled blood and continued to live on their land. "The harvest had brought us plenty of fruits and vegetables. We could've lived off of just the apples and corn alone."

Riot said that they knew that the two of them being left alone was only temporary. The authorities, school principal, and maybe even friends or neighbors would come looking for them. "How could two children just disappear without a trace?"

"Me and my brother was always the best at hide-and-seek. We used to play it with the workers' children on some weekends when they'd show up. One autumn, we were playing the most wicked game of hide-and-seek ever. It dragged on from sunup to sundown, when their parents were done for the day. *No one* knew the property better than us." Riot had her hands on her hips now, looking fully confident.

"After our parents were murdered, it was three months before Con Ed cut off our electricity. Three and a half months before Ma Bell shut down our phones.

"The telephones didn't matter. We didn't make or take no calls, and treated the phones like a trap. We'd listen to it ring one, two, seven, eight times. We also rarely used the power and tried to accomplish everything in the daylight. Lights could be seen by any curious neighbor. Lucky for us, out in 'quiet country,' neighbors were more than a mile away on both sides. We only had to be on the watch for the extra-curious ones, who now treated our place like an exciting stop on a crime/horror tour, or the land-thieving realtors who had posted a 'for sale' sign at the beginning of our land and then at the end," she said.

"The hell-copter raid had taken place in August. When the power finally shut off in November, we sparked up the backup generator that my parents had used many times in the furious country storm weather. We had gasoline stored, but not enough for more than two weeks' worth, so we used it sparingly. We put all our blankets in one pile and slept there together underneath them all. We came close to freezing to death but luckily not both at the same time. When I got sick, my brother healed me. When he was sick, I healed him. We survived the coldest winter ever, my brother and me."

Riot began howling quietly with her hands cuffed around each side of her mouth. "When the wolves began howling, and the puppies that Bonnie and Clyde had cleverly hidden and left behind went to barking, and the cans began rattling from the trip wire that my brother laid on the road as a warning to us, we were both at different places on the property. My brother was out in the fields putting down some seeds. I was coming from around the back of our house." Riot's face turned angry.

"As the stranger's car rode cautiously up our pebbled dirt road, I saw his car door first and then his license plate. The plates were marked with two of the words that our parents hated most, *state* and *government*."

The state worker man couldn't see Riot. Riot saw him. She said she read the words on the side of his car; *Bureau of Child Welfare.*

"All I could imagine was the guy trying to hurt or separate my brother from me." Her eyes were squinted now.

"I grabbed my rifle, shot one clean shot, one time, straight through his forehead." She gestured as though she was holding and aiming her rifle right there in the slop house.

"Six days later cops flooded our property and made another massive and thorough search, uncovering the murdered guy's buried body and the state vehicle parked behind closed doors, inside our empty barn where some of our stolen animals would've been if they hadn't a slaughtered them." She put her hands up halfway over her head.

"I got surrounded in the chicken coop where I was squatting," she said, finally smiling.

"I'm ten," I told the police. "Don't shoot me. I'm only ten years old." She pushed her hands up in the full surrender position.

Riot was so lucky she was only ten back then. We both knew that juvy was fucked up. But we both heard and believed that grown-up prison is much worser. At fourteen years old, any girl up here in juvy can get transferred out to an adult facility without notice. Sixteen is the oldest anybody in here could be. In juvy, no girl turned seventeen.

"I'm asking you to be one of my sons," Riot said, strangely.

"Sons?" I repeated.

"It's obvious you're younger than me. I'm thirteen," Riot confided.

"I'm ten," I revealed.

"So, you be my son. I see you're always fighting. You are young and slim. But no matter how young, big, or small anyone is, one person can never win alone."

I was thinking about her words and if they had any point or meaning to me.

"Heard you got beef with Cha-Cha," Riot said.

"What about it? I fight her. It ain't nothing." I shrugged my shoulders.

"Cha-Cha's a robot. She gives the guards what they want. She starts fights and fucks up the flow. She gives them the excuse and the reason to clamp down on you and everybody in your section," she said. I was listening.

"Say yes, and you got a crew," Riot added. I was thinking. I already had a crew.

"The thing is, our crew is smarter than the robots. We don't act like stupid girls fighting over hair and boys and visits or dumb shit. We all girls who came from families with either land, or money, or both." She rubbed her fingers together making the make money sign.

"We action figures." She gestured like she was about to leap up from the table. "We camouflage." She squatted back down and re-laxed. "We got plans and connections. We make moves." She pushed her face closer to mine.

"I'll turn eleven in July," I told her. I didn't want her thinking I was so young that she could rule over me.

"I'll turn fourteen in July," she said, letting me know no matter what she had three years over me either way.

"What you call your crew?" I asked her.

"The Diamond Needles," she said softly with an intense face that caused me to stare at her lips as she pronounced each word.

"We don't big up our name, wear tattoos, or flash signs. We don't do the daily group-up on the yard. We keep our mouths shut. If some-thing is important we send a message or a messenger with a kite. We don't do anything obvious. Like I said, we're smart. There are ten of us. We each got a number in the order that we came together."

"What's your number?" I asked her.

"One," was all she said.

"If I come in, what do I get?" I asked.

"An army," she said.

"Do you like music?" I asked her, changing the subject on purpose. I could see it interrupted her thought-flow some.

"Of course," she responded soft and swiftly.

"Name your favorite rapper, and favorite group."

"Tupac Shakur, easily," she answered, like he was a king. "My favorite group, Bones Thugs & Harmony! Hands down!" She was definite, and excited herself just by reciting their group name. "Enough questions," she said turning suddenly serious. "Are you in or out? If you're out, this is the last conversation you'll ever have with me. If you're in, I'll let you know the next move." She wasn't bluffing. I could feel it.

We both already knew I was in. I liked her story. She wasn't a broke bitch, a broken-down bully, hater, or a victim, and I wasn't either. I had nothing to lose. The Gutter Girls weren't going anywhere and neither were me or Riot. We are all prisoners.

"I got one condition," I answered Riot after a long pause. "My girl Siri gotta be down with us. It's a two-for-one deal."

"Siri?" Riot repeated. "I don't know her. Point her out."

"She's right here," I pointed Siri out, seated beside me. Riot's eyes dashed one quick time like she didn't see Siri. Then she turned straight-faced and said, "No problem. You'll both be my sons."

Chapter 4

We met in the dark, Siri and me, almost three years ago, the first night that I got here, the worst night of my life. The last items that I owned that came from Porsche L. Santiaga's world and wardrobe were taken from me: my denim Guess skirt and matching denim Guess jacket, which Momma brought for me. My deep blue Mecca T-shirt and matching blue bobos, my Taiga leather Louis Vuitton tiny handbag, that matched my leather riding boots.

At first, I didn't know who Louis Vuitton was, but Winter said he was an important man, and that if I lost the handbag she would punish me by making me wear a cheap bag for a week, and of course for that week I couldn't go out with her cause she don't hang with girls who rock cheap bags or cheap footwear, even if they're blood-related.

I held on to that bag mostly cause I always wanted to hang with Winter. Besides, she bought the bag and boots for me brand new. Her best friend, Natalie, only got to rock Winter's hand-me-downs.

I sported the boots only on special occasions and kept it a secret when they became too tight. Now all of my shit was gone. Good thing they left me in my panties.

Freezing, the floor was frozen. My freezing little body was flooded with goose pimples. The two lady guards handed me paper shoes and a baby blue jumper, all ugly.

"Don't get dressed yet. Step over there."

One of 'em ran her palms over my naked skin. Her palms felt like sandpaper and made my goose pimples crawl. Momma said lady and soft were the same damn thing. Clean, soft hands and skin and feet, she would say, as she rubbed my little body with her special creams and lotions.

"Don't get dressed yet," the guard said again as she searched and surveyed my body. Then she ordered her partner to call for the doctor.

"I don't know why they sent her here so late," the other guard muttered and picked up the phone.

I shivered and shook for an hour and twenty-two minutes till the doctor finally showed up. I got the feeling they left me there undressed seated on a cold metal stool on purpose.

The male doctor's hands were pink in his palms and were hairy on the flip side. His bushy eyebrows had dandruff big enough to see, almost as big as snowflakes. His fingertips were cold. His metal thing that he placed on my flat eight-year-old chest was cold. His pointy thing he pushed in my ear holes was cold. He shoved a stick down my throat and pinned down my tongue. He shined bright thin beams of light into each of my pupils.

Lying flat on a cold table he hit my knees with a hammer. My leg jumped.

"Sit up," he ordered me. "Hold out your hand," he said, ignoring my nervous fingertips shaking. He flipped my hand around and pricked me with a needle. Between my thumb and the finger right next to it. He squeezed my finger till my blood burst out the teeny-tiny hole that he made. He did some quick moves then wiped my blood away and Band-Aided it, as though he wasn't the one who had cut me in the first place.

"Lay down," he ordered again.

When he said, "Done," he dragged his hand down my body and touched lightly the front of my panties, like light enough to pretend he didn't do it. I peed. Even when I squeezed my legs together my warm piss wouldn't stop gushing out. It was the only warmth I felt in a room so cold my piss should of turned into piss sickles.

"You should have saved that for my cup," the doctor said now holding a small plastic container in his right hand. Now that he wanted pee from me, none would come out. What had already come was leaking from the metal table to the floor.

In a washroom big as the living room in the projects, on a cold floor that could've been made of ice blocks, one guard blast-showered me with cold water. My lips trembled.

"Pick 'em up," she told me.

She pulled a plastic bag out of her back pocket. I dropped my piss panties, the last item that actually belonged to me, inside of her plastic bag. She put a tie on it and tossed it.

"Get dressed," she ordered, offering me no towel to dry my drenched skin.

"From now on, walk on the right side of the line," she ordered. Her voice echoed in the dark hallway. Her shoes clicked out forty-three steps. She stopped walking and clicking. Then she aimed her high-powered flashlight at my feet. My damp paper shoes were no protection against the frozen floor.

"Bed number thirty-four," she said swiftly swiping her bright beam of light only one time.

I looked but couldn't catch sight of anything in that one second. She killed the light. I knew she was trying to slowly fill me with panic and fear.

"Move!" she shouted while sounding like she was acting like she was whispering.

Probably if she wasn't pretending to whisper, her real voice would shake the walls. I took my first step at the first crack of her voice raising up again.

"Keep your hands and feet to yourself," she said forcefully. "Or else we'll lock you up in the basement by yourself."

I could hear her hard shoes banging on the ice floor as she walked away. I squinted looking into the blackness in front of me. I could hear breathing but couldn't see much of nothing, just piles of bodies beneath blankets, one thin blanket on each bed. Some had their blanket sloppy. Some were wrapped tight like mummies in a horror film.

Up close, I saw one arm dangling from beneath the blanket. It looked creepy.

Swiftly, I looked back when I realized the guard's shoe sounds stopped clicking and banging. A door slam shut. Not like a door in my Long Island house. It was the sound of a door made of steel so heavy that it couldn't ever be opened without a bulldozer. The guard left me with lights out. She wanted me to walk to bed number thirty-four in the dark-dark. She wanted me to feel certain that she and anybody dressed in the same uniform as her didn't give a fuck about me. I felt it. I knew it. I would remember it, always.

Music. I was recasting Michael Jackson's *Thriller* video in my mind. I didn't need no monsters or masks, werewolfs or vampires. The people in here were scary enough. The bodies lying around, beneath blankets was like a graveyard scene. I was Michael Jackson, not the frightened girl in the video. I slid out of those worthless paper shoes and started dancing my walk through the huge black room. My limbs were fluid like Michael's. My movements were bold like Brooklyn, musical and unafraid. My heart was banging out the fast bass beats of the *Thriller* song.

As I danced, my body began to heat up. Even the soles of my feet became warm. I was up and down the rows comfortably now, even in the darkness. No one could see me or stop me. My dancing made my anger more powerful than my fears. My body began to sweat. Caught up in my movements I lost track of where I had been standing in the first place and which direction the flashlight had pointed towards to get to my bed.

As my chest heaved in and out and my heart still raced, one blanket raised up in the air. The body hidden beneath was floating like a ghost. The blanket was the only colorful crocheted blanket in the big room. When the hands popped out of each side, I saw glow-in-the-dark little lights. No! I saw glow-in-the-dark nail polish and little fingers waving me to follow her. I was Michael. So she must have been the pretty girl in the video who was afraid but still friendly.

"Follow me," she said. I did.

She stopped at an open bed so suddenly that I bumped into her back. She giggled.

"I saw you first," she said. "So let's you and me be friends before the rest of these monsters wake up. Don't be afraid. You'll never like it, being here, but you will get used to it."

She sounded nice and didn't stink. She didn't try to say or do nothing slick. She wasn't bossy either. She touched my hand. On the bed, she laid down beside me. "What's your name?" she asked.

"Porsche," I whispered, trying to get my lips close to her ear so no one else would hear.

"Pretty name," she said. "I'm Siri. We're gonna be best friends," she predicted.

"Do you like music?" I asked her.

"I like you!" she responded.

That's how me and Siri met. That night all I saw was white teeth and pretty fingers. I liked her because she liked me. She only spoke to me. She showed me things about the other girls that maybe I would of missed if she didn't say nothing at all. When two girls in a nearby bed were acting fly by speaking some language that no one else knew, Siri and me igged 'em. Then, we made up our own language. We worked on it for my first seven nights there at dinnertime, since we both wasn't eating. We made up our own alphabet using our own symbols. Each symbol stood for a sound just like each letter in English stands for a sound. We would write words and then sentences out of our symbols. If anyone found our notes they would not know what we were discussing because they didn't know our code or symbols. That meant we could write curses or our secrets and fucked-up things about the authorities.

At first, we didn't figure out how to speak our secret language out loud. So we only wrote it down after waiting in line to use one of the three pencils available in the dorm. One time when the authorities searched our stuff in our dorm, which didn't happen often but once is more than enough, they found our paper stacks. When they looked at the pages with all kinds of neatly written symbols lined up in neat rows, they asked us, "What is this about?" We didn't answer, just shrugged our little shoulders. They stole our pages and never gave 'em back.

One day at my session with the psych, she showed them to me. I was surprised to see them, so I did have a reaction on my face. She started speaking to me in the aggravating sing-song voice that I hated more than I hated her.

"Let's talk about this," the psychiatrist said, holding up a page and asking me to explain the meaning.

I told her, "It's graffiti. Ever heard of that?" She smiled that stiff smile that looked like her lips were stitched and held together by some strong string pulled tightly on the ends to make a fake smile curve.

"No, not exactly," she answered. She was never able to admit that there was just some shit she didn't know.

"It's just a bunch of pretty designs. Don't you think it looks pretty?" I asked her.

She stared at the page, paused, and then said, "I'm the one asking the questions here." She was mad that she couldn't figure me out. She couldn't get comfortable with being outsmarted by the girls she thought were the lowest, dumbest, and most craziest little things ever.

When we were around the girls on our dorm, especially the ones who were speaking their unknown language out loud, me and Siri would start speaking to each other in a foreign language that even we did not know. It made everyone pay attention to us. It made everyone want to know our language. We wouldn't tell them shit. They'd get extra red when we suddenly started laughing. We'd be like, "Yeah, we flipped it around on y'all bitches." That made them start to accuse us of shit that we had nothing to do with. They was just mad that we wasn't mad. They hated when a girl didn't need them, their clique, and their bullshit.

I fought, but Siri didn't. I fought for her, took the punishments and never snitched on anything she did or that we did together. She wasn't made for fighting.

Siri was the only warmth in a cold, cold place. She was soft and loving. She was into fashion and looked like she belonged on a Benetton's ad, draped in expensive angora or cashmere sweaters made of thick and colorful yarns. She wasn't a conceited bitch. She was quiet and exclusively mine. When I heard music in my mind, Siri would hum along with it.

Hearing her hum was real soothing and different. I mean, I was in love with music of all kinds, especially songs that made me catch feelings or remember memories. I was used to hearing the beat box, rhymes, and all types of voices and instruments. I didn't have no right name for it, but Siri was like a professional "hummer." Her voice massaged me, even when it was beneath a break-beat. She was the soundtrack to the film that I didn't want to be starring in, but was. No matter who else I met, fought, or maneuvered around with, me and Siri had been inseparable since we met in the cold, dark dorm.

Chapter 5

Chair was cemented to the floor. Ankles chained to the chair in the library. I'm a little girl, but I'm wearing the red jumper again, which means I had a recent violent episode and a stay in isolation—a small, tight cell, barely big enough for one, which the guards called *the bottom*. Normally, my age group, all girls up to age ten, wear baby blue jail jumpers. But no matter your age, if you fight, or fight back, they call it *violence*. Violent girls of all ages up till sixteen (cause at sixteen you can't stay here in this lockup no more) get locked in the bottom, in a ten-foot by ten-foot cell, sometimes naked. No matter how long you're in isolation, when you get out, the guard hands you a red jumper, and says, "Get dressed."

For two weeks after being locked down in isolation, everywhere you go, either your ankles or wrists or both sets, are chained and cuffed, while the other inmates are hands- and foot-free.

Like everybody, I still had to go to class. But in each class there were a few seats reserved for girls with ongoing behavior problems like me. All seats were already cemented to the floors, but the *hot seats* were equipped with ankle cuffs so violent girls couldn't move left or right, or even stand up straight.

At the end of each class a guard posted outside would remove the cuffs, escort me to the next class, and lock me in the same type of chair all over again.

The authorities thought they was embarrassing us "violent girls," for fighting. The warden stayed preaching that nonviolence shit, like she had no idea what was really going on, who was sparking shit up or how to stop it. She claimed that if we kept wilding, she would put through the order to build classes with cages, one student to a cage, like we were wildlife, not humans.

We young ones always did and thought opposite from the warden and them. Wearing red, in the eyes of many girls locked down, boosted my status, got me props, high fives, and favors. Some who wouldn't speak to me before would try to get next to me when I was red, hoping my style and status would rub off on them. So those were the ones I yanked around like puppets.

My eyes moved around the library, a space I had never been in before. I was searching for Riot. She sent me a kite asking me to meet up in here. She must've gotten red that I had got into another fight the day after I got ganged up with her. Although I wasn't sure if her angle was gonna be that my fighting made me look bad, or made her look bad. It didn't matter, though. I live in the C-dorm with the bad young bitches, Riot lived in the B-dorm with the eleven to thirteens. Even though I had linked up with the Diamond Needles, I still had to hold it down in my dorm no matter what.

The library was kind of empty, except for the librarian who was weaving in and out of shelves pushing a wheel cart loaded down with all types of books. There were three inmates reading quietly but all separate from one another, and an inmate who was seated behind the front desk. She caught my eyes more than the others. A beige-tan jail jumper she was wearing, which meant she was aged fifteen or sixteen. Puerto Rican, that's what she was. I could tell. Her butterscotch complexion and the tan jumper she wore were close in color. She cut her black-black hair short and had it styled nice. I noticed how the older girls up in here try to keep that fashion flow. She had dark eyes and long lashes. Her eyes weren't big and round but were wide and curved nicely. More than that she was wearing gold earrings, small ones that didn't dangle but the gold was real. It stood out to me, of course. How did she manage to have 'em, when jewels were forbidden? How did she manage to wear 'em and anybody could see 'em and then look at themselves not having none to rock? She had clout. That was my conclusion. I exhaled, tired of waiting on Riot. It didn't matter, though. I couldn't move, couldn't leave. Once I requested the library, I had to remain here and wait out the whole hour till the guard reappeared to release me.

Butterscotch stood up. She was tall. Not doofy-tall, or man-tall, a nice height, like Winter. She was slim but had that nice figure, the type that made men on my Brooklyn block call out, "Mami, let me talk to you a minute." She was coming my way. Her strut was nice. Maybe five and a half years from now, when my eight-year sentence is served out, I would have a strut more meaner than hers.

"Can you read?" she asked me as she laid a book on my desktop. I didn't answer her. She was pretty, her voice was nice, and her tone wasn't shitty or bossy, but still she had insulted me. So, fuck her. She strutted back to where she came from.

Her question *Can you read?* reminded me of Ms. Jenkins, my first grade teacher. I learned my letters in kindergarten, but Ms. Jenkins taught me to read. The first day of class she said, "If you can't read or write, you can't do anything."

We were all little and quiet, and if the rest of the kids were thinking like me, they were probably only half-listening and dreaming of being at home with Momma. When I was little, whenever I wasn't at home, I always felt like I was missing out on something, maybe even something big.

Ms. Jenkins made herself clear. She taught us one sentence: "I will be responsible for myself." She made us each write it a hundred times, and repeat it ten times, and recite it on our own five times. Close to the end of our first day of first grade, she handed out a paper and gave us a quiz on our little lesson. She collected the papers ten minutes after she handed them out. Then she gave us each someone else's paper to correct.

Next she sent us up to the blackboard in groups of four. She said we were playing a game called Challenge. She called out a word, and we had to write the word on the board swiftly. The winner was the student who wrote it on the board the fastest and who spelled the word correctly.

Her teaching style jerked us out of our dreams and made us feel pressed. As our long day with one teacher in one classroom came to an end, Ms. Jenkins pulled out a tin can of goodies and gave every student who scored 100 on the quiz, a foil-wrapped candy, like mini Reese's Peanut Butter Cups, or Hershey's Chocolate Kisses. She gave the winner of the Challenge game an unusual and pretty pencil case that was see-through on one side with a slide-down cover. It was filled with decorated pencils, and even a pencil sharpener.

On the first day of first grade, Ms. Jenkins made me want to win. Now I could get any kind of food or candy gift at home, of course. We lived in the projects, and we had everything to choose from cause Poppa kept us living and eating very well. But what Ms. Jenkins did was different. She filled us with a feeling that we had to work to win, that we had to focus to learn, and whatever was happening anywhere outside of her class didn't matter. We had to get it right or be exposed and embarrassed.

On our second day in our first grade class, as soon as we arrived she handed out blank sheets of paper and gave us our second quiz. We couldn't believe it. We just looked around at each other.

"Learning is not only repeating," she told us.

"Learning includes remembering," she said, slowly pronouncing each word. "Everything you learn should be remembered and used in your life."

When she collected our papers, she made every student stand. She called out our names and separated us into two groups. "These are the students who remembered." She pointed. "These are the students who forgot." She pointed. Immediately she gave each student in the group who remembered a bag of multicolored marbles. Then, she told the kids who forgot. "If you don't learn to read and write, you can't do anything." We stood there feeling ashamed. Shame was a new feeling for me. I was a rich girl from a rich family, the best family in my Brooklyn hood. I never had a reason to feel shame before I met Ms. Jenkins.

As we, "the forgetters," had to remain standing, answering Ms. Jenkins like we was in a chorus, I got red and redder. Ms. Jenkins called out, "If you don't learn to read and write, whose fault is it?" Then she taught us all to respond by saying it out loud: "If I don't learn to read or write, then it is my fault."

At the end of class I took my paper to Ms. Jenkins.

"I got a 95," I said to her. She looked down at me and said, "That's not 100."

When I told Momma, she said, "Fuck her! Who does she think she is messing with my pretty baby?" Later that night, Momma gave me a card plastered with gold stars that she must've got from the five-and-dime. Now I had a hundred gold stars from Momma. But, somehow, I still wanted that one gold star and that 100 percent from Ms. Jenkins.

By the end of first grade, I could read and write very well. I enjoyed reading and writing to impress Ms. Jenkins, a teacher who we spent so much time with, that one day I accidentally called her Mommy. Even though I admired Ms. Jenkins, I didn't enjoy reading books on my own, because the books were all boring. My real life was way better.

As the best learners and rememberers were rewarded daily and immediately by Ms. Jenkins, I learned the deeper meaning of what she meant when she told us, "If you don't learn to read and write, you can't do anything."

As those of us who learned to read and write well sat watching a Disney animation film on a huge portable white and silver screen, while Ms. Jenkins's personal popcorn popper popped popcorn, and her hot plate melted the butter, the forgetting, slow-learning kids sat in a corner rewriting their mistakes a hundred times. There was no movie, no popcorn, no butter, no fun, or relief for them. They couldn't even see the screen. They couldn't do *nothing*. Everybody knew who they were. I wasn't down with them. I hate feeling ashamed.

"Open it up to page 100," the pretty Puerto Rican said, standing close, right in front of my desk.

"I'm not listening to you," I told her.

"You wasted eighteen minutes already," she said.

"So what?" I answered, all blasé.

"I'm Lina, number 2, the Diamond Needles. You better start showing me some respect, little girl. Page 100. Riot left this for you. Read it," she said, then walked away, strutting.

I opened the book, thinking, *Oh, so now she knows I know how to read, huh?*

Slipped between page 100 and 101 was a folded news article. I opened it up, flipped it around, and smoothed it out with both hands. It was my poppa. My whole little face got hot. My fingers suddenly felt moist. I rubbed my palms together, and my tears fell into my hands. Nervously, I looked up to check who was looking.

Lina was looking. Her stern stare softened some soon as she saw my tears. I was angry at myself for crying. Swiftly, I looked away, then down.

The photo of Poppa had pull like a thousand magnets. I stared at it, wished I could fall or leap into the frame and talk to him as he hugged me warmly, like he used to hug Winter.

His face looked serious and tight. It was strange to see him there without Momma right beside him. How could they leave her out? The two of them were always the perfect picture. "There is no king without a queen," Poppa would say. Maybe that's why in the photo he wasn't smiling or calm, like he usually was; no queen, no Winter, no Mercedes, no Lexus, no me. Come to think of it, his feeling in the photo and my feeling right then were exactly the same.

I shifted my eyes away from the news clip. I pictured Poppa in my mind. One day he wore a black tailored suit with genuine alligator shoes. Him in his suit, dress shirt, gators, and cuff links were so handsome, he made Momma pause and go silent. She already was dressed up fly, but after she saw Poppa, she went back to her bedroom. Her door closed. Moments later it opened slowly. She came out looking "like a million bucks," Poppa said.

I liked the pictures in my head better than the ones in the newspaper, although no flick of Poppa could up or lessen his permanently handsome face.

I read,

New York Daily News

Bed Time in Bedford-Stuyvesant

by Edith Kates
BROOKLYN, N.Y.
FEBRUARY 6, 1996

Ever since the January 1994 arrest of gangster Ricardo Santiaga, and the takedown of his reputed narcotics machine, there has been peace in the notorious Bedford-Stuyvesant section of Brooklyn. In a sweep that ran through the rough streets of "the Stuy," its crack-vial-strewn alleyways, and abandoned buildings, over rooftops and stretched to the manicured lawns and mansions of Dix Hills, Long Island, 28 members of Santiaga's team were captured, cuffed, arrested, and arraigned. Charges ran from misdemeanors to murders. Crime boss Ricardo Santiaga, known for his enviable management skills and ability to command complete loyalty from his crime partners, was captured in a predawn police raid of his Long Island estate. Santiaga, who strangely had no priors despite his 10-year rise to power over a $100-million-dollar crack empire, managed to rack up a rap sheet overnight that ranged from felony weapons possession, to manslaughter, to tax evasion, and eventually came to include premeditated murder.

Fast-forward two years after Santiaga's arrest; Bedford-Stuyvesant has experienced a 50% decrease in its murder rate and an 85% decrease in drug-related arrests. Local residents, who once were completely silent when questioned by police regarding Santiaga, now appear happy to let their children out of their apartments and into the new park provided by Mayor Rudolph Giuliani, who is building a safer New York for all law-abiding citizens, replete with a visible increase in neighborhood police presence. "Now we can breathe," one Bed-Stuy resident, who asked to remain anonymous, said. He would not have been so outspoken if Ricardo Santiaga were not behind bars serving natural life.

The reporter's words were funky. I sat still for some minutes, maybe more. Then her words and all images flew out of my mind and there was just a blank, black space.

Feelings I had murdered months ago began flooding the black space in my head and then my heart. My new tears felt like boiling water. The rims of my eyes were hot. I bet the bitch who wrote the article didn't know that my father read the *New York Daily News* every day. Poppa would've looked down on that reporter for looking down on her customers. Nobody treated their customers better than Poppa. Momma and us even got into trouble with him sometimes, if we acted up around our Brooklyn hood.

Finally, I took a deep, deep breath, looked up, and Lina's arm was stretched out before me, her hand holding two tissues.

"Lina, let me get a sheet of paper—oh, and an envelope. You got one?" I asked. Instead of answering me right back, she used the tissues to wipe away my tears. She held my chin lightly and began wiping my whole face. I felt something.

Then, Lina's face changed to thought. I believed that I understood exactly what she was thinking. In lockdown it's difficult to get our hands on anything. It ain't easy like how easy it was when we was back in our homes. To get even the smallest items required us to have money on the books at commissary, something of equal value to trade, or some kind of long request process, paperwork, and explanation to some counselor authority. To get things quickly like we needed and wanted, we'd have to plot, steal, or beat someone's ass for it. I don't steal. I'd rather convince.

Lina took back the book with the article stuffed inside on page 100. She returned with the *Newsweek* magazine. She laid it on my desk without explanation and walked way over where the librarian was and began talking with her quietly. I listened but didn't turn my head around. I was flipping the magazine pages, hoping Lina had placed the news article back inside. I found it, along with two sheets of paper and one envelope. I addressed the envelope to Edith Kates, The New York Daily News, NY, NY, with no street address and no zip code, cause I didn't know it. I figured the mailman had to know it already. He probably had to drag them sacks of mail every day.

On the first sheet of paper, I wrote using the pencil that was chained to my desktop, and all of the desk tops in here. It was on a chain so short, I could hardly angle it enough to write. I wrote,

Dear Miss Kates,

I call you "miss" because you're probably not married and have no family at all. You probably are a very lonely person who thinks you know everything. But you don't know nothing at all. I don't know how you got that job at the *Daily News* because you are a liar. No one should let a liar write for a newspaper because people depend on you to tell the truth. Especially people who have no other way of finding out if their mother or father or sisters are even dead or alive. Or whether or not they are somewhere living their lives with smiles on their faces. Or even if they were killed in an accident.

My father Ricky Santiaga is a good man, a hard worker and great friend. Every place he went, there was nothing but smiles. In Brooklyn, in the summertime when the ice cream truck rolled around he would pull out a hundred dollar bill and give it to Joe, the ice cream man, so every kid outside on the block could eat. Everybody's mother thanked my father for the good things he did all the time.

My father gave the best block party every year. People who didn't even live on our block came around. One time, there must've been more than a thousand people. That party was the first time I ever danced on stage for an audience. I was 6 years old. You should've of heard the people cheer. A few of them even threw money.

I don't get it, how y'all could try and make a good family look bad? You steal their children, put them in a place that might look good but is bad.

I don't know exactly where my poppa is. From what you wrote I guess y'all got him in a cage. He can't get out so y'all comfortable lying on him. Why do you all love to put people in cages?

I can tell he's looking for me. Even in your dull black and white paper his eyes shine and I could feel his nose and mouth breathing. That's the only thing I can thank you for. After 739 days I can say for sure, Poppa's alive.

If you found my father, Ricky Santiaga, would you even tell me? You should try and meet him. Talk to him. I'll bet you'll fall in love right then and there. But you better not, cause my momma will whup your ass for definite.

I be Princess Porsche L. Santiaga #7261994 ROYALTY.

"Mail it for me," I said to Lina as she walked up on me from behind and lifted the closed magazine from my desk. I knew she would check the clock, so I did, too. There were seven minutes left before the guard would appear to release me from the chair and move me to my next class.

"Mail it for me, please," Lina repeated, correcting me softly.

"I owe you one," I told her.

"Paper, envelope, stamp, delivery, and my time," she said quietly pulling down each of her pretty fingers as she counted out my debt.

"What do you want from me?" I asked her.

"Meet me here at the library every day for the next seven days during rec."

"For what?" I asked her.

"You'll say it's for math tutoring. Between you and me, though, you gonna have to get your shit together if you wanna get up with us Diamond Needles. Riot saw something in you. But for me, I won't let you get away with no little kid tricks. You wanna walk and move with the big girls? You grown? You better act like it, mamasita." She strutted away. I watched her.

I was thinking she probably would've told me to come here to the library every day for a week *even if* I didn't ask to borrow the paper and envelope.

The guard came through. I had my eyes on Lina as he uncuffed my ankles.

"Get up," the guard said. I stood.

It all made sense to me. *Lina number 2*, I thought to myself. The name of our crew is the Diamond Needles. *That rocks,* I thought to myself. *Sounds beautiful.*

I pictured Lina standing beside Riot. She made Riot look more good. Girls love to have pretty friends. That way, one day we could all walk down the street together knowing that there was no reason for any of us to feel jealous, cause we was all doing it with our original styles, flair, and finesse. Each girl in our group having plenty of options. *Hmpp . . .* I would've picked Lina, too, definitely.

I didn't know if Lina would really mail the letter for me. I figured out not to trust even one mouth moving. It didn't matter, I told myself. Showing up at the library instead of rec was nothing to me. While I was wearing the red jumper, I couldn't do shit at rec anyway, just be cuffed and stuck.

Late that same night, I laid close to Siri thinking about Riot.

Riot must be smart, I thought. Yeah, she told me her story. But, it seems she had already known my story. Maybe she chose me cause she read the words "$100-million-dollar empire" in the news article. Or maybe she knew other things that were written in the newspapers about my family and maybe even about me. But I knew for sure that nothing in a newspaper could be trusted. Unless you are a part of someone's life every day or even just with them most of the time, you will never really know what they have and had, what happened with them and how they really are, what they do, why they do it that way and what they feel.

Chapter 6

"Hables?" Lina asked me when I showed up for my "math tutoring."

"Huh?" I answered back.

"Tu eres Santiaga, si? No Hables?" she said.

"What?" I said. Then she understood to speak fucking English. "I ain't Spanish," I told her.

"I'm not Spanish, either," Lina said. Her faced was relaxed. Her body was still, but her eyes were revealing her fierceness. *"Yo soy una Boriqua, Puerto Ricano!* Don't forget it," she said to me. But how could I remember something I didn't understand in the first place? "I can see why these young chicks wanna punch you in your face," Lina said. "You come off all wrong." She spoke calmly, but I could tell she was working hard to hold back her temper. "Maybe you won't be happy till you got a buck-fifty on your face? I know one girl up here who didn't know how to shut her mouth, so someone sliced her face open with a razor. What would you do if that happened to you?"

"I'd cut her back," I said. "As long as the one who sliced my face was walking around with her face sliced open, too, I would wear my scar. I wouldn't complain," I said honestly, then shrugged my shoulders like I do when I don't have nothing else to say.

"You stupid, stupid little girl." She said it softly but it was heartfelt. I didn't let Lina see that she hurt my feelings, but she did. I hated to be put down. I hated for anyone to play me like I'm dumb. I hated that I could tell that she really believed that I was stupid. I hated that I liked Lina a lot, and she either couldn't tell or didn't care. I hated that now Lina thought I was fighting cause I was a stuck-up, little, stupid bitch, and not because I was defending myself. I'm ten. Lina is either fifteen or sixteen. She is in the beige-tan jail jumper. Why was she coming so hard for me?

Tears bubbled up, then streamed down my face. She got up and came back with a tissue. It was the second time, on our second day of meeting, that she wiped my tears for me, while I was red, my wrist controlled on a short chain, ankles cuffed to the chair. After she did that, I was feeling hate and love towards her, and I was confused.

"Don't you know that when you are pretty, everybody expects you to be stupid?" Lina asked me.

She was seated back close to me, pretending to be tutoring me in math. Her question repeated in my mind: *Don't you know that when you're pretty everyone expects you to be stupid?* I sat thinking. Lina is saying that she thinks I'm pretty. That mixed my feelings up for her even more.

"A girl should never be stupid unless she is pretending to be stupid to save her own life," Lina said.

"I'm not stupid," I said confidently.

"How does a stupid person know that she's stupid?" Lina asked me.

I didn't answer.

"Exactly," Lina said, as if I had actually answered her question.

"Exactly what?" I asked.

"If you are stupid, you would be too stupid to know it," she said without smiling or laughing. I still didn't say nothing.

"When you meet someone who is on your side, start off by introducing yourself. That's what smart people do," Lina said.

"That's not really smart—if I am just meeting someone, how would I know if they are on my side or not? Why would I tell them my name?" I asked, and I meant it. I was looking at Lina, waiting for her to answer.

"I meant . . . ," Lina started to say. "Whatever! I introduced myself to you. I told you I was Lina, number 2, the Diamond Needles. You knew then that I was on your side."

"Okay. I'm Porsche L. Santiaga. I'm ten. I like music. I like to dance. I don't like to fight. I don't start fights with anyone. But I will fight anybody who starts a fight with me, even if I don't think I can win. I'm pretty. Lina, you're pretty, too, *so you know how it is. These ugly bitches got us surrounded.*"

We both laughed. I exhaled a lot, and then felt easier with Butterscotch Lina, who I had thought had no smile.

"I like your haircut," I said to Lina suddenly. "Did you cut it yourself?" I asked.

"No, we have a salon in Building A. My girl JinJah cut it. She's Diamond Needle, number 9," Lina said.

"She has a jail job?" I asked, all surprised.

"All Diamond Needles got a hustle. The hair hustle is the biggest payday. But chica, *I get mines done for free.* Me and JinJah in the same clique. So we take care of each other." Lina put her fingers in her hair, stroking through the soft black-black half curls, stopping at her neck where it was still silky but cut low and clean.

"And these aren't 'jail jobs.' You young, but don't forget. We're in prison, *not jail.* We're convicted, not on trial. We're on lockdown, viewed as violent and a threat to society."

I knew all of that, but it sounded even worse when Lina said it all out loud.

"To make it in here you gotta start off by choosing the right family. The family with the right connections," she said.

"Like how Riot chose you?" I asked her.

"That's not how it happened," she said, still calm and cool. "But it's true, with our clique, girls have to be chosen by either me or Riot. It's the only way to get up with us."

"JinJah number 9 can't choose nobody? And numbers three, four, five, six, seven, eight, ten, after they in the Diamond Needles, they can't bring nobody in who they choose?"

"No. *Nunca,*" Lina said.

"*Nunca?*" I repeated.

"Never," Lina translated.

I sat thinking for some seconds. I knew now that Lina didn't choose me. I wondered if that meant she didn't approve? Maybe she disagreed with Riot's choice.

"What if Riot wants someone in, and you don't?" I asked.

"*Confianza,*" Lina said. "Between me and Riot, there is *trust.* We don't argue. We trust each other's choices. We know that if either of us chooses the wrong person, both of us will suffer, then fail. Riot and me always say, '*If you tell on me, you tell on yourself.*' So we don't worry. Everyone we deal with has something to lose, something to gain, and something to protect. Riot wouldn't have chosen you if you didn't have something to lose, something to gain, and something to protect."

Lina's lesson went on like that. It was more heavy than being in math, science, or English class. I found myself doing way more thinking. Lina placed her words carefully. It seemed like every other sentence from her was laced with a threat and a challenge.

Lina told me, "There are 528 inmates locked down here as of today. In one second that number could increase or decrease. There are twenty-nine gangs in here. In twenty-eight of the crews, you gotta get 'jumped in' to get down with them. That means you gotta get your ass beat by the whole crew. Maybe they'll fuck up your face or shove a broom in your little pussy or tight asshole. Like that ain't enough, you could get ordered to do something dumb, hurt yourself or someone else you don't got no beef with. Then, your time here on lockdown doubles or triples up," Lina said, like she was disgusted. She was leaning forward in her chair, one hand pressing down on her leg and the other on her hip.

"All that shit is retarded. We don't get down like that. We're pretty, and we're smart. We make moves that the dumb ones can't figure out. We money girls," she said, and she was definitely speaking my language now.

"What if one of them twenty-eight other gangs decide they don't like the Diamond Needles girls? What if one Diamond Needle girl gets jumped? Do the rest of our clique supposed to let that slide just cause we supposed to be smarter and prettier than everybody else who's locked up in here same as us?" I asked.

"No, we pay any bitch back, but not the way they expect. We run this prison. The Diamond Needles are in all the right places. Everything runs through us or by us. Every Diamond Needle girl is in a power position. Since we got the power, and we make the money, we get the respect. If anyone crosses us, we don't beat 'em with our fist. Why should we fuck ourselves up? We outsmart 'em. We squeeze 'em."

"Squeeze 'em," I repeated.

"Squeeze 'em," she repeated.

Each day with Lina brought a new lesson, a new assignment, and a new understanding. I ain't slow, so I caught on and caught up. There were seven days of lessons. Lesson one was trust, followed by silence, loyalty, friendship, teamwork, style, and method.

On the last day of my seven lessons, Lina said to me, "Being *la bambina mas joven,* the youngest of the Diamond Needles clique, is a double-edged position. The older girls will feel even more protective over you. They might try and spoil you. Some might even expect less from you. On the other hand, since you are the youngest, you have to show all of your big sisters the most respect, answer to all the members, and you'll follow the most amount of instructions."

Lina also told me not to milk the "baby thing." If I wanted to be equal, I should work hard and earn my status.

I noticed Lina called the other Diamonds her sisters, while Riot called me and Siri her sons. I didn't think on it too long; family is family.

Even though the seventh lesson completed my training, I wanted to stay close with Lina. I liked her. She was smart and pretty, serious but still fun. She was warm if you got to know her and cold if you didn't.

For me, style and method were the hardest lessons of all. For style, I had to use manners I wasn't used to using. I had to introduce myself to each of the Diamond Needles separately. I had to remember their names and numbers. I had to learn their likes, dislikes, and requests, and be on call to help anyone on our team at anytime that I could.

I had to give each Diamond Needle a "tribute," or gift. The gift giving wasn't so bad. I understood that in here you couldn't get something for nothing. Plus I still had my candy hustle going. I dreamed up an idea that I would put in motion immediately. I'd make some little packets in arts 'n crafts. Siri would decorate them. I'd put in assorted candies, and that would be my gift. For people on the outside that might not sound like shit, but in here a little sugar was hard to obtain and could take me far.

For method, Lina explained, "You have to be disciplined enough to follow a plan of action. You have to think with all of your girls in mind and not only yourself. You have to respond to all communications as quickly as possible. You have to make sure you don't mess up or interrupt what the DN is trying to achieve."

"What are we doing first?" I asked her.

"It's your first thing, but to us is just one more thing we're doing, in the middle of doing everything else," she said. I seen that Lina liked to remind me that I was the young one. We were the last ones to be chosen, Siri and me. It seemed like she thought that I was the most likely to fuck up.

Out of loyalty to Riot, and respecting the DN code of silence, I wasn't telling Lina that I chose Siri to be in the Diamond Needles, and that Riot approved it. Lina believed that only she and Riot could choose members. But having Siri in the gang was a condition of my hooking up with dem.

"So what am *I* doing first?" I corrected myself for Lina.

"You're not going to fight with anyone else," she said, with the most mean look on her serious face since me and her first met. "You are going to let us handle the Cha-Cha beef. You are going to make it to the *Festival de la Familia* . . . ," she said, speaking Spanish again. Then she said in English, "The Annual Family Festival, which no prisoner can attend if they have even one violent episode ninety days prior to the festival date, which is on Saturday July 20, 1996."

"Okay, but . . . ," I started saying.

"You been locked down here for almost three years. You missed two festivals cause of fighting. The third one is coming up in four and a half months," she said.

"Cha-Cha is fucking crazy. You think I can schedule my fights with her? Whenever she flips out, she flips out and fucks with me. So I fight her."

"Are you smarter than her or is she smarter than you?" Lina asked me.

"You already know," I said swiftly. "Or Riot would've chosen Cha-Cha for the Diamond Needles instead of me," I said confidently.

"Good, then do as I say. Stop allowing her to deal you the same hand every time. Cha-Cha is controlling you. If she keeps you fighting, she keeps you from having any privileges," Lina said.

"She loses her privileges, too," I answered back swiftly.

"So what? She's nobody. She's ignorant. She don't make real moves. She doesn't make money. She don't have no organized team. She don't do nothing but keep the trouble brewing," Lina said, her temper showing only through her pretty eyes. "Porsche, you have to make everyone believe that you have changed, by changing your method of reacting and doing things. Even if you haven't really changed on the inside, like your feelings and stuff, you have to make them believe that you have," Lina said, and I felt at that moment that that was what she had done. On the inside she was angry and boiling like me. For some reason, she saw or learned a benefit to convincing others that she wasn't.

"Santiaga," Lina said, calling me by my last name. I liked the way it sounded coming from her lips, so different than from the warden's. "Make customers, not war," Lina said, sounding like my poppa.

"The festival is the only time of year where, for four hours and fifteen minutes, we can roam freely on the yard and mix with other people who aren't locked down like us. Some of us get only one day a year for a family member to travel all the way up here to visit us. Or, it's our only chance to see somebody we really like, not through a glass, or dirty bulletproof plastic or over a bullshit phone, or through a fence or gate. Not sitting in a small room without the chance to even touch or hug. Some girls got business on the yard on festival day. There are always competitions and prizes, good shit that can be won and sold. We Diamond Needles are all about our business and opportunities, and once a year the festival is an opportunity for us to each do something different, earn something extra, and see somebody special. You, too, Santiaga!"

Lina had me open. It was not because of no fucking festival, though. I just liked her and the feeling coming from her and the way she made me feel, like she believed in something. More than that, she made me feel like, even though she doubted me, she loved me. Of course she loved me. She sat and spoke to me and listened to me when I spoke. She taught me things I needed to know and gave me things she didn't have to give. When she got mad at something I said, she didn't give up or abandon me. She took the time to explain herself and her meaning. Even though I knew Lina wouldn't say so, she knew I was smart enough even though I was young. She wouldn't have wasted her time if she wasn't sure I was capable.

The last question I asked her before parting, "You say all the Diamond Needles have a hustle. What's yours, Lina?"

"Data," she said. I thought she was speaking in Spanish again.

"*Data* is information. It's the most important hustle, not only in here, but in total *el mundo*, the whole world."

Chapter 7

Two months later, I'm on the yard. Been in a baby blue jumper with no red interruptions, no fights, no lockdown at the bottom. Authorities are shocked at my turnaround. Instead of them leaving me alone for not fighting no more, they look me over more closer. They wouldn't get nothing new on me. I'm determined.

Getting ganged up was the best thing that happened to me since I was separated from my real family. Don't get me wrong. Prison is prison, not fun or a fucking picnic. But being connected eased some of my stresses. I wasn't silly enough to think my piece of peace would go on for the whole stretch of my stay, but even a brief break from the pressure was welcomed. It felt good to know I was not affiliated with just any group, but with the sharpest girls on the yard.

Unlike at my real home, which would always be the only real place for me, here I wasn't the invisible middle child. I was the baby, and I had ten big sisters.

True, I wasn't old enough to catch a prison job, internship, or assignment. Still I made my own hustle using what I already had, to get what I wanted and to play my part in the clique. I didn't want to stay the baby or the son forever. I wanted to even up.

So, in the C-dorm, where I had influence, I listened and learned. I sorted through and counted up the opportunities available for festival day. I had done my research and found out that there was a talent competition for us prisoners. The prize was a gift basket that had all the shit every girl in here needed every day, but most couldn't afford to get or ran out of too quick. Plus it had some stuff we never even dreamed of getting our hands on until we hit time served and walked out of this miserable joint.

The prize basket contained the latest technology that many of us never seen or heard of. We were used to cassette tapes and cassette players. While we were locked up, it switched. So the fact that the prize basket contained a CD player, along with a DVD player, CDs and DVDs donated by entertainment companies made it ten times more valuable. The basket also had three phone cards, which added up to 180 minutes, or three hours, of phone talk and stuff like lotions, soaps, deodorants, perfume, and hair products, as well as a stationery set with stamps, and some books and magazines that was supposed to be the good ones. I knew for sure that whoever won that first-place basket could open up a business in here and work each item in trade or sale or use for about a year, no doubt. I even considered that the DVDs and CDs didn't even have to be sold. If they were mines, I would open up my own version of Blockbuster and rent out the DVDs and CDs so they kept making money for me year-round. Even the books and magazines would hold weight, especially if they chose the right ones that girls from the hood would sweat, and probably weren't available in the library. The shit that wasn't being discussed was that whoever won that basket would need an army to keep it, even if they won it fair and square. The first-place winner would turn into a target in seconds, no doubt.

Riot wasn't in agreement about the prize basket or the competition. She said the authorities were "slick" and the robots were dumb. "Watch how they kill each other to get their hands on that first prize."

Riot said that the authorities paid for all that shit in the basket with money they made off of us. She also told me that the authorities would use the basket to keep the inmates in check and use the talent show to show the state what a good job they had done in controlling us, and how happy we all were to be in prison. So happy that we are up here singing and dancing for our captors.

"That's what you're gonna do, right Porsche? Dance for the authorities at the festival?" Riot asked me.

"No," I answered back swiftly. "I'm the producer and choreographer for the seven girls that are gonna grab first place. I'm gonna teach them the dopest moves. When they win, they're gonna pay me my fee."

"Pretty smart," Riot said. "How much you pulling?"

"One DVD player and whatever DVDs come with it. I'll open my own movie house. Only the Diamonds will get in for free," I said. We both laughed a little. Riot hugged my shoulders. I was working my way up to being even.

Aside from the reason I gave Riot about why I wouldn't be dancing in the show, there was the fact that Momma had said, "One day someone will pay you a million bucks to move your hips like that." Before Riot ever brought it up, I had already decided not to dance with the seven girls who I had selected after auditioning them. Prize basket or not, nobody in this fucking place could afford my dance performance.

It was windy on the yard, but we managed to get up a game of double Dutch. For us, it wasn't an average afterschool-type game. After all, there was a rope involved. That meant there was a guard posted nearby, close enough to us for her to be one of the players. But she wasn't playing. Now, I don't know if it's all right for a woman to weigh three hundred pounds, but this guard was pushing it and it was not the kind of fat that folded over then dropped or hanged. Hers was packed on her body like how frozen freezing ice cream is packed in the barrel in the ice case in the corner store. It was fat pretending to be muscle. Funny thing is, we knew for a fact that she could run like a lightweight. A bunch of us witnessed her dashing across the yard to break up a brawl, her heavy hands pulling bodies apart, then tossing them. Young ones got hurt more than they would have without her "help." Her grip only choked and crushed. So we requested the rope, played nice with it, and would return it to her five minutes before it was time to leave the yard.

One, ten, twenty, thirty, forty, fifty, sixty, seventy, eighty, ninety. Two, ten, twenty, thirty, forty, fifty, sixty, seventy, eighty, ninety . . .

We counted it out, all nine of us singing together. There was seven Gutter Girls and two Diamond Needles, Riot and Tiny. Or should

I say there were seven Gutter Girls and Three Diamond Needles, since I was in both gangs, the one I started and the one I joined on the low.

It was my turn and I was killing it. "Turn faster!" I called out as I danced between the two ropes, lifting my feet like lightning. I started crisscrossing em, and then paused, amazing myself by picking the beat back up in time to avoid losing a second of rhythm or tripping. I was gonna keep the Gutter Girl Gail's who they used to call Greedy Gail, arms turning two ropes until they were slim and sore. Siri showed up and went wild cheering for me. Both crews had to give it up to me when I bent down between the ropes and jumped out the next set from the squatting position! I'm supposed to be able to do it like dat. I'm a dancer, and rhythm and movement is my expertise.

I leaped up from my squatting, returned to skipping, then suddenly switched to the one-foot hop. As I spun while hopping, I caught a glimpse of Cha-Cha on the yard mean-mugging me. I kept hopping, and didn't miss a beat.

Riot had told me many weeks ago that "Cha-Cha has been neutralized." When I asked Riot what that meant, she said, "It means she won't fuck with you no more."

To me, that meant that Cha-Cha didn't want to fight no more cause it wasn't like she was some powerful bully and I was her scared victim who she beat up. Most of the time I got the best of Cha-Cha in our past brawls, which is most likely why the bitch kept sweating me for a rematch. I once twisted her right arm so hard I thought I broke it, but it was only sprained. I had punched out one of her teeth and lifted a patch of hair from her scalp. Honestly, she got two good shots off on me. She kicked me hard in my ribs, and pulled back one of my fingers trying to pop my bone out. I got loose from her grip quick enough before she could do any permanent damage. Still, my finger got hurt and throbbed and swelled a couple of days before it went back to the same way it was before.

It had been two months of Cha-Cha acting like I was dead. When she saw me, she wouldn't even lift her eyes or move the muscles on her face. Now she was sending off a fighting stare.

My mind started shifting. My eyes were focusing on her ugly face. It made me miss a beat and finally I was out.

"Damn, I thought you would never give up," Gail said, her arms collapsing and her side of the rope going limp.

A Gutter Girl named Brianna sucked her teeth before asking me, "What the fuck was you thinking? You were like a possessed witch inside the ropes."

Everyone laughed. I didn't get red about it. She was my girl. I knew she didn't mean me no ill will. Besides, I had taught her to read and write. That's how I hooked her for the Gutter Girls. She was steady drawing pictures and mailing them out. They weren't even beautiful pictures, just some crayon-type shit. Siri said to me, "She can't write." Instead of embarrassing Brianna, I went by her bed and said, "Let's put some words on your drawings, like a storybook. I have good handwriting. Tell me what you wanna say. I'll write it down neatly." We got tight like that.

"Get your hands up," Tiny, number 10 of the Diamond Needles, said. She was thirteen and rocking the same yellow jumper as Riot. But still, she was our same small size like she could fit in with the baby blues. She was so petite, other than her two grapefruit-sized titties. She was next up for the rope and wanted her turn. As Tiny pushed off and jumped in, Riot pulled me back some.

"The Real Bitches are trying to recruit Cha-Cha. No matter how she glares at you, don't make a move. Got it?" Riot was talking to me without looking at me. She was surveying the movements on the yard.

Chapter 8

We counted everything, and everything counted. We counted seconds, minutes, hours, days, weeks, months, and years. We counted asses in the shower and how many heads were in the gym. We counted off during head counts. We counted visits and visitors and the amount of days without visits or visitors. We counted days until hearing dates, court dates, and, of course, release dates. We counted the numbers of letters received or not received, days between connected phone calls, rejected phone calls, or no phone calls at all. We counted days since our mothers came or never came. We counted squares in the floor, lights in the ceiling, colors of uniforms. We counted the number of guards, staff, and workers. We even counted the teeth in our teachers' mouth as they talked. We counted everything, and everything counted. We counted them. They counted us. We counted. They counted.

There was a fork missing from the count in the kitchen, and one butcher knife. The alarms went off in the building. Guards charged through the halls, some ragged in riot gear. All inmates moving to the final activities of the day, and all inmates doing anything anywhere were paused as a trained reaction to the alarm. Special guards swept us up in a single-file line. The girls in the same hall area where I was standing were all escorted into the gym.

"No talking," they commanded us.

"Spread out. Both hands up." One guard demonstrated. We didn't need any demonstration. This is how we always measured space between girls on the gym floor.

"I didn't tell you to put 'em down," she barked. I knew that now she would make us hold that position for ridiculously long. In here, all adults, staff, teachers, and whatever guards were delighted by little acts of torture. There were girls of mixed ages in the gym lineup. I knew after counting fifteen rows of ten girls that they also had a lineup on the yard, maybe the slop house and in the dorm hallway in one of the larger buildings.

"Put 'em down," the guard ordered.

Me and Riot's eyes met. We were both scanning the rows, counting Diamond Needles. I seen number 7, Hamesha. She couldn't be missed. She was an Indian with a long Indian braid, tucked inside her tan jumper, the color worn by fifteen- and sixteen-year-olds. I didn't know her name before I had got ganged up, but I had seen her way before then at the hospital, which these people in here called the infirmary. She had the pretty face and the dirtiest job—emptying pots after inmate patients peed, vomited, or crapped. She got to wear gloves and sometimes a paper face mask. When she wasn't collecting the shit that no one wanted to touch, she was mopping floors and wiping down counters with some stinky smelling stuff. She had walked past my hospital bed where I was lying and locked from time to time. She only spoke to me once saying, "You are the only one who misses your ma more than I miss *meri ma.*"

"*Meri ma?*" I repeated, with my dried-out lips.

"My mother," she translated.

"How would you know that I miss my momma more?" I asked curiously. Besides, me and Siri were both bored.

"I say you miss your ma more than I miss *meri ma* because I am still holding my missing her inside. You on the other hand can not stop screaming it out."

I realized Hamesha had heard me screaming the night before when I was giving the nurses hell. But hell was my true feeling and all I had to give at that moment.

* * *

The female guards and many female staff poured into the gym. Row by row we were body-searched, fingers moving through our hair, hands moving around our necks, shoulders, arms, armpits, fingers, chest, breast, stomachs, asses, private parts, thighs, knees, calves, ankles, toes. As each row was completed, the lead searchers called out, "All clear!"

When all 150 of us were confirmed "All clear," the gym door clicked open and the warden walked in, backed up by four more guards. She dismissed the special guards. She must've felt more safe after the gymnasium body search turned up nothing.

Warden Strickland was a black woman. Her feeling was the opposite of Momma. I mean she was in good body shape, and normally wore either pants suits or skirt suits, but she seemed like a woman who had never been touched by a man, hugged by a small child, or loved by a mother and father. Her skin seemed hard, her eyes empty. Even her hair was stuck in one inflexible position, as though she sprayed it with holding hair spray every morning and never once rinsed or washed the chemical out. Her strut seemed overdone, like she had to move that way to prove she was the warden, but all of us already knew that.

"Ladies, there's one fork and one butcher knife missing from the kitchen supply cabinet. If you make it hard on me, I'll make it unbearable for you. Nobody will leave this facility and no one will be allowed in until the fork and knife are found. That means my staff, who already have worked a full shift, your teachers, the officers, no one can go home until the weapons are recovered. You're punishing them. You're punishing me. Now, *I'm punishing you.* If I don't get the fork and knife back immediately, I will cancel the upcoming Annual Family Festival. Why? Because if you don't help me, I won't help you."

A gasp ran through the gym and echoed off of the high walls. A whistle blew. "You have ten minutes. Keep your hands to yourselves. Talk to each other. Then, send the one who is trying to separate you from your fun and families on family festival day up front, where I'm standing. The guilty one will definitely be disciplined, but you will not pay for her poor violent and selfish decision."

The prisoners' talk started out as a murmur and rose to a roar. I thought to myself, *The warden is sneakier than any one of us inmates.* The lineup was broke up now as everyone took the ten minutes granted by the warden as a break.

Riot strolled over. "Lay back. It's not us," she said.

Hamesha broke her line and followed Riot. She was way calmer than everyone else. She looked in me and Riot's eyes, then stood beside us but didn't say nothing.

Tiny popped up out of nowhere. "I know you didn't see me right?" she asked all of us. "I was standing between those two tall girls in the yellow." She used her head to point them out. "So what do you all think?" Tiny asked.

"She won't cancel. She wants us to believe that she will. The festival is for her, not for us. Watch, the stupid robots will believe the warden. In a few minutes they'll all cave in and start snitching on one another."

"But they searched us all already," I said.

"Yeah, and while they were searching us in here, and the rest of us on the yard, you better know they were searching our beds, cells, and belongings," Riot said, and we four fell silent.

Brawl broke out. Instead of everybody rushing forward to where the fists were swinging, everyone except the fighters fell back leaving a huge space in the left corner that exposed three inmates. Guards raced in and attempted to yank them apart. When Warden ordered the guards to halt, the girls scuffling on the floor suddenly peeled themselves off of the other. They must've been shooken by the silence that surrounded them. Normally the inmates would've been mobbing up and cheering or choosing sides and jumping in during a breakout brawl. But the threat of the festival cancelation held everyone spellbound. No one wanted to be mistakenly included in anything that could be cited as wrong behavior. Besides, when the guards start grabbing on any one of us, if we didn't settle, and surrender, it was the stick or the shock of the taser.

We all knew that the first punishment for the brawlers would come from the warden. If the festival got canceled because of them, the second but worse punishment would come from within. The enraged girls on lockdown would hit like bullets being fired from all directions—on the yard, or in the slop house, or in the gym, places where we all gathered in groups, gangs, and cliques, where payback was a bitch, revenge was the truth and our unspoken law.

The three brawling girls were on their asses in front of the warden, their jumpers crooked and one of em ripped opened.

"Does this have anything to do with my missing utensils, or is it that you three just wanted to make sure I canceled the festival?"

"They're going to the bottom," I said casually to Riot.

"Cause they're stupid," Riot agreed.

"The warden said only the one who took the fork and knife would be punished," Tiny said.

"Did you believe her? Look how the warden caused them to fight, and watch what she does next," Riot said quietly.

The whistle blew. We froze in place.

"Hands out," one guard commanded.

We all spaced ourselves.

"No more talk," the guard barked.

The warden took one step forward. "Sit," the warden said, and we all sat down in perfectly spaced neat rows. We were all silent, nothing moving but our eyes. I could hear their hearts beating furiously. I could feel it, too.

My heart was racing for different reasons. Me and Riot, Tiny, and a whole group of us of all ages and different gangs and cliques were all "state property." We were the ones who nobody showed up for—in court, at medical offices, or interviews and hearings and, even worser, for visitations. Riot's and Tiny's parents were murdered. My parents and family were considered dead because they were all a no-show. My body began to tremble beneath my jumper. The thought of having been abandoned and forgotten was too violent. I perspired as I watched the warden. The idea that, according to them, she was my legal mother made me feel nauseous. Now I was sick and tense like the rest of them, not because of the fucking family festival where no one from my family would show. Not because of four hours and fifteen minutes of freedom, or the "best meal we having for the whole year." It was something more deeper than that going wrong inside of me.

Walkie-talkies blared at a high volume suddenly. "The A-dorm is all clear," a male voice reported into the warden.

"Move officers to the B-dorm," she ordered. We could tell her anger was mounting. She wasn't the only one.

A whistle sounded.

"Get on all fours," the warden commanded. We all looked around with questions printed on our faces. There were three hundred eye-balls moving.

"Do whatever she says," Riot whispered to me.

In a split second the gym was packed with girls on their hands and knees, including the three brawlers.

"You want to act like animals?" the warden asked. "Whatever you're going to do in life, do it well. Now crawl," she ordered.

There was a long pause and most girls began crawling on hands and knees. Riot shot me a look. She was already crawling. I saw the warden maneuvering between the rows of crawling females. I thought about Lina. She wasn't in the gym. Was she somewhere crawling on her hands and knees? She taught me to think for all of the Diamond Needles and not only of myself. I knew they all wanted to attend the festival for business, friends, or fun. I knew Lina wanted to go and that she planned on seeing someone special to her. I had the danc-ing girls who I was training and who I knew were gonna win if they perfected my routine. But I could step away from all that shit easily. It didn't mean much to me.

"If I catch you, and you are not crawling, you will get disciplined for not obeying my orders," the warden called out in a controlled and angry voice.

If I could be sure that Winter was coming to visit me, would I crawl for that? I asked myself. My eyes filled with tears. It didn't mat-ter. I was facing the floor and no one could see my tears if I kept my head down. So I did. I began crawling. I was angry that I even consid-ered that Winter would show up for me. I had promised myself many months ago not to think or believe or hope for even one visitor. That way, I could separate myself from the heavy feeling of disappointment and depression. The temperature of my body began to increase. The flow of heat within me was moving strangely because of the way I was bent down and crawling on my knees.

"Now bark," the warden ordered. "Everyone!" The gym made the barking sounds double and triple as each girl barked differently from one another, all dogs.

"Stop!" the warden called out swiftly, and crawling, barking bodies bumped like bumper cars.

"Now moo," she ordered, and there was another long pause. I was confused as to whether she was saying for us to "move." But one girl began making cow noises and soon every girl was doing it. My face was still facing the floor so I didn't moo, the same way I didn't bark. How would she tell who was and who wasn't barking or mooing?

"Does it feel good to behave like animals?" the warden called out. "Would you prefer to live like them?" No one answered because they were all still mooing.

"Quiet!" Her voice overpowered everyone's. The mooing stopped.

"How do your knees feel? Should ladies crawl on their knees and bark like dogs, and moo like cows who can only eat and poop?" she asked. No one answered. Thankfully, I thought to myself.

"Drop down flat on your bellies!" she commanded. We were all now lying flat facing the floor.

"Are you all a bunch of snakes? Are you sneaky slimy creatures? You want to ruin it for one another? Let me hear you snakes hiss!"

The hissing sounds of more than a hundred girls itched the inside of my ears, and I felt like a rash was traveling through the inside of my body. The sound was loud and disturbing. I vomited. The stinky goop landed beneath my chin on the floor I was facing. I could hear a few girls farting and a few crying.

"Stop!" the warden screamed out.

"Stand up!" she ordered next. "At the sound of my whistle all of you walk towards the wall that you're facing. Press your faces against the wall. Make your nose press against those cement blocks!" she said. This shit was getting stranger and stranger. I wiped my mouth with my jumper and stepped over my wet pile and walked towards the closest wall.

None of us could see one another or anything else because we were all facing one of the four walls, our backs to the warden, not a comfortable feeling.

From the sound of her movement and voice, she was walking towards the center with the guards.

"Close your eyes," she ordered.

I don't know if everyone did. I didn't. But I didn't turn my head left or right not even slightly. I know better than to tell on myself.

"Now, ladies, I hope we have reached an understanding. You don't want to be animals. I don't want to treat you like animals. No one can see your faces now. I want the person who knows where the fork and knife are hidden to raise her right foot. No one else will know who it is. But I will know. You will not be punished for providing the right information. You will be treated properly and rewarded kindly for saving lives. You will be the one who proves that you are not an animal living by the laws of the jungle. You are human enough to care about the safety of all of your peers," she said, politicking.

We stood facing the wall for half hour, silently. I wondered if anyone had already raised their foot even a little to signal the warden. Maybe she had already identified one or two or three snitches, but was making us stay facing the wall so she could pretend that no one had snitched. Then she would call the snitches to her office in the middle of the night or early in the morning when no one would notice that they were missing.

Her walkie-talkie flared. "Dorm B all clear." The male guard's voice bounced around the gym.

"Search dorm C. It's the last place I would expect to discover the weapons. But check carefully. Over," the warden ordered.

"Bathroom," I heard a girl's voice say softly.

"No bathroom!" the warden called back angrily. "You want to live like animals, then do it well!" I could tell she was more madder cause the guards were searching everywhere but not finding nothing. I peed. I don't know if anyone else did, but I had to pee from way back when the alarms were setting off and all this bullshit first started. I didn't dare move a leg or foot or turn my face to see what kind of puddle or stream I had made. I didn't need her calling me to her office like I had a damn thing to say to her.

"Everyone turn around!" the warden said suddenly. We all turned. "All my tans, pinks, and yellows, walk over here and line up," the warden said, pointing to the center of the gym where she was standing.

"You are the ones who are supposed to set the example for the baby blues. If these are the kinds of things that you do, what are you teaching the babies to do?" she asked, and I knew the bitch was just crazy. We baby blues weren't her babies. We were never treated in any type of way that someone who has a baby would act. We weren't treated no more specialer than any girl wearing any color prison jumper.

"Strip!" she ordered the girls ages eleven through sixteen, the pinks, yellows, and tans. But they all just looked around at one another and didn't do it.

"Strip," she repeated. "This is a matter of security. Who knows what you are hiding beneath your clothes. Now step out of your shoes and strip." I got heated cause we all had already been searched thoroughly. She knew she wouldn't find nothing through a strip that she hadn't found already. And who could hide a fork and knife in their ass or between their thighs or below their tongues?

A few girls stripped boldly, letting the warden know it wasn't nothing to them to be naked, long as they got to attend the festival. The others followed one by one, their cheap prison shoes besides their feet and the jumpers piled on top.

Tiny, the smallest girl up there, did not strip. Now she was the only one who didn't.

"Ms. Parker, are you any better than the rest of these girls?" the warden asked Tiny. That was Tiny's real name, Chanel Parker.

"No, no better," Tiny said softly.

"Then do as they have done. Or are you hiding the weapons?" she asked. Tiny didn't answer.

"I know your history, Ms. Parker. You better step out of your jumper in the next three seconds or you will pay the price," the warden threatened. I felt sorry for Tiny. Riot was up there completely nude. Hamesha was nude and in tears. Riot wasn't telling Tiny to obey what the warden said, like she did back when we were first ordered to crawl.

Tiny pulled off her jumper slowly. As it dropped to the floor, she immediately tried to cover herself with her small hands. She could only conceal her nipples. She couldn't cover the truth. Her beige skin, her back and sides and stomach were all covered with dark brown marks of different shapes and sizes. There was a long scar that bubbled on her thigh just below her butt and there were even some scars behind her knees.

In the silence of every girl seeing Tiny's life story stamped and scraped and burned and sliced into her skin, obviously painfully, I wanted to murder the warden. I didn't want to shoot her with a gun, which would've been too gentle. I wanted to cut her with a knife and burn her with a few lighted cigarettes the way someone obviously did

Tiny. I wanted to embarrass her, humiliate her, torture her. I wanted her to feel what each of us had to be feeling. It was the emotion I hated the most of all emotions, *shame*.

*   *   *

Late night, I couldn't sleep. We were all returned to our right spaces after the weapons were discovered in the C-dorm where I was housed. I was lying still, but my whole body felt like it was moving. My heart was racing. My thoughts were tangled tight like a rubber band ball that I once made. My fist and toes were balled up and stuck.

When I first met Tiny, even though I knew she was four years older than me, I felt protective over her. Maybe it was the way she introduced herself to me after I introduced myself to her. She had said, "I'm Tiny. I'm small like a dot. No, like a germ. I'm so small you can't even see me." I'll never forget that.

I knew not to ask her why she was locked-down same as me. Lina taught me that. I knew not to ask her about her past. "Sometimes it's too painful to discuss and rude to even ask about," Lina had said.

Tiny's from New York, the projects out in Yonkers. Her whole family was wiped out in a drug war, and not by the police. It was a street war over territory. Tiny's brothers were gunrunners turned stick-up. When their family gang began setting up and robbing the drug spots, it took a lot of murder before the dealers discovered who was behind it. When they did discover that it was Tiny's brothers, the war happened over a stretch of only ten days. Tiny's whole family got wiped out, parents, brothers, and all. Tiny had told me this story herself one day when I was feeling bad. She wanted me to know that her life was way worser than mine. As I listened to her details, I couldn't argue. She was right. Tiny told me she never told nobody her story except for Riot, who was the one who chose Tiny to gang up with the Diamond Needles.

Tiny told me that she was gonna tell me the "ending part," that she never even told Riot. She said she was kidnapped by her brother's enemies and tortured for six days. She told me that she was raped and taught me what that *really* meant and involved. She told me that people always say she's nice-looking, but that she feels "all nasty on the inside."

"How did you get away from them?" I asked about the kid-nappers.

"That's why I'm here," was all she said. "Make sure, Santiaga, if some nigga tries to get in between your thighs and you don't want 'em there, kill him," she said that with a straight face, no tears. "In here is safer than out there," Tiny added. After what all had happened tonight, I wondered if she still thought so.

All the Diamond Needles had stories that make the body shake and tremble. As the personalities of each of my ten sisters flashed through my mind like a dope-ass film that never been made yet, the moving pictures in my mind paused with Riot in the frame. Riot is number 1, and I been trying to figure her out little by little. As images of the warden's horror show flipped back and forth in my mind, I kept rewinding so I could figure out the events from the double-Dutch game to the warden. Forty minutes of reviewing moving reflections in my mind led me to some conclusions.

Lina is smart. Riot is scary-smart, I thought to myself. Riot some-how knew that the Real Bitches were setting up to recruit Cha-Cha. Riot also knew that Cha-Cha was my enemy. Riot probably figured that the Real Bitches were not only try'na copy her style by recruiting young ones from the C-dorm same as she did, but that they were also setting up to challenge the Diamond Needles. Riot knew it all, but didn't show it and didn't react. She didn't and wouldn't fight none of the big strong black chicks who had named themselves "real bitches." Instead, Riot put a plan together and set her army into motion, each Needle in a power position. Riot gave the orders more gentle and quietly than the warden ever could. Riot stood in the gym, innocence spread across her face. She crawled like the robots, barked like the robots, mooed and hissed like the robots, then she stripped like the robots. She even told us Diamond Needle girls that our clique had nothing to do with what was happening. I definitely believed her. I am sure Tiny and Hamesha did, too. But the fact that the fork was later found in Cha-Cha's bed, and the butcher knife tucked inside of the rubber gloves belonging to the leader of the Real Bitches had me doubting Riot. The fact that Cha-Cha and her leader were both wiped out in one incident, forbidden from the festival and confined to the bottom during the hottest month of the year made me believe that Riot had set them up as punishment for challenging her and for challenging me.

This is what my mind was working out right then. I knew our Diamond Needles clique had a girl working the kitchen detail, in the exact place where the fork and knife went missing. I had met Diamond Needle number 6, Rose Marie the Jamaican, when I first went to introduce myself and hand her my candy gift.

Riot eliminated my enemy Cha-Cha and the leader of the Real Bitches—both of em threats to our clique—without raising a fist. Like Lina said, "We squeeze 'em." A Diamond Needle only stings when it feels threatened, unlike other pests who sting as a way of life.

* * *

Almost three hours passed before my thoughts stopped their relay race, and my fingers relaxed from my fist. I was wiggling my toes now, beneath my thin blanket. Siri squatted by my bed, whispering in my ear. I was feeling a little more at ease, but I wasn't feeling easy enough to begin giggling with her.

"Where were you?" I asked Siri. "Where were you when the alarms went off?" She covered her ears with her slim fingers and painted natural fingernails. "You know I don't like loud noises and screaming," Siri said.

"So what did you do?" I asked her.

"I hid in the cubicle," she said.

"How long before you got caught?" I asked her.

"I didn't get caught," she said. "But I saw who put the fork in Cha-Cha's bed," she added, now pressing her lips against my ear.

"Who else saw?" I asked swiftly.

"No one. There was only me watching."

"Good job, Siri," I told her.

"Can I put a braid in your hair?" Siri asked me. I nodded yes. As she began to stroke my hair like Momma did when she was making sure not to miss even one strand, I felt myself slipping finally into sleep. As I fell, one last thought snuck into my mind even though I had worked hard to wipe them all away. *The guards searched through all our stuff and didn't put anything back the way we had it. They wanted us to know that nothing really belonged to us. They wanted us to know they could take and touch anything that we thought was ours, even our bodies.*

Chapter 9

"Are you from the islands?" Rose Marie asked me.

"No, I'm from Brooklyn," I told her.

"Well, you look like a lil Caribbean gal, ya know. We have gals dem who have a nice grade a hair like dat, ya know," Rose Marie said, inviting herself to reach out and touch my hair, then pulled it a little to make sure it was all mine.

"Ya, it's the genuine article," she said approving of my hair. "Yeah, Jamaica have people of all colors, all kinds. Lotta people nafa know dat. We got black, brown, gold, yellow, beige, and even tan. African, Asian, Indians, all kinds. We even have a bunch of Chinese-Jamaicans, dem come down and own a lot of tings in Jamaica. Dem give you a job, work ya hard, but never let the black ones of us come close to the cash register."

Rose Marie didn't want my candy gift, the same gifts that all of the other big sisters in the Diamond Needles had gladly accepted.

"What else ya hav ta offer me now?" she asked. "Ya have some yam, sugar cane, or coconut?" She stood looking down at me cause she was tall and I was young. I was amazed by her. She was blueberry-black and beautiful, so black her skin glowed. She had her tan jumper sleeves and pants rolled up. Her figure was feminine and strong, a small waist, monster booty, and eyes that shined like polished black marbles. Her hair was short and kinked. It had style. I couldn't see beneath her jumper, but it seemed her skin all over was smooth as silk, no scars or pimples.

"You like music?" I asked her.

"Whatcha know about music? Jamaica has the best music, ya know. Everybody copy Jamaica, our style, ya know. We got the wicked sound boys, wicked sound systems," she said, her accent getting thicker as she got more excited about her home country.

"Can you dance?" I asked her.

"American Yankee girl can't dance. Ya have to know how to make your body roll, 'n ride the beat. If me roll me body right, man empty his pockets. Move ya body like Rose Marie, make a rude boy cry, den marry me!" She laughed, her teeth all white. I laughed, too. Rose Marie was tough. Her prison kitchen job seemed to require that she be strong. Everything that surrounded her was made from steel. The pots were huge, nothing like you ever seen your mother use. The spoons were half my height. The mixer and ovens meant to feed an army. The steel cases with the knives were built into the wall and all locked. It was easy to see why at every station where a prisoner could get a job assignment, there was at least one guard to oversee the prison staff and prisoner workers. Each guard on post carried a ridiculous number of keys cause everything was a prisoner, even the shit that wasn't alive.

"We nah touch dose," Rose Marie said as she noticed my eyes looking into the knife case. "But me know how to andle dat. I cut the coconut open with my father's machete. I chop the sugar cane. Oh what I would do for some of dat right now, ya hear?"

I wasn't sure how to handle Rose Marie on our first meeting. She was the only Diamond Needle who rejected my candy tribute. It seemed like no matter what I said, Rose Marie would turn it all into a word fight.

"Rose Marie want nail polish all colors, perfume, something strong and pretty like me. Rose Marie want some panty hose, 'shampoo,' some press-on nails, mascara, lotion for hands that been scrubbing huge pots and pans or . . ." She paused. "Some Q-Tips," she added as though her list wasn't long enough already, and as though I was a fucking magician.

"You act like you going somewhere," I told her. I was getting an attitude cause I knew I couldn't satisfy her.

"Me has a date wit me boyfriend on festival day. Me, Riot, and

Camille. We tree catch the fellas' eyes last year. We boys and girls, we talk and write letters, and now dem boys come back for more this year. Me hafta get good and ready."

"Rose Marie, I'll come back when I have something for you," I told her.

"You too green to understand," she said.

"Green? Understand what?" I asked her, thinking I ain't green but I get red real quick if anyone throws me some slickass comments or insults. Rose Marie laughed. "Green means young, same ting," she said. "You too young to know bout man and 'oman ting."

In a second or so I caught on. "And if ya give me screw face, Rose Marie gon thrash ya," she said, her pretty smooth black arms on her hips. She was still smiling. I left.

I wasn't sweating no boys. I wasn't sure how I felt about them. I didn't have no brothers and never had no boyfriend yet or nothing like that. Although when I danced at the Brooklyn block party one stupid, troublemaking boy said to me, "You got a nice ass. Too bad you're flat-chested." Then he slapped his hand against his own chest and smooved it straight down to show me exactly how flat I was. Winter walked right up. She had been talking to Natalie while keeping her eyes on me so she wouldn't get into no trouble with Momma.

"What did he say to you?" my big sister asked me.

"Nothing," I answered back softly.

Winter liked boys. A lot of boys liked her, too. I liked the way she acted with them. She made 'em chase her, sweat her, buy her things she really didn't need cause Santiaga already gave her his world. But there was one who she truly liked. He was a man, not a boy like the others. His name was Midnight. First time my eyes seen him up close, it felt like I had swallowed a cup of hot sauce, with no water to chase it. The heat rushed all over my flat chest and beneath my skin. The feeling was so strong and had never happened to me even once before I first saw him. And, it never happened to me again either, with any other boy. I didn't say it to no one but I wondered, how could a man make you feel like he was doing something to you, when he wasn't doing nothing but standing still? I figured maybe I liked Midnight cause Winter liked him so much. She had a crazy crush. I could tell by the different way she acted when he was around. I wanted to ask

Winter if she got that hot-sauce feeling from him, too. I didn't ask her, though. She must've had it, cause when I tried to take my turn and sit in the front seat of Midnight's car, Winter rolled her eyes at me so hard, like we wasn't even blood related. I was seven.

* * *

Three days later, instead of candy in a designer packet, I gave Rose Marie six Q-Tips in a packet, six representing her Diamond Needle number. She told me to wait while she opened up her gift, as though she didn't trust me. Or as though, if she didn't approve, she'd make me take it back and bring her something else. I was a little nervous cause I had picked the simplest and last thing she had requested on her list of wants. When she opened the package that Siri decorated, a bright smile came bursting out.

"Until festival day, this . . . ," Rose Marie said, "will give me my good feeling. Have you ever stuck one in your ear?"

"No," I answered truthfully.

"The inside of your ear is like your pussy-hole. Stick in one of these tings and move it around slowly. Feels so good until ya get the real thing from a man," Rose Marie said.

I thought about it later. I never stuck a Q-Tip in my ear, but Momma had. She was right about that good feeling. After Momma did it once, I found myself bringing the Q-Tips to her and asking her to clean my ears "same way you did last time." Could a man make my pussy-hole feel better than that? I was confused about it. Some of the big girls talked about the pussy-hole as a place where men hurt girls badly. Other big girls talked about it like it was a place to be guarded. Then some were in a rush for a man to push up in their pussy-hole. I wasn't sure which category I was in. Or, maybe, I was in all three.

Rose Marie got on my good side cause she danced with only me one day out on the yard. She brought her music cassette. I was already out there with mine. She had me laughing as she pretended to be dancing with a boy. She got up so close on him, she started grinding on the fence and caught the attention of the guard.

"Back off," the guard shouted over our music. Rose Marie called him a "pussy clot." He couldn't hear her, of course, but her expression was clear. She forgot about the guard quickly and got back into her dance groove. She winded her waist, until she was in the down position. When her knees and thighs were each tightly touching, she would inch them slowly open, rhythmically until they were spread wide, legs positioned like butterfly wings. Then she stayed squatted and still, but made her pussy bounce. Meanwhile she began to move her head first to the right, smooth as a caterpillar. Suddenly she maneuvered it to the left. Soon her whole body was opening and closing like the fluttering wings of a butterfly. She wound her waist with no force or jerk to her movements until she was back to standing. Carefully, I watched her. I was dropping the beats and melodies of her Jamaican song "Down in the Ghetto," by Bounty Killer into my body's memory and locking it in.

When the track switched to "Ghetto Red Hot," by Super Cat, my turn came. I had cuffed my jumper all the way up to turn them into hot pants. I cuffed my sleeves to my shoulders. I danced Rose Marie's dance perfectly, showcasing my pretty dancer's thighs and legs. When I wound down into the squatting butterfly wings position, I added a bounce while I was squatting down with my legs open. I showed her I could make my pussy bounce, too. Then I stopped and bounced my butt, made it almost touch the ground, but demonstrated my control over my gentle butt bounce by never letting it touch the earth.

Rose Marie grabbed me up, swung me around, and said, "You bad lickle bitch, a real man killa. You my girl, same as my blood."

"Same as my blood," I repeated in my mind as I felt it moving in my heart.

Chapter 10

"I'd slide you a little drink, but you too little," Lil' Man said to me.

She, who wants to be called *he*, is number 5 of the Diamond Needles.

"How young are you, anyway?" she asked me.

"I'm ten, but I'll be eleven in fifty-four days," I told her.

"I started drinking when I was six," she confessed to me, as she held her paper cup filled with church punch laced with Everclear. According to Riot, the priest laced the punch and only served it to selected "older" girls in his following. He called it "a cup of mercy."

After trying to meet with Angel Johnson, aka Lil' Man, several times without succeeding, I had to ask Riot what's up with her. Riot said, "Lil' Man is a 'Highway man.'" That meant she was part of a small team of girls who get to go outside of the prison walls with guards with guns, to clean up the highways and streets surrounding the prison. Riot also told me that only the girls with the top grades in their classes and zero violent write-ups could even compete for the position. After I heard that, I had to laugh—a competition to go clean up trash.

"Lil' Man got a thing for cars," Riot told me. "She's practically a mechanic. She can put 'em together and take them apart. She love's working the highway detail cause she gets to check out everything on wheels."

I knew Lil' Man didn't really get to check 'em out, press her face against the windows and stare at the interior, open the doors and recline in the plush piped-out leather seats or pop the hood and examine the engine. She simply got to stand and watch the whips speed by.

"You're only gonna be able to catch up with Lil'Man at the prison chapel on Sundays," Riot said.

"I don't even know where the prison chapel is at!" I told Riot.

"You should find out where everything in the prison is at, even if you're not interested in it," Riot corrected me, as we jogged around the prison yard just to do something different. "Porsche, look at every place and every person as a 'potential opportunity.' Never be narrow. Keep your eyes and your mind open," Riot said, her face covered with the moisture from the spring warmth.

Now me and Lil'Man were seated in the chapel, a dreary place not too different than any other prison place, except the benches weren't cemented to the floors. More girls were arriving, looking a little more happy, and a little less hateful than the average look stamped on faces of the caught and caged.

As I peeped, a few girls were gathered in couples, interlocking fingers, sitting close up on one another. I caught on swift. The chapel was a meet-up spot.

"You see the church is open to all prisoners," Lil' Man said to me. "That's why I like it here. Every prisoner has the right to join the church."

That sounded strange to me, *the right*. Going to church was the only thing I heard of that we have *the right* to do.

A man with pink skin, wearing a long black dress entered the chapel. I tried not to stare at him. I didn't like to judge people by color, but his skin was scary looking. He was human with skin the color and texture of a mouse or rat.

"Get up Santiaga, it's Father John," Lil'Man said in a commanding whisper.

"He's not my father," I mumbled, but I got up anyway, not for him but for number 5 of the Diamond Needles.

He was saying some shit. Girls was closing their eyes, not me. I was looking at all of them. Two girls on the bench next to me were touching each other up. When I saw her hand rubbing the other girl's breast through the jumper cloth, I felt something. I don't know what.

Testify and witness were two words I didn't like. I was hearing

them both today even though I was in the chapel and not the courtroom where I had heard those two words the most.

Angel, aka Lil' Man, was in the front of the room now, talking
about Jesus, revenge, and forgiveness. The whole thing sounded like
some confusing bullshit to me. The stuff in the room looked confusing, too. Some statues were cemented and stuck to the walls. Others
were nailed into the counters just in case one of us violent girls broke
fool and grabbed one of the statues and used it to knock somebody
the fuck out.

I looked at Angel. She's very light-skinned, like my poppa. Her
hair was cut into a Caesar, like a dude. Not a short, pretty, girl style,
like Lina or Rose Marie. As I looked at her straight on, I noticed
stuff that I didn't see when we were sitting or standing side by side.
She was petite, but her personality made her seem tall and strong.
Now I could see she was small. She was small and rough. She was
using her hands to explain something up there but the same as like
how Brooklyn dudes talk with their hands to one another while
working the corner. Her face looked like it used to look pretty and
maybe it still did, but she held her mouth like a boy and her eyes
were not like girl-feeling eyes. Even her fingers were mannish. She
didn't put her hands on her hips or twist her little body like we
girls did. Her stance was solid and determined. Her legs locked and
even, not relaxed or bent or capable of flowing into a hot-ass dance
step.

" 'Porsche,' that's a badass name," Lil' Man said to me afterwards.

"Thanks," I replied, handing her my tribute candy packet.

"It's not Porscha or Portia or nothing like that?" she asked me.

"Nope, it's 'Porsche,' the name of the luxury vehicle."

Lil' Man smiled. "Hell yeah! Did your moms push a Porsche?" she
asked me, as though she was imagining.

"No, my father pushed it. Momma rode beside him and made it
look even sweeter than it already was." I laughed a little now; I was
remembering. "I heard you like cars. What did your pops push?" I
asked Lil' Man, knowing that all of the Diamond Needles come from
families that had money, land, and power.

Chapter 11

Art class only occurred once a week. The good classes and things are always rationed out to make sure we mostly feel bad. Art class was the only thing I favored that they provided, that I didn't have to think of and do for myself. The teacher was so-so. But, there was a volunteer helper, a university student, who brought some feeling to life. She would say what none of the guards, teachers, staff, and especially not the warden would say. She kept smiling and saying, "Express yourself! Unlock your thoughts and emotions. If you're unhappy or angry, excited or sad, let me see a reflection of you in your art work."

Before, most of us girls used to sit there in art class and do nothing, or scribble or rip shit apart. Sometimes we would get so bored we'd plot on how to get at each other using the art supplies, but everything was guarded or nailed down.

The college girl been here a month and now she got girls competing on the low, not for some real prize or points, but just to see her smile or look surprised. First prize would be her bragging to everyone in the class about one of our works and then posting it up in the front. The art teacher seemed glad to let the university girl, named Niecey, who swore she was from Brooklyn but living up here at her college, take over. I knew the teacher was sitting and counting the seconds and minutes and hours until she collected her paycheck and got the fuck up out of here and away from us. She must of thought Niecey was stupid for volunteering to be here working with us.

Even though there was only one pair of scissors for twenty-two of us to use, even though the one pair of scissors was on an extra-short chain bolted to our teacher's desk and had to be used standing up in the front of the class after asking for and receiving permission to use them while supervised, I liked going to art class once a week and making things with my hands.

I had an idea for my dancers' outfits for the festival performance. I expected my idea to be rejected by the authorities. However, I had learned from my father, as well as from my circumstances and from the Diamond Needles, to look at everything as an opportunity. So I was making the dress on the low, believing that once everyone saw how dope it was, they would let my girls rock it on stage for their six-minute performance. After they awed 'em and pulled first place, they could be right back in their jumpers.

Up until now, I wasn't worried about any of the other girls in the festival competition finding out what I was working on and copying or sampling my style. Some shit is so well made that it can't be copied, at least not without a long delay and study of the technique. Only Siri and me knew. Everybody else was about to see.

I got the idea for my project while thinking of Poppa. It was based on one of the gifts he once gave me. I was 100 percent sure that nobody that was living in here by force or by choice had ever received the kind of gifts that Poppa gave us. Nope, Poppa's gifts were personal to each of his daughters. From his gift choices he showed us that he knew the difference between each of us. When I asked him for my diamond earrings and necklace, he told me, "Not now. It's not time yet. Ask me for something that you want, not for something that you saw your sister receive. That would be better." Something about poppa made any anger I ever felt inside disappear, after he came to my room, sat on the chair beside my bed, and spoke and listened for a few moments, only to me.

Over the past two weeks in art class, I had already made nineteen paper birds out of black construction paper. I kept them in my cubby drawer.

The paper birds were the spaghetti straps to a paper dress made of black and gold Nefertiti heads.

As I stood up front with my back to the girls and facing my teacher, Niecey walked up to my side.

"Porsche." She said my real name nicely. We was used to the

authorities calling us by our lockdown number, or last names. "Ms. Santiaga," I would hear some authority say with angry curled-up lips.

"Are you cutting out snowflakes in the springtime?" Niecey asked me.

"No, I'm using the scissors the same way that you use them to cut out snowflakes, but I'm making something else," I told her while I kept my fingers moving and the scissors cutting out the details of my dress design.

"Should I guess or is it a secret?" she asked me, smiling.

"It's not really a secret, but a good designer doesn't show her design before it's finished." I kept my eyes down on what I was doing.

"Well, it looks nice so far. I like the black and gold color combination," Niecey said as she began to move away.

"You're hogging it," one girl said, sweating me as she stood behind me waiting to use the scissors.

"You better shut your mouth," I told her without turning around.

"Ms. Santiaga, take it easy. That kind've talk will get you in trouble," the teacher called out.

I didn't say anything back. *Focus on the festival*, I told myself. I had agreed to Lina to do that, and to let all the other bullshit go.

"Porsche," Niecey called me.

"Yeah," I answered.

"Are you done? Tyler would like to use the scissors and class is almost finished."

"Oh," was all I said as I finished up. Then I gathered up my stuff and went back to my seat.

Niecey brought me over the two pieces of yarn I had requested last week. I put nine birds on one string and nine birds on the other. One bird was left over just in case I made a mistake, but I didn't so far.

With my fingernail, I punched a tiny hole and threaded the spaghetti straps onto the Nefertiti dress and tied four pretty little knots.

I was done.

"You are the best," Siri whispered to me.

I whispered back, "We made it together. We are the best." Siri smiled and her pretty white teeth sparkled.

Quietly, I stood up and dropped off my baby blue jumper.

"You're naked!" one girl yelled out, and everyone turned around.

"So, bitch? We were all naked in the shower this morning, and the warden made girls get naked in the gym. What's the big deal?" I said it with the Lina kind of calm and casual anger. Siri helped me to put the dress over my head carefully.

"I can see your nipples," another girl called out laughing.

"I saw yours before, too," I told her. We were all baby blues.

Ms. Aaronson and Niecey were both now standing on each side of where I was standing. After their tight disciplinary faces faded, their jaws just dropped. Ms. Aaronson said, "Ms. Santiaga, that dress is really quite lovely." Then she turned towards all of the girls and said with suddenly tear-filled eyes, "You kids are so talented. What a waste, you all being locked up in here." I wasn't sure if she was happy or disgusted.

Niecey began slowly clapping for me. Some of the girls started clapping cause Niecey did. Niecey grabbed my little fingers and held my hand. I forgot about my paper dress. Hers was the first human touch I had felt since Momma and Winter. Not the same as someone slapping my face and me punching her lights out and choking her, I thought. But someone touching me like they cared for me, someone other than Siri.

As I walked with her to the front of the class to face everyone and receive "first prize," which is Niecey's bragging about me, the beat boxer from the dance class I was teaching gave me a random beat. I started moving my little body, excited to be the center of something good for a change. The girls went wild cheering for me. Even some of my rivals were giving it up. I felt moved by four forces: them, Niecey, the handmade dress, and the beat. Shockingly, Ms. Aaronson caught feelings. She had both her palms laid against her own face in amazement. Maybe that was what was missing from her life, music! As soon as the beat and my dancing began, Ms. Aaronson went from her dead self to being alive. Niecey got amped and started clapping even faster. Soon her hips started wiggling, which triggered the beat boxer to get even more live. Next thing I knew we were all dancing and having a party out of fucking nowhere!

The warden was like a high-powered vacuum cleaner. She sucked the air out of the room, like she was doing right then. It was like she removed the air and the light and now we were all standing in the dark frozen like in freeze tag and unable to breathe.

A fake smile came to the warden's face. We had never seen that before. Her smile was either nonexistent or crooked, like a villain in a cartoon. Standing behind her was some white adults. It was like she was the wicked wizard and they were her ghost goons.

Warden must've had gigantic ears the size of an elephant's and eyes that could leap out of their sockets and scurry down the hall on their own. How could she see and hear everything? I thought to myself.

"Ms. Aaronson," the warden said, the first two words spoken since the sudden frozen silence, "give me two minutes, please." She called our art teacher out. The warden turned and walked out the door. Ms. Aaronson followed her.

One tall like a giraffe white man, with whiter skin than I had ever seen, pale with no pink or red or off-white tint, raised a camera over his eye, his lens aimed in my direction, and I counted twelve clicks.

"You're not supposed to photograph the children," Niecey said politely, as though she thought she was making the mistake and not him. "It's against the law," Niecey added quietly.

The warden returned swiftly. Ms. Aaronson looked like she had just gotten one of the tongue-whippings that was regular to us. The giraffe ghost had his camera in his hand and almost behind his back, not like he thought that he was the only one who knew that he had a camera, but more like he was pretending that he didn't just use it.

I looked at Niecey. She didn't squeal on him. I didn't really know what to think.

"Little Miss Santiaga," the warden said to me in an unfamiliar tone without the angry lip-curl thing going on. I didn't answer back, just stared at her with my eyes widened. "Please follow me," she said. She was pretending, speaking like it was an invitation that I could choose to accept or reject. I knew it was a command. I was filled with a sudden terror. I had heard stories of girls who got called or sent to the administrative offices who were never seen again. What did she mean, *follow me*? I was used to being escorted by guards *but not the warden*! Where was she taking me? Why me, and why not any other girl in my art class? We were all partying together. Damn! It couldn't've been even five minutes, not a real party at all.

Fuck the warden, I thought suddenly.

What about the Diamond Needles? Would they think I crossed them, got myself into trouble and caused the festival to be canceled? Riot said the Diamond Needles don't fight over boys. So, if she was planning to see some boy at the festival, would she throw me out of the Diamond Needles for getting it all canceled? If she said I was her son, shouldn't I always be her son? And if the Diamond Needles put me out, did that mean I'd have to start back all the time fighting with Cha-Cha and now the Real Bitches, too? So, I'm unprotected now? Huh!

Then I started thinking greasy. *Fuck everybody.* I don't need none of them. If I gotta fight, I fight. So what if I'm not her son no more. I'm not a son anyway, and I hate pretense. If Momma and Winter wasn't checking on me the whole time I been locked down here, what difference did it make if Riot abandoned me, too?

"Don't worry, don't worry . . . ," Siri said softly in my ear.

"Get dressed," a guard said, handing me a baby blue and pointing me into a private bathroom, which was the first and nicest I had seen or been in, on lockdown. It was a bathroom for one. I was used to group everything now, no privacy. I hesitated. The guard pushed my shoulder from behind. I stepped inside.

Back in my baby blue jumper, I didn't know what to do with my paper dress. I didn't want to ruin it or lay it down anywhere and get even one drop of water on it. It had taken me four weeks to design and complete. Four art classes added up to six hours worth of time.

"You got a hanger?" I asked the guard when I opened the door, stepping back into the office where I had been escorted. He laughed one *ha.* "Nobody wit good sense in all of America would hand you a hanger." He gave me a stern stare. The giraffe who snapped my photos stepped out from behind a closed door.

"Water closet?" he asked with some funny-sounding English.

"Huh . . . what?" the guard asked him back. Then the giraffe squinted his eyes like he was shitting or like when you want to shit, but you can't squeeze it out.

"Oh, oh . . . ," the guard responded. Then, he pointed the tall white man to the bathroom I had just come out of.

I thought to myself *Funny how the guard was all tough when talking to a bunch of locked-up girls. Now he was talking to some guy who seemed like he could hardly speak English and the guard seemed to shrink down to my small size.* Then I watched and thought about how the photographer took his camera with him even to the bathroom. Niecey had said it was against the law for him to take photos of incarcerated minors. I wondered if that was true.

If it was, that meant he was a criminal just like us. Would they strip him out of his jeans and cashmere sweater and boots, force him in a freezing shower, give him a medical exam he didn't want to take and almost touch his thing and pretend they didn't, the way they did me, I mean us? Would they make him squat and bend or use both his hands to spread his butt cheeks open? Maybe he was in the bathroom inserting the film in his anus or underwear. What type of freak would he have to be to want photos of me that bad? And would the warden lock down the prison including her staff until the illegal film was found?

"Did he come out?" A lady came out of the same door where the photographer had come from at first.

"He's still in there." The guard was saying what we could all three easily see.

"We need to move on. The warden is becoming impatient," the lady said.

"I'll watch him. She's ready." The guard pointed at me.

"Come on, little miss," the lady motioned to me with her hand.

Terror tripled inside my small body. I counted seven adults seated with serious-looking faces and no smile. There were three on the left, three on the right, plus the warden at the head of the table. With the secretary standing up beside me, and the photographer suddenly reappearing and the guard peering from the half-opened door, there were ten of them.

"I made this dress for the festival. It's not even for me. It's for some girls who gonna dance on the stage. I know I wasn't supposed to try it on, but I wanted everyone to see it so, if the warden said so, the girls could wear it for the talent show," I explained. I felt nervous. I'd rather be punished like before, forced to wear the red jumper or left naked and locked up in the bottom listening to the music in my mind and dancing alone in the dark, than in this position right now. Surrounded by ten adults.

"I'd like to take a look at your dress if you don't mind," a man in a business suit said. The warden interrupted him. So I didn't make a move.

"Please wait. There are some rules and guidelines we all must follow. I've got a shift change to oversee in ninety minutes. So we're going to make the best use of all our time," the warden said.

The guard closed the door, minus one. Now there were nine authorities and me in a room behind a closed door. The photographer walked to a chair at the table and sat. The secretary slid the one remaining chair away from the table and over to where I stood.

"Please sit down," she said to me politely. Her friendly tone made me even more suspicious. I began thinking feverishly.

Maybe, as Riot would say, the warden was pretending for her bosses. Maybe, these people gathered here were in charge of the warden and that's why she's acting so human. She wanted her bosses to believe that she was nice and friendly to the "juveniles," or that she even loved us and cared for us well. Maybe for once the warden was frightened. Maybe she thought I would tell on her, about the way she talked down to all of us and locked us up in the basement and forced us to do things her way without a choice or say-so in our direction.

I was starting to feel a little bit better, believing now that the warden was more frightened than me. In fact, that shit felt good.

"For the record, Porsche Santiaga's guardian is the State of New York. It's our responsibility to protect her. This is the reason I have assembled all of the persons to my left. They are each involved in the ongoing protection and care of Miss Porsche Santiaga. Beginning at the head of the table, I'm Warden Strickland, next is Meredith Frankle, Porsche's legal counsel. Dr. Sally Moldonado is Porsche's psychiatrist. Karla Bussey is Porsche's in-house counselor. Dr. Dov Westinthal is a member of our board and also the top donor to our charitable sister organization. Finally, meet Paul McNamara, who is my superior and deputy commissioner. We are all on 'Team Porsche,'" the warden said.

I was confused. They were all seated in one room together but now the warden was introducing them as though they were all just meeting.

"That's not fair," a lady on the other side of the table said to the warden, with attitude but without yelling.

The warden ignored her and said, "To my right is *New York Daily News* reporter Edith Kates, *New York Times* reporter Stephen Black, and lastly, photographer Hans Stanislaus."

Greek, the warden might as well have been speaking Greek to me. I wish she was speaking pig Latin, Ubbie Dubbie, or Gutta talk, at least then I would've understood her. Or maybe it wasn't that I didn't understand her, but just that I couldn't figure out fast enough what was going on. I know I never seen any of the people on the right side of the table before today. The left side was a joke—"Team Porsche," my lawyer, my psychiatrist, this and that. The only one from "Team Porsche" I had ever seen besides the warden was Ms. Bussey, the in-house counselor, and nobody liked her frontin' ass. Ask her a question, and she'll tell you everything else but the fucking answer, boring bitch.

"Hi, Porsche. I'm Edith Kates, the reporter for the *New York Daily News*, the one who you wrote the letter to." She was extra polite and soft speaking but I wasn't blinded by her. I didn't say nothing back.

"You did write me a letter, didn't you?" she asked me. I didn't say nothing.

"As Porsche's lawyer I must say, she does not have to answer to any questions if she does not want to," Attorney Frankle said.

Frankle might as well have been Frankenstein to me. Now I could tell she didn't want me to talk to the reporter. So I definitely would. We always do the opposite of them.

"The commissioner approved this interview. Respectfully, you shouldn't block the free press," the *New York Times* reporter complained.

"If my client does not acknowledge ever having written the letter, there is nothing left to discuss," the lawyer said. Then eyes shifted back on me. I felt a cold wind coming from the warden. Man, she was cool though. Her face and eyes were blank, clothes so neat and pressed. She had one hand lying on top of a file probably filled with fucking lies about me. I hated files. Her hands were calm, not one finger tapping nervously. I fidgeted some in my chair. My belly was filled with butterflies, and empty of everything else, including today's lunch, served in the slop house, where I never eat.

"We are scaring her," Dr. Westinthal said. "Let's make Porsche feel more welcome. Let's ask her first what she wants and what she would and would not like to do."

He was right. More than anybody else, I hated doctors. So even though he was try'na play nice, he was the scariest. I hated doctors. They put me to sleep without my permission, poked needles in my arms, shoved tubes down my throat and even up my nose. I hate doctors. I hate hospitals. I hate anyone who thinks they can touch me without me wanting to be touched. Every time I woke up in a hospital, I'd move my hand beneath the thin cold sheet and place two fingers inside of my vagina, pull them back to my nose and smell it. Then I'd push one finger up just a little further to feel for a piece of skin I first found when exploring myself. I know what rape is. Girls in the group home and up in lockdown whisper about it from time to time. Besides Tiny made it most clear. No matter how few times or how many times rape was discussed, it was something no girl would forget. I check after every doctor, every nurse to make sure they wasn't poking around in my private parts and spaces after they drugged me.

In my dorm, I recruited a girl everyone called Choo-Choo. When she first heard them calling her that, she cried. She caught a case behind a guy she really liked, who let his friends, who she didn't like, run a train on her. After a couple months with the bold bitches in the C-dorm, Choo-Choo became the name that she answered to. I stepped up, pulled her in, and held her down. Most importantly, I gave her real name back, Shaleka. Then she got Gutter Girled up with me, Gail, Brianna, and rest of us, selling sugar.

"Porsche, everyone here has taken the time out of their busy work day to come and talk with you. Are you planning to answer one or two questions? Let's decide and get this finished so you can join the other girls in their activities," the warden said as if I was missing out on some type of picnic or double-Dutch competition, something exciting.

"Porsche, may I see the dress that you have there?" the doctor asked me again. I stood up and walked the dress over to him carefully.

He held it up by the spaghetti straps, and looked at it like he could even give the dress a medical exam.

"Where did you get it from?" he asked.

"I made it in art class."

"By yourself?" he asked like he didn't believe me.

"Yes," I answered. Siri helped, but I wanted to protect Siri from all of them, so I didn't bring her up.

"Do you know where your father, Ricky Santiaga, is?" the reporter spoke out suddenly, interrupting the doctor. Pee trickled down my leg and a small piss puddle formed in front of the doctor's shoe. The people on "Team Porsche" pushed back in their chairs, and stared at the floor, disgusted.

"You should've waited for our permission to begin questioning the minor," the lawyer said. The secretary jumped up from where she had been writing in her pad all along, left the room and returned instantly to soak up my piss with the mop. I ignored the stain streaming down my baby blues.

"No, will you tell me where my father is exactly?" I said, turning towards the reporter while controlling my anger like Lina number 2 does. The reporter looked across the table at "my team."

"How come the in-house counselor hasn't given this child this public information concerning her father?" the reporter questioned them.

"The last state case worker who raised the topic of Porche's family is in a wheelchair now," Ms. Bussey said with so much anger. "Talking about her family is a trigger for her!"

"So *that's* why she's here," the reporter said and asked with a mixture of shock and excited curiosity. She looked toward the second reporter.

"Still she has the right to know," the *NYT* reporter told them.

"Are you gonna tell me or not?" I said to the reporter, losing patience and blocking the others out.

"First, I have a few questions," the reporter said.

"You don't have to answer," my first-time-ever-seeing-her lawyer said. But the reporter was smart. I could tell she knew she had something I wanted. These kind of trades went on every day on lockdown so I understood the reporter wanted to make a deal with me.

"Okay, ask me one question. I'll answer, then you tell me about my father," I said.

"Ten questions, not one," the reporter negotiated.

"You don't have to answer even one question, and Ms. Bussey can give you the same information. It's our job," the lawyer said.

"I've never even seen you before." I exposed the lawyer, eager to get my poppa's address.

"You've never seen the lawyer on the other side of the table before today?" the *NYT* reporter asked.

"Nope," was all I answered.

"That's neither here nor there. I just received her file two days ago. I'm on the case now," the lawyer said.

The reporter began scribbling something on her little notepad. I didn't turn towards the warden. I didn't turn towards Ms. Bussey, either. Bussey is a bitch. I didn't trust her or nobody else either. I already knew that when these reporters cleared out, Team Porsche would attack me, and no one could stop that cause they wouldn't even know it was happening. I didn't care as long as I could write a long letter to Poppa and wait for him to write me a long letter, too. One long letter from Poppa was worth a thousand uneaten lunches, five hundred bags of candy, one hundred days of rec on the yard, fifty art classes, and ten Diamond Needles. One long letter from Poppa, and I'd volunteer to wear red, sit naked on the hot summer floor at the bottom during the fucking four-hour, fifteen-minute fucking festival.

"Ten questions, okay, I'll answer one in exchange for my father's address and nine for eleven dollars each. You can put the money on my account. The warden will tell you how to do it," I said. The reporters both laughed.

"We don't pay for our stories ever," the *NYT* reporter said.

"Okay, then I'll answer only one question, for the address," I said. Just then the giraffe ghost photographer pulled out a one-hundred-dollar bill and laid it on the table. The warden and the lawyer both stood up. The photographer whispered in the *New York Daily News* reporter's ear.

"Do you really need money?" the reporter asked me.

"All of our girls' needs are taken care of," the warden said swiftly.

"So why does Porsche feel that she needs money? Perhaps we should listen to her reasons," the doctor said.

"Everybody needs money," I answered the reporter.

"There are twenty minutes remaining before I end this meeting," the warden threatened.

"What would you buy with this ninety-nine dollars you are exchanging for an interview?" the *NYT* reporter asked.

"A box, some stamps, and some gifts to put in it for Poppa. People in cages need people to send them gifts, or else they feel like everyone who once loved them has forgotten. I never forgot Poppa, not even once." The room fell silent.

"Well, I can't pay you for the interview, but it seems Hans wants to pay you. He doesn't work for either paper. He's what we call a freelancer."

"How will I be sure that he'll deposit the money? I see it on the table, but I'll be in big trouble if I touch it," I told the reporter.

"I'll make sure," the doctor said, volunteering, and then added, "and you just made a business deal, so there will always be some risk."

"Go ahead, ask me," I told the reporters. I had heard the doctor, but didn't believe him. It didn't matter. I just needed all of them to know I knew they were all making money off of me or else they wouldn't have come up here. **So don't play me like some dumb victim kid.** I just focused only on the reporters and the photographer. I pictured them as the customers seated in the most expensive front row seats of the PORSCHE SANTIAGA, sold-out solo performance.

Q: (Edith Kates, *New York Daily News*): Are you aware that your father Ricardo Santiaga is a drug dealer?

I felt like I had been hit so hard I had no breath left. I was paused at first but told myself to toughen.

A: No, my father was a businessman. He wore expensive clothes, more nicer than anything any of you are wearing now. Ricky Santiaga is respected by everyone. I never saw him hurt anybody. He was the man people came to for help. My whole neighborhood loved him.

I swiveled my neck automatically to let them know I meant it. I could hear Ms. Bussey chuckle, and the warden made a cough sound that she wasn't making before. Bitch wanted to be funny? I'd fix her.

I only know one drug dealer. **My temper was taking over. I checked Ms. Bussey and the warden's face. Uh huh, laugh now, you rotten bitches.**

Q: (*NYT* reporter): Can you tell us about the drug dealer you know? **The *NYT* reporter was thirsty.**

A: It's the warden. She be forcing us to take drugs everyday. They don't ask us if we want them or not. They don't listen when we say no. They don't tell us why we gotta use their drugs or when we get to stop.

Warden: Deputy Commissioner, this is precisely why I was against this kind of interview. It's completely out of its proper context. **The warden was speaking to her boss. I imagined him forcing her down on her hands and knees and commanding her to bark.**

Deputy Commissioner: We'll get through it. We have to allow the press an opportunity. I'm sure these fine reporters will report responsibly and speak with all of the relevant officials as well.

Warden: Please continue and conclude. **Trying to pretend she wasn't angry.**

Edith Kates: Has your mother written and visited you? Do you know where she is?

A: **Tears were trying to flood my eyes, but I fought back to keep them from leaking.** No, you are my first visitors since I been here on lockdown. Wherever my mother is, I know she's brokenhearted. She's too sad to move, too sad to think. She's sad cause Poppa got tooken by the bad guys.

Q: Who are the bad guys?

A: Anybody who would break up somebody's family, then steal and separate all of us from one another.

Q: When people do things wrong, or illegal, Porsche, should they be punished?

A: If everybody who does something wrong would get punished, well then, I guess that would be okay. But if some get punished and other people who do the same kind of things don't, then it's all bullshit, ain't it?

Q: If you could see your father standing right here today what would you say to him?

A: I'd say 'I love you, Poppa. I'm sorry we can't talk right now cause for some reason all these people is all up in our family business.'

They all shifted in their chairs.

That's it, now give me the name of the place and my poppa's address. Say it out loud, I'll remember it.

Q: (*NYT* reporter): That's only six questions.

"No one can count better than us, ask the warden. We count and they count. In here everything counts. You asked me seven questions just now and three before. First you asked, Do you know where your father is? Second, you asked if I'd ever seen the lawyer on the other side of the table? Third, you asked me if I really needed money? When you asked me about my mother, you asked two different things—if she ever visited or wrote me, and if I know where she is. See?" I put my hands on my hips.

The doctor and the photographer laughed. The reporter looked confused, then thoughtful, then insulted. Then even she laughed a little.

"Your father, Ricardo Santiaga, is in Niagra Correctional Facility. It's four hours north from here, in Erie County, NY. His prison number is . . ."

I pressed the information into my permanent memory. *Me and my poppa, separated by only four hours,* I thought to myself, my feelings swelling in my chest.

"Is there a record of any inquiries or requests made on Miss Porsche Santiaga's behalf by her immediate or extended family?" the *New York Times* reporter asked "Team Porsche." This one question leaped out at me. It was separate from all of their other chitter-chatter. I didn't look at the warden, but I listened for her answer. My back was turned, and the guard was about to walk me out.

"A Mr. Bilal Ode made several requests, but he is not a family member of record," Ms. Bussey, the counselor, answered.

"Do you know Mr. Bilal Ode?" the *NYT* reporter's voice raised up to ask me as I was leaving.

I turned around. "You used up all of your questions," I told him quietly. I had enough and didn't know no fucking body named Bilalode. What kind of name was that?

Chapter 12

My superpowers wore off as soon as I was being escorted back down the corridor to my dorm in my pissy baby blues. My temper is my protection and my trouble spot. My temper is taller and wider and heavier than me. When it takes over, all I can do is sit back and enjoy at how it seeks and distributes revenge to the people who are so comfortable never being told off or hit back. Tougher than me, my temper is unafraid of the warden, loves the color red, doesn't mind being trapped and alone, and eats brains and guts instead of food. Adults in the system, the authorities, always tell me I'd better get rid of my temper. The truth is, I'd rather my temper get rid of them.

I was a nice girl when I was home with my family. They, "the children snatchers," interrupted me, aggravated me, and pushed me into a more rougher state of mind.

Ask Mercedes and Lexus, my twin baby sisters, how nice I was. When Winter wasn't home, *I* was their big sister. I took care of them. I thought they was a hundred times better than my eighty-six stuffed animals whose names I could recite rapidly cause I made the first letter of each of their names spell out one long sentence.

When I looked into the twins' eyes, I could see something moving on the inside of them, that wasn't moving in the eyes of my stuffed animals no matter how long I stared or no matter how close I placed my face in front of theirs. I loved the twins cause they could laugh and smile. If I poked them like they were teddy bears, they would even cry. I didn't poke them, though.

My stuffed animals were better at keeping secrets than the twins.

No matter how many nights we talked, not one of the eighty-six of them would spill one word of it. Siri is like that, too, and since Poppa bought me all eighty-six of those stuffed animals at separate times and from different places, I adored each of em. Poppa said he was gonna prove to me that even when he was not home, he was always thinking of me. So everywhere he went, he always brought back something. Since Poppa always took care of me, I took care of my eighty-six, kept them clean, fur combed, and even shined their eyeballs with a touch of Johnson's & Johnson's baby oil. They each had their own seats on my shelves, and I kept them in order, made sure each was seated beside his best friend or same clique.

Maybe the twins told about how I put the medicine powder on their tongues the afternoon that the "children snatchers" showed up. It was three days after the police had raided our palace. I had seen the strange car and the stranger driver from the third-floor window. Normally a car like that would've been stopped at the gate by our security, who stayed way outside in a tiny house small enough for either a full house of midgets or only two big body guards. But Poppa and all of his workers had got tooken, so strangers like her could ride straight into our home up the driveway that only Winter and Momma could usually use without bothering with security check. At age eight, I didn't know she was from the Bureau of Child Welfare. However, I did know she was there to take something from my family. All strangers are takers. Over the last two weeks, every stranger had taken something of my father and mother's; Poppa's car, Poppa's money, and Poppa's guns; Winter's photo, which I saw one cop slide in his back pocket, and even Momma's peace and happiness was gone—taken away, stolen.

I didn't trust Magdalena, our housekeeper. I was home when Momma hired her. It was when we had just moved into the beautiful house, leaving behind great memories and deep feelings and plenty of relations in Bedford-Stuyvesant, Brooklyn, where we had spent our lives. Momma had interviewed several women for the job. Magdalena showed up with one of the young female workers. She was the worker's mother, just sitting around waiting for her daughter to finish answering Momma's questions. I could tell Momma didn't like the daughter. Momma was good at secret funny faces. She would signal to me with her funny faces whenever anyone who didn't belong to our family came around. Soon as Momma saw the young worker's mother, named Magdalena, she offered her the job instead. When they was gone from the front room of our palace, I asked Momma why she picked the older lady, who she had seen last after interviewing all of the others. Momma said, "Because she's good and ugly!" We laughed so hard. Momma didn't even have to explain. But she did anyway. "There's only one queen in each palace," Momma said. Still smiling, I thought about my oldest sister, Winter, and quietly told myself, *I think we already have two queens.*

From my invisible middle-child life, I watched everything. I most likely saw even more than Momma, Poppa, and Winter saw. Magdalena seemed to know everything, but she pretended to know nothing. That's one of the biggest reasons I didn't like her. I noticed that she played dummy around Momma, mixing her words up and opening her eyes wide and blank. When she was watching me and the twins, she was way different.

So when I saw the stranger driving up our driveway after our place had been raided, I told my young sisters, Mercedes and Lexus, "Hurry, we have to hide." They got excited because they loved games. I told them I was gonna show them one of my favorite secret hiding spots that no one else knew. Mercedes, the quicker twin, said, "If you show us your best place, you can't use it no more cause we'll know where to find you."

"That's okay. I have hundreds of hideouts," I said, grabbing both of their hands and rushing through the double doors that opened into Momma and Poppa's room, where we were never suppose to go before 11 a.m., or after 7 p.m., without permission, and definitely never when our parents were not home.

"*Sshhh,*" I quieted them, and closed the doors back. "C'mon," I flagged them over while I grabbed one of Momma's six medicine bottles off of her night table. Momma had been hurting. Poppa said she had fallen down. Midnight and Winter worked really hard to convince me, Mercedes, and Lexus that Momma had fallen, but the invisible middle child always finds out the hidden things, cause no one pays her too much mind. Momma had been shot in her face. She had surgery. Her many medicines were for sleep and pain. That's what I found out while being silent and listening real hard. It made me extra sad on the inside, not because Momma's beautiful face was scarred, but because Momma was hurting and sleeping so much, too much, and I kept wondering if the jealous motherfucker who did that shit to Momma got a bullet in her head or not? Even while young, I liked to keep things even.

"*Uh-un*," Mercedes warned. "You gonna get all of us catched."

"I promise I won't," I told her. "*Momma wants me to hide you now. It's an emergency.*"

I pushed open Momma's closet doors. It was a long closet filled with fashions, some bought just a week from then, others over the amount of years I been alive. Momma said they was the kind of fashions that get more expensive the longer she kept them, instead of the other way around. She warned me not to play in her fashion closet and said even if I thought she wouldn't find out, she would.

"If you get one smudge of baby oil, or one strand of your hair, or one glob of gum on any of my fashions, they're ruined and won't be worth a dime. I'll have to throw them straight into the garbage." Momma would make the angry face so I would know she meant it. Then she threatened to sell everything in my luxurious bedroom, just to replace the value of one outfit of hers that I might have ruined.

Still, one day when I was feeling invisible I went in there and found the best hiding spots behind Momma's full-length coats. I leaned against the wall that day, when some fur accidentally rubbed against my face, I pushed back because of the feeling it gave me, which was different from the feeling I got when I rubbed one of my stuffed animals across my cheek. The wall behind me pressed in a tiny bit. Curious, I turned around and pushed it with both hands. Behind a big square was a big small space, closed in but empty, so I went in and sat there for a while.

Now that the twins and me were being hunted by the takers, I lured them into Momma's forbidden closet with two Charms lollipops from my lollipop jar in my beautiful designer bedroom. When we all three were inside, I dropped down to the crawling position, so they did, too. We crawled, and I pushed the square in gently. Once we were all three stuffed inside of the small space, I placed the square back in its place, just in case Magdalena came looking for us.

"What's that?" Mercedes asked me, her eyes searching through the dark space where we three were gathered together.

"What's what?" Lexus asked. "I can't even see anything in here," she added.

"It's like a Pixy Stix," I told her. I knew they both loved pouring the colored sugar from the Pixy Stix candies on their tongues. I broke Momma's medicine capsule open and said, "Stick out your tongues." I sprinkled the powder on Lexus's tongue first.

"Taste nasty," Lexus said.

"I don't want none if it's nasty," Mercedes said.

"You get a lollipop," I said to Lexus, peeling the wrapper off a cherry Charms. "Now suck the lolly," I told Lexus. She did.

"It tastes good now, right?" I asked Lexus.

"Cherry, yum," Lexus said.

I dumped another capsule into my hand and broke it open.

"Mercedes, stick out your tongue," I whispered quietly.

"Nope. I only want the lollipop." Mercedes resisted.

"Poppa said family sticks together. We all gonna have some," I whispered.

"You first," Mercedes said.

I cuffed my hand and put it towards my mouth, spilling the powder on purpose. But I knew she couldn't see the tiny crystals in the dark.

"Okay, your turn," I told Mercedes, wiping the extra powder stuck in my palms onto my pants. "Stick out your tongue," I said, still softly.

"Let me see yours first," Mercedes demanded. So, I stuck out my tongue knowing she couldn't tell in the dark space.

"Stick out your tongue," I commanded her with a stern whisper. I pulled out a capsule and sprinkled it on her four-year-old tongue.

"I knew it was nasty," she complained, spitting. "Lexy was right."

"Now suck your lolly," I told her, unwrapping the wrapper quickly and pushing it into her mouth. But I missed her mouth in the darkness. It dropped.

"Where is it?" Mercedes asked. We both felt around the small floor for the lolly.

"You dropped it," I said reversing it on her.

"You dropped it," Mercedes said. "I want water, I don't wanna play no more." Mercedes reached over me to tug at Lexus, who was fast asleep.

That's all I was tryna do, make my two busy twins sleep and stay still while the takers were coming in our house. Asleep they would be safe. Awake, they would give us all away by accident.

I had already buried my best things in our backyard yesterday. I had told myself, if any more strangers showed up the way the cops had, they could come and take anything else except the things I had already buried and the twins who, no matter what, I couldn't replace.

As they both laid on my lap after sucking the powder from Momma's sleeping medicine, I tried keeping my heart from racing and then bursting out of my chest. I tried to think happy thoughts, but I kept getting flooded with worries.

Hot. I had just began to notice how hard it was to breathe in here. It was like summer in the secret hiding space, even though it was winter outside, real winter in the dead of January the 31st, three days after my sister Winter's seventeenth birthday.

I pulled out the square, tilting it to let some air in but not wanting to pull too hard causing it to cave in and show us if someone was searching. Even with the small opening, I couldn't hear nothing. Should I crawl out and see what was happening? Maybe it was a trick Magdalena was pulling, being extra quiet to lure me out. My mind went back and forth. Then I put my ear down towards each twin's mouth, to listen for their breathing. Now I was sweating like crazy. I shook 'em a little and finally heard something, but both their bodies were heavy and still.

I heard a noise. I removed the square completely and went to crawl out. My legs felt extra heavy. I felt like I was working too hard to lift even one of them up so I could move. The noises I heard stopped. Maybe the stranger left already. Did Magdalena go with her? Did the stranger come to take Magdalena in the first place? Now there was no one left except me and the twins?

My head felt heavy. I didn't really take the medicine, I had pretended to make sure Mercedes would take hers. I couldn't sleep. I was in charge, their only protector, their big sister. But a little bit of the powder did touch my tongue as I spilled the rest out onto my shoulder. I had tasted the nasty taste that Lexus complained about.

"Police."

I saw a white head, a red face, a bright, bright light. My eyes closed on me, tears squeezing out both sides. I felt him drag my sister's weight off of my legs. My own body felt like a bag of rocks. "My sisters, my sisters, the twins, Mercedes, Lexus," I was saying. But I couldn't even feel my lips moving. Lifting my eyelids were like lifting heavy curtains with my little hands. They opened into half-moon slits. I saw some type of lady cop, a woman, and ugly-ass Magdalena staring down at me.

When I woke up, I was in a hospital. Ms. Griswaldi, the lady who said she was my "caseworker," was there, coming in and out of the room staring down on me and checking her watch. I looked left, no Lexus; right, no Mercedes. Turning sideways, my tears squeezed out, and I was angry at myself for falling asleep. In fact, I was furious with myself for the following two years and five months, up to this exact second, for not protecting the twins and being their best big sister.

My temper is seven layers above my anger at myself. I hoped in my heart that even though my young sisters and I were separated for what now felt like forever, that they knew my true feeling and understood my real reasons for hiding them that cold winter day.

I didn't know what exactly was in that thick file that my psychiatrist, the warden, and counselor, and lawyer had. They might try to tell my story a different way. But not one of them bitches was there. I don't know. I don't care.

* * *

I was surprised that I never got punished for that day with the paper dress and the dancing, although I got questioned a few times about who told me to write a letter to the *New York Daily News*. I didn't tell them shit. I was insulted by their doubt. For some reason, they couldn't believe that writing the letter was my idea. I hated how they always played us like we were fucking dumb. When they questioned me about who mailed the letter to the *NY Daily News* and so on, I played dumb like they thought I was anyway. I played super-duper stupid like Magdalena, but I didn't dime no one out, unlike Magdalena. I stayed true to my clique.

Of course, my paper dress idea got turned down and no one bothered giving me back the one I had already made. Now the dancers I trained was as good as they was gonna get, but it's bullshit dancing in a jail jumper. Everybody knows a real performance is never complete without the right fashion. Especially for a dancer, clothes have to sit softly on the skin and ride her curves so the audience can see the beauty and skill of her body movement.

I didn't know if they would cancel my festival participation. I didn't give a fuck. I was waiting for Poppa to write me back after I sent him a seven-page letter so personal the envelope seemed to contain a piece of my heart, one eye, and one of my fingers.

Chapter 13

The night before the festival, instead of finally getting a letter from Poppa, I got a kite from Riot. It was delivered to me by Diamond Needle number 4, a sixteen-year-old slim, but really strong, Asian girl named Ting-Tong. She worked the laundry detail. All of us got fresh baby blues for the festival. Riot had written the letter in the secret language that Siri and I made up, which I had taught to her little by little on our days on the yard. As girls in my dorm braided each other's hair, showered and re-showered, lotioned and creamed up their little bodies, rehearsed routines in complete excitement for the big family day, it took me all night to break down my own code and language. Once I could read Riot's note, I was shocked into silence, so silent I didn't say nothing, not even to Siri.

* * *

Early morning, everybody was noisy and busy, more noisy than ever. Girls were showering again. The lotions and creams they put on the night before were rinsed away and rubbed back on again. Girls were sharing hair grease with girls they never usually shared nothing with. Everybody was on their best behavior.

Sound check was happening on the yard. We could hear the loud buzzing from the system as they tried to get it right. One chick was singing and re-singing a song she was gonna perform for the talent show. I heard it so many times, I wanted to punch her in the mouth. Gail swore she could smell the meat cooking outside on the grill.

"It might rain," I said to Gail, Shaleka, Brianna, Siri, and them.

"Don't say that!" they all said, like a chorus.

We came to attention for the count. They counted. We counted. The heavy doors opened up, and we went pouring into the sunlight. Way across the yard were people's families, the authorities, the stage, the huge speakers, and the rows of food tables.

Barbeque and barbed wire, does that even go together? Then suddenly, *"Woo ooh ooh, woo ooh ooh, ooh ooh ooh, woo ooh ooh . . ."* It was the melodic voice of Lauryn Hill. She was that pretty, dark fudge brown Fugee girl. It had to be a new joint cause I had never heard it before. Her voice sounded pure and was pushing through the sound system and filling up the air and floating towards the sky. Her voice held me standing in place in the grass as though my feet were glued to the ground.

"The best-smelling food ever cooked and served in this lockdown institution was being cooked today. To give people's families and state officials the false impression that they feed us right and don't abuse," Riot said. "And of course the robots are all cleaned up and grinning, so their families will believe that nothing is wrong with this place," she continued. But, I was listening to Nas jump on the track. That nigga was weaving his words together so perfectly, spitting so nice, my body started moving. Brooklyn's Notorius B.I.G. was the best, but on the low a Queens dude had put all our hoods on the map painting authentic scenarios with words rhymed more better than Shakespeare.

"I gotta take a dump," Riot said and walked away.

Listening, it wasn't too hard to figure out that the title of the new magnetic track was, "If I Ruled the World." And whoever thought of pushing Nas and Lauryn Hill together was a musical genius, I thought.

"Don't worry, don't worry," Siri said to me as I watched each girl matching up with her "peoples"—grandmothers, mothers, fathers, brothers, sisters, boyfriends. My eyes teared up. Something about that one Nas and Lauryn Hill hip-hop song was doubling—tripling my already exploding emotions.

I imagined Winter walking across the yard to see me. She didn't give a fuck that it was a long trip from our home. She came because of love, her love for me, her sister. Winter was so beautiful, high heels sinking into the soft earth, dressed so stunning the crowd divided to let her walk through while they watched. Even though I had tears, I smiled some at what I imagined.

My nerves stirred like someone was inside of me twisting my intestines.

I walked to an available Porta-Potty and stepped in, closing the door behind me. With both hands, I lifted the metal square with the big hole in the middle and looked in. Nervous about wasting time, I stepped in and curled my body into the green toilet water and lowered the metal lid over my head until I heard it click. I could smell piss, but not shit. Chemically stinky smells raced up my nose holes. I squirmed a bit to settle into the space. I held my head a few inches below the metal lid and a few inches above the water level so I could breathe. I was used to being closed in and uncomfortable.

When I heard the Porta-Potty door open, I was excited that it was swift. Then I realized it wasn't. Ass cheeks were being lowered over the hole and rested there. In the wet darkness, I was losing air, same as I lost air when me and the twins were stuffed in the closet space and also while dancing at the bottom when I was locked in isolation.

"Don't sleep, don't faint, don't sleep, don't faint . . ." Siri's voice said softly in my ear. A slight trickle of pee came down, then a small shit dropped into the green water. Then a burst of gas exploded and loose shit splattered.

"DJ Jazzy Joyce on the turntables . . ." I heard coming in from outside. Then the hole was uncovered and tissue dropped down onto me. The stench thickened. The Porta-Potty door opened, letting some of the stink escape. The door closed. Whoever it was didn't wash her hands.

"You bitches must've been born in the gutter," a guard once yelled down on us in the C-dorm. Now, I was lying in the sewage curled tightly like a baby inside of its mother. But I think the inside of the mother is clean. I was soaking in filth.

The Porta-Potty rocked. It was being lifted. I could hear the machinery drowning the sound of anything else. The metal box raised up, shifted some, then eased down and was dropped gently onto something. No more rocking. Steady now. We were moving.

"Keep moving, keep moving . . . ," Siri whispered. It worked for a while. Then shortly and suddenly we stopped.

"ID," I heard the familiar forceful voice of a guard say.

"We have a pass," another male voice answered.

"What's in your load?" the guard asked, but it sounded more like a command.

"We got four Porta-Potties. That's it."

"The festival just got started," the guard replied.

"We called ahead and put in an order to pick these up. We gave you guys too many, and these are the more expensive luxury models. Gotta get these back, or the boss will have my head."

"Let me see the order form," the guard demanded.

"Right here. Small mix-up."

Then I heard the walkie-talkie sound but not the exact words coming through it.

Even though I was lying in the water, I wasn't cold no more. The water had turned warm, and my face and neck was sweating.

"Open up. Let's check it," I heard the guard call out as though to another guard. Fear froze me even though I was sweating. I began to pee in my wet jumper into the pissy-doo-doo water. I heard other doors opening, creaked, unlocked. But the door to my Porta-Potty was still closed.

"Fucking stinks," I overheard the guard's voice say.

Then I felt the slight wind from my Porta-Potty door being opened. The lighting was altered from how it had been when the door was still shut. My right leg caught a cramp. "*Shh* . . . it's okay, it's okay," Siri said. It wasn't okay, though. It hurted. My face was stuck in the screaming sound position, but no noise was coming out. My tears were spilling. My hair was soaked with perspiration. My own muscles were attacking me.

Four Porta-Potty doors were now slammed shut.

"All clear!"

"All clear!"

"All clear!"

A creaky, heavy metal door slammed down hard. We were moving again. The pain of the cramp was punishing me. I was afraid to pass out as I had done many times before when shit was too fucked up for me to bear. If I passed out in here, I knew I would drown.

Ten-year-old girl with six days left till she turns eleven, found drowned in the portable toilet. No one came to claim her body. The state, her legal guardian, threw her in an empty field where thousands of forgotten, abandoned children are dumped in unmarked graves.

"Come on out," Riot said softly as she held the metal lid and stuck her head in only a little bit.

"She can't move," Siri said.

"Do you like it down there?" I heard Tiny's tiny voice asking me.

"I can't move, cramp." I moaned my words out.

Tiny and Lil' Man grabbed my legs and shoulders and lifted me out and laid me on the truck floor. Forcefully, I swallowed my own screams. They were stretching me out.

"Oh shit, she needs water," Riot said.

"We're all soaked," Tiny said.

"No, she needs water to drink. She's dehydrated," Riot explained.

Lil' Man was just quiet, watching me. I imagined she was thinking I wasn't tough enough. She must've been saying something like, "Take it like a man." But I'm not a man. I'm a young, young girl.

"Which leg?" Riot asked me. I looked at my right leg.

Riot began to push both sets of my toes towards my head while my heels were pressed against the floor. She was pressing, then moving, my toes around, massaging my feet. "Point your toes toward your face," Riot said softly. I liked that, even though I was painful and panicked, Riot was not panicked. Tiny was wiping away my sweat with her small, soft fingers. Suddenly the pain disappeared as swiftly as it came in the first place. They each stopped and stepped back as they felt and saw my legs and body relaxing. Slowly I got up.

"You okay?" Lil' Man asked.

"I'm good," I said.

"Walk back and forth. Hurry up," Riot told me.

"For what?" I asked.

"Just do it. Pace!" Riot said, pointing her finger in a back-and-forth motion.

"You look like you got born in that toilet. Or like you gave birth down there," Tiny said, giggling nervously.

"We all look wrecked," Lil' Man said.

"And we all stink," I said, walking back and forth. Riot was squatting in the corner rocking with the movement of the moving truck, her jumper dripping. She was thinking.

"Six minutes," Riot mumbled. Tiny and Lil' Man took off their jumpers and began wringing the dirty water out.

"Don't look at me," Tiny said.

"Naked don't mater. We all girls," I said.

"It matters to me," Lil' Man said.

"See, I knew you was looking," Tiny said in her baby voice and jumped back into her damp dirty jumper. As they did, the truck stopped suddenly, jerked once. We all tried to balance ourselves from falling. Two seconds later the heavy creaking metal back door was lifted.

"Seventeen minutes. I made it," a young-faced, blue-eyed guy said. He was a worker I figured from his filthy boots, blue khakis, and dark blue shirt. He's in the "doo-doo" business, I guessed. Looked like he worked hard and owned nothing. His plastic wristband on his cheap watch was a second away from snapping.

We were all jumping down now, jogging in a line behind Riot. We were used to staying and moving in a line formation. We were inside of an empty building—no, in a factory or some type of warehouse with no windows. We jogged into a room with walls made of cinder blocks.

The blue-eyed guy turned a knob, pulled a long hose off the wall and sprayed us with some type of foam even though we had our jumpers on. Tiny laughed nervously; Lil' Man didn't laugh at all. Riot began pulling up her sleeves and pants and rubbing herself with foam. We did the same.

The guy switched hoses and sprayed us with a second hose, all water. Riot took it from his hand and began spraying us instead. We spun around to get all the foam soap off. Then she used the hose to clean herself. Next Riot brought the hose close to my lips and said, "Sip some water. You might not get the chance until later tonight." I held the hose, placing my hand next to hers, and gulped some down, maybe three glasses full, I thought.

The guy left and returned in seconds. He tossed a plastic bag to Riot.

"Turn around," she told him. He did. She signaled us to undress. She threw us each a T-shirt and a cheap, thin no-name denim skirt from out the plastic bag. The kicks she tossed out were "skips," the type you get your ass whipped for wearing back in Brooklyn. If it was all you had, you wouldn't even dare come out to play. No double-Dutch, or hopscotch, or anything that would bring more attention to your feet.

We scrambled over the cheap sneakers, all try'na get the right fit. We weren't dumb, though. We knew whatever it was we had to make it work, make it fit, quickly!

As Riot collected our dirty jumpers and put them all in the one plastic bag that we had just emptied, the rest of us started looking around at one another. Nothing was funnier than seeing Lil' Man in a cheap micromini that revealed her bowleggedness. She was pulling at her tight tee, which wasn't long enough to conceal her belly button, which was the only dark part on her extra-light skin.

When I checked myself, I got red cause my T-shirt had TOUCH ME written on it in tall, thin script. I was taking a snapshot of all of us in my mind. I never wanted to forget. Once I get back all my riches, I'll be able to look back and laugh it off. Right now, I couldn't even recognize myself as Porsche L. Santiaga, daughter of Ricky and Lana Santiaga.

A rhythmic knock came from the one closed metal door, like a break beat, and the sound bounced off the bricks. The guy who was still turned away from us went to open it. We all fell completely silent and scattered to the side-wall corner, like rats trying not to be seen or captured.

The blue-eyed guy opened the door but guarded the entrance with his body. A stuffed envelope was handed off through the small opening. The guy pulled it in and put his foot against the door while he counted the contents. Stacks—it had been almost three years since I had seen real money like that, especially not a stack or pile like what he was flipping through in the fat envelope. He pushed it in his back pocket and nodded his head to the left. Riot caught his signal and stepped right over, standing in front of him. I could tell by the way he looked at her, different from the way he didn't look at the rest of us, that he liked Riot a lot. Was he the boy she was planning to hook up with all along on festival day? Was he the reason she was crawling and barking like a dog on all fours with no resistance that day in the gym?

"I'll see you soon, right?" he asked her.

"Depends. If you keep your word," she said, giving him a serious look with no flirting mixed in it.

"So far, I'm doing alright," he said.

"Yeah, because if you tell on us, you tell on yourself," Riot said, looking into his eyes. He didn't say nothing back. "It's true what they say about us, you know," Riot told him.

Then they were interrupted by another intense rap on the door. Riot ignored it.

"That we're violent—a gang of girls who will attack without warning and murder our enemies if we don't get our way." She stared him down.

I didn't know if she was trying to shut him down, the blue-eyed boy, or slow him down or turn him off or threaten him, but after she said that, he seemed to like her even more.

One by one, he let each of us out through a too-small opening of the door where he still held guard, as though he didn't want to see what was going on, on the other side.

On the other side of the door and outside of the huge warehouse, a car was backed up to the door. The trunk was wide open so we couldn't see what model of year, or type of car it was, or who was sitting inside.

"Climb in," Riot said, nodding towards the trunk. We got in without hesitation.

"Don't worry, you can breathe through that hole." Riot pointed. We shifted around until we were lying side-by-side, fitting ourselves together like mismatched puzzle pieces. Riot reached and when she pulled her hand back, she was holding a gun. It was small, like Momma's piece, the one Poppa brought her, with the pearl handle. Our eyes followed the burner. She handed it to Lil' Man. They looked at one another like they both already knew what was up. As Riot lowered the trunk I realized she wasn't jumping in with us. When her face disappeared, slowly I felt the seriousness of what was happening and a little uneasy about not really knowing nothing about the details of this move we were making. She pushed the trunk closed.

The car sped. I could hear the wind pushing in and sucking out and swirling around our "breathing hole." We were in a dark, closed-in, cramped space again. Unlike before, I was not laying in water. Our bodies were on top of a warm blanket with a fleece texture. It would've been perfect for the fall breeze, but we were speeding through the summer heat.

"Porsche, are you scared?" Tiny's voice asked.

"No," I said.

"In twenty-six minutes it will be one o'clock," Tiny said.

"I know," me, Lil' Man, and Siri all said at the same time. We counted seconds and minutes. The top of the hour always meant something to us and for us. At one o'clock the festival would have been on for a full hour. There would be three hours, fifteen minutes, remaining—and then, of course, the head count. I could feel Siri's heart beating heavy. I was lying between Siri and Tiny.

"Tiny, how long did you know about all of this?" I asked.

"About a month. Why you askin'?" she said.

"How 'bout you Lil' Man?" I asked.

"Since last year around this time," Lil Man said. "What difference do it make?" she added.

"How bout you, Porsche?" Tiny asked me.

"Late night, I just found out last night," I told them truthfully.

"Don't be mad," Siri said to me.

"That's cause you the baby," Tiny said.

"Plus you a little crazy," Lil' Man laughed. "We had to be sure nothing slipped out, or the Diamond Needles would've of been fucked." Lil' Man disrespected.

Then the ride got silent.

I'm a "little crazy"! I repeated Lil' Man's words in my mind. "Who's crazier than her?" I thought to myself. I mean, I understand the killing part, that someone hurt her mother real bad, so she sent him to the cemetery. I didn't understand the rest, like how come she acted like a man, looked like a man, made everyone call her Lil' Man. I didn't understand why I once saw her holding her crotch like she had balls, diddy-boppin' so hard she looked like she might fall sideways. Why was she acting like she all about church, while she was getting sauced up in the bullshit sermon? I understood why she might not like men or want them for boyfriends after what her rapist father did to her mom. But if she hated men, why did she act just like 'em? Why did she become one?

I'm a little crazy. Her insult repeated in my mind once more, and I laughed out loud.

"What's funny?" Tiny asked.

"Nuphin," I mumbled. I didn't forget Lil' Man had the gun.

"You acting like this shit was some little schoolyard secret that nobody told you. This shit is serious. Me, Rose Marie, Hamesha, Tiny-Tong, we were all about to get shipped out of juvy to do *real time.* You know what that's like, waiting for the warden and them to snatch us up anytime she felt like it and send us into a worser hell, where we had to start all over again with bitches that's madder and meaner than us?" Lil' Man said.

I didn't answer back.

"I'm serving out premeditated murder. You know what that means? Did you know that some killing is considered worse than other killing? Premeditated murder means I knew all along I was gonna kill somebody. I thought about it, planned it out, set it up, and then made it happen. It wasn't an accident or incident or self-defense. I am considered the worse kind of murderer: murder one. I was to serve out the maximum," Lil' Man explained, but to me she was just bigging herself up, which wasn't necessary. Then she started up again. What could I do? We were stuffed in a locked trunk together.

"Yesterday, July 19th, was Riot's birthday. Did you know that? Today she would've become eligible to get transferred out of juvy. Once you become eligible for transfer, you got to serve your time on pins and needles, kiss the warden's ass even more. *That shit is stressful.* So we bounced. And you *lucky you got to ride with us,*" Lil' Man said. But I wasn't lucky. I'm Diamond Needle number 11, and I was down with whatever we had jumping off, from the moment I agreed to be down.

"Porsche," Tiny said, softly changing the tone of our talk. "Me and Lil' Man bout to jump out. Hope you not scared to ride alone."

"I'm not scared of shit," I told her, still red at the way Lil' Man was putting her words together.

"Alright, big girl, I'm just checking," Tiny said in a light joking voice.

"Tiny! I thought you said it was safer on lockdown than in the real world," I challenged her.

"I changed my mind," was all she said.

I didn't push any further. I figured the warden made Tiny make that decision when she forced her to strip in front of everyone.

"Where are you and Tiny going? Are you two staying together?" I asked.

"You digging too deep young-young," Lil' Man said. "Our drop-off is coming up. We flashing out. That's all you need to know."

"I'll stay with her until I don't want to no more," Tiny said. "Right, Lil' Man?"

"That's right. *Ain't nobody forcing nobody to do nothing.* But after you see how good I'm a treat you, you gonna wanna stay with me, watch," Lil' Man said. Tiny giggled.

"Is that love?" I asked Tiny.

"Damn, why you ask that?" Tiny said after a long pause.

"Cause I thought we could talk about anything," I said softly.

"We could," Tiny said swiftly, but she still didn't answer if it was love.

"I don't know too much about that, Porsche," she said in an even softer voice than her normally soft way of speaking.

"Porsche don't know shit about love either," Lil' Man said. "If someone loved any of us, we wouldn't be in this predicament." Her words were like bricks.

"Porsche, keep your mouth shut, that's rule number one. Don't repeat nothing you seen, or nothing you heard. Keep it in your chest," Lil' Man warned.

The car came to a stop. In seconds, someone knocked on the trunk. It popped open, no one was standing there, and Tiny and Lil' Man leaped out. Swiftly, Lil' Man slammed it shut. She wasn't playing. She was in a worried hurry.

"Porsche, it was nice knowing you. You're so pretty and a real cool little girl. Don't let nobody ruin you. It's nice that you still believe in love," Tiny said through the breathing hole.

"C'mon," I heard Lil' Man bossing her. The car sped away.

"It's better when it's only you and me," Siri said. But now I was thinking of Lina. Did she get out? I loved her most of all the Diamond Needles.

* * *

We rode for two hours, or a bit more. I hoped it was long enough for me to reach close to New York City. I didn't have no money. I didn't know where I was, who was driving the car, who was riding in the seats, or whether the car was moving south, north, east, or west. I didn't know the details of the plan, but I knew if I could get close to our Long Island mansion address where Momma was, nothing else would matter. If I could see her, hug her, spend only one week with her, if the authorities hunted me down and shot me through the back of my head, it would be okay, cause I'll have had seven more days with Momma than I ever expected to have.

The car was pulling over now. The speed dropped, and we went from a smooth highway type of ride to driving over what felt like rocks or pebbles. Then we came to a complete stop.

There was a too-long pause, say three and a half minutes. Inside that time, terror gripped me. What if Riot was gone, and I was left alone with some stranger? What if it was more than one of them, and they tried to do me like Choo-Choo? What if they kidnapped me like how they done Tiny, marked my skin up, and slashed me a few times? I didn't have no weapons. I began feeling around, telling Siri, "Let's look for something, a knife, a screwdriver or wrench or even a spray can, so I could squeeze the nozzle and blind 'em."

The trunk popped opened as I was crawling in the limited space, lifting up the rug below the blanket, bout to grab the black iron tool that was pressed inside of a small wheel.

"Santiaga!" Riot said. "Put the jack down. It's alright."

I was relieved to see her standing there. I was relieved to be breathing better now that the trunk was wide open.

"Everything good?" a male voice asked from a short distance.

"Porsche, pull your skirt down, your butt is showing." Riot laughed. "Hurry up, jump out!" She turned back to business.

Soon as I was standing on my two feet, I peeped a green-eyed white boy in a hoodie with the drawstring pulled tight and a bandanna running across his forehead. Less than a half second later, Riot was tightening a blindfold around my eyes. "This is to protect you," Riot said.

"If anything goes wrong, just blame me. I give you my permission. Tell the police and the authorities that I forced you out. You don't know nothing. You couldn't see nothing. This way you won't be lying either," she said.

"I'm not no snitch," I told her. "You should know that by now." I was red, but I wouldn't fight Riot. I loved her, too.

"I know you're not. *But you are my son.* If you knew too much, the authorities would target you to snatch up all the Needles. You don't have enough experience to deal with them head up," she said as she put what felt like a knapsack on my back, and one hand on my shoulder. She pushed a little, and we began walking.

She trusted me. I could tell. She didn't tie my wrist, and I could've easily yanked off the blindfold. She didn't tie my ankles to prevent me from running. If I wanted to I could've bolted easily. As we walked I listened to hear the car that we arrived in pull off, but I didn't hear nothing but what Riot had once described as "country quiet."

We weren't walking on level ground. It felt more like a dirt path. I could feel one or two sticks cracking beneath my cheap shoes, and an occasional rock pressing too hard against my soles. Riot moved me with her hands as a guide, pulling my shoulder left or right when she needed me to move even slightly in one direction or another.

"Step over," she would say when a boulder was in our path, or "duck down," when I was about to walk into some dangling branches. I didn't have to be too smart to know we were walking in some woods. I had never been deep into the woods before in my little life. I'm a city girl other than the big back yard at my Long Island, New York, palace.

Fuck it, we were hiking. It couldn't have been a little cut-through. We had been walking almost a half hour. Riot was quiet. I could hear the birds singing their songs and Siri had been humming the whole way, her pretty voice calming me down some. I was sweating. The bandanna was soaking it up.

Forty-five minutes in, Riot said, "Stop." She began untying my bandanna.

"Water," I said.

"It's in your knapsack. Sip it slow," she warned.

When I stopped gulping instead of sipping, I looked around.

"It's an orchard," Siri said. "It's so pretty. Let's play."

We was surrounded by beautiful, tall trees. A powerful sunbeam slid through an opening and spread light. As my eyes adjusted, I saw a gang of white butterflies, birds diving, squirrels dashing, and little small creatures scurrying.

"Chipmunks," Riot said when she saw my eyes following one of them as he moved about. In the distance I saw a deer. All my breath left me. The long-necked animal had the biggest, darkest eyes and a stare that captured me. I did not feel any fear. I don't know why I started crying. I was mad at myself because of it.

"I'll be back," I told Riot. "I gotta pee."

"Don't go too far. You can pee anywhere," she called out. Then she said, "I'm a pee, too."

Peeing out here in the wilderness felt different than peeing as a prisoner. It didn't feel like my vagina muscles were fighting me dropping out only a few droplets or splashing out uncontrollably. Now a steady stream of warm piss was coming out and taking its time. It kept coming, till finally it finished.

Why were my tears still streaming? I asked myself. Siri said, "You're crying because we are so lost. You're crying because we are hungry and we have been hungry for years. You are crying because we have left nothing behind and we have nothing to look forward to."

"I have Momma, and Winter and Lexy and Mercedes," I murmured.

"You know better. We promised not to ever expect to see them. It hurts you too much when we do. We promised to only believe it when they were standing right beside you and even then, only after you reach out your hand and felt their skin to be sure they were really there. We gotta keep that promise because that's the only way we made it this far."

"I remember, you're right, Siri," I said, wiping away my tears with a piece of my thin T-shirt.

When we skipped back to where we had parted with Riot, I didn't see her. I stood still, spinning only my eyes over each leaf and space looking for her. Next I spun my whole body around in a complete circle checking for her. Then I heard her laughter. "C'mon, we'll follow the sound," Siri said.

The trail led us to a wooden dollhouse with no glass where the windows were supposed to be. Riot was there inside, leaning on the wooden frame looking out at us.

"Come on in," she welcomed us.

"I like it out here," I told her truthfully. I was definitely curious about the dollhouse. I wish I had asked Poppa to build me one of these in our backyard at home. But I never got the chance.

"This house has a roof. If the hell-copters come, they won't see me," Riot said, convincing me and Siri to dart inside.

Inside she had her knapsack open. In it were a couple of bags of chips, and chocolate bars, some nuts, raisins, a banana, and her bottle of water, a flashlight, a candle, and a jar of something like Vaseline but not Vaseline. She also had a pocketknife and two books of matches.

"Somebody hooked you up," I said, seeing all she had now that she didn't have before. As I really checked it all out, Riot was wearing green cargo pants and a green T-shirt. Her hair was unbraided and yanked back into a long flowing ponytail. Each strand was crinkled like hair does when you unbraid it after it's been braided for a long time. The two tied-together black bandannas that she had used to blindfold me were now wrapped around her forehead, headband-style. She definitely had been wearing the same fucked-up cheap miniskirt outfit that we were all wearing a few hours ago. Now, not only was she chilling, she even had a Timex on her wrist.

"Psyche," she said. "No hell-copters should be coming out here. But I'm glad you came inside anyway. We should talk some."

"It's 4:15 p.m.," Riot said with a bright smile stretched across her face. Her green eyes were glued onto her Timex.

"PANIC, walkie-talkies blaring. The volume pumped all the way up. Cell doors slamming shut. Guards scrambling, officers calling the library, the clinic, the visitation hall, the commissary, the slop house, the gymnasium, the dormitories, the classrooms, the tower. Officers reporting 'missing bodies.' That's us," Riot dramatized with exaggerated body movements as she acted out the scenes described. Serious faced, she was reflecting on what she knew for sure was happening back at lockdown. Me and Siri got caught up in her storytelling. We knew it was dead on. Riot continued.

"It's 4:18 p.m., First Officer calls the Captain." Riot was using her fingers, pretending to be on the important phone call.

"It's 4:20 p.m., Captain calls the Assistant Deputy Warden. He tries to keep it a secret, get to the bottom of it, gain control, collect more info."

"Now it's 4:30 p.m. Assistant Deputy Warden calls Warden Strickland."

"It 4:30 and three seconds. Warden places entire facility on shutdown. No one leaves out. No one gets in. Shifts don't change. The workers, officers, staff, and administration all feel tense, aggravated, imprisoned, angry."

"4:35 Yellow alert."

"4:45 Orange alert."

"5:00 RED ALERT!"

Riot threw herself back on the dollhouse floor. She laid out flat next to her picnic items. Riot placed her hand over her mouth and screamed into her palms. "You motherfuckers! You assholes! You perverts, creeps, bloodsuckers, liars, cowards, punks! We fucking outsmarted you! We did it! We did it! We did it!"

Her face turned a pale pink with fury. She laughed. She cried. She shook.

I understood.

"Porsche, I couldn't sleep last night. Now I'm exhausted. Forgive me if I knock out. I trust you. Watch over me while I rest. Don't worry about the authorities. They won't be coming here anytime soon, and probably never. We are on Seneca land. This place is not technically even America. We're safe here. The New York State Police cannot even come here. Even the hell-copters won't come here. And please eat something. Me and you gotta start eating now that we're gone from that nasty prison."

* * *

I wanted to talk to her. I had a slew of questions and plans I wanted to make. I already decided when I was lying in that trunk, thinking, that I was gonna change my relationship with Riot. It had to even up somehow. I didn't want to be kept in the dark on the most important matters anymore. I felt like a fool seeking out each Diamond Needle and offering my candy tributes while they were doing big things, serious schemes, making dangerous and necessary moves.

And what is "Seneca land" and is it possible there is a place that was a few hours from lockdown that wasn't in America, where cops couldn't come? That shit blew my mind. If Riot had gotten us to such a place, she deserved to sleep well, word.

I knew that Riot didn't know about my eating matters. The psych on lockdown called it my "eating disorder." I didn't give a fuck about anything the psych had to say. I knew what I was doing and why. A person gotta have rules for themselves, I think. If other people don't understand another person's rules for themselves, it doesn't matter and shouldn't affect them. I don't have no eating disorder. I just don't like to eat around people who I don't trust. I don't like to eat food prepared by people who I don't trust. I don't like to eat any food that anyone offers to me. I want to get it myself, choose it myself. I'll eat it if it's random enough. Otherwise I'm stubborn enough to starve.

Siri was right. I was hungry and I'd been hungry for years, at least for all the years that I been away from my home. I always knew that I was hungry. I ignored it cause not trusting was heavier than hunger.

So in that moment, I ate. I didn't touch any of the things that were in my backpack. I ate the candy bars and chips and the honey bun that Riot had. I chose those foods cause they were not given to me. I chose them for myself, right or wrong.

Chapter 14

Garlic. I didn't smell like myself. I woke up naked in a warm bed in a wooden room, covered by a pink sheet. The sunshine was pouring through a window. "A window," I thought to myself. The dollhouse doesn't have glass windows. This room didn't feel familiar like a prison or hateful like a hospital where they forced tubes up my nose, needles in my arms, or cuffs around my ankles locking my feet in one stiff position. I lifted each leg, exhaled, and laid them back down. I rolled left, then right, testing my freedom. I was rolling over something beneath me. I reached in and felt around the sheet. When I pulled my hand back, I was holding pieces of garlic. Garlic like in Poppa's famous black beans, which he liked to eat. I put my head beneath the sheet and looked around. I opened my legs and pushed a finger between my thighs and into my opening. It was still closed. I exhaled. I pulled my fingers up to my nose and smelled the moisture. It smelled the same way it did whenever I performed a pussy check to be sure no one had fucked me in my sleep. *For three years I've been nervous about sleeping,* I thought to myself. I knew it was a time for anyone who wants to take advantage, to do things to me that I never agreed to. I had promised myself that no matter what happened, and even though they stole me from my family, and traded me around from place to place before throwing me into a cage, no one would fuck me if I didn't agree to it. I had zero plans to agree to it anytime soon. So normally, I fought sleep and never would until either I collapsed or they drugged me. So they say I have a "sleeping disorder."

Eating disorder, sleeping disorder, anger disorder. Eating disorder, sleeping disorder, anger management problem, and those were nice and simple words. Oh, they had long ones like *Skitzo-frena-paranoya*, but I never listened to people who purposely try to talk over my head. I knew that it's a slick way to make themselves seem smarter and better than me while making me feel dumb.

I peeled back the sheet. My stomach felt nervous, but I didn't feel captured. I knew well what that captured feeling feels like. Sitting up straight now, my eyes roamed the room looking for my clothes. It took seconds to remember "my clothes." Not the baby-blue jail jumper or prison pajamas, but the skimpy, cheap jean skirt and baby T that read TOUCH ME. They weren't here. There was another bed a few feet away from the one I was in. I wanted to believe that Riot had slept there, cause I could see that somebody had. I got up walking softly on the pretty polished wood. I was used to cold cement and rock floors.

I pushed in a wooden wall that led to a closet stuffed with lady things. Relieved, I stood on my tiptoes and grabbed the first thing I could reach that my fingers touched. It was a dress made of soft silk. I smelled it, then slid it over my head.

"It's too long, but it looks nice," Siri said, giggling. "It doesn't matter, as long as we are not naked," she added.

"I'm not keeping it. I'm not a thief," I told Siri.

"I know," Siri said quietly.

My fingers turned the wooden knob slowly and pulled the room door open gently. I wasn't used to opening doors or doors being unlocked and opened.

I poked my head out. The hallway walls were wooden. No one was walking around, and I didn't hear no sounds of life. The smell was very nice, the kind of fresh smell like pine needles from a huge Christmas tree we once had back home. I was used to noisy, busy, wide corridors and stinky dorms. Should I walk out, or should I go back and wait in the room for something to happen? Cautiously, I stepped out. I took a few steps and jumped a step back, when I looked left and saw a wooden hanging thing. When I looked right I saw another one. They were wooden masks of faces of horror. It looked like it was put there to scare the shit out of little kids. I squeezed my legs together. I had to pee. Rushing with my thighs still pressed together, I found a toilet. I stepped in. My pee splattered out before I could sit.

"There's a window," Siri said. I pulled down a towel from the thin rack. I cleaned up my pee. I wasn't used to cleaning it up. I'd leave it there on purpose, a puddle for the guards to clean. I rolled the dirty towel up neatly, then hid it in a small space behind the toilet. I turned the faucet on, a sparkling clean silver faucet. I cleaned my hands.

Glancing at the window, I wondered if it was wired with alarms or a booby-trap or if there was a secret tower outside with snipers who shoot kids for moving two feet beyond the lines. Or maybe there was no tower or lines, but I'd be electrocuted or bagged by the warden. Siri lifted the window. I leaped backwards one step. No alarm rang, but a string of bright green leaves dangled in.

"See, it's safe," Siri said.

So, I approached. I jumped out to the ground level right beneath the window. My left foot arched a little, over a rock hidden in the green grass. I looked up. It was a brick house covered with green leaves. The leaves climbed over every section and even up the roof, leaving nothing but the door uncovered. But even the door was almost completely hidden by two tall bushes.

The yellow sun was blazing up, but the forest blocked its strength. The green everywhere was only shown up by the blue sky. I began to cry. I didn't know why. Why not? In my last conversation with myself I didn't know who I am. Now, I also don't know where I am. Even in prison, I knew what would happen next, was locked into a schedule, could count up everything and reduce it to a pattern. Siri wiped my tears. I turned tough again and started away from the house into the forest, more pee trickling a trail as I stepped.

We walked and walked until I heard and then saw water, a stream sliding down some gray rocks and around the trees.

"Good, let's drink," Siri said.

I squatted, cupped my hands, and just as I went to splash my face Siri said, "Maybe we shouldn't."

With water leaking from my face, I asked her, "Shouldn't what?"

"It's okay to wash your face, but maybe we shouldn't drink it, though," Siri said.

"I have to drink water," I told Siri as I cupped my hands and drank. Besides I liked it like this, finding water for myself instead of someone handing me a suspicious cup of something with a suspicious fluid inside, maybe even small bubbles that could've easily been some spit. I found some berried branches, big purple fruits, not grapes but dark like em. I pulled a few down. Some busted in my fingers and turned my tips colors. I licked the busted ones and ate the others. I found lettuce growing from the ground. I grabbed some, washed it in the stream and ate it with a tomato, which was growing from the ground nearby. Had some more water. Seemed like a few minutes later my stomach was rumbling like thunder in a powerful storm. I squatted by a tree and pooped a pile of poo, loose like a bowl of chili. Disgusted but relieved, I wiped myself using some leaves, dug in the dirt, and buried them. Then I walked back to the stream to wash my hands and body with the cold water in the warm heat while the red dress hung on a nearby branch.

The fog had now passed out of my mind. My thoughts cleared up and came rushing to me. *I, Porsche L. Santiaga, am free. I'm going home. I'm almost eleven years old. I'm going to see Momma, Winter, Lexy, and Mercedes. After that we will all go and see about Poppa.* Holding my arms straight out in front of me, I began to inspect my skin.

"Wish we had a mirror," Siri said.

I didn't want Momma to be disappointed with my appearance. She taught me to keep my skin moisturized and to especially care for my feet. I looked down at my toes. They were still pretty, but not moisturized, just drips of water left over from the stream. Of course my nails were unpolished. I stroked my hair. It was thick and wild and longer than it was before I had cut it off and threw it at Cha-Cha more than a year ago.

The thought of Cha-Cha triggered a dark memory. But I was glad that now it was a memory, not a reality. I didn't want dem girls touching me. That jealousy spreads like germs. I would never know who caught it next. I wish jealousy was like the chicken pox and showed up as bumps and rashes all over faces and body parts, or made jealous people's skin turn green so they could stand out and be stayed away from. I don't know where all my Gutter Girls are right now. I felt bad for bouncing on them without notice. But I didn't feel bad enough to have stayed and ridden my time out side by side with them. The Gutter Girls was my little battling squad. We had a nice little hustle that helped me make it through each day in the C-dorm. I taught them well enough for them to continue the grind if they had the heart. The

Diamond Needles, however, was many levels above the GG cause their reach was stronger. In my crew, I carried the weight. In the Diamond Needles every girl played a key position. I did figure out that Riot seemed to know everything about each of us, yet we really didn't know enough about one another. I mean we checked for one another, had each other's back, held one another down, but beyond that, the details we didn't know at all. Or at least I didn't.

I needed a ride to Long Island to my house, the Santiaga palace. Or I needed some loot for a train or bus ticket and a nice outfit that won't make me seem suspicious or "wanted." Something that would make Winter see me and welcome me in and let me hang out with her, proudly. I wanted to look so pretty that Winter wouldn't lose me again, and even if she accidently did she'd search for me forever.

"Someone's coming," Siri said.

Maybe it was dumb for me to choose the red dress, I thought to myself suddenly as I stepped behind a wide tree. Maybe my brown skin would blend better with the bark. Maybe I should leave the dress on the branch and just hide in the nude.

"What if it's a man coming?" Siri warned whispering. I snatched the dress down and put it on. Her words caused me to stand statue-still.

She was moving cautiously, using the trees as her hopscotch hiding place, looking up towards the sky, checking for the hell-copters that she said wouldn't come. Riot's green eyes lit up like lightning bugs. I shifted my head and called out like back in Brooklyn, a mean game of hide-and-seek or hot peas and butter. Then I pulled it back and hid.

"Porsche, quit playing and come on out," she said. "You okay? Feeling better?"

"Meet me halfway cause you don't look like yourself," I called out to her.

She was walking my way, her black hair gone, her long braid clipped off. Her hair was short and blonde in a buzz cut.

"You look like a boy," I told her, shooting out from my peeking place.

"They'll be looking for girls," she said serious-faced.

"I thought you said they weren't coming?" I reminded her.

"They won't. We're on Seneca territory. But when we travel off this land like I did this morning, we'll be back in regular American territory."

"Alright, Riot, let's sit here and go over some things so I'll know what's up same as you," I said.

"Your dress is on inside out," Riot noticed. We both sat down on the ground surrounded by trees. "No problem. I planned to tell you some things and answer some things yesterday, but you got stung by some yellow jackets. They must've smelled all that sugar in your blood. You ate all my candy and the honey bun! You passed out and your whole body got all swollen," Riot explained. I felt bad about passing out. I knew it was shit like that which made it hard for me to even up with Riot and the older Diamond Needle girls.

"So is that why you kept me here with you, because I passed out and got stung by bees? So if that never happened, you would've sent me home to Long Island where I want to go?"

"You can't go home no time soon," Riot said calm and serious again.

"What do you mean?" I asked her. I was serious, too.

"Nobody went back to the places where the authorities are gonna show up first," Riot said.

"How would they know?" I asked.

"Because the authorities got thick files on each of us. They know all our business, our family addresses, the schools we used to attend, the phone numbers we would call, everything," she warned.

I didn't say nothing for a few seconds. I was thinking.

"Do you think we're at my farmhouse right now, on my parents' property?" Riot asked me.

I still didn't say nothing. She seemed comfortable enough to be at home, but I was still thinking.

"We're not. I knew and I know I can't go back there for at least a year. Even if I did go back, it would just be out of curiosity. The authorities stole the land from my parents. If I went there, I'd be trespassing. But I'm smart enough to know they still expect me to go there," Riot explained. "Porsche, you know I'm not a liar. We're hours away from where I used to live. We are on a reservation," she said.

"A reservation?" I repeated.

"We are in America, but not really. This is the land that the American government had to set aside for the Native Americans, who they stole it from in the first place. Now the Native Americans own this land. They have their own government and way of life. They own their own businesses. They have their own police. The American government and the New York State Police are never supposed to come here. That's why I chose this place for us to be safe," she explained.

"How long do you plan on chilling here?" I asked, getting red.

"Porsche, you gotta think. You're young, but you still have to think everything through, every detail. That's how we pulled this caper off. We stayed calm for a long time. We made moves quietly. We let our pride go so we could get our goals accomplished. I was serving ten years. You were serving eight. If we didn't get out on our own, we wouldn't have seen nobody we know or loved for a crazy long stretch. Now this place is real nice, even though it ain't where you wanna be. It's not home but it's better than prison." She gave me a stern stare. "*You* put yourself in the Porta-Potty. Nobody pushed you. *You* had the choice. *You* wanted to walk. You could've stayed, I didn't have to convince you, right?" she asked me.

"True," was all I said.

Her words were true and I couldn't front on even one of them. Still I was mad about the parts that I did not already know and understand before Riot brought them up and broke them down. I didn't want to be treated like a kid and have everything hidden from me until it's too damn late. I didn't want to know everything except what someone older thought I didn't need to know.

"What about Lina?" I asked.

"Lina is straight," Riot responded, again without telling me nothing.

"Hamesha, Rose Marie, Ting-Tong, and Camille?" I asked.

"None of em could fit in the Porta-Potty or the trunk of the car," she answered.

"So they all still locked down?" I asked, feeling like if we are all one clique, nobody in the clique should get left behind and forgotten.

"No," is all Riot answered.

She had secrets. I could see she had plenty of secrets. I had my secrets, too, but less than she did.

"So it's just you and me?" I pushed. Thinking there had to be a reason she only kept me. Then a feeling rushed over me.

She kept me. I repeated my thoughts to myself. *Riot kept me. She did what Poppa and Momma and Winter were all unable to do.* It made feel closer to her. Then I warned myself, *She kept you so far . . .*

"How long before you and I split up?" I asked Riot.

"Why? Do you want to split up?" she asked me. "I'm not the warden, Porsche. Leave if you want to. But I thought it would be better if you and me stuck together."

"Why?" I asked.

"Because we're the same, except you're younger than me. Right now you are the same age I was when I murdered a man. We both fight hard. We both love hard. We both smart. We both will never ever give up."

"True, but my main thing is to get back to my family . . . ," I said.

Then we were both quiet. I felt fucked up because I didn't mean to put Riot down because she had no parents or land or house to go back to.

"So you're trying to get back your people and your things. I'm trying to get back the same, except my parents can never come back to life. That's why I have no fear. The worse thing they could do to me they already did it. Now I'm ready to fuck the authorities. Everything they ever thought they controlled, I'm aiming at that. The money they love the most, I'm taking it, making it. I'll use it to punish them," Riot said.

Only the word *money* stood out to me from what she had just said.

"Yeah, let's make a plan to get money," I said.

"I already got a plan," Riot said.

"I said 'let's.' That means you and me make the plan together," I told her. I knew she was right about the fact that we could work together.

"You got some ideas?" Riot asked, as though she was sure that she was the only one with ideas.

"I got some money," I told her. "How about you, Riot? Do you got some money?" I asked her.

I was trying to get my weight up in Riot's eyes. I needed things to get more even between me and her even though she was four years older. I needed to show her that I was really smart, not just because she says so, but because I am. Besides, if I thought that she secretly thought I was dumb, I would think of her the same way I think about people she calls "the authorities," and that wouldn't be good.

She paused before answering me.

"I used my money to get us out, almost fifteen thousand dollars. That all I had. But I got a plan to build it back up," she said.

"I have five thousand dollars," I told her.

She stared at me serious then laughed.

"I do," I said, and I didn't laugh.

"Where is it?" she said.

"I have a money tree," I told her.

Riot squatted down and looked up to me.

"If we're gonna be a team, Porsche, you gotta cut out all of this imaginary shit. It's the only way you and I can build up more trust. I trusted you. That's why I chose you for the Diamond Needles even though all the other members thought you were too young and might get us in an unnecessary mess."

I ignored the burn of the thought that all the other older sisters were against me and swiftly said, "No, you chose me because of my hustle, cause I already had a crew in the C-dorm before you came along." I reminded her of my status. "I agreed to be one of your sons because your hustle made my hustle easier and because . . ."

"And because I'm white, you knew I'd get more privileges," she said, believing that she had finished my sentence. That wasn't what I was thinking.

"No," I answered swiftly. "I don't even think like that."

"*You should*," Riot said swiftly and calmly. "That's how the authorities think," she added.

"Even though I was an inmate same as you; even though I murdered a man and you only assaulted a woman, they still saw me as being better than you and every other girl that was your same color or even close to it. I hate them for that. I used it to choke 'em though. And me and you plus all the Diamond Needles can keep using that race bullshit against them until they cough up everything they owe us." She was calm but angry.

"I have a money tree buried in the backyard of my house in Long Island. If we can get to my house, I can get what I want first, to see my family. I know you can understand that," I said sternly. "And you got a brother to see. That's right, isn't it? When I first met you and you told me your dope ass story, you left out that part. You killed a man, shot him with your rifle that your parents left in an underground bunker. The authorities captured you in the chicken coop on your family farm. But you never said what happened to him, your brother." I gave her a stern stare.

"He got away. He was smarter than me. He stayed hidden right in the space where we agreed to hide in case there was another invasion," she said.

"I knew he had to have gotten away. How could you have done all that you did to set your plan up and get us gone from the prison without him?" I said, revealing to her that I am smarter than she might believe I am. "I mean, you didn't have fifteen thousand dollars from no prison hustle, right?" I asked, but I felt I already knew the answer. Riot didn't say nothing. "See, you said you trusted me but now you're not saying nothing. You knew that I couldn't see who was in that car yesterday, but one of the people *had to be him.* The guy with the green eyes same as yours, right?

"After that ride, you had clothes that fit you perfectly, food, two knapsacks, and a watch. After we dropped Tiny and Lil' Man, the car didn't even make any stops. I'm just saying. You saw your brother yesterday, right? So you understand that *I have to see my family, too,*" I told her. "So let's set that up. If you can set up a prison break for twelve girls, we can definitely pull off a trip to a Long Island backyard. If you help me get there, I'll give you all the money as an investment. We will go in on a plan we both come up with, fifty-fifty. I'll go from being a son to being a partner." There was a long pause. I wasn't sure if it was filled with doubt, suspicion, insult, or regret.

"Alright," Riot said thoughtfully. "We can both compromise. I think we should stay here for one year. That's when the authorities will start to pull back and forget about us if they haven't made any captures, or maybe not forget but some other big thing will happen to shift the attention off of us," she schemed. "My compromise is I'll set it up to leave here in forty days instead of a year, right after the Autumn Festival. Tomorrow would be day one in the count. This gives me a chance to put some money together for our trip down to the city. Also, we gotta be smart and establish a new identity. We won't be able to use our real names when we travel. We'll need some type of picture ID, shit like that. That will take some careful planning. Let's take one month and ten days, then we'll travel to your Long Island house. If the money is there, we're partners. If the money isn't there and anything goes wrong, we'll come back up here to the reservation together, where it's safer. If that's the case, I can work up here until you grow up some more," she proposed.

"Cool, the money *is there*. It's a deal," I told her.

"Porsche, no bugging out if things at home are not the same way you left them. And until we get to your house, you still gotta respect the rules that's already in motion. We don't make any phone calls to any family members or friends. We don't read any newspapers or watch any television for the first three months."

"No newspapers, no television, why?" I asked Riot.

"It won't help us, that's why. It will just cause us to panic. Then we'll be acting nervous and end up giving ourselves away," Riot said thoughtfully.

"True, but then we'll never know if our pictures are in the newspapers or on the television, same as my Poppa's. We'll be walking around, everyone will know us, but we won't know that they know!" I pushed.

"Our pictures will not appear on television or in any newspapers. We are juveniles. It's illegal for them to post our names and photos," she said like she was 100 percent sure. I thought about how Niecey had said something like that, too. I believed them both.

"We keep our code of silence. We don't leave the reservation for any reason without letting each other know first. When we do leave the reservation together or alone, we dress and pose and move as though we are boys. We don't bring new people to our temporary house. We take good care of ourselves so our health and mental problems don't get us caught. That means, we both gotta eat and sleep. We respect the people on the reservation and don't ever call them *Indians*. They're not Indians, they're Native Americans. Last, we don't discuss our past with anyone who is not a Diamond Needle."

"Whose house is that anyway?" I asked.

"You'll see, come on."

Chapter 15

Me and Riot grew tight on the reservation although the woman who owned the house, who Riot called "NanaAnna," said her hidden house was actually next door to the territory owned by the Native American Seneca Nation. NanaAnna said her house was prime real estate that the State of New York and the feds would never have allowed the Natives to get their hands on without a hefty price tag and tax. She said she had the deed and property tax receipts to prove it. She said the Natives living on the reservations didn't have to pay property tax to the United States government.

"So why didn't you get your free house?" I asked her.

"*They* don't pay property taxes to the U.S. government, but *I do.* I never trusted no blue eyes. Seems like they was driven by some powerful evil spirits that got mightier with every moon. Our fight to get a piece of what was already our land was so bloody. So many souls were lost from this world. I figured even though the whites signed a treaty *and* said that the reservation land was ours, it would just be a matter of time before they snatched it back and started unsettling and resettling and shuffling my people back and forth again. I figured, soon as they seen what crops we could raise, what businesses we could build, what good we could do with our territory for ourselves, they'd show up suited and shooting, and stealing, wagging that lying tongue and hiding their devil tails," she said straight-faced.

"She's great, isn't she?" Riot asked me, smiling brightly.

The truth was most of the time I didn't know what NanaAnna was talking about. Momma and Poppa didn't talk this type of business with Winter and us. I didn't know nothing about who owned the

Long Island palace where we lived before we lived there. I just knew it was big and expensive and better than any house anyone we knew ever owned.

Riot loved to listen to this Native woman talk. Whenever Nana-Anna was home and still, which wasn't often, she would spit fire. NanaAnna said that she bought this property "fair and square," and paid her portion to "the devils," instead of being tricked into believing that the white man would honor any special reservation agreement with the Natives.

"I figured if I bought like the whites, paid taxes on it like the whites, I could keep it and defend it and even have rights like the whites. No one could show up saying they did me any charitable favors," she said.

NanaAnna was brown-skinned like me, with long jet black and gray hair. She was an antique, but her skin appeared teenaged young, without wrinkles. Her eyes were brown, bright, and clear. Her gaze was strong, steady, and still, like if she looked at anything for too long, she could burn a hole in it with those eyes. She was medium height and size, not bent over in any direction. I could tell that if anyone had the time to sit still she could tell 'em a gazillion true stories. I could tell she used to be considered a stunner like Momma and Winter. I wondered why I didn't see no husband moving around her property or heard no mention of one either. I started imagining that maybe all husbands get tooken and locked in cages and all women, especially the pretty ones, get left lonely and heartbroken. Maybe all pretty women get punished for being pretty? But I didn't really know the rhyme or reason to life.

I was still trying to put one and one together on how the old woman hated and distrusted whites, but trusted and protected Riot, and whoever Riot loved and trusted.

NanaAnna kept guns and knew how to use 'em. She didn't walk slow, although she did talk slow. She'd be bent in the garden, climbing on the rocks, carrying heavy things, always moving and working. Maybe she hears music in her mind like I do.

One night, in the comfortable bedroom that we shared, I asked Riot, "How come NanaAnna likes you so much?"

"NanaAnna was one of my parents' corporate customers," Riot answered.

"Corporate," I repeated, lying on my bed on my back in the dark.

"NanaAnna used to hustle weed. She was a distributor."

"She doesn't look like no hustler," I said.

"The real smart hustlers never look like the hustlers," Riot said calmly. "NanaAnna used to run distributions to medical marijuana houses. They supplied smoke to patients with chronic illnesses and pain. She's a healer, a natural healer. Fuck the doctors. NanaAnna knows more than them. She saved you from all those bee stings after you collapsed. I carried you here on my back and NanaAnna healed you," Riot said.

"So does she still hustle or not?" I asked, ignoring the debt I now owed to both Riot and NanaAnna for saving me. That's what happens with debt, it seems. When you owe more than you can ever imagine paying back, you ignore it until being able to pay it back becomes a reality.

"Small scale, nothing big. When my parents' land got raided and the weed crop got burnt, a lot of good people like NanaAnna got put out of business. My parents were the largest and most trusted suppliers. NanaAnna was a distributer. The people who NanaAnna distributed to were the retailers and dealers. The people buying weed in small amounts, they are the customers or users depending on how you like to say it," Riot explained.

"*Hmm,*" was all I said, but my little mind was moving, comparing my candy hustle to the weed hustle and wondering about my poppa's business as well.

"What about her husband?" I asked after a long pause.

"Husband and daughter are both dead, car accident. Me and you are both wearing the daughter's pajamas," Riot said softly.

I didn't say nothing but Siri whispered, "I knew it."

I felt crazy laying in a strange bed in a strange place wearing the dead girl's clothes, but it was better than prison and just a stop on my way home to Momma in forty more days.

Chapter 16

We stood staring at the missing children posters on the wall in the entrance of Walmart's where NanaAnna dropped us off while she parked her pickup truck.

She walked up behind us as we stared, and grabbed both our hands and yanked us forward like we were both her children.

"Don't worry, those same children are missing every year. No one finds them cause no one's looking. No one's looking around here for you two either," she said softly as we pulled out a shopping cart and began to stroll.

We were not confident like NanaAnna that no one was looking for us. It was day three since we escaped. We are not missing children, we are "wanted juveniles," or as Riot said, "fugitives from the law." On the low, this was one time that I didn't mind pretending I was someone else, even a boy. Porsche L. Santiaga shopping in Walmart for fashion! No way could it ever be forgiven. I braided, then bandanna-ed up my hair and wore a cap over the bandanna. Rocking my cheapass sunglasses worked for me. They concealed the prettiest parts of my face. In baggy jeans and boy tees, we looked mannish. I thought of Lil' Man and tried to move like a dude. It definitely didn't come natural to me. Riot had it worse. Before getting dressed she had to bind her half a cup of titties down on her chest each day. That was funny. She better be glad she didn't have big ones! So far, all I had were swollen nipples. But I did have hips and pretty legs. NanaAnna said we both looked like fools. We figured she thought so, only because she knew what we actually looked like as girls. No one else up here did.

On a list we gave to NanaAnna was all of the lotions and creams and girly stuff we needed. I was gonna get myself ready to be super gorgeous for my return. Riot had cut her hair off, but I couldn't cut mine cause Momma said never cut it. I had already broken that promise once. I wouldn't do it again.

We were in the boy section on our own, searching for a couple of pairs of pants and shirts to use while the only pair we had so far was getting washed. Plus, I needed a hat. We only had a hundred fifty dollars between us, donated by NanaAnna. I convinced Riot for each of us to save a few dollars so I could buy some magazines. Siri wanted to check out the fashions and all the stuff we missed on lockdown. I did, too.

Afterwards NanaAnna took us on a tour of the area. "This is theirs. That's ours. This is how we do it. That's how they do it. This is what it cost on the reservation. This is what they sell it for in U.S. territory. *And there is that damn casino!*" NanaAnna pointed as she drove and spoke.

"Why don't you like the casino?" Riot asked.

"We built it. We own it. It's on Native land. It makes millions, maybe even a billion, but it brings all type of people on to our land, not as welcomed guests, who love and know us, or our culture, but as *gamblers*. There's a lot of traffic twenty-four hours a day, and a lot of liquor. Drinking and driving, never a good combination," she said. I remained quiet since I now knew that her husband and daughter were killed in that kind of accident.

"That's a whole lot of money, and the casino probably created a bunch of small business as well," Riot said, and I saw her mind moving.

"Yes, and that same money divides us Natives. Families that had been united forever were broken over that damned casino." She frowned like she was caught up in a dark memory. "Because of that casino and the money it generated, all kinds of people started popping up claiming they was Natives when they weren't. Even some of our enemies started saying they were entitled to a share cause they had one drop of Native blood, that they say came from their great-great-great-grandfather, who they couldn't never prove ever existed!"

As I looked around I noticed several signs advertising cigarettes by the carton at very cheap prices. I wondered how the Natives could sell 'em so cheap when they were so expensive back in Brooklyn. Aunts and uncles and everybody else used to complain about cigarette prices that kept going up and up. I thought to myself, if I could get someone to cop a couple of cartons for me, purchased up here on the reservation, I could shoot to the city and sell 'em as "loosies." I could make some real paper. It wouldn't be risky like selling weed, I figured. After all, smoking cigarettes is perfectly legal, right?

As her truck eased by the residential section of the reservation, I checked it all out. So these were "the Natives"? I asked myself, not really fully understanding who they were. Their houses were small and cheap, not too impressive. In some parts there were a group of trailers. The few men I saw walking around rocked cowboy boots. Cowboys and Indians, I thought to myself. But the Indians, who were not Indians, were dressed like cowboys? NanaAnna's skin color was darker than most of the Natives I was seeing. With the Natives wearing the same fashions as everybody else, I couldn't really tell them from the average white people. NanaAnna spoke like there was a big difference. I couldn't see it, though.

"Our people living on the reservation don't pay property taxes to the United States government," NanaAnna pointed out as we toured.

"Yes, but are the people here poor?" I asked NanaAnna.

"What is poor?" she asked me strangely. I didn't say nothing back. Maybe I had insulted her after she had helped me. "We are fighters and survivors. We are here. We are alive and breathing, living and loving, birthing and caring, working and earning. The sky is above us. The earth is below us. We can never be poor," she said.

"You shouldn't of asked her that," Siri said to me. "Let's just be mostly quiet," Siri suggested.

Chapter 17

"That was a real dangerous thing you did escaping from the white man's prison. It was even more dangerous because you brought others with you. That's why I love you. You're not like them. You're fair skinned and unselfish. It's like the great spirit of evil didn't swallow you up. Your family, especially your mother, was good and strong. I'm sure she watches over you. She may even be sitting right there." NanaAnna pointed. Riot's body jumped. NanaAnna continued focused strongly on speaking to Riot.

"Have no fear. Our ancestors are on our side. Your mother probably was the spirit leading the way when you young ones were journeying through the forest to my home. You used to run through there when you were little. Remember, you and Revo, you two were smart enough to find your way back here after being away for four or five years. That's your youthful minds working for you, led by your departed elders," she said. Then her eyes shifted some to include me in her talk.

"Just remember, their law says that you are children. I'm the adult, which makes me responsible for both of you. You let yourselves onto my property. *But I let you stay.* That means I'm laying my life down, for the protection of your young lives and your freedom. That's one of the things that any elder is supposed to do. But whatever you two do out there in this world, they'll trace it back to me. *Be brave but not stupid.* Walk humble, instead of puffed out with pride. Be unafraid but not careless or casual. *It is the highest level of civilization when you realize that you are connected to others*, and you live your life not just for yourself, but for one another," NanaAnna said. I did catch that she was saying something like what Lina taught me, about living for the Diamond Needles and not just thinking of myself all the time.

"Now that you are fleeing from 'the Great White Hunter,' you are the same as us," she said to Riot, I guess because Riot is white. Then NanaAnna pointed to me and then to herself, to say like Riot was now with us brown-skinned people who were always running from the Great White Hunter anyway.

NanaAnna gave Riot a tall gift. Riot stood up and unwrapped it. It was a mirror. I was glad to see that. I had been wondering why there were no mirrors on this property. I needed one to check myself out.

"A mirror," Riot said.

"It is the first mirror on this property," NanaAnna said. "Lean it here and take a look at your whole body," she instructed Riot. Riot leaned it, then stood in front of the mirror looking at herself.

"Remember that the mirror can show you a reflection of what you are wearing. It can show you an image of your body that you will only mistakenly compare to the image of someone else's body. The mirror cannot show you your soul. The fashion and styles and even your disguises will change many times. Your body will mature and age, then retard. The mirror can show you your clothes, image, and body. It cannot reveal your intentions or your beliefs. The soul is eternal. Your beliefs are your guide. Your intent and actions are your judgments. Parents and ancestors surround you. They have passed on to the spirit world, where the great evil is *powerless* and can never go. While you are on the Mother Earth, fight against all forms of evil. Never sell or surrender your soul. It is the only thing that lasts forever. If you sell your soul to the devil, if you become evil, you will live in eternal hell. If you fight the great evil while living on Mother Earth, even if it kills your body, your reward for resisting is paradise." Riot's eyes were wide open and her face was frozen. She didn't say a word. I definitely didn't either. What could we say? These were words that were foreign to me. I guess she was saying be good and not bad. I thought it was too late for me. When they busted into my house and destroyed my family, there was already nothing I wouldn't do to get them back. Everyone said that was my wrong attitude, my anger-management problem, my schizophrenia paranoia illness and dysfunction. Everyone had already decided I was a bad girl. I wondered if bad and evil meant the same thing. If it does, fuck it. I'll be dat.

Late night, Siri and me were sitting outside speaking softly. NanaAnna appeared without making no noises. It's her property, I thought to myself. She knows where every pebble and rock is. Through the dark night I could only see her eyes. "These are for you," she said. I didn't see her arms or fingers handing me anything, but a colorful sack appeared. Because of the countryside darkness, it seemed to hang in midair, like in a magic show. Now all I could see were her eyes and the floating bag. I reached for it.

"You seem to like the dark night," she said. "So I'll talk to you here where only our eyes seem real. That will make the truth softer for you."

"We can talk," I said.

"She's spooky," Siri whispered, her lips pressed against my ear. I touched Siri's leg to quiet her. I was sure NanaAnna didn't notice her seated beside me in the dark.

"The spirits suggested that I give these books and items to you. I know you can read and write. They said to me that you are so young in your journey, and have so much more to figure out," NanaAnna said.

"Maybe you can talk regular to me so I can know what it's about. I like regular talk better," I told her nicely.

"You pretend not to know many things that you surely know," Nana said.

"I'm not a pretender," I defended.

"The spirits say that you are carrying many injured broken bodies on your eleven years young back."

"Huh?" I said. I wasn't even eleven yet.

"You believe that it is loyalty to be just like the ones who you are carrying. But your soul knows that *you are different*. Otherwise *they* would be carrying and protecting you, instead of *you* carrying and protecting them."

Siri tapped my leg. I knew what she was thinking: *Let's get outta here.*

"The only way you will be successful on your journey on Mother Earth is if you accept and acknowledge that you are different from your loved ones, and use it as a strength and a weapon to save them. If you refuse to open you heart and listen to your soul as it speaks to your heart and mind, you will fail and become the same as those who you are trying to save. Then all of you will suffer until your collective and complete defeat. As it stands, while you are pretending not to know what your soul has *already told you*, everyone here on Mother Earth is afraid to tell you the truth."

"I don't know, NanaAnna. But I do know I won't stay here long and I'll pay you back every cent for everything I use that belongs to you. It will take me a little time, but I'll add on some money if it takes me too long."

"We are not discussing money, credit, or repayment. I discuss these things with the government. They are not my friends or children or people," she said in her way, very calm but with a little angry feeling along with it. "*Na-ho-ten-ye-sa-na-tenh-gwa*," she said, speaking some foreign language. I wondered why people thought that they could just suddenly start talking any language other than English to me. I didn't say nothing back. What could I say to that?

"What do they call you?" NanaAnna said.

"Porsche," I answered back.

"Porsche, we believe a child's name should reveal a piece of the meaning of their life journey. You were named after a car, right?" she asked.

"Not just any car," I responded. "An exclusive car, an expensive car, a fast car, a beautiful ride." I said my words slowly, softly, and confidently into the air. They were not really my words, though. They were Poppa's. Was she trying to disrespect my father because of the name he gave me? I started feeling red.

"So what's the meaning of *NanaAnna*?" I shot back.

"It's the name of my second face," she said oddly. "It's the name that those who don't truly know me call me. I only answer because they call me this name with affection. Also, I know that they would not take the time to truly know me well enough, for their tongues to call me the name of my first face, given to me by my people, *Oshadagea Oronyatekha*."

NanaAnna was right. Who's ever gonna be able to repeat that name comfortably? In the hood they would just name her *Big O* or *Little O* if she came with all those letters and sounds. Only the first letter of her name would count. On the other hand, I took it like she was try'na challenge me. No, I took it like she doubted that I could ever speak that name either. I was being underestimated again.

"Say it one more time, please?" I asked her.

"*O-sha-da-ge-a O-ron-ya-te-kha,*" she said, pronouncing it slowly. "It means *Rain Water.* Many people express anger when in rains. Some even become depressed by the rain. Rain is regarded as an interruption to more important things that need to be done. But without rainwater, nothing grows. Everything dies before blossoming," she said. I sat quietly, thinking.

"What language is that?" I asked her because it did not sound like anything I had ever heard in Brooklyn, Long Island, or on lockdown where there were a lot of different girls speaking different ways.

"It is the language of the Iroquois people of the Seneca Nation," she explained.

"Iroquois." I like that name. "What does it mean?" I asked her. She paused.

"It means, *the killing people.* But we are much more than that. Sometimes when you fight back, your enemies name you things like *the killing people,* when we should have been called *the fighting people,*" she said.

"The fighting people," I repeated. I liked that, too.

"The fighting people who will kill you if you're hunting us, our spirit and offending Mother Earth," she said. "Porsche, in the bag are some of the things you will need to use to become stronger. Stronger in your health and in your understanding." She paused. "Remember, your body is the vehicle that your soul is using here on Earth. If you don't pay attention and take great care with your vehicle, it will break and become useless. Then your soul will be released and return."

I murmured, "Thank you." I was getting uncomfortable with that word, though. I don't like *thank you,* because it means somebody did something for me that I'd rather I had done for myself, or that my family should've done for me instead.

"I like you, Porsche, for many reasons. You remind me of my daughter of many years ago. When she was your age, she had your face and fire. Secondly, you and I both speak to the spirits. Even out here in the dark there are many more sitting besides us than just you and I, right?" she asked me.

"Huh?" I responded.

"And like myself, you prefer to be with the ones you love the most, but if they are not giving you the love that you need and that you crave and the same love that you give them and gave them, you are prepared to be alone." NanaAnna laughed a little. "Yes, that's how I am also. You and I are capable of creating our own little world, a safe place for ourselves," she said softly. *Oronyatekha*, the second part of my name, means *between villages*. It describes my life journey so well. Always, I am caught between 'the world of the hunter and the world of the hunted.'"

NanaAnna left quietly like she came in the first place.

"Who talks that crazy to little kids?" Siri asked me.

Then Siri began to talk greasy about NanaAnna. But I checked her.

"We shouldn't say nothing bad about her. She's strange, but she helped us out when no one else would."

That night, I decided that anybody who helps me out, I'd pay them back more than they gave me in the first place. I don't care what nobody says. *Money makes shit happen*, same like Riot's money made us get free. Same as money made girls on lockdown have anything they needed or do anything to get it. If NanaAnna didn't have no money, they'd kick her ass right off of this property. She said so herself—"property taxes," right? And if someone gives you something for free, they can show up anytime and take it back or lie about it and switch it around. She said that, too.

That's why she didn't want to live on the land where the government told her to live. But then she didn't want to leave it either. Caught "between two villages," she bought the property from "the hunter" that was right next door to the hunted, "the killing fighting people." She bought the house hidden in the wilderness. That's gangster to me.

Chapter 18

We were on our hands and knees picking strawberries, in a field of 15,000 strawberry patches, as the sun rose up, incredible.

"You said you wanted to work," NanaAnna said.

Me and Riot and Siri rose up in the country morning dark without complaint. We had money on our minds. The morning air was chilled. We walked, instead of riding in the pickup truck.

"Walking is good for your heart," NanaAnna said as she weaved and worked her way leading us through the woods and into the strawberry field.

"Take deep breaths. Inhale, and exhale," she said. She was wearing a pretty, long denim skirt, with a short apron tied around front. She wore expensive leather walking shoes and a cotton long-sleeve blouse. Her hair was wrapped in a floral scarf and tied beneath a quality hat, not fitted or floppy, and very feminine. Me and Riot had on the cheap shit we got yesterday. Our Walmart jeans were stuffed into our tube socks. Our tube socks were stuffed into our skips. Hoodies protected our skin and us from the early morning breeze. We both wore work gloves that NanaAnna told us to put on. Riot tied down what little hair she had left with a blue bandanna. I tied mine with a black one. We were not going into town, so we were girls today. Riot suggested that me and her should use the names off of a song that her mother used to like. It was written and performed by Stevie Wonder and Paul McCartney. The song was called "Ebony and Ivory." I told her that was fine, but I'm Ivory cause that name was the bomb to me. We agreed. Immediately, we told NanaAnna our new names. She smiled. I said, "It's the name of my second face."

Out in the fields nobody bothered too much about names. It was picking those berries and getting them in the wide wooden baskets and how many baskets we could fill by noon.

"Put your hands in the soil," NanaAnna told us. "Ivory meet Mother Earth," she said, introducing me to the dirt. "You city girls gotta get country smart. Country smart is more useful than city slick," she said. I didn't mind cause NanaAnna picked while we picked. She taught us how to sort and select the darkest red plump little strawberries and how to handle them carefully so that they wouldn't bruise.

"The bruised ones are just as good to eat or cook, but harder to sell. Some customers are silly like that," NanaAnna said. "They think if anything isn't perfect looking there's no good inside of it, or use for it."

After demonstrating how to place each strawberry in the basket, and how high to stack 'em so that the ones on the bottom of the basket didn't get crushed, we got busy. Me and Siri was slow in the beginning, and dropping strawberries here and there. Before the first half hour disappeared, we were quicker than the others who were mostly older ladies. My body is flexible like that. I crawled easily on my knees up and down the rows. I didn't care about destroying the jeans. Soon as I left this area headed home, I was dropping every cheap labeled thing in the trash.

We got paid a dollar a basket. I did fifty-four baskets so I had fifty-four dollars. I didn't think they paid enough cause I counted how many strawberries were in one wooden basket so I could estimate the total in all of my baskets. In the basket I used for the calculation, there were 175 strawberries, so I multiplied that by fifty-four baskets, which equaled 9,450 strawberries. My mind was going crazy with numbers. How many strawberries are in those little green containers in the supermarket? It couldn't be more than twelve, and how much does a small container in the market sell for?

NanaAnna said her strawberries were natural, organic, and precious. She told us that other farms and farmers were spraying poison on theirs and selling them to innocent unaware families and people to eat. She said the chemicals on those other strawberries would kill people slowly as the cancer crawled and creeped, attached, grew, and then exploded in their insides. I never heard nothing like that before until today. On the walk back from the field through the woods to our house, I ate a pocket full of those natural organic precious bruised strawberries. They were the ones I chose and picked. It was the only food I had all day. They were the only natural organic strawberries I ever ate in my little life. Sweet and juicy, they tasted better than candy. I never thought nothing natural could taste better than candy.

Riot and I raced to the bedroom. We all three fought to get in the bathroom first. When we were cleaned up and wearing our second set of cheap clothes, NanaAnna called us out to the kitchen.

"Time to cook," she said. "I'm a little hungry and you girls worked on an empty stomach as well." Riot quickly agreed to cook, but NanaAnna rejected her.

"No, you sit down. Porsche is going to prepare lunch for the two of us," she said.

Riot laughed. "I guess we're gonna starve then," she said, doubting me.

"She'll do just fine," NanaAnna said. "And I noticed that she won't eat anything that anyone else prepares. So from now on, she can prepare the meals," NanaAnna said softly. "We will gladly eat what her hands prepare for us."

"It's okay, you two can eat. I'm not hungry," I said, declining the cooking offer.

"If you want to pay down your debt, you should accept every decent job and do it well," NanaAnna said.

She was looking into me, and I was looking back at her.

"I'll do it. It's nothing," Riot stood up volunteering.

NanaAnna touched Riot's hand, saying, "No, I have something else for you to do."

NanaAnna asked me, "Where is the journal I gave you?"

I didn't know what she was talking about.

"You didn't look inside of the sack I gave you last night? The gifts that the sprits told me to give to you?" she asked. I made a face at Riot then ran to go search the sack that I had thrown on the floor in the closet without opening. I came back with two journals in my hands.

"Which one do you like best?" NanaAnna asked me.

"This one," I pointed to the purple.

"Okay, so we'll use the orange one for the recipes. I've never written any recipes down before for anyone. So, consider this an introduction to our friendship," NanaAnna said.

"Thank you, but it's only forty days and there are only thirty-six days to go," I reminded her, Riot, and myself.

"Thirty-six days is more than enough," she said as she wrote out a recipe for strawberry pancakes with maple syrup and beans. Then she handed me the journal. I liked pancakes and beans but not freaking together.

I was left in the kitchen alone, after she put a flame beneath the griddle, and left the soaking beans in a pot on the stove.

"Gather up your utensils first, then your ingredients. Once you have it all organized, begin cooking." She placed one hand on my shoulder and left the kitchen confidently with Riot following behind her.

Standing at the center of a large pretty kitchen, in a long and wide wooden house covered with bricks, and ivy leaves, I felt panic. As I watched the flames crawling beneath the iron griddle and sprawled out slightly below the bean pot, I began to sweat some. Realizing I was left with fire, matches, gas, and an entire knife collection, a drawer filled with forks, spoons, and more knives, unlocked see-through cabinets packed with clay and glass plates, unlocked closets filled with foods of my choosing, I felt crazy and unfamiliar. As I looked up to the ceiling it seemed the whole room was swirling. I had never in my life cooked anything before, or received a cooking lesson even. The room spun a little faster. And no one would leave me with all these weapons alone without sending the guards, calling the police, or chaining my wrists and ankles together. Would they? I began to cry. I was alone, so crying was okay. Siri was walking up the hall towards me. It's always okay for her to see me cry, I thought.

"Come on, let's try," Siri said. The spinning kitchen slowed down its spin.

"You can sit, I'll do it," Siri said. But I didn't want to sit.

"Okay, we'll do it together," Siri suggested as she pulled over a footstool to stand on to see better. We made small piles of the seasonings because they were all in separate small glass containers. Me and Siri stuck one finger in each in every pile till we tasted seasonings that we both liked. When we agreed on four different tastes I put a tablespoon of each in the boiling beans. The recipe had said, "Season to your taste." I added chopped onions, which Siri had trouble slicing with a butter knife. The strong onion sting made her spill tears silently.

"Don't be embarrassed," I told her, of course. I chose a tomato and washed it then dropped it in the boiling beans. I figured the hot water would turn something so soft into liquid even if I didn't chop it up. I considered adding garlic cause Poppa would've liked that taste. However, after wakening up the other day with garlic pieces all over my body and bed, I was all garlicked out. Me and Siri held up the sticks and leaves NanaAnna had left there on the counter. "Are we supposed to put those in the boiling bean water?" I asked Siri.

"I don't know," she responded. "Let's smell them," she suggested. Each stick and leaf had different smells. Siri and I each chose our favorite. Then we hesitated and put them back. "Flowers smell good, but we wouldn't put flowers in our soup or food, right? So, let's not put these sticks and things in either," Siri said. So we didn't.

Some of the pancakes were really big and others were really small. They all ended up crispy, cause the griddle grew hotter than hot while we were taking our time preparing the beans. None of 'em was burnt though. I had sliced the strawberries up and laid them nicely on the plate where I piled five pancakes each for the four of us, twenty all together.

"Four plates?" NanaAnna asked curiously.

"Everybody's eating," I assured her. Maybe she thought I wouldn't, but after preparing my first meal ever, I was definitely going to test it out.

"It's so good," Siri said first.

"I can't believe it," Riot said, stuffing a forkful in her mouth, her second one.

"I can," NanaAnna said. She was watching me eat. I felt a little uncomfortable but the sweet maple syrup—soaked pancakes on my tongue made me too happy to remember that I was uncomfortable.

"What about the beans?" NanaAnna asked me a little while later. She and Riot had eaten all of theirs but me and Siri didn't.

"I eat beans, but not with pancakes," I told her.

"Beans are protein and calcium. If you only have sugar, you'll be out of balance. Protein gives you strength. Calcium is for your bones and teeth."

"My bones are fine," I said. "Thank you for caring about me," I said politely.

"How much did you remove from my debt? How much more do I owe?" I asked straight-faced. I needed to know how much the cooking job paid.

NanaAnna paused. "Since you have turned me into a debt collector I'll put a chart right there on the wall. We will keep track of every expense just like you wanted, and credit you for each thing that you agree to do, just as you require."

I agreed. I needed to keep count on everything in my life and on everything I owed and everything that was owed to me.

"Ivory!" Riot called me as I was leaving the kitchen.

"I fixed the tire on a little bike outside if you wanna ride it," she said.

I looked at NanaAnna.

"How much for a ride, NanaAnna?" I asked. She took a good look and a long pause and a deep breath, then said, "A dollar a day."

"No matter how long I ride it for or where I go?" I checked.

"You gotta stay on the reservation with it," Riot jumped in.

"No matter how long and no matter how short. Even if you take for five minutes or five hours, it cost a dollar," NanaAnna said.

"No problem," I said.

I guess she didn't know that paying was the only way I could ride without feeling like I was child without parents who loved me enough to keep me, and buy me a bike.

"School tomorrow," NanaAnna said.

"School?" I repeated. Didn't she understand our situation? I thought.

"Okay, learning tomorrow. First work, then learn, then ride the bicycle," NanaAnna said, emphasizing each of her requirements.

"Okay, learning . . . ," I said.

"Thank you for the bike, NanaAnna. Riot, thank you for fixing the wheel," I said as me and Siri were leaving.

"Thank you for the meal. You are a good little cook," NanaAnna said.

The bike was old with a rusted fender. Colored pink with a white basket in front with plastic flowers woven on it, didn't have a banana seat, back rack, or sissy bar. *Where will Siri sit?* I asked myself.

"I'll run along the side," Siri said.

I told myself I'd let her run on the side just for this time, but when we got back, I would look for a wrench or something to knock off the basket. Then Siri could sit on the front handlebars while I pedaled.

I took the trail on NanaAnna's property that led right to the reservation. This way I didn't have to go on any outside streets to arrive there. I was gonna peddle up and down all the back and side reservation roads to get familiar with the place. Between the housing area of the reservation, NanaAnna's house, the strawberry fields, and the woods, I liked the wilderness the best, especially the dollhouse. Maybe I loved the dollhouse cause it was the first safe place for us in the middle of nowhere. I never knew that "nowhere" could look so nice. I loved the stream and wondered if it led to even more water, like a pond or something. I'm not an expert swimmer, but I can swim enough to have fun and not drown. I wanted to go back to the doll-house, but I didn't know how to get there.

Riding with a hot summer wind blowing onto my brown skin, I felt relieved like someone had taken one of the seven bricks off of my head. First I sat. Next I stood pedaling, still holding the handlebars. Then I stood with my arms spread wide out on each side, coasting. Rocking the bike like an acrobat is something we used to do back in Brooklyn.

"School kids . . . ," Siri said. I saw them walking casually like they didn't have no worries, no bricks on their heads, no cages for them or missing parents or sisters. I kept going, noticing them noticing me. Siri was waving at them.

"We should've brought some water," Siri said.

"We'll head back," I told her. I was just as thirsty as her, too. "Next time we ride, we'll fill up the backpack with water and treats. We'll ride until we're exhausted. Then we'll jump off and have a picnic!" I promised Siri.

Chapter 19

She was standing outside of NanaAnna's, by the bushes that concealed the front door of the big beautiful brick place, covered with
leaves, the good-smelling, wide house, with the wooden walls and
floors. Soon as she saw me riding up, she closed the book she was
reading and pushed it into her back pocket.

"I was waiting for you," Riot said.

"I'll run in and get me and Siri some water. Then I'll come right
back out," I said as I got off the bike and sat it on the kickstand.

"I'm going into town. I waited so I could let you know before
leaving out, just like we agreed," Riot said.

"I'm coming," I told her.

"Not this time. I'm going on a mission," she said.

"A mission . . . ?" I repeated.

"I gotta follow up on something and check something out," she
said.

There was a pause, just me staring at her and her looking away.

"You going by the casino?" I asked her.

"We'll talk when I get back," she said.

"Good, cause I gotta idea, a good hustle," I told her, thinking of
the possible profit on the cigarettes.

"Me too," she said. "NanaAnna said we only got four more days
left of the strawberry picking job, and that's it till the next crop," Riot
informed me.

The figure $270 popped in my head. That's five days of picking
at fifty-four dollars a day. That's the minimum I would earn picking
berries. But I didn't say nothing.

"Okay, when you get into town, see if you can ask around about the mall. They must have one, like a Macy's or something like that. Eventually, I'll have to get a going-home outfit," I told her.

She laughed a muffled laugh. "Okay, Santiaga," she said.

"You gotta get used to calling me Ivory!" I reminded her.

"Yeah, well, I'm not Ebony right now," Riot said. "I'm going into town so I'm Rod," she said. I looked at her. She didn't have to tell me she was posing as a boy. I could always tell by the way she rocked her hair, and her stance.

"You really getting into this boy thing?" I said.

"This shit is serious," Riot answered back swiftly.

"Which do you like best, being a boy or girl?" I asked.

"I like both," she said, giving up a half smile. "Boys get more respect, especially from other boys. When I'm looking to make a few dollars, I can pick up an odd job faster and get paid more than a girl would get paid for doing the same thing. When I'm a boy, I can get girls to do whatever I tell em. When I'm a boy, I don't have to worry about boys trying to fuck me," she said. I smiled.

"At least not yet," I told her. We both laughed. "And, you don't seem to have no trouble getting girls to do what you want us to do. You have a whole army, the Diamond Needles, and you're number 1," I reminded her.

"Yeah, but damn that was a lot of work! When I'm a boy, I can just tell a girl, 'Come here,' and she'll come. When I'm a girl, I got to do a lot of talking and convincing. I got to answer a slew of questions. Just like when I'm kicking it with you, Porsche. You got a million questions. If I don't answer them right, you start to distrust me," she said and then silence fell between us.

"That's right," I told her, breaking the silence. "You gotta answer them right or I will start to distrust you. Why did you close that book and push it into your back pocket when you saw me coming?" I asked her seriously. She pulled the book out and showed it to me. I read the title: *Four Arguments for the Legalization of Marijuana.*

"Where did you get that?" I asked her.

"From NanaAnna's library. It's in the back room. You should check it out sometime," she recommended. "See, the girls out here don't care what I'm reading when I'm a boy. They just look up to me and think I'm about to be a successful businessman. But between girls, there is usually this layer of distrust. It's hard work breaking through that and keeping girls tight and unified with one another. Porsche, me and you gotta get tighter, and more unified, okay?" she asked, her green eyes shining in the sunlight.

"Trust is feelings and actions stretched out over time. I think you can organize plans, actions, and girls or boys, or whatever. But no one can organize feelings. They just come when they come and grow little by little. As far as me, my feelings come very slowly, but then they grow so wild like the leaves that cover this house. And they grow roots so strong like that tree right there, that probably been standing right there for more than a hundred years," I said, without thinking.

"Porsche, you are a fucking pretty little girl," Riot said suddenly. "And, it's so much more than the way you look."

She left.

"Should we get water from the stream or the faucet?" I asked Siri.

"Let's go inside and use the faucet. I'm tired from running," she said.

After drinking water from Siri's palms, water that flowed from the faucet, we both lied down on our bed. Siri was curious about the sack. She began picking through it.

"Two journals, a pack of pens, pencils, cocoa butter, shea butter, three bags of almonds, three bags of raisins, peanut butter, a long heavy thick green leaf, a bag of beans, a stalk of corn, and some 'feminine pads'?" Siri called out the names of each item. "That lady NanaAnna sure is strange," Siri said. "Remember you gave her a list? She didn't buy anything you asked her for."

I looked in the bag. Siri was right. I didn't ask for none of this stuff on my list.

"Take the envelope," Siri said, handing me a pretty pink envelope.

I opened it. On the cover of the card was a pretty eyeball with long lashes. On the inside of the card was a handwritten letter with nicely drawn lettering. I read.

I gave my daughter Tallahee a journal to write in. She never did. I wish she had. Right before her thirteenth birthday she was killed in a car accident. If she had written in her journal before *then, I would be able to hear her voice in her own words. I would know her thoughts and be able to hold on to her feelings for my lifetime. I would read and reread them every night. It would soothe me so much. Your life is an adventure and a journey. Your story may one day become the most valuable thing you have, other than your breath, body, and soul. Now, I am giving you a journal to write in. It is your choice.*

"She's nosey . . . ," Siri said. "Does she want you to write about your real life and feelings so she can read it every night? You're not her daughter," Siri reminded me.

"You're right. I'm not her daughter," I said.

* * *

In what felt like the middle of the night I woke up. There were piles of clothes on my bed and a few hangers poking my legs when I moved around. When I flipped over, I saw Riot asleep in her bed a few steps away. She wasn't back when I had first fell into my sleep. It wasn't the hangers or the weight of the clothes and shoes that woke me. It was the sound of the drums. The driving rhythm was calling me. My body heard it first, my heart and insides, and then my feet next. My toes were tapping. My mind was the last one that caught on. The beat had me going, heart racing. My feet were already moving a short way down the hall and out of the bathroom window, so as not to disturb Riot, NanaAnna, or nobody else. Outside, in the country black dark, I looked up through the trees and saw so many stars glowing. I never seen stars like that before. The moon was full and bright blue and white, lighting the dark sky like a sun. The shining stars and ferocious beat made my chest swell with feelings. I followed the sound of the drums. It wasn't coming from the direction of the reservation housing, or from the direction of the strawberry fields. It was pulling me on a path I had not explored yet. It was light in the sky but dark on the ground. I was filled with feelings and not thinking. So fear had no space to spread out. The intensity of the drumming sound grew. I imagined that the earth beneath my feet was thumping, a rhythmic earthquake. I liked it.

My running feet paused right before a small clearing that was lit up with three torches. Below the fire sticks sat a Native drumming. His hands were moving like music. It wasn't a familiar break beat or song he was playing. It wasn't hip-hop. Still it had deep feeling. Siri's humming could not compete with the thunder of his drumming. Maybe if there was a volume button somewhere or a fader, I could equalize it like on Momma's expensive sound system. With my clothes peeled off now, I felt the warm night breeze. Without clothes, nothing was weighing me down. My body began to heat up. It was dancing, moving only on feelings.

"There's a girl over there sitting on the ground beside him," Siri tried to say to me. But I let her words drift away. I was moving inside the beat where no one could reach me.

Collapsing on the ground, burning with sweat in the dark wilderness, beneath the trees that looked way larger in the deep night, I wondered if Momma could feel my heart race. I wonder if she had sent a thousand of Poppa Santiaga's soldiers to search for me, telling them to never return until I was found. I wondered if she had a hole as wide and deep as mine on the inside, an emptiness that could only be filled by her and my true blood family relations.

Chapter 20

"Me, the raccoons, squirrels, chipmunks, and bears have an agreement," NanaAnna said as we weaved through the wilderness towards the strawberry fields once again. She was speaking to me.

"Our agreement is that I live inside the house and they live in the wild. If you leave the bathroom window open, they'll all think I've changed my mind and invited them in!" she said to me. "Especially when they smell your sweet strawberry maple syrup pancakes."

"Sorry." I spoke that one painful word. "I didn't mean to leave the window open. I was getting some air."

"The front door works." NanaAnna made her point.

"Let's get us a dog," Riot said. "NanaAnna, you could use three or four dogs on your property."

"Why dogs? I have a treaty with the wolves, two rifles, two shot guns, a pistol, and a hundred knives." She laughed some, playfully. But, I believed every one of them words.

When we reached the fields, instead of older ladies like the day before, there were bunches of school kids of different ages.

"School's out," NanaAnna said. "Yesterday was their last day."

"School in July?" Riot asked.

"Native school, our cultural place for the youth," NanaAnna explained.

It was 5:00 a.m. dark, and I was excited to see kids my age, but I had my eyes focused on picking without wasting one second. I was earning my way back to Momma, my going-home money.

On my hands and knees, with my basket at my side, I was crawling. NanaAnna and Riot had not even began yet. A small group of little kids were gathering around her. Meanwhile Riot was introducing herself as "Ebony" to some teenagers.

An hour in, and some little girl was quick picking from the row of strawberries besides me. When I took a swift glance at her, she would already be staring at me. It seemed like she was trying to keep my same pace and work in my same section nearby. I kept it moving. She ended up being good for me. We were racing one another, actions without words, young rivals. As the sun heated up I wanted water and had some in my side pouch. I worried about how many strawberries I would miss out on if I stopped for even a moment.

A cold splash shocked me and I looked up. The young girl was standing over me, spilling her water onto my face now.

"You have to break for water," she said.

She was tan and pretty with dark eyes and a bright smile. Her face was dirty and her hair was wrapped. We both wore T-shirts and jeans. I didn't get red. Her icy water was already warming, then drying on my skin. "Thanks," was all I said. I went back to picking.

Seconds later, she was one row over and back trying to catch up.

Fifty-eight baskets. I was red with myself. If I hadn't stopped to look up, to the girl who splashed me, maybe I could've made sixty. My tongue was so dry, it felt glued to the top of my mouth.

"Drink water," Riot insisted. "We're not moving till you drink all of yours. Do you want to get dehydrated, catch cramps, and collapse?" she reminded me quietly enough not to embarrass me. After I drank, I felt way better. Still I was glad I didn't break for water before, losing time. *Fifty-four dollars plus fifty-eight dollars*, my mind kept repeating. I had $112 dollars and only three picking days remaining.

Why were two girls and one boy walking back towards NanaAnna's place with us?

After peeing and washing up, I returned to the kitchen for lunch. No one was there. The chart was on the wall, taped to the tile loosely with a tiny piece of tape.

15 dollars for each cooking day. Debt $75 for clothing, $3 Per day
for summer stay. One dollar per use for bicycle.

I stared at it, thought, and reread it a few times. I penciled in what I thought was missing.

*$5 a day for dishwashing and clean up, which is separate from
    cooking.*

I would point that out to NanaAnna. My five-dollar clean-up fee would take the sting out of her three dollars a day summer-stay fee. Now I would be earning two more dollars per day than I originally thought, rather than losing three dollars a day, which was too steep. My swift calculations led me to a total of what my strawberry picking, cooking, and cleaning earnings would be by the fortieth day with all my expenses deducted. It came to $811: nice. And who knows, maybe I'll pick up some other odd jobs here and there.

A huge pot of water was on the stove beneath a medium-sized flame. On the long wooden eating table was a paper. I went and got it. I read.

Pasta, Pasta sauce, Salad

The instructions were written out neatly in the same handwriting as the day before, which was pancake and bean day.

"Gather you utensils and ingredients first," NanaAnna had said.

Before I finished setting up, they all came bursting through the door, hands filled with tomatoes, onions, lettuce, and peppers.

"I want peppers in mine," Riot said, smiling.

"No onions, please," the teenaged boy said.

"I want everything," the girl said. She was the same girl, my rival.

NanaAnna reached for an empty basket and collected the vegetables they had picked from her garden.

"Lunch for six," she said.

Lunch for seven, I said in my mind.

She had forgotten about Siri, again.

"Can I help?" the girl asked me. "I'm Onatah, the one you call NanaAnna is my great aunt. You are Ivory: nice to meet you," she said, introducing me and her without my help.

Big O and Little O, I thought in my mind.

"Did you wash your hands?" I asked her.

"All clean." She held up her palms, and then flipped them. Her little face wasn't dirty anymore. "Except for picking tomatoes." She smiled and walked to the faucet and washed her hands again.

"You chop the tomatoes," I told her.

"Let her chop the onions; they burn my eyes," Siri whispered.

"I'll chop the onions," I said to Siri.

"Okay," Onatah said, rinsing the tomatoes and getting started.

I needed the help since I was cooking for seven. As long as not one penny was deducted from my fifteen-dollar cooking fee, I was good. Would NanaAnna pay me less cause I allowed her niece to help and hadn't prepared the meal on my own?

"Aunt said you and Ebony are summer campers," Onatah said as she was chopping. "How long are you staying for?" she asked.

"Not long," I answered.

"How many years are you?" she asked me.

"Almost eleven," I told her.

"I'm almost eleven, too," she said. "Can you swim?" she asked me.

"Yes," I said.

"Wanna go swimming later?" she asked me.

I paused. NanaAnna had said I had to go to do some learning after lunch. I didn't know if I could or should agree, but I felt curious.

"I'll ask Aunt. But do you want to go?" she asked, searching me for feelings. I don't know what she expected. I had just met her.

"Okay, if it's okay," I said.

When the seven of us were seated for lunch, I had a strange feeling. I looked at the faces one by one. Everyone was talking, joking, and seemed happy, even Riot, who sat by the teenaged girl and boy. I felt like a stranger in a nice foreign family. I missed my real family. I needed Poppa. There was no father here. I felt good that I had prepared the pasta, especially the sauce. I liked salad. It would've been better if I had cooked this same meal for my real family. Wouldn't Momma be so impressed? Winter would think I was showing off. The twins . . . I felt choked up. I gathered all of the energy in my body and I pulled back the tears before they could get organized and race to my face and spill from my eyes. I felt a pressure, but I held back. I did not cry. I did not even let water fill my eyes and make them look like I wanted to cry. Dry-eyed, I won the battle against myself, this time.

"What's wrong?" Onatah asked. "Why are you puffing up your cheeks like this?" She was imitating my face. I exhaled.

"If you don't have a bathing suit, I can lend you one," she offered.

"She has one," NanaAnna jumped in and said. "And she can go swimming with you Friday, not today."

"Yes, Aunt," Onatah said softly.

* * *

Back in the room after my learning session with NanaAnna, me and Siri flipped through the magazines I got the other day from Walmart.

"You would look pretty in this," Siri said, pointing to a real colorful dress designed by Emilio Pucci, a designer I was just finding out about. I knew I couldn't afford the big designers yet.

"Should I wear a dress or just a nice pair of jeans and a pretty blouse? Should I get kicks or shoes?" I asked. "My first pair of heels?"

"Just get rid of those dirty strawberry picking skips." Siri laughed.

I looked down at my disgraceful sneakers. I laughed, too.

Yup, those will be the first things I replace, I promised myself.

We cut out clothing we thought would look good on me. We taped them into the back pages of the journal where I already had two days worth of recipes and five pages of leaves and sticks that I learned about earlier today in NanaAnna's herb class. I was surprised to learn that all of those sticks and leaves were foods; that each created different tastes and brought about different kinds of healing in a person's body. There were even flowers that could be eaten. NanaAnna taught me to take notes. She said if I was smart and continued cooking and learning classes, I would get to the point where I could use all of those herbs and sticks without even looking at my notes or reading and following printed recipes.

"Am I going to do your hair for your trip home to Momma?" Siri asked.

Where would I get my hair done? Momma always said, "You can't let just anybody play in your hair." She also said that "a jealous hairdresser can do all kinds of dirty tricks if you let her." I was used to Earline's in Brooklyn and I went to only one other place in Deer Park, Long Island, to get mines done.

"Let's cut out some fly hairstyles and put 'em in the journal," I told Siri. "I'll choose the one I like best in thirty-four days when it's time to go home."

"You're back," I said when Riot walked in after having been gone too long. "We were supposed to have our business meeting last night, but I didn't see you," I reminded her.

"Well, I saw you," she said. "I pulled you out of the closet, picked you up off of the floor and put you on the bed. What were you doing in there and why did you take all the clothes out and pile 'em up on your bed?"

"Look, I put them all back," I said, jumping up and sliding the closet door open. I knew I was ignoring her real question. What was I supposed to say? I was in the closet because I'm used to being closed in. So I cleared it out, went inside, closed the door, and dreamed and danced and listened to the music in my mind in a dark empty space. Should I tell her that sometimes I had to exhaust myself to fall asleep? Or that sometimes I sleep only after I pass out? No, I wouldn't say those things about myself, which were reserved for only me and Siri to know.

"How was your trip to the casino yesterday, and where did you disappear to after lunch today?" I asked Riot.

"Well, you know I didn't leave the reservation today or I would've mentioned it to you first, like we promised each other. I walked with the girl, Monica, back to her place. I was squeezing out as much information as possible, getting familiar," Riot said.

"What'd you find out?" I asked.

"Regular shit like, the Native youth like to drink, smoke, party. They don't have too much violence on the reservation except after everybody gets all liquored up. They swim at the waterhole down the way. The boys like to fix cars; drag race and you know . . ." Her voice trailed off. "If I wanted weed, Monica could get it for me," she added.

"You selling?" I asked.

"Nah, if I wanted to get heavy into that business I wouldn't fuck with Monica. She's just offering a joint to puff, or maybe a nickel bag. If I wanted to get into it as a business, I'd talk to NanaAnna even though she ain't really in that line of work no more. I'm sure she still knows a whole bunch about it."

"What about when you went to the casino?" I asked.

"Yeah, I went over there, but I didn't go inside. I didn't have to. I found out the first time I had gone over there, that there were enough people hanging around outside to get what I want," she said.

"What's that?" I asked.

"Identity," she said. "Porsche, you and I are juveniles. We need somebody eighteen, nineteen, with a driver's license, social security number, all that. Around here we could just tell people our names are Ivory and Ebony but when we take a trip downstate, if we get pulled over, we gotta have someone with ID and all their paperwork in order. Someone who can cover for us."

There was a long pause.

I felt bad for thinking Riot was out bullshittin'. She was really working on getting me home and I felt that.

"Did you find someone? What about the driver who drove us here?"

"Porsche, anybody who was involved in getting us out will never see my face again."

"I thought that one boy who drove us to the warehouse . . ." Riot cut me off before I could finish.

"He will never see my face again," she said with no regret and no smile in it. "He doesn't know where even one Diamond Needle is located today. He doesn't know where I am or who I'm moving with. He doesn't know nothing, he never will," she said from her gut and her heart.

I began thinking about the green-eyed boy who wore the hoodie and black bandanna. One glance and I could see he had more swag than any white boy I ever seen, and more swag than the one who drove us in the doo-doo truck.

"Your brother, Revo," I said. When I saw Riot's shocked look I told her, "NanaAnna said you and 'Revo,' used to run through her property. So I know that's your brother's name." I was straight-faced. Also, I wanted to be taken seriously. There was a pause.

"His name is Revolution, Revo, for short. He's my same exact age, so he doesn't have a license and can't make a six- or seven-hour driving trip to New York City. It's too risky," she said with no room for debate.

"Riot and Revolution, the same age, you have a twin?" I asked.

She didn't answer so I knew it was true. I understood she wanted to protect and defend him. I understood how close twins are. You could poke one and the other might cry instead. But I never poked my twin sisters.

"NanaAnna," I said. Riot interrupted me immediately, again.

"NanaAnna has already done more than enough. Even if you or I were ever captured, we will both protect her. We will both say that she didn't know who we were. She never knew we escaped or were on the run. We will say, we ran onto her property and pretended to be kids from around the way. She was kind to us, so we took advantage of her and stayed a while."

When Riot's mind was in overdrive her body seemed to heat up and be surrounded by a heat wave that I could see floating in the air around her.

"I understand," was all I said. I wanted to dead the conversation for a while. She was in too deep and way too dead serious.

That evening, dressed as boys, we traveled to town with NanaAnna. In a side shop stuffed with ugly country fashions that I would never wear, I chose a cheap red one-piece bathing suit and handed it over to NanaAnna. She paid for it. I added $9.99 onto the debt column on the list that was on the wall in the kitchen. I had my own copy of the list I wrote for myself in my recipe journal.

Chapter 21

On Friday after strawberry picking, where Onatah had not showed up, we returned to the house. NanaAnna told me that after I showered and changed, I would not be cooking lunch because Onatah would be having a swim party barbeque. When she saw me screw up my face at the thought of losing even one day of a fifteen-dollar cooking fee, she added, "You can cook lunch and dinner tomorrow, to make up for the money you're losing today." She sounded a little aggravated, but I ignored that and accepted her offer.

* * *

Neither Riot nor NanaAnna got out of the pickup truck when it stopped at Onatah's place. NanaAnna pointed.

"It's there. Walk up some and turn into the left. They're expecting you, Ivory, and Onatah is very excited," NanaAnna said.

I was standing on the road at the driver's window looking up to NanaAnna and glancing towards Riot who was sitting behind her.

"You're still on the reservation," NanaAnna explained.

"And I'm headed to town," Riot added as her window eased down. She really didn't need to tell me when she was going to town. I could tell by her appearance, gestures, and the direction she brushed her hair.

I must've looked nervous to them as I stood there, because that's how I felt.

"I'll pick you up right here at 8:00 p.m.," NanaAnna said.

"The sun will still be up, although I know that doesn't matter to you," she added.

I looked at Riot. I didn't want to ask her any questions in front of NanaAnna and end up blowing up her spot. She picked up on my look and told me, "I'm getting dropped at the barber shop. I'll catch the bus back. See you later." They pulled off.

As Siri and I walked up the road, I imagined that NanaAnna was watching us through her rearview mirror. She would be watching to be certain that I was safe, I felt sure.

Onatah lived in a palace that stood alone on the farthest corner of the reservation. A palace lit up by the sunlight and not hidden beneath the leaves or trees likes Nana's. There were no trailers there or short small cheap houses lined up in an overcrowded row. The design of the place was unlike any of the homes that I had seen while walking, bike riding, or being driven around the reservation. *I knew there had to be some rich Natives,* I thought to myself.

"Wow," Siri said. "She has a really fly house."

"Don't get too excited. Wait till you see mine," I told her.

Suddenly the door opened before I even got the chance to knock. A not-too-old, not-too-young lady leaned towards me.

"You must be the little one who is called 'Ivory,'" she said.

"Yes," I answered.

"C'mon in and welcome." Onatah came racing down some stairs like I was her best friend.

"Who do we have there?" A male voice trumpeted from another room. The lady who opened the door walked me towards the sound of the male voice. Onatah grabbed my other hand, held it, and walked with me.

"Ivory," the man who just had to be Onatah's father—from the way he sat, spoke, and felt like someone important who owned a palace or two might sound—said, "Let me take a good look at you."

I didn't pose or spin or even really understand his request.

"She does look like . . ." I heard a voice say. When I looked to my right, there were three more heads peeking out. I heard another sound and I looked behind me. There were two big boys who had just walked in.

"Ivory, meet my dad, my three sisters, two of my brothers, and my mom," Onatah said happily.

"Hello, everyone," I said softly and shyly unlike myself.

"Let's go swim." Onatah pulled my hand.

"We're not done talking to Ivory," her father said to her.

"Daddy, please, she is my friend, and I found her," she said in a baby-like voice like she was five instead of about to be eleven like me. It worked.

Riot had mentioned a waterhole where the teenaged Natives swim. Onatah had a long and wide pool in the ground behind her house. It was filled with crystal-clear clean water.

"Let me see you swim first," she said, testing me. "Stay on this side," she told me. These must have been instructions her parents gave her. Besides, her older sisters were all watching. I stayed on the side where the water rope divided the shallow water from the deep. The water felt good. I went under, holding my breath, and stayed squatted below on purpose. Beneath the water I felt lighter weight. It was like underwater I didn't have any problems. Or maybe I just had less.

I thought of Poppa who invited the whole Brooklyn neighborhood and all of his family and friends to Orchard Beach one year. I thought of Momma lying on her back in the sun, her oiled skin glistening. Poppa was so proud, he must've rented out a whole section of the beach. Only people with us laid their blankets in our area. Brooklyn had taken over and everyone was popping open their coolers and bringing out baskets of sandwiches and fried chicken and watermelons. I remember, I was six. My cousin and me took turns burying one another in the sand and scaring everybody. We also laughed at four of Poppa's workers who stood watch in the ninety-five-degree weather, their expensive shoes sinking in the sand. Their suits were really nice looking but completely wrong at the same time. Me and my cousins joked, "If one of us starts drowning, which of those guys will jump in and save us in those hot suits, hard shoes, and sunglasses?"

Onatah pulled me up from the bottom of the shallow side of the pool.

"What are you doing?" she asked, panicked.

"Just holding my breath, getting used to the water," I told her.

"Swim," she ordered. She was a little too friendly and too bossy at the same time.

I swam to put them all at ease. Once they saw that I could swim and even float on my back, it turned into a fun time. Onatah's poppa was working the grill. Onatah was floating on a gigantic plastic frog wearing oversized yellow sunglasses like a movie star.

"So how did you get to become a camper at my aunt's place? You are so lucky. The other day was the first time I had been there in a year," she said, still laying back looking into the sky.

"How come it was the first time in so long?" I asked. I was getting good at not answering any questions that I didn't want to.

"Because of a big reason," she said. She was good at not answering also. "Besides, my aunt is a busy person. She is very important in our tribe. She is a healer. You know what that means?" she asked me.

"Like a doctor," I said dryly. I hated doctors.

"No, a healer is way better than any doctor," Onatah said confidently. "My aunt has cured people who even the best doctors could not cure."

"How come you didn't come pick strawberries today?" I asked her, switching the topic a little bit.

"I only came the other day cause I heard that my aunt was there the day before. I thought it would be great to see her and I didn't believe that the owner of the strawberry fields was picking strawberries," she giggled.

Ignoring the new information that NanaAnna was the owner of even the strawberry fields, and had a thriving strawberry business, I asked Onatah, "Do you like music?"

"Music is okay. My brothers listen to a lot of it. I like to ride my horse," she said as though it was nothing unusual. Purposely, I didn't react, but inside I felt a wave of excitement. I swam off to calm myself. I spun underwater and swam back.

"Is music your favorite thing?" Onatah asked.

"I like to dance," I confided to her.

"That's so funny. I like you, but we're unmatched," she said sadly. "I can't dance at all. Our parents and the elders force us to practice a traditional dance at the Native school, for our Autumn Festival, but we don't want to. It's not like cool music. It's like drumming and we are suppose to do this spiritual thing," she complained.

Spiritual thing, I repeated in my mind. NanaAnna likes the word *spirit. She uses it all the time,* I thought to myself. I didn't know what Onatah had in mind when she said spiritual dance. But I was sure of a couple of things: I could dance to any moving drumbeat. If the drummer was tapping it right, it was cool music to me and my whole body was in love with the beat.

"What's that?" Onatah asked.

"What?" I asked her.

"Right there! It's red," she pointed. I looked down. There was red water where I was standing.

"I don't know," I said, genuinely surprised. But, when I walked away through the water, a thin red stream followed me.

Shame had returned. I bought a cheap red swimsuit and now the dye was coming off of it and ruining the water in her pool. We were on the deep end by the stairs that led in and out of the pool. I walked towards the steps.

"Wait a minute!" Onatah pushed in front of me and stepped out first. As I walked up the pool steps she came running back with a towel wrapped the towel and her arms around my waist and held them there.

"Ivory wait, don't move," she warned me.

"The food is ready!" her father's voice called out. A big family crowd gathered by the barbeque pit. One of Onatah's sisters came to see what we were doing. Onatah spoke to her in another language. Her much older sister answered in another language. Instead of going towards the grill where everyone was, we walked towards a really small building, bigger than the dollhouse but smaller than a one-car garage.

In the "pool house" packed up with nets and sticks, pumps and hoses and cleaning supplies, they sat me on a wooden bench with the towel beneath me. Her big sister said something that sent Onatah off running and her and me were alone.

"Would you like to call your mother?" Big Sister asked me.

I was shocked at the question. *Yes! Hell yeah! I wanted to call Momma!* I thought to myself.

Then I remembered and said out loud, "No thank you."

"Do you know what is happening with you right now?" Big Sister asked.

"What do you mean? I'm a little cold in here," I said truthfully.

"Did your mother talk to you about getting your menstruation?"

she said, and asked, "Are you dizzy? How are you feeling?" She was asking too many questions back to back.

Onatah came rushing through the pool house door with her hands full.

"Stand up," Big Sister said. She unwrapped the towel from my waist and showed me my blood.

* * *

"There are reasons why we are best friends," Onatah said to me. I didn't say nothing cause it was impossible to me that I could become best friends with someone I had only known for four days. I also didn't say shit because we were sitting in her stable besides her horse, the most beautifullest thing I ever saw that wasn't human. I felt guilty. I felt guilty because I wanted her horse, and maybe even her life. I mean, I didn't want her same life, but I wanted to rewind mine back to my house, erase the police and the raid and the kidnappers and the terror. I wanted to continue from my last request from Poppa: to get me a pony to trot around our property. I wanted the smile on Onatah's mother's face on Momma's face. I wanted the confidence and control from Onatah's father's feeling, to be in my poppa the same way it used to be, but even more. I wanted love from my sisters, all three of them, the way that Onatah's sisters loved her. So I felt guilty for going along with this little rich Native girl's idea, that she and I could already be best friends, or friends even. Siri wouldn't allow it. Then there's Riot and Lina and the rest of the Diamond Needles. Not to mention my Gutter Girls.

What makes a girl a best friend in the first place? I asked myself as Onatah began brushing the beauty.

I think, in order to be somebody's best friend, you had to be right there with them when shit was happening. You had to be there for the good shit, laughter and all that. You had to be there through the shame. You had to be there through the blame, pain, and guilt. And not just be there like you're watching a fucking movie. You had to be in it, feeling the same things, pain or pleasure. Could anyone whose life is all good be friends with someone whose life has been tossed and dragged and hurtful? I would say no. Still, I was planning to use Onatah. I felt bad about it, but not bad enough not to do it.

"Reason number 1 is because," Onatah began, explaining why her and me were best friends. "Reason number 1 is because you know my great-aunt. She's my favorite even though I'm not allowed to see her often. Reason number 2 is because you look like my great-aunt's daughter. I never met her, but she died in a car accident with my oldest sister. They died together. Reason number 3 . . ."

"Your sister was in the car?" I asked automatically, interrupting without thinking.

"Yes, my eldest sister was, and my parents loved her so much. Great Aunt's husband was driving. He was drunk. Everyone in the car was killed."

"Sorry." That word slipped out from my tongue. I *was sincerely* sorry that her sister was killed. When I thought of Winter, and if she were killed, my heart dropped. Maybe *she was killed*? Maybe she was killed and Momma and Poppa were so heartbroken for Winter, that they couldn't even remember me? Maybe Winter was killed and that's why she never wrote me a letter saying how she missed me or how she was on her way to get me from the group home or from the fake foster-care people. Yes, that could be the *only* reason she never visited me for almost three years at the juvy prison.

"Are you okay? Please don't cry for us. It happened a long time ago but father can't forgive Great Aunt, and they don't speak even though they are related. And my sister's mother never recovered from their loss, and . . ."

Onatah went on and on . . . I wasn't really listening to her. I had my own thoughts and feelings.

"Don't you have any friends?" I asked Onatah.

"Yes, of course," she said.

"How come they didn't come to your barbeque?" I asked.

"Because I wanted to get to know you, the little girl who made Great Aunt want to pick strawberries, and gave me an excuse to visit Great Aunt's house comfortably. The girlfriend who made my whole family curious and want to see you and caused Great Aunt to call our house and speak to my mother. The same girl who made Great Aunt drive almost all the way to my house, which she never does, and . . ." Onatah took a deep breath. "The girl my same age who had her womanhood in my pool!"

* * *

Later that night I made a decision and a promise. I would crack open the journal that NanaAnna gave me. Bit by bit, I would write the story of my life. I wouldn't go back into my past. I'd start from this point forward. But I would not write the boring details. I would write, from now on, only the most exciting, confusing, craziest, truest, or scariest best parts.

Why would I write a diary all of a sudden? I got *shook* thinking for the first time ever that Winter was actually dead. I got *possessed* by the thought and locked myself in the bedroom closet for four hours.

If Winter *is dead* how would I ever know what her life was like? If she had a diary or journal like NanaAnna suggested, at least I could read it and find out how she really felt about me, what she really thought. What her real life up to the point of being killed was actually like. I would be flipping through Winter's diary like crazy looking for love. Did she think I was aggravating? Or did she just treat me that way because big sisters think they're supposed to do that? Did she secretly see something special in me? Did she think that I was smart or dumb? I hope not dumb. That would make me red and I didn't want to get red with my sister Winter. And fuck anybody who does.

How can I predict what will happen with me? Riot and I already made a plan to protect NanaAnna, but I failed to make a plan of what to do about my own family if, say, the authorities swooped down and recaptured me, or if I was riding home to Long Island in a car and some drunk bastard slammed into the vehicle and killed me. How would Momma know what my life was from age eight through eleven? How would she know my most personal feelings? She wouldn't. How would Winter know how I worshipped her and how much I wished she would appear and save me? She wouldn't. How would the twins know that I wanted more than mostly anything to apologize to them for not protecting them from the kidnappers although I tried really hard? They wouldn't. So I would write my diary to my family, whichever one of them I felt like talking to at the moment.

I would tell NanaAnna and Riot if anything ever happened to me, give this purple journal to my people.

Chapter 22

THE DIARY OF PORSCHE L. SANTIAGA

Dear Winter,

Riding the bicycle on the trail wasn't nothing like riding it on the smooth straight road. I hit a rock and flipped over my handlebars. The last thing I saw was treetops and the wheel spinning a few inches from my face. The bike landed on top of me. I saw glimpses of sky and sunlight through the spokes. I blacked out.

Head pain, a little more drastic than a headache, my eyes were opening some, just slits. Again I was in an unfamiliar place, not home, not foster care, not prison, not NanaAnna's. I must've still been on the reservation cause everything was wooden. The Natives seem to like that kind of design better than aluminum siding or any other material. Even I was lying on a slab of polished wood, like someone had laid me on a tabletop.

When I lifted my head a little it hurt. So I laid it back down. I moved my fingers just to check and make sure they were working right. I slid my hand over my thigh and in between. I needed to check if someone had fucked me in my sleep. When I smelled my fingers, I panicked. The smell wasn't the same.

I heard sounds, heavy breathing and skin rubbing together. I felt terror. Slowly, I turned my head in a way not to make it hurt anymore than it already did. The first thing I saw was three heads without bodies. Not real heads but styrofoam ones made out of that same material they use to make cups. Each head was wearing a pretty black-black wig, long flowing straight hair, the kind ghetto chicks would kill for. I knew the sounds I was hearing were not coming from any of those fake heads.

I stretched my neck some. Even moving my eyeballs was work. I saw a man's naked body moving. I watched. His legs were strong looking and his ass cheeks were moving in and out. Most of all his skin was tight and nice. It was tan, like the inside of a Milky Way with a teaspoon of chocolate mixed in it. I liked his muscles moving. There was a body below him. Her legs were open. Her feet were flat against the bed at first. She pulled 'em up some, and then wrapped and locked em around his butt. I couldn't see his or her face, but the dancer in me knew they were moving in a rhythm together, not like a fight or a rape. My fear evaporated.

So this is sex, I thought to myself. Those sounds, after a while I closed my eyes and I made them music in my mind. Meanwhile, I tried to imagine the feeling they both felt. I couldn't. She looked like she was feeling so good in those moments, like if she had one worry before he touched her, she didn't have it now and wouldn't until he separated his body from hers.

I drifted into sleep cause I was running real fast while I was knocked out on the wooden tabletop. I was chasing a feeling I just couldn't capture.

* * *

THE GUY I MET.

Dear Momma,

You already know, today is my eleventh birthday. You would be surprised to see what I would only show to you: my little titties, which are mostly only big swollen nipples. I know there is so much more to come.

And I have hair down there, not a lot. It's like the light fur on a peach. I know it will only stay like that for a little while. Soon it will become a bush. I've been told that I had my womanhood. Seems too soon to me. I wanted you to be the one telling me all that. Then you and I would keep it a secret from Poppa.

Momma, listen to this. A few days ago, I woke up in a tree, a tree house in the wilderness, closer to the sky than usual, with unusual neighbors if you know what I mean. When I first looked out of the door I saw a beautiful but nervous blue jay and a red robin. When I saw the ground it was way, way below where I was standing, I got dizzy. No one was home. I didn't see a way out besides jumping and breaking my little legs. I didn't know who put me up here, if they were joking or trying to kidnap me. I was getting used to being kidnapped, but this wasn't the authorities' doing, I knew.

It turned out a handsome drummer lived in this tree. I know you wouldn't say he's more handsome than Poppa. But he's damn sure fine. He's Native with a Caesar cut and a tomahawk tattooed on his neck. He has dark eyes and dark brown lips and a strong body. He holds his drum between his knees and touches up those skins with his magical, musical moving hands.

When I saw all the heads and hair in his tree house I thought he was some type of murderer or, worse, a rapist serial killer. Turned out, he's a hair hustler. He's a real hustler from the top to the bottom and from the beginning to the end. Charming like Poppa, with a real pretty smile, he travels to neighborhoods and talks girls into giving up their hair. He pulls out a stack of paper (Momma, the kind of money stack that we're used to) and he pays them a price they agreed on. He cuts their hair off and bags each head separately. On one block, some girls lined up soon as they saw him coming. I get excited over him but mostly for his style. I like that he lives in a tree, owns his own business, makes his own money, and looks good while doing it. I got fascinated with his zip cord and how he glides from another tree to reach his own tree house. He seemed sure that he wanted to live his own way in his own space in a hidden and unpredictable location. I like that he found me when I blacked out beside my bike, but didn't take me to no hospital (long story, Momma, I hate doctors and hospitals) and healed me. He didn't touch me in any of my private spaces as far as I could tell. At first I thought he did because of the smell between my legs, then I remembered that I had my womanhood and that made things different. Besides, he has a girlfriend and she's really crazy over him, I could tell. She said she's the one who washed my body clean and changed my clothes. She was cool at first. Now she wants me to get out.

Last night I danced for him, but not really for him but for his drumbeats. His drumming is more than music and coming from me, Momma, that's saying a whole lot. It's like his beat is driving me or pulling me like a puppet. She wants to be his only puppet. I understand, but sex and dancing are not the same things, right Momma? And the drummer and her are grown, like seventeen and eighteen, and I'm just eleven. So there shouldn't be no problem, true? She says that if I had my womanhood, I can have a baby and that's too grown to be staying with her man in a tree house. I been here for like six days but I couldn't tell him where I live because I promised Riot I wouldn't tell people where we are staying.

For three days I was sick. For two days I was enjoying watching them.

She was making wigs—not cheap ones, incredible ones, that you might see on the head of some type of rich and glamorous movie star. I helped her wash the hair he collected. I combed and blow-dried it, too. She paid me a fair price for my help. For the last two days I was rolling with him, checking his hustle. His haircut was clean and sharp but he showed me a photo of himself with long, straight, black, beautiful hair lying on his back and flowing all the way to his bottom. I gasped and asked him was it his real hair growed from his scalp? He smirked and said, "Of course, I chopped it off and sold it." I asked him why would he cut something so lovely. He said he sold it to the father of a young girl who had cancer. He sold the hair that he cherished, to replace the lovely hair that the little girl once had but lost to the horrible illness. It was his most special human hair wig.

Don't get angry, Momma. I asked him how much he would pay if I chopped my hair off and sold it to him. He told me it was too beautiful and I should keep it. He said the same thing you used to say! "Never cut it."

On my last night staying with them, he was drumming in the clearing in the woods, and I was dancing. These Natives up here seem to always have a reason why they are dancing, something they are trying to say, or someone they are trying to talk to, or something they believe that I don't understand. So I was doing a wicked dance. My reason was for him to never forget me.

I'm going back to NanaAnna's house today. Now I'm confident riding across the forest on the zip cord. Once I saw how fearlessly the girlfriend did it, I had to be brave also. I'm leaving at sunup and I'm going alone. But he promised me that I could come back if my mother says so! My dance last night must've worked because he also asked me if I would dance in the Autumn Festival to his drumbeat. I told him I would.

He doesn't have a million dollars to pay me for moving and shaking my hips like you used to suggest. But please don't worry, Momma, I'm just killing time. I learned how to do that in prison. I'm killing time until I get to you, in sixteen days.

* * *

To my Twins, Mercedes and Lexus,

Should I write each of you a separate letter with a separate topic? I thought about that for a couple of days before I actually began writing this one to the both of you. I thought about how now you two are both seven years old, so amazing. I tried to guess how your little faces may have changed. More than that, I tried to imagine your personalities. People don't realize that seven year olds have their own personalities. I had one when I was seven so I'm sure both of you do, too. How are they different from one another? I miss getting to see those changes happening to each of you. A friend of mine got a puppy today. She said it was a late birthday present to herself. It's not one of those small ones that can fit into Momma's pocketbook. It's a Rottweiler that will grow big and rough. I think my friend wants someone who is completely loyal to her and on her side. She already said that her and the dog are breathing in the same rhythm. She takes him outside and trains him for a few hours every day. I think she wants him to be more ferocious than a real wolf or a mountain lion. She's really smart so she might get her way. The Rottweiler's name is Blood. You two would be surprised. I made my first birthday cake from scratch. That means I had to get all the ingredients, measure them out carefully, and blend them the right way. My friend chose one of the most difficult cakes for me to make. It sounded like it was gonna be real nasty at first, but it turned out to be delicious. It's a carrot cake with buttercream frosting. Don't worry, I know you girls don't want no vegetables. You know I use to be the same way. But a carrot cake doesn't taste like a raw carrot. Besides I learned a lot here in summer camp. Vegetables are only nasty tasting when a farmer sprays them with poisons called pesticides. I know that sounds like a crazy thing for a farmer to do, but most of them do it. They want the bugs to stay away so they could have a bunch of good-looking vegetables. This way they make more money. The poison they spray on it, kills people. It makes little kids like my two pretty sisters hate vegetables because of the nasty poison taste. When I come home, I'm going to cook for our family. First month or so, I'll cook all by myself to spoil Momma to make her think I'm her best daughter! After the first month, I'll teach both of you how to cook, too. Guess what? I can even make homemade ice cream. So far I only made strawberry ice cream, but it's sweet and good. I love you, Lexus. I love you, Mercedes. I love you better than food, candy, and even ice cream. I hope you love me back.

* * *

AUTUMN FESTIVAL

Dear Momma,

Dancing at gunpoint. That's what I would've been doing if I had agreed to perform in the prison family festival or at least that's what it would have felt like. The festival with the Natives was the opposite of prison. I was young and completely free. I didn't have to get permission to make a costume. The Natives believed in costumes and had all types of leather work, beaded clothes, embroidery, wooden masks, and shoe skills. Everything they handmade and built on their own got me thinking.

Momma, Siri is my close friend. I hope you don't mind when I bring her home with me. She has nowhere else to go. Anyway I hope you'll love her. She's warm and fashionable like you. She can sing but her best skill is humming. Some say when Siri hums it gives them goose-pimples or "the chills." Many nights when I was missing you, Siri sang to me, and caressed me. Always when I was in danger or trouble or deep sadness, Siri comforted me. She's so quiet. She sits for hours watching me when I'm dancing and sometimes when I'm asleep. She thinks she loves me best but I tell her Momma loves me best and of course Poppa, too.

Siri made me a meanass minidress made of feathers. I didn't wear shoes because I wanted to show the beauty and power of my feet, calves, and thighs while they were moving. My arms were bare and my neck and back open. Instead of the wooden masks that some Natives wore, Siri painted a cosmetic facemask over my eyes that concealed my identity, or at least confused it. I wore a feather cap as my hairstyle. We made it out of a bathing cap so it would hug the shape of my head and lay gently against my pretty skin, which I got from you. The cap was badass, please believe me, Momma. I probably can save it and wear it one day in a superstar video.

When "my drummer" began tapping, touching, and pounding the skins of his drums, I took flight like a pretty, proud peacock. It was only me and him surrounded by hundreds. He had told me I was doing a "salute to the Sun." Remember, the Natives need a reason to dance. I don't, but I ripped that place down. Believe me, Momma, I danced my ass off. I wish you could've seen me. There weren't any cameras though. The Natives said it was a "spiritual moment." Their moment lasted all day and into the night. My performance lasted eleven minutes. (Momma, 11 is becoming a lucky number for me. If you need four digits to play the numbers like back in Brooklyn, you should play 1111.)

When my dance was complete the crowd closed in on me. It was hard to shake the crowd of followers who wanted to know me, meet me, touch or pluck one or two feathers off my skirt, but eventually I shook them all.

Running back to NanaAnna's in the feather-wear, even the deer and birds were checking me out like I was a new breed of animal moving through their territory.

Tomorrow, NanaAnna's giving us a going-home party. Everyone believes we are campers going back home because August is coming to a close. Onatah, a Native girl who I met, will be one of the many kids who NanaAnna invited. She believes she is my best friend. Somehow me and Onatah keep getting connected back together. It turned out that my drummer is one of her brothers. He's the rebellious one who didn't want to live with his family in their mansion. I don't know why. So he made his home and ran his business in the trees. The whole time I was in his tree house worrying if NanaAnna and Riot was worrying over me, she already knew exactly where I was. Momma, Onatah chills like how we used to chill before Poppa got tooken. She even has her own horse. Up here people go horseback riding like how we play cards or dominoes. I know you didn't want me to get a pony or a puppy. Poppa told me so. He said you couldn't stand even imagining the piles of poop. But I learned that sometimes to get to something really beautiful, you gotta stand in, lay in, or inhale a little poop! I'll see you, Momma, in three days!

* * *

Dear Poppa,

Tense, that's how I'm feeling. How about you, Poppa? Are you tense? I know, you are more tense than me. I always know and understand even the slightest difference in things. (You and Momma helped me with that.) So you are still in a cage? I have been out of my cage for forty days. I'm tense because now that I've been out for what seems like a long time to me, if I get captured, it will be much harder for me to cope and deal. I'm sure of that. So I am planning to not get caught to the best of my ability. I have been thinking, Poppa, of pretty heavy things for the past twenty-four hours straight. For example, how serious am I about not getting caught? Am I so serious that I would kill to defend my freedom? I have been fighting a lot for three years now, Poppa. I know some murderers but I don't think I'm one of them. I hope the authorities never push me so hard and so far that I have to kill. And if I can't kill anyone else no matter who they are, I can and am willing to hurt them enough to stop them from coming after me.

The toughest question is, could I kill myself as a means to not getting captured ever again? It's hard to measure suicide. How does a person know if it's better to be dead or alive, when life can switch up in a heartbeat and become so scary and painful? And if I get captured, I can still get released one day after time served. I can still then see you and Momma, Winter, Lexus, and Mercedes. If I kill myself, I won't be able to see any of you unless there's really a place called heaven. Heaven or hell, if I kill myself, I'll be waiting there alone till any one of my loved ones passes away and arrives to join me. The problem is, I have already been alone for too long. Poppa, tomorrow we ride. You said you have a tight team. Me and my girl call ourselves Ivory and Ebony. We are definitely tight. If you knew Ebony, even you might want her to become one of your soldiers. She got a nineteen-year-old girl to ride with us. We call her Honey. That's not her government, but that's the name she wanted to be called. She's driving, got a license, and a Social Security number, a credit card, and she's renting a vehicle. She's not doing us any favors. My girl met her outside a casino. Honey had a black eye and a habit! We have been using her habit against her. My girl Ebony says she been training Honey the same way she trains her Rottweiler. She makes her do tricks for treats. She starves

her at the right time; "feeds" her at the right time. At first
Honey thought Ebony was a man. She was used to having a pimp
so she followed orders nicely and expected to get punched
when she didn't. Afterwhile, she got used to Ebony. When my
girl showed Honey that she was actually a girl, Honey laughed
a lot and says she knew she was too good to be true. "No man
is so good," Honey said about Ebony. By that time she was
hooked on her trainer. I met her once. I don't trust her, but I
trust my girl. When I saw how nice my girl was treating her that
one day, I thought the chick should have been named Money
instead of Honey cause she ate and drank too much, plus she
got a habit to feed. Honey said that Honey is her stage name.
She caught it cause the men can't leave her alone. Once they
meet her once, they stick. That's what she said. Now she say's
she tired of men. (Nineteen and tired of men. How does that
happen, Poppa?) She wants to go to Hollywood and "Young,"
that's what she calls Ebony, is her manager. Poppa, Honey used
to get beat up a lot. We don't beat her, though. We treat her
good even though it's not good to feed her habit. I've learned,
Poppa. Some people gotta get used. The weaker you are, the
easier it is to use you. I hope Momma doesn't get startled when
we ride up to our Long Island home. I wouldn't want her to start
busting shots at us. Since she's definitely not expecting them
or me.

Poppa, remember that time I fought with cousin Stacey
over Aunt Sheila's house? Remember Aunt Sheila spanked me
and yelled, "Money don't grow on trees?" I know you remember
it well. Momma was so mad that Aunt Sheila had the nerve to
spank me. I remember after Momma told you the story, you
didn't really react or bring it up again to me or none of us. Then
on a late Saturday night, you walked into my bedroom with a
money tree. When I woke up early the next morning I didn't
believe I had a real potted small tree at my bedside. Each thin
brown branch had leaves made of real cash folded and dangling
like birds. The lowest branches had ones, then fives, tens,
twenties, then hundreds close to the top. The top branch had

a new pair of gold earrings for me. I wasn't sure what I was most excited about, the fact that you thought about me and took the time to do something so special to make me feel better, or the money, or the way my money was folded into the shapes of birds and other animals. Yes, the 24-karat-gold earrings were really pretty, but I'll admit I thought about Winter. She would've gotten diamond earrings from you. But if you had put diamonds on the top branches of that money tree, I probably would've blacked out from an overdose of happiness.

I wanted to tell the whole world about my poppa. How could people not know how real you are? How big your heart is? You told me, "Sometimes when you have a good thing that no one else has, and everybody wants, you gotta keep it a secret. Hold it in your chest," you said. "Keep it for a rainy day." So I planted the tree out back. I listened to your instructions. Poppa, I know I pressed you to teach me how to fold the paper like you folded the cash, and wasn't satisfied until you taught me the origami. It took so long for you to teach me, I figured you had to go find out and learn it for yourself first! But you did, Poppa, cause you always came through. Now I can make those origami birds and shapes easily. Poppa, to this day you are my only hero.

When you got tooken, Poppa, it was the darkest, coldest night ever. My plan was to give that money from the tree to Momma so she could help you. Then Momma got tooken. Then I got tooken. Mercedes and Lexus got tooken. I did one thing that might make you proud. Before I got tooken I thought ahead like you used to try and teach me to do. I took each folded bill out of the beak of my stuffed bird named Pretty. I buried the cash from my money tree in our backyard somewhere near where I had first planted the tree in the ground.

Tomorrow we ride. If anything bad happens to me, capture, murder, suicide, I want Momma to have that money, and to give it to you. I want your commissary to be endless. I don't want you to even have to lift a finger, or to do what anyone else says for you to do, just to earn. I'm familiar with the cage, Daddy. Your middle daughter loves you more than you may ever know.

Early tomorrow morning, I'll bury this journal. I already set it up, so that if I don't make it, this journal will be dug up and given to Momma so she can collect the money. I already know that anything I give to Momma is the same as I gave it to you. I am your middle daughter. If you receive this diary journal, this is my true voice and true feelings.

The end of Porsche L. Santiaga's on the reservation journal.

Chapter 23

We met Honey at 10:00 a.m. in the additional parking area on the side wall of a local boutique. She was sitting in a rented white Volvo. Riot and I both did an eye search of the vehicle before we got up close. We had already done the same of the surrounding area. As promised, I had smoked the clothes I had worn for forty days, except for the one cheap outfit I had on. Tossing those items into the big blazing campfire the Natives had going the night before was easy. Wrapped in a couple of brown paper bags, the forty days turned to ashes in less than five minutes.

My memories, however, are permanent. Leaving NanaAnna, the land, the sky above, the reservation, and the people was only outweighed by returning to Momma and my family. I couldn't explain how a total of forty-two days had turned into real feelings. The fresh air, the stream, the lake, the organic gardens, and fruit fields caressed me. More than that, the first-time incidents were situations that flipped me over from young child to young woman. So many things that I could never possibly imagine happened. Having four Native girls from age ten to twenty-four celebrating my womanhood the same as if it was their own was awkward for me but it moved my heart some. So much so, I became uncomfortable in the cheap boy outfits I had been wearing. Onatah's big sister, taking the time to explain the meaning of it all, how to keep myself super clean, and in what ways women are special, made womanhood desirable to me. I used to hate pretense. Now I hated it even more. I was liking being a young woman, falling into the feeling of my growing body and swirling emotions. It was already impossible to conceal the curves of my hips and backside in the first place. Now I had no desire to wear a too-big tee to make my small waist and young breasts disappear from sight. I didn't want to flaunt it, seriously. My friend Ebony hated girls who only thought about their looks, kept messing with themselves and couldn't stay out of the mirror. She hated them as much as she hated the "robots." She believed that all dumb girls, no matter how good or ugly they looked, were exactly the same, worthless. So I tried not to be that and never wanted to be associated with being dumb or inferior even before I met her.

I buried my journal as I promised Poppa. I dropped it inside an empty cornflakes cereal box along with Momma's address and a special thank-you note to NanaAnna. I buried it under the soil closest to the eleventh tree on the straight path from the ivy leaf—covered, wooden, bush-blocked door of NanaAnna's brickhouse house, simple.

In my hand I held my recipe journal that contained almost fifty recipes for lunches and dinners and desserts that I had made myself. It saved me from my "eating disorder." The recipe journal also contained thirty-one days of learning from NanaAnna, which turned out to be better than any school on the planet. Inside I had cool things like pieces of sage and oregano, rosemary, bay leaves, cilantro, lemongrass, aloe vera, thyme, and peppermint. Also, I had a tiny bag of repellent, which I renamed "Back the fuck up." It was a concoction of cayenne and other secret things that when blown in someone's eyes or nose caused them to not see or balance themselves long enough for me to get away. All the ingredients were legal. If I got searched and found I'd shrug my shoulders and say, "Seasonings for our Labor Day holiday barbeque." My recipe journal was the first book I ever wrote, the first book I ever read from cover to cover, and the first book I ever loved.

I would miss Onatah after all, although I would miss her horse more than her. Her horse was the first one I ever got to ride without some adult holding the reins. Her horse was the first one that actually galloped with me alone riding its back, instead of walking in small ovals or circles at the zoo or in the blocked-off street at a block party or carnival. I only got to ride like that once, right before my time on the reservation was over.

I liked Onatah's father. He owned a construction company. His company had built many of the places on the reservation, even part of the casino. He was tall, heavy but not fat. The best thing about him was his voice. It was an instrument. I imagined if he wasn't a construction guy, he'd be a singer, the type of singer who the whole audience turns completely silent for in anticipation of his voice coming from his gut and pouring out into the room so powerfully it shook the walls. One afternoon after my learning lesson with NanaAnna, he was out watching Onatah ride. As I waited for my turn, he sang and Siri hummed some. I think his voice made her feel safe, and her voice moved him to tears. I had never seen any man cry before. Not even my strong poppa when he got cuffed and tooken. When I looked at this tall big Native mountain of a man, his tears didn't seem like a weakness. He didn't feel nothing like a sucker or bitch-ass nigga. That same afternoon, he walked out his house with me and Siri. He walked us to NanaAnna's pickup truck. It was his first time ever doing that. We all stood there silently facing NanaAnna until me and Siri climbed in and NanaAnna pulled off. The next day Onatah was so happy that she promoted me to being her best-best friend.

My drummer was not the first man who ever rescued me. But he was the first man who drummed a beat only for me. He tapped in precision with the movements of my young body. He was the first one to ask me what my body was saying while and when it was moving. My drummer was the first person I ever met who lived in a tree. He was the first one to place me in a box and slide me on a zip cord across the forest, giving me that first-time flying feeling, a rush so nice and tingly. My last day seeing him he said, "Now go and grow up, then come back to see me, before . . ."

All my little mind was thinking was, before what? Before what? Before what?

They say a person's first time at anything good is the best feeling in the world, a strong high, a feeling a girl or guy would chase forever. I wasn't sure if that's the truth, but I know all of the first-time good feelings I had in those forty days made me feel good enough to stay alive, become strong, and smile for more than a few quick seconds.

* * *

In the parking lot, we were leaning over and looking inside the Volvo right before the automatic lock opened. Me and Riot got in.

"Honey, you got everything?" Riot asked.

"Yep, right from the dollar store," she answered.

"Pop the trunk," Riot told her. Me and Riot both got back out.

"Baseball bats?" was the first thing out of my mouth.

"Just in case, you never know. We might have to knock somebody out. I'm not holding. Bats are legal," Riot said in complete seriousness.

"A beachball, a baseball, a water cooler, a flashlight, a jump rope, a grill for two . . . ," I laughed. "A box of matches, charcoal, and a bunch of boxes of pampers. Pampers!" I said, pointing.

When I looked inside one of the pamper boxes, there were neatly packed and stacked cartons of cigarettes from the reservation and not diapers.

"You remembered." I clapped for Riot. I liked that she listened to what I suggested even though I was younger. Riot didn't smile. She was serious like how she is on any mission. Before closing the trunk she showed me a small shopping bag, which held a sack which held a clay pot. "A gift for you from NanaAnna," Riot said. My eyes welled up with tears.

Inside the car Riot checked under both seats in back, then in front under the driver's seat. Honey lifted her legs for her.

"Damn, don't you trust me?" Honey asked her.

"Let's go," was all that Riot replied. I understood.

I thought to myself, *Poppa would say, "Always be good to a good worker and a good customer."*

But Momma would say, "Never trust a fucking dope fiend crack head!"
Now the Volvo was moving down the road.

Chapter 24

Almost seven hours. Of course, I slept some. Funny thing, it was only when the car stopped that I would wake up. When we stopped at the gas station, me and Siri stayed laying down on the back seat on purpose. Riot stayed seated in the car while Honey raced around pumping gas, going inside paying and coming out with a coffee cup bigger than her head and a few chips and sweets.

Riot and I was camera shy. Or should I say we were camera smart. Same as she never stepped foot inside the casino because of cameras, and wouldn't take me to the nearest mall because of cameras. She also wouldn't let us enter the service stations or the rest stops heading home. I'll tell you one thing, we were definitely going shopping at Macy's on Thirty-Fourth Street in Manhattan across the street from Madison Garden, a place that was crystal clear in my memories. I chose the place. We figured they had cameras also, but Riot said she agreed to it because "New York got ten million people and nobody gives a fuck about anything except money. So, as long as we're not stealing (and we *are not stealing*) nobody will look twice at two white girls shopping with their pretty black daughter. I had switched from being her son to becoming their daughter. A cokehead blonde, with a blonde-head girl dressed as a boy, posing as the cokehead's husband and their pretty black daughter, whatever. Me and Siri were already unbraiding my Allen Iverson, long front-to-back braided boy hairstyle. I was lying in the back turning from a caterpillar to a butterfly. We had agreed I would blossom soon as we seen the city lights.

* * *

We parked at an extra expensive pay lot down the block from Macy's. I could've copped a pair of kicks for the amount of that rip off parking fee. We had to park there. It was Friday night. Cars of every make were circling Madison Square Garden looking for parking. Every other nearby lot was filled. All the streets surrounding the famous Macy store said no parking, no standing, and no stopping with threats of seizing vehicles. Cops were stationed here and there, sitting and reclining and snacking in their cruisers. Tow trucks were laying and waiting for victims.

"Give me your handbag," Riot said to Honey.

"Why? Okay . . ." Honey handed it over. "There's no money in it." Honey laughed like, *gotcha.*

"I know. I have all the money," Riot checked her.

"You promised . . . ," Honey said in a teasing voice.

Riot gave her 150 dollars—one one-hundred and one fifty-dollar bill. I couldn't believe the high price Honey had obviously demanded for driving us down, and driving her and Riot back upstate. That was three days on our knees picking strawberries for eighteen hours!

I began to hope Riot wouldn't blow the five-thousand dollars I was investing on this "money chick"!

"Stay by my side while we shop. Don't go nowhere," Riot told Honey.

"I won't. I'm so excited. This is my first New York visit. We're close to the famous Forty-second Street. We gotta go there!" Honey said.

"We gotta get the kid some clothes. I told you that already."

We weren't shopping thirty minutes before Honey disappeared.

"I gotta pee . . ." was all I heard her say.

Riot stayed by the rack where I was flipping through dresses instead of following Honey to the restroom. She didn't even glance at her as she left.

"You better follow her," Siri whispered. Riot didn't budge.

An hour later we were done with our Macy's shopping. Even Riot had picked out a few items.

"What about Honey?" I asked.

"Don't worry about her," Riot said casually.

In a nearby Foot Locker I chose some kicks, and got an overpriced pair of tennis socks with a fuzzy white ball on the back of my ankle.

"Do you mind if I change in there," I pointed, asking the Foot Locker salesman, a young dude. "We got a birthday party to go to." I smiled. He agreed.

* * *

Riot smiled. "You look nice, like a different person."

She was right. Fashion makes a pretty face and figure go from gray to fluorescent. In my new neon green Airmax, my feet lit up. My denim Guess dress stitched to my young shape. I was feeling nice about myself.

* * *

In McDonald's I stood at the register ordering our food. Riot went to the bathroom. One side of my mind was asking me, *What if she doesn't come back?* I felt a little panic easing into me. I kept my eyes on the bathroom door and turned away from the register and cashier, waiting.

"That's $8.25," the cashier said with an attitude as though she was repeating the price for the tenth time.

"One minute," I told her, reaching into my side pouch. I counted the money, my eyes checking the amount, bouncing back to the door. I couldn't let Riot slip past me.

"Here go your change, take it," the cashier based. She turned around, grabbed my white bag off of the back stainless steel counter, and turned back towards me, plopping it down. As I walked towards the bathroom with the bag in one hand, orange juice in the other, Riot came out wearing a dress like mine, and some pink ACG kicks. She was a girl. I could tell she had wet her hair and combed it down into a short bob.

"I can blow-dry it some more with the McDonald's hand dryer. Check me out. How am I looking?" She smiled a free and soft and pretty smile, like she had finally taken a brief break from her constant calculations.

My green-eyed Diamond Needle was a pretty butterfly. As we

walked back to the parking lot where the car was, I thought of Lina. I always wanted to walk down the street with twelve Diamond Needles in a row fluttering. But I especially wanted to walk besides Riot and Lina and Rose Marie.

"What about Lina?" I asked Riot as we walked. There was silence for a long while.

"She didn't escape like us," Riot said. "She had already served out the majority of her time. She'll be home before Christmas."

Riot handed the man the ticket. We stood to the side while he pulled our Volvo out. I didn't say anything. I know Riot was the queen of plans. I figured Honey would roll right up, on time.

"Get in," Riot said to me.

I climbed in the back. Riot got in on the driver's seat, pulled the gear into drive and pulled out towards the down-ramp that led to the street. We waited there. I was looking left and right for Honey. Riot opened Honey's handbag, opened her wallet, then laid it on the seat. She pulled out a napkin and Honey's lipgloss. She used the napkin to clean off a layer of the gloss, then stuck one finger in and spread it on her lips. She took out a case of colored powder and dabbed on some eye shadow. She then lined her eye with heavy black eye liner. A car honked behind us, as she was finishing up. She pulled out into the crowded New York streets.

"A promise is a promise," she said. "Let's go." She turned on the music.

At the red light she opened the map. We were on our way to my house. It was 7:15 p.m.

* * *

The Dix Hill, Long Island, nights were dark. I remember Winter lying on our palace roof facing the sky, puffing a blunt. As we weaved around the jigsaw curved corners, one ways, dead ends, and alcoves, all of the street signs said NO PARKING AFTER 6:00 P.M. It's an exclusive neighborhood. Every resident owned luxury vehicles and had long winding, gated driveways to park themselves, their relatives, and guests easily. Any car lurking on the main streets instead of parking on the private properties would raise suspicion.

"It's there!" I said, excited. "That's my house! Stop the car!"

"I see but . . . I can't just let you off. I gotta park and make sure you're alright," Riot said, moving slowly on past my house.

"I'll jump out," I said, with my hand on the handle.

"Please don't! Give me two minutes," Riot said.

Around a couple of neighborhood corners, she found a house that was obviously under renovation. Where there was supposed to be grass, there was dirt. A Porta-Potty was plopped down to the side.

"There's a sign," Riot said laughing. "You know we gotta trust the Porta-Potty!" She pulled in and parked the car on what seemed like an empty property. We both got out.

"We'll walk," she said. "Don't forget nothing in the backseat."

"I got everything," I assured her.

She unlocked the trunk, grabbed the flashlight, and dropped it into her side pouch. She was also clutching Honey's handbag.

With each step closer to Momma, I felt my heart pound. It felt like what a heart attack should feel like, I thought. And I felt like I had to pee. Instead of being a beautiful butterly, I felt like the butterflies were in my empty stomach. My stomach rumbled. We both laughed lightly, nervously. Neither one of us had touched the McDonald's. Guess we bought it for show.

My driveway was gated up and locked. We walked past to the smaller gate that led to the walkway to my house. A metal plate lodged into the bricks had some words engraved on it. We stepped in closer: MARIO AND MARIA SCHETTINI RESIDENCES.

"Mario and Maria Schettini?" Riot read aloud. "Are you sure this is the right address?" she asked, turning to me. That's when she saw my tears and my face, which was the face of a girl who was 100 percent certain.

"C'mon, we can't just stand around like this," Riot warned.

But I couldn't move.

"C'mon, Porsche. We'll put together a plan B," Riot said.

I walked to the mailbox and reached in the mail hole.

"Don't put your fingerprints on nothing," Riot warned.

I pulled out a flyer from a pizza delivery place. All it said was "Resident" and it had the right address on it, my Long Island address that was engraved in my memory. The same address I had recited out loud a hundred times to Ms. Griswaldi, the kidnapper caseworker. I

walked to the closed gates that stretched across our driveway. I looked
up the driveway for Momma's red Mercedes Benz or any fly ass whip
I would recognize as Momma's, or maybe Winter had her own ride
by now. Either no one was home, or the cars were parked round back.

"Where are you going now?" Riot asked.

"To the other side where my money tree is at," I told her. She
followed me.

Soon as I rounded the corner to the other side I could hear the
thunder, then the rumble of a pack of high-speed dogs charging in
our direction. At the same time, a bright spotlight came on, piercing
through the night darkness.

"Let's be out," Riot said. I didn't move. I wasn't afraid of dogs, and
I knew Riot wasn't either.

"Those are motion lights. They'll know someone is near their
yard!"

They were stuffing their faces between the iron bars barking
hatred, flashing fangs and spilling spit. Riot grabbed my little hand
and yanked me. "Four German Shepherds, they might even be police
dogs," she said as she pulled me away. After we got off my block, we
ran a block before we slowed down to walking like nothing happened.

Inside the Volvo, rolling in reverse, I yelled, "We gotta get my
money tree!"

"Porsche, take a deep breath. Slow it down some," Riot said. "We
gotta get moving. In neighborhoods like these you never know who's
watching."

She was almost on the Long Island Expressway.

"Please, take me to Bed-Stuy, Brooklyn," I said.

"I don't know the way there," Riot said.

"Use the map!" I yelled. I was hurting.

Chapter 25

Could I read faces four years later? That's how long it had been since I stepped foot in Brooklyn. I knew the exact location and addresses of every one of my relatives, especially Momma's sisters. I even still knew some of their phone numbers by heart. They were the same numbers on my emergency contact list at school. I knew my sister's friends and definitely where Natalie's apartment was at, although she used to be all up in our place.

Crazy, soon as I got on my block, it looked unfamiliar, smaller, dirtier but still busy and noisy. Me and Riot stood still for some seconds as people passed by us this way and that.

"Can you still trust whoever's apartment you think you're going to?" Riot asked, still looking calm although she was the only white girl on the streets of Bed-Sty at 10:30 p.m.

"You said you didn't want me to call ahead to nobody. So, I gotta trust it this way." I started walking towards my old building. Riot followed close behind me. Then I stopped, and began walking in the opposite direction.

"Smart decision, you know how many famous hustlers, gangsters, and revolutionaries were turned in by their own families?" she said.

I was standing still in the same spot all over again. I was remembering how I had called all of the phone numbers I ever memorized to my aunts, cousins, and uncles. I had snuck and called collect from the group home and from the homes of each of the foster-care fakers. None of my aunts, cousins, and uncles ever accepted any of my collect calls. I had told myself that they must've changed their numbers. I believed that it was strangers declining my calls, not family. If it was family, of course they would've of accepted my call because they knew it was me, Porsche.

"What now?" Riot asked.

"I got a better idea." I started walking towards the corner store.

I went in looking around, same old guy behind the counter.

"You buying, investigating, or moving in?" he asked me.

"I'm buying." I grabbed some grape Now and Laters and a pack of Bazooka's Bubble Gum.

"Mr. B, did my mother come in here?" I asked him.

"Who's your mother?" He was looking down over his counter.

"Santiaga," I said. "You know her. Has she been around here?" I asked.

"Oh, she's around here all right, but I can't tell you where. This is her time of night," he said strangely. I wanted to press him but the rest of my questions were locked in my jaw and wouldn't come out.

I paid and left.

I walked over to Earline's where Momma and all of us Santiaga girls got our hair done. She stayed opened late for the weekend going-out crowd, and styling for special events. She would definitely know. Maybe Momma was there right now.

"Ms. Earline, Ms. Earline," I called out over the noise of the blow-dryers and videos playing on the new flat screen that was on the wall. It wasn't like that four years back, I thought. When I stepped up to her occupied chair, she switched her blow-dryer off.

"Yes, honey, how can I help you? We're not taking even one more head tonight. Come back in the morning. We open at eight." Earline said all those words and asked all those questions without even listening to me or taking a good look at me.

Typical, I thought.

"Have you seen Lana Santiaga?" I asked.

She stared at me for a second, then busted out laughing.

"Who wants to know?" she asked.

"Me, I'm asking," I said.

Earline looked around like she was searching for Momma with her eyes.

"She ain't here," she said and turned her blow-dryer back on. I cut my eyes at her. I had watched her kissing Momma's ass for as long as

I could remember. She would even push a customer out of her chair in the middle of perming their hair, just for my momma, Lana Santiaga, well-known queen and wife of Ricky Santiaga.

As I was leaving the shop, a lady who had her hands beneath the fingernail dryer called me over with her eyes.

"Why you looking for her? Does she owe your people money?" she asked me with a straight face.

"No, nothing like that," I said. "But she been around here right? You seen her recently?"

"Check the park," she said after glancing at her watch.

"The park?" I repeated.

"Yeah, the round caves in the old park," she said.

We left Earline's.

"Maybe we should try in the morning," Riot said.

"Why should we? If Momma's in the park, we don't have to worry about you going in anybody's apartment who you think I shouldn't trust, even if we related," I said sarcastically.

We were stepping back down the same block, walking on the right side of the curb, both of us out of habit. In juvy we had to walk to the right side of the line.

* * *

I was going one way. She was going the other. She gave me a stare, then the ghetto girl up and down. I gave her the same. When I noticed my bite mark on her face, I knew it was my cousin Tammy. I was about to get excited. Her expression shifted swiftly. I knew that she recognized me now, but she wasn't acting like she was cool with it.

"Porsche," she said, like it was a curse word.

"I know you not still mad cause we fought once when we were little. We blood related, remember?" I said to her with enough heat in my words for her to take me seriously.

"Your father murdered my father," she said with more heat in her words. "What you doing round here?" she asked me like a threat. I didn't feel threatened. I was still tossing the info she just gave up around in my mind.

Poppa murdered Uncle Steve? I was thinking.

"Don't look all shocked. You knew," she said. I pushed off. Riot followed me. There wasn't no way for me talking to her now to end up right. I pushed my hand in my side pouch. Juvy taught me well. I'm not no fucking late responder.

"You looking for your stinking dirty-ass momma? Aunt Lana, that cock-sucking, low-life bitch?" she yelled behind me.

I was on her smashing her face with my fist and smearing her eyes with my tiny pouch of Back the Fuck Up cayenne concoction. Whatever hate she had, I had double. She already had my tattoo on her face, a warning she obviously never learned from. She was wilding, coughing sneezing, throwing punches in the air that weren't landing on me cause the bitch couldn't see. They pulled me off her right after I punched her eye further back into its socket. My eyes dashed to see who was pulling me. It was everybody! But only Riot was familiar.

"We gotta move," Riot said.

"Fuck you, Porsche Santiaga. You and your momma," my cousin yelled, feeling false confidence now that she was being restrained and cleaned up by the crowd.

"We gotta bounce," Riot said. But I was headed to the old park down the block, and I definitely wasn't running.

At the park I dipped in the kids' area where I used to go diving and crawling through the painted, round cement caves and swinging on the swings.

There was someone sitting in the last cave. I leaned in, smelled piss and the stench blew me back out.

"You got something for me?" a woman's voice asked, calling me back. Riot shined the flashlight. I looked again. It was a broken, filthy, finished Momma. My tears spilled like raindrops. I crawled into the cement cave and hugged her. I couldn't stop hugging her, and I couldn't believe. We both kept crying and our voices echoed around and bounced off of the cave walls. Or maybe it was just me crying and my voice echoing. Many minutes passed, or maybe it was only seconds that felt like minutes. Riot was in the cave now, seated on the other side of Momma.

"We gotta move before that one girl comes back with ten more girls. I don't have a burner, a bat, or a blade. We gotta go," Riot said forcefully.

"What girl? Who? Oh child, please I gotta stay here. Somebody got something for me. They coming. He coming, in a little while," Momma said, fast talking.

"Whatever he got for you, I got for you. Whatever you got coming, I can get it," Riot said to Momma swiftly as she pulled open her side pouch and pulled out the rolled-up jeans and T-shirt she had been wearing before she changed in the McDonald's bathroom.

"What you gonna get for Momma, Riot!" I yelled. "You gonna feed her coke like she's Honey?" I screamed. "You tryna train her like your fucking puppy?" Riot ignored me, pulled off Momma's top and started putting her old T-shirt over Momma's head. Somewhere between seeing Momma's ashy skin, skinny bones, drooping titties and feeling hurt, shame, and betrayal, I began beating Riot. Momma began fighting her, too. Riot pushed and tried blocking our attack. She took our blows and punches but wasn't swinging back. We three tussled in the round cave barely big enough for the three of us to sit quietly and designed as a crawl space for kids.

Riot jerked off Momma's stinky shorts while Momma was kicking and screaming. The stench was stronger than bleach and fouler than the backed-up toilets on lockdown when the plumbing system once failed. I stopped fighting and resisting when I seen Riot desperately trying to get her jeans onto Momma's tiny legs. Momma kept kicking and squirming so I held her arms and shoulders down until Riot got the pants up.

"C'mon, let's be out," Riot said. Me and Riot were both standing at opposite sides of the caves now and Momma was still laying there in the middle with her ripped up old clothes tossed beside her.

"Who is she?" Momma said, pointing at Riot with her eyes. "Whose side is she on?" Momma made a stank face.

"Come out, I told you I got you," Riot yelled at Momma, pulled out her short money stack and shoved it inside the cave as bait for Momma to move. As Momma began moving, Riot pulled her money fist back slowly and stuffed her money in her side pouch. Riot then ran over to the trashcan and started rifling through the trash. She pulled out a empty forty-ounce bottle, slammed it on the ground, and kept the top part with the jagged edges. She concealed it in her side pouch, keeping one hand on it like it was a gun.

"Let's get a cab," Riot said. Momma laughed.

"One might stop for you," Momma said. As Riot ran into the street to hail a cab, I looked down at Momma's feet. She wasn't wearing any shoes. "Damn!" I screamed. I took off my new Air Max, dusted off the shit on the soles of Momma's feet. I stuffed Momma's toes into my kicks. They wouldn't fit.

"Walk on the back of'em, Momma. Fold'em like flip flops," I said. She did.

Me and Momma walked down the sidewalk on my Brooklyn block while Riot walked in the streets facing the traffic searching for a taxi. Me, in my tennis socks ignoring the rocks and pieces of glass I was stepping on, and Momma dragging my new kicks. I saw people watching. I didn't give a fuck about them or me. I was destroyed and distraught over Momma. I cared for her above anyone and anything.

We rode silently in the cab. I began feeling grateful to Riot, although I thought she already seen way too much. And the things that she had seen so far, that I never expected to see myself, could never be taken back or erased from Riot's mind's eye. I wanted Riot to leave. At the same time I didn't want to see her go.

Soon as we jumped out the cab I shot into the drugstore buying everything with Momma in mind. Momma wandered into the aisle with the toys and bought herself a bright yellow wig, part of a princess Halloween costume set.

Chapter 26

ROOM, that's all the sign said on a piece of cardboard posted in the window in a building on the side street on the West side of Forty-second. Riot checked us in, flashing Honey's driving license. The creepy old man didn't even check it.

"How many hours?" he asked, his teeth stained with coffee, tobacco, or both.

"Overnight," Riot said.

"That's twenty-eight cash, no checks, no credit cards. You girls play nice, that's all it cost. Bring back a man, it's double, fifty-six cash, no checks, no credit cards. Bring back two men, that's triple, eighty-four cash, no checks, no credit cards. I'll be setting down the door and the windows don't open. If you're expecting some fellas, might as well pay up now before you girls gets too busy . . ."

"No men!" Riot said angrily. She peeled, then pushed him three ten-dollars bills. He took 'em and handed her the keys, disappearing without offering her two dollars change.

After she opened the door, she stepped to the side and allowed me and Momma to enter first.

"Check it out. See if it's okay," she said calmly, with concern for us.

I looked around first with only my eyes. Then I walked in. Walking into the bathroom, I could see the place was better than a prison cell, larger than a closet. It had a tub, shower, and the hot water faucet that came on without delay. It had a bed, desk, mirror, and a chair. It wasn't no type of fancy, but it functioned.

"It's cool," I told Riot.

"I'll be back," she said, closing the door slowly.

"Where are you going?" I pulled the door before she could shut it completely.

"To meet Honey," she said.

"Where?" I asked.

"At the same place where we parked the car."

"You expect her to be there?" I asked.

"When she runs out of whatever she used her money on, she'll go to the place we three have in common, the parking lot where the rental car is. That's why I parked it and left it back in that same old expensive lot. No other reason." Riot left.

I was sitting on the bed, face-to-face with Momma. She was in an uncomfortable-looking chair, looking uncomfortable.

"Momma, let's switch places, or we can both sit on the bed together," I said.

"When do you think the girl is coming back?" Momma asked about Riot.

"Soon, so let's you and me talk some," I suggested gently.

"What's there to discuss? You already seen everything," Momma said.

"Don't be like that, Momma. We haven't seen each other in so long. Are you comfortable? Are you hungry?"

"I don't have any money to get nothing. I told you I was waiting for someone to bring me something. I don't have my handbag or my clothes. What was the sense in us leaving Brooklyn and coming all the way over here?"

"Momma, where are your clothes? Where have you been living?" I asked her.

"Girl, I'm a gypsy, can't you tell?" Momma smiled, revealing one missing tooth. Luckily, it wasn't in the front. But it was close enough to the front that a smile would show the opening.

"A gypsy?"

"I move around, especially cause funny people be acting funny," she said strangely.

"Funny people?" I asked.

"Especially if they family. They be acting the funniest. One minute they with you, next minute they against you. Back and forth all day and night long. That's why I move around."

"So who keeps your things, your clothes, shoes, handbag, family photos? Your record collection?"

"I got a little space. Got some cleaning up to do. It's okay, though. Hot in the summertime, cold in the winter," she said.

My tears welled up, and so did hers. We both knew why. I wanted to ask. But Momma seemed so fragile, like something about to break. So I focused only on her. It was crazy. If someone would describe my momma as looking like she did right now, living the way she seemed to be living, I would've punched 'em dead in the mouth, paralyzed 'em, maybe even killed 'em. What I was seeing was something only I had to see for myself with my own two eyes.

"Momma, remember you used to put lotion on me and clean out my ears and wash my hair?" I asked as I got up from the bed, grabbed one of my drugstore bags from the table, and disappeared into the bathroom.

I turned on the bath water, checking the temperature with my fingertips. I swished the water around, cleaning the tub before I put in the rubber stopper. I pulled the bubble-bath balls out from my CVS bag and dropped the lavender balls into the warm-hot water. Leaning over the side of the tub, I watched the balls dissolve, creating a nice scent and pretty purple bubbles.

"Do you think I'm filthy?" Momma said, startling me some, standing in the bathroom doorway.

"No, but I want to take my momma to dinner. I'm hungry so we should both get pretty. Come in, I'll help you. I can wash your hair, too. I'm good at doing hair these days," I told her softly.

"I got my wig, it's in your bag," she said.

"I know, undress, get in. I'll give you the beauty treatment." I was speaking so softly not to agitate her. I wanted her to relax, trust me, and confide in me. I looked away so she could undress and step in the tub. She did.

I began cleaning Momma with the squishy sponge I had just purchased, cleaning her shoulders, raising up her arms, cleaning her armpits, tickling her on purpose.

"Don't it feel good, Momma?"

"It's alright," she said. As I cleaned each of her fingers, I overlooked the dark patches on her skin. I cleaned her neck and her back, her stomach with soapy water. I cleaned her thighs, legs, calves, and toes.

"What color would you like me to paint your fingernails?" I asked her. She drew her hands back and hid them underwater.

"I aint got none," she said.

"Yes, you do, I brought you some press-ons and some eyelashes." I smiled. She was sweating. Racing through her beads of sweat were her tears.

"Do you want your toes and fingers to match colors?" I asked her.

"I don't want no press-ons on my toes," Momma said. We both broke into our first laughter.

"I know, Momma," I said. "I just asked about the colors." I began clipping her toenails carefully.

I wrapped Momma in a towel and walked her to the sink. I washed her hair with Herbal Essence. It was short, about five inches long, but I was happy that she was not bald.

"All done," I said after a warm rinse.

"But we only got one towel," I said.

Momma removed her body towel to dry her hair.

Sitting naked in the uncomfortable chair, momma put her feet up as I first weaved tissue in and out of each toe space to separate her toes. I began to paint them a pale pink color. I blew on all ten toes until they were dry enough.

After I completed her fingernails, I removed the tissue between each of her toes. I washed, then dried, my hands in the air. Next, I told her to tilt her head back so I could do each lash. I concentrated really hard to line them up just right. As Momma's eyes were closed, and I could no longer see that vulnerable, insecure look in her, I asked, "Momma, where is Winter? Why isn't she taking better care of you?"

Momma's tears squeezed out of her shut eyes. I paused, then dabbed them away with toilet tissue. My own heart dropped. Was my big sister dead? She had to be dead. No other way all this could've taken place with Momma, unless her first daughter and closest friend was dead.

"She's locked up, doing fifteen years . . . ," Momma said. My fingers shook. I dropped a lash or two on Momma's skin. I tried to pick it up with my fingertips without pinching or scraping Momma.

"For what?" I finally asked, but it was hardly possible for anyone to hear, not even Momma, whose face was only inches away from mine. Maybe I only asked it in my mind.

After a long pause, Momma said, "Conspiracy to distribute crack cocaine." She sounded like a courtroom lawyer. "And some other shit, too . . . ," Momma said bitterly.

"When did this happen?" I asked my most important question. Used to keeping count, I wanted to know how many days my big sister was walking around free, without coming to check on me. Or had she been arrested immediately after the last time I saw her and that's why she never came to see me or better yet to get me?

"About a year and a half after you got tooken, your sister was arrested right there in Bed-Stuy on our Brooklyn block. She was sitting in a car dressed up real rich, and balling real hard. She almost could've gotten away, but she was chasing after your father's letters. I had 'em. Winter wanted 'em, and then the police came. It was a mess," Momma explained.

"Poppa's letters? Letters he wrote to you, Momma?"

"Nope, letters he wrote to her, bout ten of 'em," Momma said.

Tears were streaming down my face. I was happy Momma couldn't see them.

Ten letters kept repeating in my mind. Ten letters to Winter. I didn't get one bloody fucking word or even a sentence on a postcard.

"So where are the letters?" I asked her.

"I told you, I gotta little living space. They in there, inside of my bags," she said.

"Is that where the twins are, too? Are they living there with you in your living space? Do they have a good babysitter who won't let anybody steal them away? Can I go see them in the morning? Would that be okay?" I asked.

Momma's eyes popped open, half short lashes, half long. She gave me a strong stare. She never answered my questions. Silently I cried, still trying to get her lashes on straight. After some silence between us, Momma said, "I used to be just like you, Porsche. I used to walk around thinking everything was so special, me, Winter, the twins, and of course your poppa. But I found out that in this life, ain't nobody shit, even me. I ain't shit and things come and go. Don't try and hold onto shit, and you can be happy. Try and hold on to it and you'll end up with nothing but a gigantic hole in your heart."

Numbers paraded through my mind. Winter was free for 545 days walking and riding round Bed-Stuy without checking on me. Poppa wrote ten letters, without writing to me. No one knew where the twins were: if they did, it was a place too terrible to mention.

We were silent until Momma's lashes were completed.

Momma pulled on her yellow wig. Naked, she spun left and then right, shaking her hair, checking herself in the mirror. She extended her arms and wiggled her fingers, admiring the press-ons. She checked her toes, and then pressed her face up close to the smoky mirror, batting her eyes, flaunting her new lashes.

"I wanna wear that dress," Momma said, pointing.

"The one I'm wearing?" I asked, as I pulled it off and gave it to her. Her body was so slight; she fitted her eleven-year-old daughter's dress with room to move around.

"I should give it back to you, right?" she asked, but I could tell she didn't want to.

"Momma, whatever I have, you can have it," I told her. "It's yours." I slipped into Riot's old outfit; the one Momma had taken off before bathing.

* * *

Dawn was coming, a different dawn under a different sky in a cheap rooming house with one permanently locked window, no breeze, and no view.

Momma was asleep. She went to bed after she knocked back four glasses of "Moet Peach Nectar Imperial Baby!" at twenty dollars each at our late night mother-daughter reunion dinner. She ordered filet mignon. My heart swelled with each forkful she ate, even though she didn't eat much. It was my first time buying a meal for her with money I had earned on my own.

I didn't say much. Momma did the talking. She'd go from depression to comedy in less than seconds. Then she switch to cursing about beefs with people I didn't know and never heard of. Then she'd cursed out family members who I did know all my life who she used to be close with. Next she'd be yelling too loud to be sitting in a restaurant.

She didn't know Riot's name even if she had overheard me saying it. She didn't remember. She'd just throw back a drink and say, "That little white girl is a liar." The she'd switch, laugh, and say, "But she ain't the only one!"

I sat, not eating the food I ordered. I was waiting on Momma to really see me. It never happened. I had confirmed at that late night–early morning dinner on the infamous Forty-second Street, that I am Porsche L. Santiaga, the invisible middle daughter. No one came for me. I lived my young life fighting to get back to Momma and my family. I crawled on my hands and knees, barked like a dog. I worked my young ass off. I cried, cramped, spit, cursed, vomited, and even laid down in fucking doo-doo. I fought, fainted, starved, wrote letters of protest, letters of love, even wrote a book. I made money, saved money, beat shame, blame, guilt, and humiliation.

For Momma, who I love so much it burns, it seemed like one ordinary night. She didn't say I did well, am good, look good and dressed up for her real pretty. She didn't recognize my fight or my effort. She didn't even ask me about it. Momma didn't recognize my dancer's legs, little lady hips, or my new pretty titties. She didn't say my hair was long and lying on my back like a bad bitch would rock it. More than that, she didn't recognize my pain or my love. Momma didn't explain herself, turning heavy topics into light jokes. She didn't apologize for even one thing. She never said sorry, didn't seem sorry for abandoning me. Momma was too hurt for her to care about me.

Chapter 27

Riot walked in with the sun, her hands filled with clothes and shoes. She dumped them on the desk before I could even help out. Honey walked in behind her, with another black eye.

"Santiaga!" Riot said to me with whispered excitement. "Get up! And let's roll." I pulled myself up. I had not slept for even one second all night and early morning long.

Honey collapsed on the bed next to Momma, in the space I opened up soon as I stood.

"I paid the old guy downstairs for one more day. Let's let them sleep it off." As I walked to the door, wearing the same clothes Riot wore yesterday, including her old skips, I looked back at sleeping Momma. Would she be here when we got back from wherever we were going? Maybe I should stay on guard right at her side?

"They're not going anywhere. I promise," Riot said.

I opened the door and walked out into the hallway. Right now Riot was the only reliable person in my little fucked-up world. She came out the room smiling.

"Wake up. We gotta get that money tree!" Riot said, cheering. "And why did you switch back into my old clothes?" Riot asked me. We were walking. I didn't turn to look at her. Instead I kept my eyes in the straight ahead direction. It was a cloudy morning.

"I wanted Momma to have my new dress. It was a gift from me to her."

"You didn't have to. I was bringing clean clothes for your mom and for Honey, too. New York City is an incredible place. Business never stops. It's convenient," she said.

"So you want to chill here?" I asked.

"No, I didn't say that. I'm just saying whatever you need to get done out here, gets done triple time. You don't have to wait for stores to open. They never close! The lights are always on." Riot sounded excited.

"That's cause we're in the Forty-second Street area," I told her, remembering the bright lights and packed crowds when my whole family went to dinner and a late-night film together. Momma, Poppa, aunts, uncles, cousins, and all to see *The Lion King*, Poppa's treat.

"It's gonna rain," I said, looking up.

"It's perfect," Riot said. She opened the car door. It was out of the expensive lot and parked in a regular money-meter curbside space.

"Not really. Today is Labor Day. The rain gonna mess up the parade," I said in a sleepy mumble, as I settled into the backseat.

"It's going to fuck up the parade, but heavy rain is gonna help us out." Riot started up the car and pulled off. "Porsche, you know exactly where this money tree is located in the backyard? Right?" She was watching me through the rearview mirror.

"Exactly," I assured her and collapsed into sleep across the back-seat.

* * *

I thought it was a nightmare when I woke up hours later facing the Porta-Potty. Was I just gonna keep reliving the same shitty scenes? When I looked down, I had on Riot's clothes. So I was sure I was awake instead of dreaming. But why was I alone in a parked car in a rainstorm, the windows so soaked all I could see was the portable toilet, a memory that I'd like to forget.

My back car door opened. "The dogs are inside!" Riot said in an excited voice. "We gotta move now!"

The cold water shocked me into a clear reality.

"Put this on." Riot slid a rain poncho over my head. When the poncho was covering my whole body, she shoved an object underneath and said, "Keep it hidden."

I held the handle, slid my fingers down and felt the shape of a small shovel.

"We'll walk fast. No one will think twice about two girls trying to hurry out of the rain."

No one would even know we're girls, I thought to myself. We both now had our black rain hoods up and our bodies covered in black plastic.

When we reached my Long Island house, Riot said, "Stand over there in the driveway. I'm gonna open the gate. Then, run in and get the money. If I'm not here when you get back, walk, but don't run, to the car and lay down in the backseat. Got it?"

"Got it," was all I said. I saw Riot reach in between the bars of the front walkway entrance. She didn't enter. I couldn't see what she was doing with her hands. The gate opened. I ran in.

My tree had multiplied. It was more wide than tall. The branches that used to have money dangling from them were now filled in with dark green leaves and yellow blossoms. I looked up, rainwater beating down onto my face. My bedroom window was there, in Poppa's house, where Momma, Winter, Lexus, Mercedes, and me lived. Who the fuck told these people they could live in the house my poppa bought for his family? I felt cold water on my neck sliding down beneath the plastic poncho and over my breast. When I looked straight, there was Siri. She was also standing in the pouring-down rain facing me.

"Siri," I said. "Where have you been?"

"Porsche, your feet are sinking in the mud. Hurry up and dig. We gotta get out of here," she said.

I looked down at my feet. They really were sinking. I ran to the tree, turned around and walked out the combination that I would never forget. I started digging at the right spot.

"Don't worry, don't worry," Siri sang to me over and over again, but I was worried about her. She didn't have on a rain hoodie.

When my shovel hit the metal I knew it was my moneybox. I used my fingers to push away the rest of the mud. Siri and I pulled the thin handle of the box together, until it moved some. Then we wiggled it and pulled it out.

"You got it!" Siri said, clapping with soft excitement. I started to run.

"Walk, don't run," Siri reminded me. "Even though we're soaked we have to walk," Siri said calmly. Even though her hair was soaked and her clothes were drenched and clinging to her pretty skin, she walked the same as if it were a sunny day. We both ignored our feet squishing in all of the dog poop piles, which had become a part of the soil. We left out the backyard and through the gate, which was left opened. The metal box was concealed beneath my poncho.

The car door was unlocked. We crawled into the backseat from squatting down and laid on the backseat both shivering. The car started, although I didn't see Riot. I lifted my head to peek over the seat. Riot was sliding up from the floor.

"You got it?"

"We got it. Siri helped!" I said.

"Where's the shovel?" Riot asked. She was looking back at us, as she drove the car in reverse out of the driveway.

"We left the shovel?" Siri said.

"Did you forget the shovel?" Riot asked.

"Yes," I told her, sitting up.

"We gotta get it," she said. Because of the way Riot spoke those words, I *knew* we had to get the shovel. As she rounded the corner to my house, driving at a low speed through the downpour, two police cars were coming from the opposite direction. Me and Siri ducked down. Our hearts were beating so fast it felt like an attack. It was as though someone was throwing rocks at my chest. No, like someone was burying me and Siri. Smothering us with pounds of rock and gravel. Siri began stroking my hair like Momma would when I was little. Riot wasn't saying nothing. She wasn't stopping or slowing down the Volvo. She didn't slam on the brakes.

In the back, in the uncomfortable small space on the floor, we were shocked into silence. The cold plastic poncho was pressed against my already wet clothes. My lips were shivering. My head was pounding. I smelled shit. I knew I hadn't shitted. I peed on myself all the time, but never shitted. My sneakers were covered in dirt. "It's dog shit," Siri whispered. Her lips were pressed against my ear. We held hands. All of our fingers were dirty. Mud was caked beneath our nails. Momma must be right, I thought to myself. *I ain't shit either.*

* * *

Storm turned to drizzle. The gray-black clouds still churned. We were parked. "We're here," Riot said. I unfolded my legs from the locked position I had held them in for the more than an hour drive. I peeled off the poncho and still shivered in my damp clothes.

"It's a holiday. We can leave the car here as long as we move it before 6:00 a.m. tomorrow morning," Riot said. "Are you okay? You look like you caught a cold." She placed her palm on my forehead.

"You got a fever," she said calmly, like a mother in thought. "Go ahead up. I'll get you some medicine and be right there." I couldn't argue or even tell her I didn't want no medicine. I felt drained of all of my power, even the energy to talk. I used whatever strength remained to hold the handle of my metal money-box. As I walked down the street to our motel room, I thought about how people would mug me if they knew I had five thousand dollars cash. But they didn't know. This is New York. I'm a shitty little girl wearing skips soaked in watery dog poo and someone else's cheap ugly clothes.

When I opened the door to our rented room, Momma and Honey both had angry faces. "Porsche, get over here," Momma said. I had not explained to her not to call me "Porsche," that my name is Ivory. I didn't even tell her why I needed a new name and that I'm an outlaw. She never asked where I came from or how I got my way back to her. Through my feverish eyes, I looked a little closer and seen Momma and Honey were handcuffed together at the feet and Honey was also handcuffed to the bed.

"They won't leave, I promise," Riot had said to me when we left out this morning. "A promise is a promise," she had said just last night. I thought to myself, this bitch is crazy, smart, loyal, and very scary.

Chapter 28

Down by the dirty-ass Hudson River where the water was still, black, and greasy like oil, we grilled chicken breasts and roasted corn and marshmallows. Honey drizzled on some borrowed barbeque sauce from some Latino men who were playing dominoes among the Labor Day evening crowd, which swelled after the rainy afternoon. Momma was grooving to someone else's throwback jams. She was wearing one of the summer dresses that Riot had brought in her pile this morning.

Riot, the vegetarian, was eating marshmallows and so was I. I tried the corn but it didn't taste no way as good as the organic corn on the cob at the reservation. I couldn't pretend to like it or eat it. So I laid it to the side and left it in the flimsy paper plate, while Momma and Honey began grubbing like this thrown-together meal was gourmet.

"What made you buy that stack of chicken breasts? I was surprised to see you with a bag of meat," I asked Riot.

"Oh, it was for the dogs in Long Island," she said casually. I didn't say nothing for some seconds. I was thinking of how she was feeding Momma dog's food.

"Luckily, I didn't have to use the chicken breast, my dog whistle, the stick, the bat, or the pizzas. When the radio predicted rain, and then there was a Long Island area afternoon flood warning, I knew they would pull their dogs out of the yard until it all cleared up. I used it as an opportunity," she said softly like it was nothing.

"The pizzas?" I asked. "You were gonna feed the dogs pizza, too? I never heard nothing like that," I said. Riot laughed a little. "Remember the flyer you pulled out of the mailbox? The one advertising pizza deliveries in that neighborhood? Well, I kept it. If the weather prediction was wrong, I would've used the pizza delivery guy at that exact shop to get onto your property. While he and I created a distraction at your house by delivering pizzas to them that they hadn't actually ordered and then opening the gates and letting the dogs escape, you would slip in the yard and grab the money tree."

I just looked at Riot. Was she serious? There so many things that could've went wrong. "That wouldn't have worked," I said.

"Sure it would've. I had a slice of pizza with that delivery guy while you were asleep in the car. I convinced him I was looking for a job, and he agreed to let me ride with him for a few hours," she said, straight-faced. "I had another plan, too. I would watch the house to see what time the owner or one of their kids walked the dogs. I would've followed them and delayed them with my talk about how much I love dogs and dog training my Rottweiler. We would've traded training tips, while you slipped in and grabbed the money tree," she said confidently. "That's how I found out how to open their front, back, and driveway gate anyway. I watched till someone came out. I saw a boy push some buttons right before he left your house." I liked that she kept calling the property my house and not theirs. She was right. It is mine.

I could also see that she was going to get us onto my family's property no matter what. She was a girl who it was best to have on your team. Once she started scheming against anyone, anything was possible. I knew she was down for me. I knew she was down for us getting money and making moves. But was Riot against Momma? The question raced around my mind, and I started feeling red.

"And the clothes. Where did you get all those clothes?" I asked.

"From the charity. There was this all-night church. They let anybody shop. Well, it wasn't really shopping. The cost was "a small donation," for however much you could grab and hold without a bag. The clothes are used, but I got all that for three dollars." She smiled, impressed with her find.

Riot had Momma eating food she had brought for some meanass attack dogs, and wearing somebody's thrown-away dress. She obviously didn't understand how I felt about Momma or about my family. Not to mention she had cuffed my momma like a mangy mutt. I didn't know what she thought about Momma after all she had seen last night in the old Bed-Stuy, Brooklyn, park. What she saw wouldn't change my heart. I'm gonna rescue Momma the way I wanted someone to rescue me. I'm gonna get her back to where she used to be, looking like a million bucks. I'm gonna take her to see Poppa, proudly. *I will prevent him from seeing her broken.* I am going to get the twins and love them. I want them to see that I am a good big sister. I can protect them. Moreover I'm gonna get back all of Momma's stuff, one by one, over time. When I help Momma in this way, she is gonna see me clearly and love me deeply. It won't matter that I'm the middle daughter. Like in a game of freeze tag, Momma is gonna unfreeze me.

Black-eyed Honey and Momma in her yellow wig were exchanging words with two older guys with the grill next to us. We could easily see that the guys had lured them over with a bottle of Ray and Nephew Rum. Momma's press-on fingernails were wrapped around a Dixie cup. Her thin arm was extended, as a man Momma would never be attracted to, or never even talk to, poured her a drink. So what, I told myself. It's a holiday and Momma is celebrating. That's a good thing.

"Riot, we got to talk some," I said. I was mixed with feeling red, feeling shame, feeling pride, and feeling anxious.

"I wanted to talk, too," she said. "I wanted to wait until your fever broke and your mind had cleared. Also, when it was only you and me speaking and hearing."

"I understand," I said. "About you cuffing my moms to the bed like that . . ."

"Hold on. Who am I talking with right now?" she interrupted me and asked strangely, staring into my eyes. "Am I speaking to Porsche the little girl, Porsche the big girl, or Siri? Which one?"

"What?" I asked automatically, buying time to figure out exactly what Riot was trying to pull now.

"If I'm speaking to little Porsche, my son, I know I gotta hide all of the information that I'm sure she can't handle and ain't ready for," Riot said. "If I'm talking to big Porsche, I can give it to her straight, no bullshit, no tears. We can make some decisions and take action right away, like I'm used to doing," she said stone-faced. "If I'm talking to Siri . . ." She leaned in, staring closer into my eyes. "Where is Siri?" she asked me. I paused. I didn't want to be the first one to blink

my eyes and break our stares. Riot was definitely trying to test me. I
didn't know why. I did know that Siri wouldn't want to speak directly
to Riot. Siri only likes to speak to me, and that's how it had been for
all eight months since we got ganged up in the Diamond Needles.
So why was Riot asking about Siri all of a sudden and threatening to
speak with Siri directly, instead of me?

"What are you doing, some freaky shit?" Momma asked, breaking
up me and Riot's close-faced intense feeling. Riot stepped back and
away. Even that insulted me. Why was she walking away as though
Momma stunk or something? Momma was clean. I had cleaned her
myself, and she was wearing the clothes Riot brought in.

"Momma, I need to talk to her for a few minutes. We gotta make
some decisions," I said.

"You too young to make decisions," Momma said. I knew she
couldn't see me clearly. I'm young but I can do so many things and
had made so many decisions, alone, already.

"I gotta get back to Brooklyn, check on my little space, get my
handbag. You got some money, so give me some. I'll leave and you and
that crazy bitch can talk all you want to," Momma said.

"Don't leave. Give me ten minutes, Momma. I got the money.
Don't worry."

"Well, you should've told me you had more money in the first
place. Then we had no business sitting around playing with her,"
Momma said, nodding her head towards Riot.

* * *

Seated in the backseat of the rented Volvo, separated by nothing but
my closed moneybox, which I was leaning on with one hand, me and
Riot began our meeting. Momma and Honey sat on the hood of the
parked car beneath a tree.

"You're talking with me, Porsche L. Santiaga, eleven-year-old girl
who feels like she been living, fighting, hustling for twenty-two years.
Say whatever you want to say. Don't leave nothing out and make sure
it's all true," I said.

"Your mother . . ." Riot's first two words came out quick and
forcefully. Then she slowed down some. "Your mother and Honey are
addicts, users, crackheads," she said.

My little body tensed up. My mind told my fist and legs to relax.

Riot continued, "I can't carry them. I can't work with them. I can't fuck with them. They will get us caught. They're not smart. They attract too much attention. I'm down with you, Porsche, me and you," she said slowly and clearly. I could feel her sincere emotion.

"But you *been fucking with Honey*," I told her.

"I *used* Honey for her identity. I'm still using Honey for her identity. I can't use your mom, because she is your mother. I can see you don't think straight when it comes to her. I cuffed her to the bed because she is a fiend. Fiends can't be trusted. They go with whoever got the product, crack, coke, weed, alcohol, whatever. Every one of their secrets and our secrets are for sale for the price of that rock. They don't care about nothing but feeding their habit. They're weak, Porsche. Even if they're relatives, we gotta treat 'em like an infected finger, that gotta get cut off, or it will kill the whole hand." Riot was using all her energy to convince me.

I refused to cry. Holding back my tears felt the same as the feeling of not shitting when you absolutely have to. But I did not cry.

"What do you want to do?" Riot asked me. "We can put your mother in the rehab until she gets better. I'll help you to find the best place. I'll stay down here till we set that up." Riot was wide-eyed, searching me for my answer. "Or, we can let her go back to Brooklyn like she wants to. Me and you can go back to the reservation. If you give her any money from five dollars to a thousand she'll smoke it in one or two days and be back to square one," Riot said like she would even bet her life on it. "We can move her out of that Bed-Stuy area where we found her and set her up somewhere where at least she don't know everybody and no one knows her. Then she can try to start over. But you saw how quick her and Honey find what they looking for even in an unfamiliar location. What do you want to do, Santiaga? Whatever it is, me and you are Diamond Needles, sisters for life," Riot pledged. I was grateful that through her words, she had promoted me from son to daughter to sister.

I couldn't accept the idea that Riot was more real than me. It felt that way, though. I never front on the feelings I feel. I opened my money-box, unfolded and counted out my money. I put the bills in order according to amounts, faces all facing the same direction, smoothed 'em out and stacked 'em. I pushed the tall stack over to Riot. "A promise is a promise," I said, quoting her. "You got me back to Momma. I give you the five thousand. We became partners, fifty/ fifty. The five thousand is the investment. How long will it take you to flip it?" I asked her.

She sat still. Finally I had silenced Riot. I had done my part. I had been as real with her as she was with me all the time.

"I'm staying with Momma. How long before I see you? I trust you, Riot. You are the only one I ever didn't leave my handprint on, for talking about my family. It's only because you been family to me during the worse times," I confessed.

"I can't leave you with nothing," Riot said quietly.

"I had $1,100 from working jobs on the reservation," I said truthfully. "Oh, minus the things I bought for myself and for Momma. Now I got $750 left over," I said, counting in my head.

"I don't want to leave you at all," Riot said, looking regretful. I guess my silence, our silence that fell on us and remained for a minute, confirmed our separation.

Riot counted out one thousand dollars in twenties and gave it back to me. I counted out three hundred dollars and slid it back to her. "Buy me some more cigarette cartons," I said. "You hustle on your side. I'll hustle on mine."

"We're fifty/fifty on a four-thousand-dollar investment," Riot said. "I'll meet you in sixty days on Halloween, Thursday, October 31, in Manhattan. Let's meet in front of Macy's since we both know it, at 6:00 p.m. If I don't show, I'm captured or dead. No matter what . . . ," she said. I already knew, so I interrupted Riot.

"No matter what, we never give up NanaAnna. We always protect her, and her property. We lie or die with our secrets. If you tell on me you tell on yourself."

Chapter 29

Relieved and stressed, is it possible to be both things? I was. The only solution was music and dance. "Momma, do you still have your record collection?" I asked as we rode the train back to Brooklyn. We were carrying all of my possessions packed into four sturdy shopping bags, plus my side pouch. Me and Momma each carried two.

"Yeah, right," she said, rolling her eyes and turning her head in the opposite direction.

"Let's go to the record shop before we head home."

"It's the CD shop or the music store. *Where you been?*" she said.

"I know. I was just saying . . ." My words trailed off.

Momma roamed in between soul and rhythm and blues. I was excited in hip-hop. I had been playing music mostly in my mind for the past three years or listening to no-name rhyming chicks on lockdown. Or, hearing a girl in the bed besides me beat boxing or Siri humming beautifully, sometimes even surprising me, by singing a song. Being able to choose my own music, instead of having to listen to whatever the upstate DJs spun while we were using the Department of Corrections' radio in limited time amounts, under supervision, was so sweet to me. Seeing the CD covers, the artwork and images, instead of passed-around bootleg cassettes, was fascinating to me. Hearing a Brooklyn neighborhood record shop's speakers booming and blasting into the Brooklyn streets even on a holiday made me feel alright.

"Why didn't you tell me you didn't have a record player?" I asked Momma.

"A CD player," she corrected me.

We were both overlooking and purposely ignoring the fact that

Momma's "living space" had no front door. Momma had stopped on Fulton Street in the Ft. Green section of Brooklyn, she made a left and walked behind a store in a slim alleyway. She bent down and pulled a thin rusted metal bar out of a lock holding together two rusted iron slabs that laid slanted over the cement sidewalk. Her thin arms lifted one side of the iron gate. It creaked. Momma took six steps down the cement stairs and into the ground.

"Come on, what you waiting for? These bags are heavy," she said impatiently.

I stepped down slowly, feeling déjà vu. *I'm headed back to the bottom*, I thought to myself.

Once I was down and in, Momma let go of the iron gate and it dropped down, eliminating any light from the street lamps and store signs. It sounded final and permanent, like prison doors slamming shut behind my back. Doors to enter and never exit, with locks that had no keys that I could ever hold, touch, or be in charge of.

"Stay still," Momma said. She began moving around in the darkness. "That's why I don't be here a lot of time. I gotta look all over for the damn light," she said.

I wasn't afraid of the dark. I stood still cause she said so. I heard her fumbling, something falling, glass breaking open, then being crushed beneath the weight of a shoe or sneaker. I was used to listening carefully to sounds in the dark especially, footsteps coming from down long corridors, or keys jingling, or breathing, heavy breathing of overweight officers, greedy guards, or horny authorities. I could even hear the sounds of rubber-sole shoes, sneaky nurses, and drugging doctors. I knew the sounds of dirty mops swishing around the dirty water on dirty floors. I even could detect slight sounds, like someone withholding a burp or fart or letting it rip. Or, the gentle pull of a smoker smoking in the dark in a no-smoking area. I was an expert in listening for the sounds of secret crying, someone else's tears or, sometimes, my own.

"There it is," Momma said. A switch got flipped. No, a string got pulled, the light of one bulb swinging on a wire flashing here and there. Momma tried to catch it and stop it from swinging. Soon she steadied it over her head. Now I could see clearly a living space bigger than a living space for a prisoner, but too small for anyone who had never done anything wrong. There was a mattress on the floor, a dirty sheet half hiding an ancient pee stain. There was a stove covered with grease and gook, two rusted pots with molded and maggoty burnt leftovers left sitting on two opposite burners. There was a half refrigerator, perfect for half a human.

Momma snatched the dirty sheet off the mattress and tossed it in a corner, where empty liquor bottles lined the wall. The sheet landed on top of them. Did she think I hadn't already seen them? Or did she toss the sheet as a distraction for my eyes to follow, while she hurried and grabbed the pipe and empty vials, pushing them down into the front pockets of her charity dress. Nervously, she searched for and found the broom. She grabbed an envelope from a stack of envelopes and papers and newspapers. As she swept the glass that had just shattered beneath my new Air Max, which were still on her feet, I saw the seal of the court on the envelope she was using to sweep the glass onto. It was an unopened court notice of something. My eyes surveyed the floor. There were stacks and stacks of unopened mail; some of them were stained with red Kool-Aid or maybe wine or something like that.

There were no windows. There was a second set of iron steps leading up to somewhere. Momma pulled off the yellow Halloween princess wig.

"I did say I had some cleaning to do," was all she said to me.

"I'll do it," I said, sounding upbeat so Momma wouldn't turn too sad.

"Where's your record player?" I asked. "Why didn't you tell me you didn't have one when we were both just in the music store?"

"I don't know how much money you have. I don't have none! There's a store upstairs. I get paid when I work. When I don't work, I don't get nothing," she explained.

"What do you do?" I asked.

"Stack newspapers, tie them up, so he could put them on the curb. I sweep up the floors and dust the shelves. I wipe down the canned goods and put 'em in perfect lines, labels facing outward. I wash dishes and clean up in the back room of the store. *But I ain't been here in ten days or so.* Big Johnnie be acting funny sometimes," Momma said.

"Like what?" I asked, wanting to know everything we were dealing with.

"Sometimes he keeps that door locked so I can't come up into the store. How am I supposed to do my job if I can't get in?" she said.

"How come you don't go out the same way we just came in and walk around to the front door to the store?" I asked.

"Because I'm supposed to do my job from 3:00 in the morning till 6:00 a.m. before the front door opens for business and the customers start arriving. He acts like he don't want nobody to see me, like he don't want to admit that I'm working for him. And one week that nigga tried to pay me with four cans of Spam and a pack of cigarettes. He lucky he keep that register empty. He takes all the money with him when he leaves every night. When I'm cleaning and working up there, there's not a penny in the whole place! When I'm done up there, I gotta get out and stay out from when the store doors open at 6:06 a.m. every morning until it closes at 11:00 p.m. each night. So I can't come back here till after eleven. How that sound?"

Momma was making a strange and funny face, her hands on her hips and one leg bent like she was about to leap.

"I can do that job. You don't have to work. From what you're saying, I go up these stairs and could be in and out. He wouldn't even know," I planned.

"How you gonna get up and go to school if you been working from three in the morning?" Momma asked.

I moved from the last cement step where I had still been standing still. I pulled the one wooden chair away from the one-woman wooden table and said, "Please sit down, Momma."

I explained in detail that her daughter, Porsche L. Santiaga, is a girl gangster, a Gutter Girl and a Diamond Needle. Her daughter won't be doing nothing official, like school, or going any place where anybody official might be looking for me. Her daughter won't be telling anybody her real name or showing them her real feelings or sharing any information about our family or family business.

"I'm here for you, Momma. I'm gonna work till I drop. I'm gonna hustle like crazy. I'm gonna make you love me," I said, staring up to her.

"I don't know what you talking about. I love all my kids," Momma said casually. I couldn't feel her words swelling in my chest or racing through my veins and into my heart.

"Please believe in me, Momma. I'm gonna take back all our shit that got tooken."

* * *

Early morning I came up from the underground and into the Brooklyn streets. This definitely wasn't Bed-Stuy where the Santiagas were infamous. I was glad. The man Momma called Big Johnnie was first on my work list. I needed to take a look at him and his store. I had tried to climb up the iron stairs and through the ceiling door that led to his store at 3:00 a.m., but like momma said, it was locked down tight. My little mind was organizing my opportunities and my necessary lies.

"Do you sell peanut butter?" I asked.

"Second aisle in the back," the man at the register said. He had to be Big Johnnie, I thought. He was big and black and serious looking. I went and got peanut butter. The price was way too high. I wanted to put it back, but I knew I had to buy something to get a decent conversation going. I got peanut butter and a loaf of bread and walked it up to the counter.

"That's whole wheat," the man said.

"I know," I said without an attitude.

"Good, cause you can't bring it back. No refunds," he said. Then he pointed to a sign behind him that read NO REFUNDS.

"I won't bring it back. This is for me. I'm gonna eat it," I said, laying my five-dollar bill on the counter.

"That's even better," he said, and smiled.

I took the smile as an opportunity and jumped right in.

"How much for a pack of cigarettes?" I asked.

"Five-fifty but I don't sell cigarettes to kids." He placed my change on the counter.

"My aunt said . . . ," I started explaining.

"Who's your aunt? She knows better. Everybody round here knows. You ain't from around here," he said. The store door opened. Two customers walked in.

"I'm visiting. My aunt's the lady from downstairs." I pointed down as in through and under the floor. His face turned sour. His eyes were following his customers as they each moved down different aisles.

"Who left a nice little girl like you with her?" he asked without looking.

"Aunt's nice, too. She's been down there trying to come up to work, but the door has been locked." He placed one big long finger over his lips to signal me to stop talking. I did. He rang up the two customers and they left.

"So, you say you just visiting?" he asked with a serious face and a suspicious look.

"Yes," was all I replied.

"For how long of a visit?" he asked.

"One month," I said swiftly, surprising myself. Then I added, "My mother is in the hospital. Before they took her into an ambulance, she told me to go to this address and stay with her sister-in-law."

"She gave you this address?" he asked doubtfully. "What about your daddy?" he asked. I didn't answer, just gave him a sad stare. A few more customers came. I stayed quiet since I seen that was the game he was playing.

"Does my aunt owe you some money?" I asked after they left.

"Why would you concern yourself with that?" he asked me.

"Oh, I thought that was the reason you keep locking her out. If you don't open the door so she can work, how can she make some money to pay you back for what she owes?" I asked sweetly, my two hands up in the air. He laughed a big laugh.

"She doesn't owe me no money. She doesn't want to work either. But I see that you do," he said.

"I can help her," I told him.

"She *needs* some help," he emphasized with some disgust.

More customers came. I stood to the side watching them. Watching him. Cigarettes, coffee, chips, and candy were the main things moving.

"Let me get a baloney sandwich, hurry up, I'm late for school," one kid disrespected.

"A baloney sandwich, please," the man corrected the kid. "How many times do I gotta tell you? One of these days I'll take you out back and kick your little ass like your daddy should've done," Big Johnnie told him with no fears.

"I'll make it!" I volunteered, to break up the tension. The kid placing the order looked at me like he didn't care who made it.

"Just hurry up," he said. I looked towards Big Johnnie for approval. His eyes said, "Let me see you try." I quickly scooted to the back, washed my hands, and put the sandwich together all in less than a minute and fifteen seconds. The schoolboy paid, grabbed the wrapped sandwich, and taunted Big Johnnie on the way out. "If she was ugly, I'd ask you if she was your daughter." He laughed.

"That's what a compliment from a fool sounds like," Big Johnnie told me.

Our conversation was interrupted by a steady flow of customers. I used each gap in time to check things out. I acted like I wasn't searching for anything. My eyes, used to searching and counting, caught it all, even Big Johnnie's two guns, one big, one small.

"I'll wake my aunt up on time. I'll help her clean. I could make sandwiches and wrap 'em in Saran wrap so they already ready. They would be fresh. Made on the same day of business, ready to sell at 6:06 a.m. each morning. Please, Mister. It seems like you need some help in here. I noticed you don't get along too well with nobody." He laughed.

"For one month?" he asked me for the third time.

"One month," I said. I already knew I would tell him a new lie later.

"Okay," he agreed.

"How much do I get? I mean how much do you pay for jobs, my aunt's, and for the sandwich maker?" I asked.

"One hundred a week for your aunt. For you, it depends on how the sandwiches sell. Customers might take to 'em, might not. I'll pay you fifty cent a sandwich," he said. I looked at him like it wasn't enough. Then I switched my face and agreed.

"And listen . . . ," he said. "Every item in my store is counted and accounted for. If I'm missing one lollipop, one slice of deli meat, one can of tuna—"

"I don't steal. We don't steal," I interrupted him.

"Good, then we have an understanding," he said.

"Has anything been missing before I got here?" I asked.

"Only thing been missing is your aunt. She comes and goes. She's not reliable. You look reliable," he said.

"How much does she pay you for rent?" I asked.

"Don't concern yourself with that," he said strangely.

"But if she earns four hundred a month are you gonna deduct—"

"I said don't concern yourself with that. Your aunt never made four hundred dollars in one month. She never showed up four weeks in a row, Monday through Friday."

"But if she does show up . . . ," I pressed.

"If she does what she suppose to, she'll get what she's suppose to get."

"Thank you," I said. "Can I start tomorrow?"

"You already started today," he said, pressing a button on his register. He placed two quarters on the counter for the baloney sandwich I made. As I was leaving out, he asked me, "Kid, don't you think you should tell me your name?"

"It's Ivory," I said instantly.

"Like the soap," he joked.

As I checked out the whole block of businesses, only one store next door didn't have a sign and was filled with old junk that I guessed needed fixing. Bernard the Butcher, Esmeralda's Beauty Salon, World of Flowers, and The Golden Needle were clean and neat places. I wondered why the rent was something Big Johnnie wouldn't discuss with me. I would find out from Momma when she got back. She left out last night saying, "I gotta go get something." She wouldn't allow me to come and she wasn't back in the morning. I wouldn't let it get me down. I was gonna make her living space a place she could be happy returning to, so she would come home each night and sleep beside me. I was gonna treat her like a queen.

The Golden Needle! I had been standing in front of the place lost in my thoughts. Then it dawned on me, what a pretty name for a store. I looked in. The sunlight made it impossible for me to see. When I pressed my face against the glass, I was face-to-face with a woman working her sewing machine. She looked up. Her expression soon as she saw me was like I was peeping in on her while she was doing something real personal. I pulled my face back, embarrassed, and kept it moving. *Oh, like needle and thread,* I thought to myself. *The Golden Needle, it's a sewing shop.*

As I crossed over to the apartment building directly across the street, I decided I would buy something small from each shop and use it as an opportunity to see what I could get from it. The same way I had to meet and greet each Diamond Needle, I would do the same on my new block. Instead of bringing them each a gift to break the ice, I would just let my purchase from each of them serve as my tribute.

Six blocks down, at the dollar store, I found everything I needed for a thorough cleanup at the right price. I was ready to get started, even excited. Hell, I could've been mopping floors at the C-dorm for a bunch of bitches I didn't love. Now I'm here making things sparkle for someone I did love.

As I balanced a broomstick, string mop, and sponge mop, the dustpan, three plastic bags, and a box which contained my used radio/record/CD player, it took me twice as long to reach the back alley to Big Johnnie's store, where we lived beneath the floor and iron gate.

Listening to Junior Mafia's joint "Get Money" got me amped. I cuffed up my jeans, tucked my tee, and threw on my rubber gloves. It took about an hour of hard work before I got dizzy. I didn't know why. I ran up the cement stairs and pushed open the heavy iron gate. As air rushed in, my dizzy feeling began to disappear. I stood there at the top of the stairs, huffing and puffing. The bleaches and cleaning chemicals were so strong. I guess I could've passed out. I should have done like NanaAnna and cleaned things with lemons, limes, and lavender. I weighed the situation. If I left the iron lid open I would not faint. But, I might get robbed or raped by an uninvited creep. If I kept them closed, I would definitely pass out. So I left one side open and kept my new box cutter and my back-the-fuck-up pouch on me. If someone came down, I would see them first, blind 'em and slice 'em. I knew a lot could go wrong with my plan, so I cleaned as quickly as I could without missing a speck of dirt, grease, or crap. The minute I was done, I threw open both sides and kept them open as I sat on a crate in the alley out back, so the place could air out nicely. I was close and listening to my music float upstairs.

* * *

"A dozen roses," I said to the woman in the flower shop.

"What color?" she asked.

"Some of all the colors that you have," I said.

"Shall I arrange them for you?" she asked.

"Sounds good, thank you," I said as I glanced around.

It smelled so nice in here, I thought. I wondered if twelve roses were enough to make this type of smell in the underground. The woman had disappeared into a back room, and then returned carrying three vases.

"Which one do you choose?" she asked. I pointed.

"Good selection," she praised me.

Red, pink, white, yellow, and black were the options she had available for the beautiful roses.

"Give me five red, and five pinks. Then give me one white and one black," I requested. "Oh and wrap the black and white separately." I asked.

"No yellow, no problem," she said politely.

"Get yellow for me," Siri suggested suddenly. I don't know how she knew that the black and white flowers represented me and Riot's friendship.

"Have you seen these before? Would you like some?" the flower lady asked, pointing to some sticks speckled with teeny white blossoms. "They're called baby's breath," she explained.

"No, thank you," I said. "But could you give me one yellow sunflower from over there? That one." I pointed.

"I'll finish the roses first. Then we'll get you the sunflower," she said.

I smiled. Siri's flower would be the sun that was missing in our underground.

As the flower lady arranged them nicely I asked, "Wouldn't you like some help in here?"

She smiled. "I've been doing this on my own for six years now. I can handle it. As you see, there's not a crowd of customers."

"Oh, but I'm sure you have lots of customers. All of the businesses on this block seems pretty busy," I said with made-up cheerfulness.

"The rent for these shops is high. Most of us are not in the position to hire. I'm lucky, my grandson helps out on weekends," she said.

"So you don't own this place?" I asked, looking around. I wanted her to tell me the amount of the rent. I knew she wouldn't, so I didn't ask. If I knew the amount maybe I could figure out from that what amount of rent Momma should be paying, or even if she might be getting cheated.

"No, I don't own this shop. One man owns all these shops on this block and the building across the street. He's really nice, but business is business," she said. "I still have to pay him every time on time."

"Do you have someone to help you carry these?" she asked, placing the wrapped-up vase, the separately wrapped black and white roses, and the stem-wrapped sunflower on the counter.

"I don't need any help. I'm staying with my aunt a few doors down. My name is Ivory. Nice to meet you." I extended my hand. She seemed surprised at something.

"I figured you were new to our neighborhood. You sure ask a lot of questions. And you're a pretty little thing, prettier than all the flowers in my shop." She smiled, accepted my hand, and shook it lightly. "That's $79.99," she said, in a tone that was the same as though she was saying seven dollars. My shocked expression spread before I could hold it back. She smiled and said, "I told you the rent here is expensive." Then she pointed to a sign on the wall, SUPPORT BLACK BUSINESS. Right next to that sign was a sign saying BUY BLACK in bold letters.

I pulled out a one-hundred-dollar bill and laid it on the counter. She picked it up, pressed a button on her register, and handed me my change.

"Thank you," I said. Even though I told her I didn't need help, she walked me to the door carrying my vase with the ten roses, as I carried the other flowers.

Thinking quickly, I said, "Could you give me a chance to earn back some of the money I spent in here today? I can clean up, fold down used boxes, tie them up, water your plants, sweep your floors, even clean your windows," I offered. "Even though the person I am buying these flowers for is really sick, I might get into trouble if I don't have enough money left over to pay for her medicine." I stared at the lady sadly.

"Well, you seem really smart and very well-mannered. I like

that. The lesson in all of this is that you should always ask the price of something *before* you order it. Once these flowers are cut and arranged at your request, they're yours, no refunds." She folded her arms in front of her. "Oh," she said. "There he is." She pointed through the front glass door of her shop.

"He owns everything. His name is Mr. Sharp. Maybe he'll give you a little after-school job. He certainly can afford it. He works in The Golden Needle even though he certainly doesn't have to. Ask your aunt first, if it's okay to ask to work for him. Then, see if he agrees," she recommended.

She pushed open the door. I understood her polite way of saying, "Get out! You're not getting your money back." I still forced out a smile and left. I cursed myself out all the way back. "Eighty fucking bucks!"

I could've got pretty flowers from the little Spanish men for eight or nine dollars. Then I thought of Lina. In my mind, she was setting me straight.

"Not little Spanish men, Latinos or Boriquas!" whatever that meant. I told myself that these expensive flowers better make Momma smile so bright, love me so much, and accept Siri, who I was gonna introduce to Momma tonight when I prepared all of us some chicken soup.

NanaAnna had taught me that soup prepared properly, with organic ingredients, healed the body. She had explained to me that garlic is a natural antibiotic and the many healing uses of garlic were in my recipe journal. Momma seemed a little sick to me. I hate hospitals. I was gonna try my best to heal Momma with foods that NanaAnna said are natural medicines.

"So this is our new place?" Siri asked me. We were underground. I had arranged all of the flowers and set them in the best places.

"It's okay," she said. "But will Momma like me?"

"Momma loves music. So hum and sing her your most beautiful song," I honestly recommended.

It was almost four in the afternoon now. I had the filthy mattress cleaned up and lying up against the wall outside in the alley in the back of Big Johnnie's store. With the living space cleaned like brand new and the stove looking like brand new, and the flowers smelling nicely, I raced down a bunch of blocks to buy sheets, pillows, a lamp, two plates, a frying pan, and the groceries. Racing and running back and forth, I was sweating and thirsty. I didn't eat that morning and my stomach was empty.

"A handful of almonds and raisins or three spoons filled with peanut butter to keep yourself from fainting," NanaAnna had said to me after noticing my peculiar eating habits and fainting and collapsing spells. "If you don't feed your body the right nutrition, your own body will attack you," she taught me. "Poor nutrition leads to a sick body. A nutrition-starved brain leads to all kinds of psychological problems," she once said before breaking it down so carefully, so I could understand her. "If you don't eat right and it develops into a starved brain, then psychological problems, they'll give you chemical medicine that will steal your smile, jumble your thoughts, then kill you."

The smell of the healing chicken soup filled up our place. "It better work," I said to myself. I was recalling how many blocks I had to walk to find foods that were organic: tomatoes, potatoes, garlic, ginger, onions, carrots, and celery. Not to mention, organic thyme and chili peppers. The cost of the organic vegetables, herbs, fruits, and other seasonings was so extreme that I began to panic in the expensive organic market. The money from my money tree was drifting out of my hands triple time in that store.

Siri got me to take deep breaths in the bakery aisle. She told me to smell the sugar! I inhaled the scent of organic apple pies and oven-baked cookies and cupcakes. I calmed down.

"See, it works!" Siri cheered. "We don't have to buy this stuff. We can just smell it and fill our bellies." We laughed together. That's when a nappy-headed boy my age with a pile of pretty kinky hair and with skin more better than suede and a natural bright smile came walking up the aisle.

"Do you see anything you want?" his expensively heeled mother asked him, as she held her Epi Leather bag close to her side.

"Not yet," he said casually.

"Well, look around. Get whatever you want. Put it in our cart." She was speaking to him like he was a young king.

Get whatever you want: the phrase kept repeating in my mind.

Without any gold jewelry, he looked rich. In addition to his eyes and skin and teeth, all glowing, he wore Evisu jeans and a Polo Rugby. His Nike Air Force 1s were crisp. I wondered if he shopped in this overpriced organic market with his loving mom regularly. Maybe they could buy easily the foods that were priced so high it had pushed me to panic.

He seemed like an opportunity.

Siri pushed the cart into him on purpose in the juice aisle.

"Sorry," I said.

"No problem," he said. Then his mom appeared.

"Elisha, what's going on?" she asked, seeing my cart pinned up against his legs.

"Nothing," he answered casually, turning the cart around and positioning it back to me.

"Hello," she said to me. "Is she a friend from school?" his mom asked him.

"No," he said.

"And what's your name?" she asked me.

"Ivory," I said.

"Well I'm Mrs. Immanuel. He is my son, Elisha."

That's how we met.

* * *

Momma didn't return for me, or for her beautiful refreshed apartment, or my menu of organic, healing chicken soup prepared in the clay pot that NanaAnna gave me as a going-home gift. Siri and I ate together instead. We shared soup, brown rice, salad, and slices of organic apples for dessert.

I unscrewed the mop head from the stick. Then lodged the stick on the two cement beams. I made it into a place where I could hang Momma's few clothes. With all of her stuff removed from her only clothing closet, I crawled into the empty space and danced till I collapsed. I had not done that in a long while. I had learned to sleep naturally in the last two weeks on the reservation.

When I woke up on Momma's empty closet floor, I was all wet. My throat was dry, and I needed water. I jumped up, grabbed a bottle from the half refrigerator, and drank it all. I checked my dollar-store clock, 3:38 a.m. I raced up the iron stairs and pushed at the floor door. It was unlocked. It opened.

You never seen nobody work like me and Siri did that early morning. We busted our little asses. We cleaned that place, and it needed it. There was dust hiding behind the cans and foods on every shelf. The back room was piled high with dishes, empty boxes, disorganized old newspapers, and mess. I wondered if one man could've used all this stuff or if Big Johnnie had a worker in the later afternoon or evenings that I didn't know about. Or did he leave his place like this on purpose to see if I was a good worker or not?

I didn't have time to daydream. I cleaned and cleaned. I even unplugged and turned his toaster upside down. Weeks of old breadcrumbs spilled out. I wiped down his microwave oven, and cleaned out his refrigerator. I washed all of the dishes and made his few pieces of silverware sparkle. I tied up the newspapers and stacked them up front.

When we were finished, I ran down and spooned out some organic chicken soup for Big Johnnie. I put it in one of the clay bowls I bought the day before. I covered the bowl with one tight sheet of saran wrap and left it on the front counter where Big Johnnie sits. I left a simple note.

> Good Morning, Thank you from me and Aunt. Enjoy my homemade organic chicken soup.
>
> From, Ivory.

I soaked my sponge mop with hot water and soap, and raced it down each aisle carefully. I walked myself backwards with the mop until I reached the floor door. Seconds later, me and the mop were back in our underground space. It was 6:00 a.m., whew . . .

Chapter 30

It was three o'clock that same day. I waited to approach Mr. Sharp, who was the owner of The Golden Needle, five more stores, and an entire apartment building. When I was buying roses yesterday, I noticed that Mr. Sharp was just arriving to his shop in the afternoon. I could've been wrong, but I imagined that since he was big balling, he chose to have a big breakfast with his attractive wife. They slept in a huge comfortable bed with silk sheets and satin pillowcases. They had a huge television and play-fought over the remote. He wins all of the play fights and keeps the TV on sports. She doesn't like sports but also doesn't complain. Instead, she reclines and counts and admires all of the jewelry that he bought for her, cause he could do it like that. When she's not counting jewelry, she's counting her secret money stacks, cause Momma used to say that a real bitch always has and keeps a secret money pile.

Speaking of Momma, she still hadn't returned. I pulled down two pieces of her not-so-nice clothes. I would carry them with me over to The Golden Needle as bait for the lady who sits in the window sewing. I didn't want her to think I was some aggravating beggar hanging around the store, since she had seen me pressing my face in the window just yesterday. If Mr. Sharp wasn't there, I'd ask the lady to stitch Momma's jeans and the dress that I just ripped a tear in. I wasn't worried about Momma getting red that I took her clothes. I planned to buy her plenty of new ones.

Also, our underground apartment doesn't have a bathtub. Momma used to soak in her pretty, marble, Long Island tub, with candles and perfumed water. I promised myself I would take Momma to a nice hotel once a month. We would go shopping for pretty things until our feet got tired. Then we would head back to our hotel with our purchases. I would run warm water in the clean, deep tub, dash in a few drops of Momma's favorite scent and maybe even some rose petals. Momma would be so relaxed and happy. She would love me.

I looked back at the roses as I climbed the first cement step to exit the underground. They were young and gorgeous. The petals were smooth and tight. They had not even blossomed yet.

"Momma will be back before they blossom," I told myself, then left out.

* * *

"*Un momento!*" The Spanish-speaking lady leaped up from her chair where she had been sewing when I arrived.

"*Espera aqui!*" she said and pushed passed me and through the shop door. Standing alone in The Golden Needle shop, I turned and watched her sprinting down the block in her skips.

Maybe it's an opportunity, I thought to myself. I looked around. They had the things I guess anyone would expect to be in a sewing shop: two gray dummies with lady figures and no arms, and with plenty of pins in their shoulders; a stand with spools of threads of every color, displayed and lined up like rows of nail polish in the manicure shops; folded fabrics, tape measurers, yard stick, scissors, the works!

My eyes landed on the pretty gold curtain that had shiny gold sequins on it. Maybe Mr. Sharp was behind that curtain. I walked over, pulled the curtain back a little and was surprised to see a room in the back much larger than the small reception area in the front. The back was carpeted even though the front area was not. The carpet was white and completely clean. There were racks of men's suits that looked brand-new, three dressing rooms, and a wall of photographs.

"Mr. Sharp," I called out just to be sure, but I could feel that I was all alone in this space. I am familiar with that alone feeling wherever I go.

I began looking at the photos of rich-looking people, luxurious cars, and tailored clothes. I liked the world the photos re-created. It was a different world than the one I lived in now. I looked closely, amazed when I saw a photo of Sean Combs, dressed in a tailored suit, looking like he had a billon bucks. Iron Mike Tyson's photo got me pumped, cause like Notorious B.I.G., he repped hard for Brooklyn. Ball players, and well-suited boring politicians, singers, and men built like athletes, they were all on that wall, amazingly. As I eased down, I found a section of photos covered with thin plastic as though the owner wanted to be sure those pictures didn't fade or tear. I couldn't see the photos at the top even though I was standing on my tiptoes. I could see the ones in the middle. In disbelief I pushed my face up close to five photos of Momma! She was styling, rich and glamorous, smiling cause she knew it. Her handbag was more exclusive than anything on the wall and prettier than everything except Momma's hands. Momma's long, manicured perfectly painted zebra nails complemented the summer silk white gown she wore, which fit her body like skin and showed off her pretty shoulders, long neck, and nicely shaped breasts. I touched my own little breast wondering, would they turn out like Momma's. I put my hand on my little waistline. Momma's was small and tight same as mine is now. Momma had woman's hips and the silk of the dress clung to her thighs showing the shape of her pretty, long legs. Her pedicure, French Black, complemented her heels. Her heels complemented her handbag. Heels so lovely it seemed she bought them from a shop that was selling only that one pair, for ten thousand dollars. After Momma came in for a private showing, the one pair of shoes fit her perfectly like Cinderella. She pulled out eleven one-thousand-dollar bills, paid ten for the shoes and threw the salesman a thousand-dollar tip. When Momma walked away with her threaded and embroidered shopping bag with the leather handles, the shop closed down forever because they only existed to find the perfect woman for that one pair of exclusive high heels.

"What are you doing?" a man's voice said calmly. But still he shook me out of my thoughts. I turned quickly, and was facing Mr. Sharp, a well-dressed, handsome older man.

"Why are you crying?" he asked me. Then I heard the bells jingle from the front door opening.

"Step into the front office," Mr. Sharp said. As I walked through the gold curtain, the sewing lady was back and giving me a suspicious stare. Mr. Sharp walked out behind me. He was tall, towering over me. His presence made her relax her face muscles.

"*Lo siento,*" she mumbled.

"Linda, have you been out arguing with the meter maid again?" Mr. Sharp asked her calmly.

"No, *no* . . . ," Linda said, answering with her hands and her face. I knew she was lying. What else could make her bolt down the street like that, leaving the store with a young stranger?

"Give Ms. Linda your clothes, and tell her what you want done," he said.

"In English?" I asked. He laughed two short laughs.

"If you are telling her in English and showing her at the same time, she understands."

"Mr. Sharp, about the photos on your wall . . . ," I began.

"Yes, I can see you recognize that kind of elegance . . . ," he said. "So do I. I must admit, of all my clients that ever looked at those pictures, you're the first one to be moved to tears," he said.

"The pretty lady in the dress," I said slowly.

"Which one?"

"The prettiest one on the wall," I said. He smiled a bright smile like he knew something no one else in the world knew.

"Must mean Lana." He turned and walked back through the curtain. I followed.

"Senorita," I heard the sewing lady say. She followed me. Now we were all three in the back.

"It's okay, Linda. Come on in," Mr. Sharp said to her. She did, remaining close to the curtain like a security guard.

"Show me the prettiest one on the wall," he said to me.

I pointed to Momma. I heard him say *Lana* so I knew he knew her.

"Do you know anyone else on that wall?" he asked.

As I searched, Siri whispered, "It might be a trick question, be careful." But I was too busy searching the wall to consider Siri's warning. I stopped still, in front of a photo of my poppa, which I had not seen before. More regal than the president or the king of any country, so handsome was Ricky Santiaga that he was prettier than Momma.

He was prettier than anybody and everybody else. I put my finger on the photo and slid it to the right. There was another photo of Poppa standing beside a younger-looking Mr. Sharp.

"Can I have this one?" I asked automatically without thinking. "Can you make me a copy? I can pay you for it," I said, feeling anxious, nervous, delighted, and depressed all at once.

"What's your name?" he asked me as though he might already know the answer.

"Ivory . . . ," I said, to protect myself.

"Ivory . . . ," he repeated. "Ivory, you are crying again."

He got up from the tall stool he was leaning on and walked over towards me. Ms. Linda's eyes followed him like eyes follow a main lead actor in an emotional film. Mr. Sharp reached in his shirt pocket and pulled out a clean and pressed folded handkerchief with embroidered edges. He wiped away my tears.

"Who is he to you?" Mr. Sharp asked me.

"Who?" I stalled.

"The man in the photo?" Mr. Sharp said.

I took two steps to the left and pointed to momma's photo and said, "Ms. Lana is my aunt."

Mr. Sharp stared at me some, smiled, and walked away.

"I'm staying with my aunt for a month . . . ," I said.

"A month?" he repeated.

"I want to help her out. I'm looking for work," I added.

* * *

The Golden Needle was the golden opportunity. More than my fake story about being Momma's niece, it was my truest emotions that captured Mr. Sharp and opened his heart to cooperate. He didn't offer me a job, but I was building a trust. After that afternoon, every day I skipped down the block with my bag of quarters and fed the parking meters. I had matched the faces of all of the shop renters and workers with their vehicles. I never let the EXPIRED sign hit any of the meters where their cars were parked. I became the number-one enemy of the villain, the meter maid. But what could she do about it? Was she gonna write an eleven-year-old a ticket for preventing business owners from receiving expensive parking tickets?

My hustle was in full swing, one hundred dollars a week from Big Johnnie, plus sandwich-making money. I collected service fees from each of the shop owners for my meter-feeding job, five dollars a week, twenty-five dollars a month. A ticket from the meter maid would cost them twenty-five dollars each time and some of 'em had piles of meter tickets! I also received tips and gifts from all of the shop renters for my excellent manners and customer service (thanks to the lessons from Lina, Diamond Needle number 2). Every day, Monday through Thursday, I went to Mr. Sharp's place from three to four. I'd sit and talk to him for an hour while watching the meters and the streets. His stories kept me alive.

"Ricky Santiaga was an upstanding cat, a man's man and all-round great guy," he would say about my poppa. "He was the sharpest man I ever tailored suits for. He spent a fortune on my business. Every man wanted to be him. That bought me more business. Even the athletes and superstars envied his position. That bought me more business. Ricky Santiaga never played with credit or debt. Whatever it was worth, he'd pay me double. Soon as I handed him the goods, he paid out in cash, always large clean bills." Mr. Sharp was trapped in those memories. I understood. So was I.

"How much is an apartment in your building?" I asked him one day out of the blue.

"Who said I own a building?" Mr. Sharp asked.

"People talk. . . ." I smiled. He laughed a short laugh, the way strong men who don't overdo it do.

"Depends on the size," he said. "Why do you ask? Thinking about moving in?" He stared into me for truth.

"How could I think about moving my aunt over there when I've never even seen it?" I asked, setting him up for the offer.

"I'll show you around, c'mon," he said.

He tapped Linda to follow us and turned The Golden Needle store sign to BE RIGHT BACK.

It was hard to believe that Mr. Sharp was a tailor. He was bigger than Big Johnnie, who he called just "Johnnie." I looked at his hands and tried to picture them threading a needle. His fingers seemed too thick to steady a tiny needle and thin thread. But he said himself that he was the tailor who made all those clothes for Poppa, and that he had only ever made one dress for Momma, the one she was wearing in the photo on the wall. Maybe that's why he had her pose in so many stances. He said he used the photos to show new clients and potential clients the detail and level of his skill.

I asked Mr. Sharp why I never saw him actually sewing. He said, "I'm comfortable. Styles change, not only styles, but people change, too. I keep this store open out of habit. It's not my main moneymaker. It was fun when our people had an eye for decency and elegance."

Mr. Sharp told me that these days Linda does mostly alterations and repairs. He added that if any old customer came along, he would gladly serve them, or he would willingly outfit a lavish wedding, debutante's ball, or graduation.

"Debutante's ball?" I repeated. I never heard of that.

"Wealthy families had this tradition. Fathers would introduce their daughters to society at a grand ballroom affair. Everybody who was anybody would be there. There would be dinner, music, and dancing but most of all the fashions were 'immaculate.' It was a competition of dressmaking, suit tailoring, and a mean, mean shoe game. If a man had a feminine beauty for a daughter, man his chest would swell with pride. She would walk gracefully down the aisle arm in arm with her father. He would take her to the platform. She would lift her beautiful gown and walk up the stairs. On the platform she would bow to the audience while the master of ceremonies announced her full name, the name of her father and mother, as well as her education, talents, and accomplishments. Eligible bachelors would battle over the young debutantes. It was the ideal place for them to select a wife from the moneyed, connected, and unbroken families." He smiled, remembering. "That was one thing. Also, the bachelors were battling over the 'head turners,' the greatest beauties. But they had to get approval of the fathers first." I could tell he preferred those times and kinds of affairs.

Mr. Sharp seemed to like me a lot and I noticed certain things about him, like that he always made Linda sit nearby when he was talking to me. Or he would have her come along if we went anywhere outside of the shop. I could tell she wasn't his wife and didn't seem like a girlfriend, but I guess he had his reasons. I was always upbeat when I was with him for one hour, but he had no idea about Ivory's, aka Porsche L. Santiaga's nights.

By the third night that Momma didn't show, I was out dressed in Riot's boy clothes, jeans, a jacket and a fitted searching for her in Bed-Stuy. Because of the 3 *F*s, I was nervous: fear, family, fugitive. I was not afraid of the Bed-Stuy neighborhood, family, or friends. I was more fearful of what I might find, but not afraid enough not to look. I didn't ask nobody nothing. I just roamed the streets each night and kept going back to check the colored round caves.

By the eighth night I was crazy red. I couldn't understand what was so important that Momma would choose it over me. I considered that she could be sleeping at any one of our relative's apartments. But I doubted it based on what she had said about them, and what my cousin had accused Poppa of. I wouldn't approach no one in my family for fear that they might turn me in to the police. Momma had made me believe that things had gotten that hateful. Maybe Momma forgot me, again.

I had two buckets from the dollar store. I filled one with Momma's opened mail and one with her unopened mail. I sat staring. I didn't like feeling like I was the same as the authorities who searched through our stuff in prison. They would do it any time they liked, but mostly while we were away in classes, or rec, or work. At the same time, it seemed if I didn't read Momma's mail I'd be a young fool with no answers to the many questions that marched through my mind. I compromised. I began reading only her opened letters, and left Momma and Winter's sealed letters alone. First I checked the addresses. I would write them down and go into the night and see if Momma was there. It turned out most of the addresses were the same. I knew because when we lived in the Brooklyn projects, for most of my young life, we had the same address as the ones on these envelopes. Only the apartment numbers were different. So these letters had been sent to Momma's sisters' and brothers' apartments. When I matched the dates up I discovered that for two and a half years the mail went to my mom's brothers and sisters. Maybe she had lived with each of them for a while. After that pile, all of her letters were addressed to an unfamiliar Brooklyn address. I jotted it down. I noticed that none of the letters were addressed to our Long Island mansion, or to the underground apartment beneath Big Johnnie's, where I was. On the ninth night I went to the one unfamiliar address in a cab.

"Okay, son," the driver said, when we arrived. I paid him and got out. It was dark-dark, an autumn night, but there were swarms of people outside of where I was about to enter. When I reached the door my body jumped. Blocking the entrance was some type of security guard. The last thing I wanted to see was anybody official, or anybody wearing a uniform. I didn't want to start running away and cause suspicion.

"I'm looking for someone," I said in my boy voice.

"This is a women's shelter facility for single women," the guard said. I was about to say something back but remembered I was dressed as a boy. Some girl came up behind me. She showed a pass and got in, no questions asked. I left and went to the side of the huge building. I removed my fitted, crushed it into my back pocket. I pulled out the ten long cornrows that Siri had braided for me. I combed my hair with my fingers. Then, I tucked my T-shirt so my little hips would show their feminine curves. For five dollars I rented a lady's pass who was outside begging for change. "Stay right here if you want it back," I told her.

Smiling, I reapproached the guard as a young woman, flashed the pass, and went inside.

A football field filled with women, more women than the C-dorm and all the juvy dorms and cells put together; more women than I ever seen on the yard. There were rows and rows of them, sitting, standing, leaning, and laying on beds. They talked, cried, laughed, shouted, argued, packed, unpacked, and slept. I stood still, stupid, with my mouth open and in shock.

What the fuck had happened? Were all of these women the same as Momma? Were all of their husbands and daughters and sons locked up while they were left to fall to pieces? I counted twenty rows across, and couldn't see any further down. I started walking up row one. Stupidly, I called out "Momma," and a thousand heads turned to answer my call. So I changed. I started saying Lana halfway up the aisles, and then switched to saying, "Santiaga," hoping Momma would jump up and be happy to see me. After I told her how I had made her place clean and fresh and pretty, we would go back to the apartment I prepared for her beneath the floor.

On the last and twentieth row now, I began to accept that Momma wasn't in here. I finished it off anyway. I left outside to return the pass.

"You found her?" the lady who rented me the pass asked.

"No," was all I answered.

"Is she an addict?" the lady asked me. It felt like she had stabbed me in my chest. I didn't want to say Momma was no type of "addict." I didn't even like the word.

"What's she using? Drink? Pills? Heroine? Crack?" she asked me. "Where she from in Brooklyn? Cause everybody here is from Brooklyn. You have to be from Brooklyn to stay in here." I listened to her fast-talk and I looked at her thinking to myself, *You look like the fucking addict!* Then my mind switched. Maybe that's why she could help me. I began thinking.

"The lady I'm looking for is from Bed-Stuy," I said.

"Okay, stand right here," she said and ran off like a rabbit on the reservation.

"She can help you," she said when she returned. She had a woman with her who was definitely an addict. "She smoking that rock, right?" the second lady asked me. She was sweating and jittery. "Give me a yard, I'll take you right to her," she said.

I walked off without saying nothing back. I definitely wasn't giving her no one-hundred dollars! She looked like she'd do anything for half of a glazed doughnut.

"Wait a minute, wait a minute, wait a minute," she ran behind me. She kept touching my shoulder with her filthy fingers.

"I know where she's at!" she screamed.

"You don't even know her name!" I said through tightened lips and gritted teeth.

"I know where the area crack house is in Bed-Stuy. That's where I'm from. That's why she came and got me. I'll take you there," she said with full attitude and confidence as though it was the only thing in life she was sure about.

"I won't give you a penny if she's not there," I said.

"*Un-un* nah that ain't right," she said still jumping around, her lips more ashy than her knuckles. "Twenty if she dere. Ten if she not," the lady offered me.

"You went too low," the lady who rented me her pass complained.

"Deal," I said. We three walked off. I followed them. I might look like a lost sweet little girl to them, I thought. Used to being driven around by Poppa, it was true that I didn't learn my way around the Brooklyn or New York train system yet. But, I would know for sure when I was on my blocks in Bed-Stuy.

* * *

As low and awful, cruel and cold, empty and upside-down as my last three years of lockdown had been, I couldn't say what I saw in a language that anyone else besides Siri could understand. I thought of regular words like *horror* and *terror, shame* and *embarrassment, guilt* and *disgust, insane* and *fucked-up.* But when I uttered those out loud they were whack-overused words that couldn't capture my true feelings or the real life images that my eyes saw.

I flashed back to a time when Winter made me go inside of the haunted house at an amusement park. She was stuck babysitting me. Her and her friends were complaining that I was with them, so they acted like I wasn't and went everywhere that I shouldn't, with me. Crooked staircases and demons in cosmetics, hands without bodies and necks without heads, couldn't compare to the crack house. Even though back then at six years old I was afraid, at least I knew that it was all make-believe.

No one was pretending in the crack house. No one was black, white, or Latino. Everyone was the color of ash. Eyeballs multiplied in size by three, knuckles, fingertips, lips all burnt up. Everyone was sucking on something. Their hair was hard like straw. Everyone was in their own corner of their own foot of space, or plopped down dead in the middle of the floor. Each of 'em got nervous when anyone approached them, even a kid, a little girl. There were no welcomes, smiles, hellos, or even questions asked or answered. Sounds of sucking and inhaling, angry dogs chained and barking, old wood cracking, and collapsed plumbing pipes leaking; a stink-stank, foul odor. Every face I looked at in the damn darkness looked exactly the same.

I put my jacket over the naked body of someone shaking, nothing left but bones and a pipe. Still, he, she, it was still smoking.

"Don't give her your jacket. She'll sell it," the crack-house tour guide said to me. I ignored her, wouldn't take it back.

Eight floors of searching, now we were headed down. A skeleton with one layer of gray skin left, brushed by me on the stairs, hand in front of its face, fingers spread like arrested people who don't want to be seen on the news, wool hat pulled down. It was running like it believed it was being chased. But there was no one on the stairwell but me and the crack tour guide and the bag of bones that sped ahead of us.

"Here you go. Your ten dollars," I told the crack-house tour guide when we met back up with her friend, the one who first rented me her shelter pass. She had stayed outside the crack building, playing lookout.

"We can show you some more places," the guide said. "This is the biggest, but it ain't the only one," she pushed.

"It's late. I seen enough," I said.

"If you ever need anything ask us two. We'll give you a good price," the pass renter said. "We always be somewhere outside the shelter at night," she pitched. "Next time bring a picture of your mother. I'll find her for you. You don't even have to come. Door-to-door service. Just tell me where you want her," the crack guide said. I stopped walking.

"Cash on delivery," she joked.

"I didn't say it was my mother," I turned and told her, feeling red. The two of them giggled nervously.

"Our bad, we all somebody's mother. Make sure you check us!" they called behind me as though they were real businesswomen. As I headed down the subway stairs, leaving the same way I came, it dawned on me that they weren't following behind me. I had supplied them with crack money for the night, and the crack house had plenty of rocks for sale.

When I reached the underground, Momma was back. She had thrown on a dress that was hanging up when I left earlier to go look for her. I guess she thought I was still six. I had seen my ruined Air Maxes, just a flash of fluorescent green running down the Bed-Stuy crack building stairs. Besides, *me and Momma both stunk*. The smell of the place I couldn't describe was in my hair, on my clothes, and making my skin crawl.

We showered together. Momma was just standing there in the warm water as I cleaned her body, her butt, vagina, underarms, and hair. It was better in the shower. You couldn't tell our tears from the drops of water.

We weren't saying nothing. I turned on some music to make Momma feel better. Oddly, in a frightening way, the first cut that came on was "Dear Mamma," by Tupac Shakur. It was September 13, 1996, the exact day the bullets finally killed him. I wondered if he felt relieved. Can being dead be a relief? Is there is a possibility that even after death, there would be more pain?

Tupac believed that a crack fiend could still be a black queen. I looked at Momma, hoping his words could possibly be true.

I don't know if Momma, the music lover, was listening. I don't know what Momma was thinking. She looked as small as a kindergartner and held her legs with her burnt hands and hung her head to her knees. She was sitting on her bed. It was made up with new sheets and blankets, real pillows and decorative ones. I had not used her bed in eleven nights. I thought she should be the first to enjoy my gifts to her.

She didn't even notice. She didn't say nothing. I looked at the roses I had purchased for her almost two weeks ago. They were like me and Momma, I thought: stuck in one pose, one position, dry and dead.

Chapter 31

I had cooked and served eleven organic recipes to Big Johnnie. Each night, I'd have one whole meal left over from mine and Siri's. It was meant for Momma. Big Johnnie received Momma's portion every early morning after I was done doing Momma's job at his store, and before he arrived at 6:06 a.m. After the first meal I left for him he began paying Momma one hundred thirty dollars per week, instead of the one hundred dollars he had agreed to pay Momma when I first met him. I wasn't sure if it was because he knew it was really me doing Momma's job, or because he loved my cooking, or because he noticed that I worked weekends even though I wasn't scheduled and didn't have to. Thirty extra dollars, *humph* yeah I'll take it. I wasn't spending any of the money I was earning. I was still surviving on the money I earned at NanaAnna's and the seven hundred dollars I kept from my money tree. Plus, I was still walking around wearing my "handwashed in the bathroom sink clothes."

* * *

"You was touching my stuff," Momma said to me when I returned from upstairs doing her job.

"Momma, I was trying to figure out where you were for all those days and what happened to you," I defended.

"What for?" Momma asked strangely.

"I was worried about you. You were gone for a long time," I explained.

"So," she said. Silence fell on both of us.

"So I wanted to be sure you were okay," I said.

"You see me, right?" she asked, as though nothing had happened. But more than that, she talked like she thought that we weren't even related. Or she sounded like she thought I was the mother putting too much pressure on her, and she was the daughter who had to make excuses.

"I see you Momma, and I'm so happy to see you. Please don't leave me again," I asked her with no trace of bossiness or disrespect.

"We can't go everywhere together," she said.

"I know. But we can spend *some time* together, *can't we*? I want to cook a meal for you. Wait till you taste it! Big Johnnie tasted my cooking and every time I clean up, his bowl is empty."

"Did he bring his big ass down in here?" Momma said, suddenly alarmed.

"No, Momma, after I was done working up there I would leave him the food I had cooked for you, since you weren't home."

"That means you got some money," she said. "You worked. Did he pay you?"

"He did."

"How much?"

"One hundred dollars."

"Where is it?"

"I spent most of it." My first lie to Momma. Then I added truthfully, "I'm going to the market with what money is left. We ran out of groceries."

"You going out? I'm a wait here," Momma said.

I didn't trust her. This was a new feeling between Momma and me, distrust.

"Please come with me?" I asked sweetly.

"No," was all she said. I wanted to change my mind and stay and watch her. At the same time, I needed to get the ingredients for the healing soup to heal Momma. I wasn't sure what to choose. Should I stay? Should I go?

"What you standing there for? Go get the groceries," she said. I left, hoping I wouldn't regret it.

What are the chances of me seeing Elisha? Probably zero, I thought as I walked to the faraway organic market. What did I want to see him for anyway? I asked myself. No answer came to mind.

He wasn't there. As I pushed my cart around, I looked down at my cheap, ugly sneakers. Then, I looked at myself, the part that I could see. I'm glad Elisha isn't here, I thought to myself. Look at me. All this time the businesspeople on the block kept calling me "pretty little girl." I looked a cheap mess.

WE ARE A HEALTHY COMMUNITY was on the message board, which was posted on the wall right before the exit at the organic market. I walked past it with my expensive organic foods packed in expensive organic foods shopping bags. Then I took three steps back, and posted a note:

Elisha it's me, Ivory. I shop here on Fridays at 3.

I pinned it on the board where there were many postings, and messages.

Momma was gone when I got back. I believed she would return soon. If she didn't, it would be too cruel to me and too bad for her and too sad for us. She needed the healing soup. She needed me to take care of her.

I washed, peeled, sliced, chopped, and crushed, preparing the ingredients for the soup. In my deep clay pot, I placed a few stalks of thyme and poured in the purified water and, by accident, spilled a few tears.

Chapter 32

October 2, 1996

Big Johnnie,
    I know my month is up and I'm supposed to leave. My mom died and I'll be staying downstairs with Aunty for a lot longer than I thought.

Love Ivory.

That was the big lie tucked inside the little note that I left for Big Johnnie. I laid it on top of a bowl of homemade vegetable stew, made with organic red beans, onions, tomatoes, garlic, ginger, tumeric, sea salt, cumin, coriander, and three big soft organic potatoes. I left a hot, fresh slice of cornbread, made with fresh organic corn for him to dip in the delicious stewed gravy.

I had been dodging a face-to-face with Big Johnnie for a month. Although I cleaned his place thoroughly, organized his inventory, matched up his labels, trashed his expired foods, cut, collapsed, and tied his empty boxes into neat stacks, organized his old newspapers, packaged twenty-five sandwiches per day plus ten buttered rolls and five peanut butter and jellies, and knew his store like the palms of my hands, I did all of that from 3:00 a.m. until 6:00 a.m. each morning. He didn't see me. He didn't have to. Purposely, I wanted him to believe that Momma, aka my aunt, was on a good streak. I wanted him to imagine that "Aunt" was doing all those jobs while I prepared the sandwiches. I wanted him to believe that aunt and niece worked together preparing his special morning meals. Big Johnnie would leave my pay each Friday, in a white envelope with my name on it, at the front counter. I'd take it down below with me at 6:00 a.m. when I was finished with my work, and do the same routine the next week.

I wanted to face Big Johnnie at the end of the month with Momma standing at my side, wearing one of the three new outfits that I had purchased for her. Now I would have to face Big Johnnie myself and alone, and pretend not to be living alone underneath the floor of his store. I knew no adult would allow two eleven-year-old girls, Siri and me, to live underground alone. At least no adult would, except Momma.

Hesitantly, I entered the front door of his store for the first time in thirty days.

"Big Johnnie," I said.

"Princess Ivory," he said.

"I'm sorry I had to extend my stay living beneath your store."

A customer rushed in. He served him. He left.

"Maybe now you can let me know about the rent," I asked.

"Don't concern yourself with that. You have a wake and a funeral to attend. When my mom passed away it was the saddest year of my life. It didn't matter what anyone said or did. Mom was all I could think about. That's why I can sit in here eighteen hours a day," he said. "I just think of my mother and how grateful I should've been while she was alive, that she didn't raise me to be one of these crazy fools I see out here every day."

I began to feel bad about my lie.

"Your momma must've been one incredible woman, too. She raised an incredible daughter." My eyes teared up on their own, with guilt and thoughts of my real momma.

"Thank you," I said softly. "So is it okay for me to stay?"

"Please, please, don't leave me," he dramatized. We both laughed, me wiping away my tears.

* * *

"I heard your mother died," Mr. Sharp said. He was so sharply dressed in a suit and shoes shined so well I could see them reflecting the sun. He was sitting in his Mercedes outside of his store with the engine running. "Go get Linda. Tell her I said to lock up and come on out."

I ran in to tell her.

"You get in the back!" he said to me through the window. I got in, surprised and embarrassed by my cheap shoes on his plush interior in his throwback Benz. I fidgeted some. Even Linda looked a little uncomfortable.

"Seat belts," he said to both of us. "You see the box in the back?" he asked me, as he pulled away from the curb. "Open it."

I reached over and picked up the gift-wrapped box. I sat staring at it for some moments until I noticed Mr. Sharp was staring at me through his rearview mirror. I peeled the gift-wrapping away. It was a gold-framed picture of Poppa looking like king of the world. Beneath the tissue paper was a gold-framed picture of Momma. Her pose was so mean, she could've been a cover girl on *Vogue* magazine. Again, my tears turned on me.

"A woman's tears are beautiful to me," Mr. Sharp said. "Every time I see them I'm amazed. Wish I could do that as easily as you all can do that. I'm forty-four. I've seen all type of things. I've never cried, not even one time."

He was talking nice, but his words made me have confusing thoughts. *How could tears be beautiful? When a woman is crying it means she's hurting, doesn't it?* I thought to myself.

"Whose father is that in the photo in your hand?" he asked. I didn't say nothing. "Whose mother is that?" I didn't say nothing. "Is she dead?" he asked. "Is the woman in the picture dead?" I didn't say nothing.

"I loved your father. It would be my honor to help his daughter. In these times, a black man has to be careful. They always got us walking a tightrope; I find that we just have to become the best tightrope walkers in town. As a man, people look at me suspiciously if I say I love my brother. Men are supposed to love their brothers, work together, and fight together. When one falls, his brother gotta step up and take care of his brother's wife and family. That's how it supposed to be. But now, if a man makes any kind of gesture to a woman, he's viewed as a pervert, someone who wants something, someone suspicious. If a grown man shows compassion to a young girl, he is seen as a molester and a rapist. They've closed down all the avenues for real men to express real love as a brother, as a father, as a friend. So we have Linda here, to break up the suspicion. To confirm that I'm just a good man doing a good deed to balance out some other deeds I done that wasn't so good," Mr. Sharp said, in a slow, steady, manly voice.

Up until that day, Mr. Sharp had given me plenty of learning lessons, but had not offered me a job, or given me a copy of the photo off the wall that I asked for the first day we met. He said, "I been watching and waiting to see if you were gonna be sticking around." Now he was taking me shopping.

"Choose two pairs of shoes, and two pairs of sneakers," he said. "We used to call it our 'nice shoes' and our 'play shoes.'"

In the Saks Fifth Avenue store he said, "Show me your style. Once I know your taste, I can make you something even better." He was confident.

In the Gucci store, he warned me, "This is a one-time, all-day, shopping spree event. I don't want to spoil you. I already spoiled my own two daughters. Now they grown spoiled women. I don't want to rob you of your enthusiasm, your work ethic, or your understanding of the true value of each penny, and every dollar. After today, you'll come and earn some money working for me after school."

I wanted to work. I appreciated him. But I didn't want to be exposed or to admit to anything either. I wanted to refuse the shopping event, but I felt it would ruin everything between me and him if I did.

"Mr. Sharp, what if I say, it's okay if we talk about some things but not other things? What if I make up a sign like this . . ." I manipulated my fingers. "And anytime I flash this sign, it means I don't want to answer that question." I smiled. "So when you see it, you don't ask that no more," I said softly.

He laughed a hearty laugh. Linda began laughing, too. I wondered what she was laughing at when she always spoke only in Spanish. I decided she was just happy he was happy. It was one day of seeing him as a man and not a boss. I didn't know if it was her first time like this or not.

"What if I don't agree to your sign language?" he asked.

"Well, Mr. Sharp, you're a nice man. I don't want to lie to you."

"That's the Ricky Santiaga I know. You don't have to tell me you're his daughter," he said.

I flashed the sign.

* * *

In Esmeralda's Beauty Salon, a few doors down from Big Johnnie's, I was having my hair done for the first time since lockdown. Used to Siri or me doing it myself, I felt a different feeling when Esmeralda touched me. The warm water in my hair, her fingers massaging my scalp, clearing away the shampoo suds, and even the way she kept securing the plastic around the front of my body so my clothes wouldn't get wet felt unfamiliar. *No one touches me*, I thought to myself. While the shampoo bubbled up in my hair, some tears did flow from my eyes, even though they were closed while enjoying the feeling of the wash.

The ladies in Esmeralda's liked me a lot for saving them and some of their customers from getting those parking tickets.

"Who did your nails, *mami*?" one of 'em asked.

"I did," I said, but really it was Siri who had the patience to paint on unique designs, blow them dry and wait and apply a top coat. Holding a mirror and showing me all the angles on my hairstyle, three beauticians stood still for some seconds admiring my new look.

"*Que linda!*" they said.

When I went to pay, Esmeralda refused my money.

"No, *mami*!" she said. "Today for you is free," she whispered while walking me out the front door of her shop. She wouldn't even take the tip. I knew that was big. Sometimes I sat inside their shop when it was raining. I'd be flipping through fashion magazines. Their tip game was crazy! They started with an empty clear jug each morning, and counted out a bunch of ones, fives, and tens and a few twenties every evening. I was plotting on getting in good enough with them for me to become their "hair wash only girl." I thanked Esmeralda four or five times. She stood outside her shop door watching me walk down the block for some seconds.

As my feet moved light and comfortably in my new Nikes, my legs in my Guess jeans, my breasts in my new North Face jacket, my new Gucci bag on my shoulder, I dropped my last quarters of the day in the meters, and passed The Golden Needle on Mr. Sharp's day off. I admired my manicured natural nails, clear polish with a razor-thin purple line across the tips, a la French manicure. As I waved at Linda, my mind realized that Esmeralda and them had probably heard from Big Johnnie, or one of his customers, that my mom had died. No wonder everyone was treating me extra-extra special. Every person, the men and the ladies, knew that the loss of a mother was the worse feeling and possibility. Only Mr. Sharp knew the real truth, the truth I never confirmed for him.

As I walked, I thought about how every day I feel the same sadness a child whose mother had actually died would feel, I believed. If it were not for Siri's singing and beautiful humming, I don't know how I would ever be okay enough to make it through each day. Even in lockdown, laying awake in my bed at night in the C-dorm, I felt like I had a hole in my heart. But at least then, I was still surrounded by plenty of other little crazy girls who each had a hole in their hearts, too. In the underground beneath Big Johnnie's floor, I got real familiar with extreme and continuous loneliness. Death and loneliness seemed the same to me. At least they had to be cousins, I thought to myself.

For two back-to-back Fridays, Elisha had not shown up to meet me at the organic market. The note I left for him would always be removed by the time I returned. I'd post another one each time. This Friday I was hoping I'd be lucky. Since a few things had begun going my way for the last twenty-four hours, and since I did not have to spend one dollar of my savings on these new clothes, I thought it was a possibility that Elisha would be there this Friday, and he was.

Chapter 33

"My mother liked you," was the first thing he said when I walked up. He handed me a copper-gold box of chocolates. More importantly, it was Godiva, the kind of chocolate Poppa used to give me one piece at a time, to prove a point.

I smiled. Then he handed me another gift, a round wooden box. I opened it. It was an assortment of olives and cubes of cheese.

"I wanted to give you some options," he said. Then a bright smile began beaming naturally across his face. His teeth were perfect, like the day after a person gets their braces tooken off. I smiled again.

"I like her, too. Is she inside the market?" I asked him. He took back the wooden box, pulled a tiny shopping bag from his North Face pocket and put the wooden box inside and held it for me.

"No, do you need to go in there?" he asked.

"*Uh-un,*" I said as I opened my Gucci backpack that I carried like a handbag, and placed the box of chocolates inside.

"Ivory, what do you like?" he asked. Him saying my name made me tingle some, even though it wasn't my real name. I don't know why I was tingling.

"Music," I answered softly.

"Speak up!" I heard Siri's voice in my ear. "Don't turn all soft just because he's a boy," she said.

"But you're soft," I said to Siri.

"Huh?" Elisha said.

"Do you like music?" I asked him.

"Everyone likes music," he said. "My mother started me on guitar lessons when I was five. I'm twelve now, so I guess you could say I play pretty good."

"I dance," I said.

"All girls say that," he said.

"I'm not the same," I told him. "As them . . . ," I added softly.

"I know," he said. "That's what my mother said about you."

"So did you come to meet me cause your mother said so?" I asked him.

"Yep," he answered with full confidence. "C'mon, let's walk," he said.

"Do you like sports?"

"Not really," I said. "You?"

"I ball, but it's not really my thing," he said.

"What's your thing?" I asked.

"Movies," he said.

"You want to go to the movies?" I asked, a little excited at the idea. I hadn't been to one in more than four years.

"No, I want to make movies," he said.

"Oh, that's dope," I said, and then I turned a little quiet, imagining.

"You seem like you might make a good actress," he said, staring straight ahead. I was just trying to figure out if that was a compliment or an insult.

"Why you say that?" I asked.

"I told my mother that you *acted like* you accidentally pushed that shopping cart into me," he smiled half way.

"I did not," I said, swiftly switching suddenly fierce.

"See, that's what I'm talking about. You would make a good actress, because you made my mother believe you!"

I stopped walking and turned towards him, getting red.

"Why would I do that!" My attitude burst out. He laughed.

"See, that seems more like the real you," he said calmly.

"You don't know me!" I told him.

"Not yet," he said. "But because I'm gonna be a movie director, I'm good at watching people." He held his hand up and gestured like he was looking at me through the lens of a camera.

"This is my school," he said. We were standing in front of Brooklyn Boys Academy. Then he pointed diagonally across the street.

"That's my house, right there." It was a Brooklyn brownstone. He pointed again. "That's the church my mom goes to. The organic market is right back there." He pointed in the direction we just walked from.

It must be easy, I thought, for him to feel so free and relaxed that he'd easily say *I live here, I go to school here, this is my plan for life.* I wouldn't and couldn't. But I admired that he could.

"Your turn," he said.

"For what?" I asked.

"You live where? You're twelve or thirteen? Your family?" he asked.

"I live way down there," I pointed. "I walked twenty-eight blocks to meet you. I go to the organic market because I was taught that non-organic fruits and vegetables were sprayed with poison. I want my momma to eat well. It's too expensive for me, the organic market, but I shop there for Momma anyway. I'm a year younger than you, but I feel older than I am. I just moved to Brooklyn. Most of my friends are age forty and up. So I'm so happy to meet somebody young like me."

He busted out in boy laughter. "That's crazy! Most of your friends are forty and up?" he questioned.

"It's true," I said, thinking of Big Johnnie, Mr. Sharp, Esmeralda, the flower lady, and Bernard the Butcher. Now I was laughing, too.

I felt nervous when Elisha opened the door to his school and walked me inside. He knocked on another door and then two boys came out.

"Stephen and Maurice," Elisha introduced them to me.

We four left the school together. We met up with two girls, two blocks down from there.

The girls, Atiyah and Karla, looked me up and down. After I was introduced and said hello, I didn't glance their way or feel fucked-up because of them. Today, as far as looks go, I was fucking flawless except for the big hole in my heart, and they couldn't see that.

"What school do you go to?" Atiyah asked.

"I just moved to Brooklyn. I didn't register yet," I told them.

"Private or public," Karla asked.

"What?" I said.

"Are you going to a private school like rich boys like Elisha attend? Or a public school like ours?" Karla pushed.

"Mind your business," Elisha jumped in. "She didn't decide yet."

I liked him more when he said that.

"Where are we going?" Atiyah asked.

"There's a party at our school tonight at eight. Wanna check it out?" Karla invited.

"Nope," Elisha said swiftly. He seemed to say whatever he thought without hesitation.

"Ah, y'all are punks!" Atiyah said.

"We not ready to die for you two," Elisha said.

"On the strength," Stephen and Maurice said. I noticed now that they were both dressed in their school blazers. Elisha was not.

"I got an audition in the morning. I don't want no bullet holes in my body." Elisha and the guys laughed. An audition? I thought to myself. I wondered what that was all about. I didn't ask, though.

We didn't do much, but I could tell they'd rather do nothing together than doing nothing alone. It was October. The cold came creeping in but wasn't full blast yet. We walked around pointing out which cars we wanted to drive when we each got old enough to drive. Atiyah chose a kitted-up Corvette. Karla chose the Cadillac. Maurice was content with the Pathfinder, but Stephen wanted the Suburban and said he would run Maurice off the road. Elisha waited to make his choice. Then he said he wanted the hunter-green Range Rover with wooden steering wheel, rims, and the buttercream-soft leather interior with the evergreen piping that he just saw.

"And you?" Elisha asked me.

"I didn't see one I liked yet," I said.

"You must know what you like. Tell me."

"A Porsche," I said. He smiled. "Nobody on this block could afford one," I added, smiling.

Downtown Brooklyn, Karla wanted cheesecake. I didn't cause I never had it before. Me and Elisha sat outside of Junior's.

"Let me see your book bag?" I asked him.

"For what?"

"I wanna look at your books, see how far behind I am. Or maybe I'm way ahead," I teased, but I didn't mean it. I believed I was too far back to catch up. In prison classes I was too angry to learn. At NanaAnna's, I couldn't stop learning. Now that I knew for sure I wouldn't be going to no more school, I had been telling myself it didn't matter. As long as I could read and write, count, add, subtract, multiply, and divide, I knew enough to not get beat outta my paper.

Elisha unzipped his bag and handed it to me. "You sure you looking for books?" he joked without laughing or smiling. I didn't answer him.

The first book I pulled out was *Vocabulary*. He smiled. "I gotta test on that on Monday."

"Are you ready for it?" I asked him.

"Why, you gonna be my tutor?" he asked.

"I'm okay with words," I said, feeling challenged but not confident.

"My school is no joke. The words in there, we wouldn't ever use in no conversation," he said. I wasn't sure if he thought I was dumb. I was sure that I didn't want him to think I was dumb. I couldn't like anyone who thought that way about me. We definitely couldn't be friends.

"What page?" I asked him.

He took the book from me, flipped some pages and said, "Right here, page 34. I gotta know the definitions and use the words in sentences." I looked at the first word and the definition his book gave:

Anomaly—a deviation from the norm, unusual.

I had never heard that word before. As I scanned down the word list on page 34, I felt a pinch of panic. Nothing looked familiar. I was behind, too behind to catch up. More than that, I was embarrassed. I didn't want to be embarrassed in front of him.

"I told you. Forget it. Let's do something else," he said.

"Anomaly," I said aloud. "Use it in a sentence." I reversed the challenge onto him. He paused then smiled, his white teeth perfect. I could tell he was thinking.

"Some people consider my parents' marriage an anomaly, because my mother is a Wall Street lawyer, and my father works for UPS," he said.

I thought about it swiftly. I guess he used it right. The word really just means unusual. I guess he's saying his mother earns more money than his father. To me, that was unusual.

"Good!" I told Elisha. "You got that one right. The next word is . . ."

"Now you use it in a sentence," he said, folding his arms across his chest.

"I don't have a test on Monday," I said softly, trying to ease out of it. He didn't say nothing back. I tried to think quickly.

"I hope love never becomes an anomaly," I blurted out. His eyes widened some. He stared at me for a moment.

"What's the next word?" he asked me.

"Duplicity," I read aloud. Then I looked at the definition, so I would know. I read to myself.

Duplicity—Deceitful in speech and conduct by acting in two different ways to different people concerning the same matter.

I kept my eyes on the page of the book instead of looking up at Elisha. I was feeling naked and guilty because of that word.

"My mother says that when money is involved, a lot of people deal in duplicity to make a higher profit," Elisha said.

"Yep, that's right. That fits the definition," I told him. "You must've studied already. You don't need me."

"Your turn," he said, ignoring my escape route. I sat thinking.

"Don't look at me," I said suddenly.

"Why not?" he asked.

"Cause," was all I said. Silence fell between us.

"She was sincere in her duplicity." I said my sentence softly.

"What does that mean?" he laughed. "Duplicity and sincerity are opposites," he said.

"Not really . . . ," I disagreed.

"How aren't they opposites?" he asked.

"Because someone could say two different things to two different people about the same thing, because the person has a different relationship with one of the people compared to the other," I explained myself.

"You could say two different things, true. But that would be duplicity if the two things weren't true."

"No," I said softly, wishing I had taken his offer to do something else. "If you asked me if I was happy right now, I would say yes. It would be true cause I'm happy to meet you and have a new friend. But I could be happy to meet you and sad at the same time. Depending on who asked me, my answers would be different about the same thing, but they would both be true," I said, still looking down. He was quiet now.

"What's the next word?" he asked.

"Let's just quit it," I said.

"I'm learning . . . ," he said.

"But I can tell you know all of the definitions already," I said. "So we should do something else."

"I'm learning about you . . . ," he said. "One last word, then that's it," he said.

"**Perfunctory . . .** " I read aloud, hardly able to pronounce it correctly.

"I don't know that one. Choose something different," he said.

"You know it! Now you're dealing in deceit and duplicity!" I laughed a true laugh. He smiled.

"Seriously, I don't know that one," he said, smiling. I still didn't believe him. I thought he was just trying to make me feel better by pretending that he didn't know something. So I read the definition aloud to him.

"*Perfunctory*—Lacking interest, care, or enthusiasm. Merely performing a routine without feeling." Then I read the definition silently to myself over again. I thought of Momma. That's what was happening between Momma and me. Momma was lacking any interest in me. She didn't even seem to care about me. She came home when she needed something. Otherwise she didn't come home at all. Even when she was sitting right in front of me, she didn't seem to have any feelings. She was perfunctory, just going through the motions.

When I looked up, Elisha was staring at me and my tears. He wiped them away with his fingers.

"Eat a piece of chocolate," he said. "My mother said chocolate makes girls happy. That's why I gave it to you. And give me back my books. I never meant for my exam to make you cry," he joked. I didn't tell him how much I hate my tears for telling on me every time.

Leaning on a car that was old enough to lean on, I handed him a chocolate. "They're for you. I'll eat one if you eat one," he said. So we did.

"What time you gotta be home?" he asked out of the blue. His questions kept making me pause. There was no one at my "home." There was no one telling me to do anything any particular way. The thought reminded me that I'm not cared for enough to be scolded or looked for if I went missing for too long.

"Why?" I asked.

"Cause I want to take you somewhere with me. I don't want to get you in no trouble with your moms," he said.

"Eight o'clock," I said without pausing or thinking.

"Good enough," he said.

When his noisy crew came pushing out of the doors of Junior's, they saw a photographer selling Polaroid shots. Maurice flagged him over. They all jumped in but I stayed back.

"C'mon, get in the picture," the girls waved me over.

"No, that's alright," I told them.

"Elisha's girlfriend must be 'America's Most Wanted,' and shit!" Atiyah said. They laughed.

Elisha stayed leaning on the car and said, "The best pictures are the ones when we ain't posing."

"Take the shot!" Stephen ordered the photographer. Maurice paid for it. The photographer stood shaking the photo, then framed it. Stephen grabbed it and gave it to Karla.

"We bout to bounce," Elisha said to his friends.

"Where y'all headed?" Maurice asked. "What's up with the arcade?"

"Check y'all Monday," Elisha told them. "C'mon," he said to me. We walked over one block. Elisha stopped at the bus line.

"You know your way around Brooklyn?" he asked me. Before I could put together my answer, he said, "You just moved here. I'll show you around."

When the bus rolled up, he moved me in front of him. "Get on.

I got you," he said. I climbed the two steps. And walked passed the driver. Elisha flashed one bus card and dropped one fare into the machine. The bus was packed. We stood for some blocks. I began thinking how I never rode a Brooklyn bus. When I lived here, for all of my young life, I rode in Poppa's car.

In my mind, I was writing down my firsts. It was the first time I met up with a boy. It was my first time receiving a gift from anyone besides family. It was my first Brooklyn bus ride.

When I came out of my thoughts, Elisha was staring at me.

"What?" I reacted.

"Nothing, I'm just watching," he said. As I began watching him, watching me, I noticed that he was watching everyone, not just me. He seemed like a person who was always studying. I wondered why.

"Sit there," he said when a seat opened up. I sat down. He stood over me.

When a seat next to me became open, he sat down.

"What do you think that lady right there is thinking," Elisha asked me, pointing out a lady who, now that I looked, seemed upset about something.

"I don't know," I said. "Why does it matter what she's thinking?" I asked.

"If I want to make great movies, I have to be able to capture great scenes, unusual and ordinary people. A great writer and director has to be able to go inside of his character's mind."

"So are you the writer or the director?" I asked.

"I'm the director. So I should learn how to do everything. The man in charge shouldn't be someone who's just guessing," he said.

"So where we going? You said you were gonna show me around."

"This is it. This is Brooklyn, real people doing real things," he said. Then he smiled. "I'm checking out locations, too," he added.

"Locations?" I repeated.

"Yeah. I gotta match up the right scenes with the right locations, to get the right feeling. Different parts of Brooklyn have different feelings, and different things going on. I know the whole place, but every now and then, I walk or ride around like this to check out the changes. Things change a lot, you know. Things change quick. Don't be surprised," he said, like he was absolutely certain.

We rode quietly. I was used to paying attention and watching people for my own safety. Trying to figure out what random people had on their minds, that was new. I realized that I was usually trapped in my own thoughts. How could I get into anyone else's? Why should I? Elisha's the director, not me.

But I did watch Elisha get up and give his seat, the one right next to me, to a pregnant woman. I watched how easy he was with people. He was the opposite of me. He didn't seem suspicious of everyone. He acknowledged other boys his same age with ease. That was an "anomaly," I thought. He didn't have that Brooklyn murder stare that Brooklyn boys walked with. Hell, we were known for Notorious B.I.G., "Who Shot Ya!" and shit like that. We were known to be rough. Elisha wasn't rough. He wasn't a sucker either. He had something that I couldn't put into words right then.

It was 8:00 p.m. by the time me and Elisha were back to where we first met, the organic market. It was closed now. Elisha kept walking. I asked him where he was going.

"Twenty-eight blocks in that direction," he said and pointed. "I'm walking you home."

I didn't want him to leave me. I liked the feeling of something completely unfamiliar to me, a boy. I grew up with three sisters, no brothers. Before I was old enough to think of boys I was locked down with all girls. Now here was a boy I was meeting who was a year older but almost my same age, something different and it felt okay. We walked.

In the colder wind of the October night, my skin began heating up with worries. Worries of him finding out I lived underground, beneath the store floor where there are no windows. My poppa's doing life. My momma's doing crack. My sister's doing fifteen. My little sisters are lost somewhere, and no one is looking for them. I knew that even though Elisha liked to know what other people were thinking and going through, there was no way he would guess my thoughts or my life.

We stopped in front of the building Mr. Sharp owned.

"That's twenty-eight blocks," he said.

"This is the building, but I can't have company!" I said swiftly.

I didn't want him following me into the building towards an apartment where I don't really live!

"I wasn't inviting myself in. Let's just chill right here for a minute," he said, leaning against the green mail pickup. "What's your phone number?"

I broke out in a sweat beneath my clothes. I never even considered putting a phone in the underground. I had not made one phone call since my escape. Of course I didn't receive no calls either. Embarrassed, I blurted out, "I can't get no calls. Give me your number?" I said to him.

"You can't get calls, but you can make calls?" he said, smiling.

"Yes," I said.

"*Um*," he said, pulling out a pen and scrap of paper from his long side Guess jeans pocket. He wrote his number down, folded it, and pushed it into my front pocket of my jeans. I felt something.

"Do me a favor?" he said. He went inside his jacket and pulled out some sheets of paper. "Oh no," I thought to myself, not more vocabulary words.

"Before you go, help me practice my lines for my audition tomorrow."

He handed me three sheets. "You be Yvonne, the mother. I'm auditioning for the son's role. Read your lines first. Try and act it out," he said. I guess he really thought of me as an actress. But I actually hated pretending.

"You don't have a script," I said, waving the papers he gave me.

"I memorized it already. Go head, test me." He seemed to like tests.

I read my first line: "Nothing is more important to me than you are, my son."

Emotion began racing throughout my body. I wished Momma would say something like that to me, her daughter. Maybe she would've said those warm words if I was a son? Maybe Riot was right. Maybe being a boy is better, with more benefits and more love.

Then Elisha said his lines like he really was the son in the script named Byron. Elisha's face even changed. He was making gestures as though his mom was really standing there in front of us. I was no longer Ivory. I was Yvonne, his mother. He was Byron, my son.

When I read my last line on the third page, "Tell him to wait. I'm talking to my son," my tears fell down. Elisha stood staring at me.

"I knew it," Elisha said calmly and thoughtfully without a smile. "You're an actress." He gave me three claps. But he was wrong. I wasn't acting. What he was seeing was my true feelings exploding.

"I gotta go in now," I told him, wiping away my tears and handing him back his script.

"I'll walk you up," he said.

"I live on the top floor," I told him.

"I'm healthy. We can walk or take the elevator," he said, patting his leg with his right hand as if to show how strong and sturdy it was.

"I'll go up and wave when I reach so you'll know I'm good," I told him, trying to hurry off.

"Okay but when will we meet up again?" he asked, handing me the shopping bag he had been holding for me.

"Next Friday at our market, same time. Is that alright?" I asked.

"Cool," was all he said. He stood watching me enter Mr. Sharp's building.

Waving from the hallway window way upstairs, I wasn't sure if he could see me. But I saw him standing glued to the sidewalk facing the Brooklyn night sky.

I waited till he began walking away, then took the stairs down, went out the back door of the building and down the alley and into the ground. Friday night, 8:18 p.m. I was alone again.

By midnight I was back on the streets. I was out of my new clothes, dressed down and searching for Momma.

Chapter 34

Not impressed by monsters, ghouls, or ghosts, I was trying to choose a Halloween costume. It was October 31, morning time. I had already worked Big Johnnie's, and was feeding the meters, walking and wondering. I was excited too, about meeting up with Riot later on, October 31 at 6:00 p.m. as we promised one another. I had already taken myself through all of the emotions I would feel if she didn't show.

"Captured or dead," Riot had said would be the only reasons she wouldn't be there to meet me.

I told myself I needed the costume because Riot and I are two fugitives showing up in one same spot.

"Things change quick. Don't be surprised," Elisha had said.

Even though he wasn't talking about my situation, I knew that true words spoken truthfully could fit almost anywhere.

"Let me pick you something pretty," Siri said. "Just because it's Halloween, doesn't mean you have to look stupid and crazy," she added.

"I know, but I don't want to look too pretty. That boy I made the baloney sandwich for been trying to get with me lately," I told Siri.

"You made the sandwich for your job, not for him. We don't like him. So we'll wear a mask, and we'll slip out the back alley like alley cats!" she joked. "That's it, we'll be cats! You'll wear a mask like Cat Woman. It gets dark by 5:00 p.m., so we'll just walk light and sneak past him," Siri suggested.

In long painted black fingernails, my real fingernails, black tights, a black Danskin, a black ballerina skirt, a black Cat Woman mask, wearing black lipstick, black eye liner, and black mascara, I slid into my black high top Prada kicks, the ones I chose and Mr. Sharp paid for. I selected my black Lady North Face, cause I liked the way it was cut to hug and outline my shoulders and waist.

"Wear the tail!" Siri said, cheerleading. I had debated about the cat tail that Siri got from the Halloween specialty store. Then I decided that a girl's butt already gets too much attention. I rocked one thick black braid from the center of my head going back. My hair had grown so much, even with Siri catching all of my hair in the French braid, the braid still fell past my shoulders and into the crease in the top of my back. That would be the only tail I was wearing. I was blacked out like a luxurious black Porsche. I felt powerful in the disguise, unlike one of the "hunted people," that I normally felt like without the disguise. With the disguise, oddly, I felt like Porsche, not Ivory.

I rode the train with all types. When I reached the crowded corner of Thirty-fourth and Seventh in Manhattan, I purposely kept walking. I decided I would remain one block over and watch for Riot's arrival, just in case. When I saw her arrive, I would prance across. But what outfit would she be wearing? Would she be a boy or a girl? Probably a boy, I thought to myself.

At six sharp, I saw a green-eyed teen soldier in camouflage pants and an army jacket. Timberlands on his feet, he was rocking a green bandanna. Wearing a green duffle on his back, that looked like it weighed more than him, he was pacing around moving in between people who were moving, but wasn't crossing over when he had the green light in his favor. So I crossed, crushed in the crowd. I walked up and stood besides him. When he moved, I followed. I felt good that he didn't recognize me. I said one word, "Revolution."

He turned swiftly, and then tried to slow his reaction to my recognizing and reciting his true name. Maybe he was supposed to recognize me first. "Too late," I thought to myself. He didn't have a mask on or war paint or anything like that. His eyes were greener than Riot's. They were big and clear and obvious in the lit-up streets of Madison Square Garden.

"Pretty fucking little girl . . ." He said his intro under his breath. "That's what my sister said about you."

"Where is she?" I asked.

"Follow me," he said.

"I'll walk behind you. Go ahead," I told him. I stayed a few paces behind.

"Hope everything is okay," Siri said.

Riot's fourteen-year-old naked feminine body was facedown on a metal table. I could see that she had recently made some new black friends, from her pretty perfect blonde cornrows beginning at her neckline and flowing upwards into her braided bun. In an unmarked store that was behind a store that was marked Denim Den, there was hardly enough space for three in the narrow room. Other than one opened window, the walls were plastered with animations, not simple ones like Mickey Mouse or Bugs Bunny. They were drawings etched with rage and revenge by an artist who loved aliens more than people. The air smelled like cleaning detergent and was filled with the sound of buzzing. A tall, slim, white girl with lady hips, wearing a belt with silver spikes and a hairstyle that matched her belt, was crouched over Riot's naked body. I checked her black spiked riding boots, trying to calculate if this was just her holiday costume or her everyday way to chill.

"Ivory, I wanted you to see me," Riot said, speaking over the music that was filling the tiny room and without looking up or changing her position even slightly. Even the spiked girl didn't turn.

Riot reached over and lowered the volume on the CD player. They were listening to a cut named "Me and My Girlfriend," off the *Makaveli* joint by Tupac Shakur.

"How did you know it's me?" I asked her.

"Cause Revo, me, and you always do what we promise. And those dancer legs . . . ," she said.

"So what's up with me and you for today like we promised?" I asked, feeling red.

"It's six o'clock. I wanted you to see me like this," she said strangely. "Step around and check out my tattoo."

I eased around to the other side of the table. I didn't remove my mask. I didn't need the artist profiling me.

"You see it right," Riot asked.

"*Uh,*" was all I answered, agreeing that I see it.

"So when you see me, you'll always know if it's me by what you see now," she said, confusing me.

I knew better than to talk too much. I said "okay," and left it at that.

"You can bounce with Revo. He got something for you, and we can all three meet back here around ten, when I'm dry," she said. I leaned over and picked up the cloth that I guessed should have been covering Riot's ass. I shook it out once and laid it over her cheeks. The artist shot me a first look with her deep blue eyes. I didn't throw her no heat. I hadn't touched her and caused her to make a mistake, or placed the cloth over her design. She had painted a beautiful Diamond Needle across and down my girl's back. The design of the wings was already amazing, colored, and detailed like stained glass in a window. Now she was easing right above Riot's crack, finishing what I guessed was the long black stinger, or maybe it was the tail. The fact that the design was on skin made it beautiful to me because the body already had its own design and curve. The body was a more-better canvas than some flat piece of paper, cloth, or wall. A kid could tag up a wall with graffiti. But graffiti on a body would be something to make jaws drop.

When I am dancing, I am also doing body art, I thought to myself. In addition to hugging and riding beats and rhythms, and expressing and releasing all kinds of deep, dangerous, dark, sorrowful, or joyful feelings, I'm showcasing the body through movement. When I am dancing, if I am not alone like I usually am, I am showing whoever's watching something so heartfelt and captivating that it would remain in their mind for as long as a memory could exist. It would sit in their gut, like a craving, like when a person really needs or wants something that's hard to obtain, like true love.

Riot would be happy to know that I definitely wouldn't forget her skin art, even if I never saw it again.

"Is that for me?" I asked Revo, who was standing outside the Denim Den door. He nodded. "Let me take it then, thanks," I told him.

"You can't carry it. That's why I got it. Tell me where you want it. And there's one more bag just as big as this one," he said calmly. I stood thinking.

"Where's the other bag?" I asked him.

"Follow me," he said.

At the Port Authority bus terminal on Forty-second and Eighth Avenue, Revo said, "Stand right here." He dropped the heavy duffle off his back and left it on top of my Pradas. "Lift your right foot," he said. I did. He took the strap of the duffle and laid it below my raised foot. "Now set it down," he said. I did. "Don't lift it again. Don't move. Don't talk to nobody. I'll be right back," he said. He's the same as Riot, I thought to myself.

Less than three minutes later, he returned with an identical duffle on his back. "Lift your foot," he said. I did. He grabbed the straps, carried both duffles a few steps, then hailed the cab from the taxi line in front of us.

"Tell him the address," he said to me. We were seated in the cab.

"My address?" I stalled.

"Wherever you want your luggage," he said.

"I can take it to my job, but not to my house," I told him. Then I told the driver the address for Big Johnnie's.

On the expensive ride in from Manhattan to Brooklyn, thoughts raced around my mind. I didn't want Revo to know where I lived. Would he believe this was not my house like I said? Would he remember my address? Would he tell Riot? He should believe it, since it's a corner store. I'd get out on the side street avoiding the store front door and even the back door that led beneath the floor. Then I wondered why I didn't want Riot to know my address. I obviously trusted her more than anyone else. So what was wrong?

The answer came slowly. I was uncomfortable with anyone who was uncomfortable with Momma. I didn't want anyone to see her and misunderstand or judge her. I didn't want anyone to just show up to the underground and maybe Momma would be there looking or feeling too vulnerable. Even though I didn't love the space beneath the store floor, I wanted it to be the one private place where Momma would come, because I made it special and, most importantly, because I was there waiting for her.

"How young are you?" Revo asked, breaking what had been a silent ride except for the driver's radio, which was stuck on the sports channel where there was no music.

"Too young," was my two-word response.

Revo handed the taxi driver the fare.

"Wait, don't pay yet," I told him. He looked at me confused.

"Take him to Madison Square Garden," I told the driver.

"Push the duffle bag out," I told Revo as I dragged one of them out on my own.

"I'll stay with you until your luggage is safe," he said, leaning over while pushing the duffle.

"It's safe. I'm here. I'll meet you back at ten. That's what your sister said," I told him, slamming the door. Of course he could've jumped out if he wanted to. But I knew I had said the magic words, "That's what your sister said." Even though he was the male, everybody who knew Riot knew she was the boss in every situation, even when you're in it with her fifty-fifty!

Cartons of cigarettes couldn't be too heavy, I thought to myself.

The sound of meowing took me out of my thoughts. "Shorty, you want some help?" The Baloney Boy rolled up to the side of Big Johnnie's store soon as the cab pulled off.

"No, I'm good," I told him.

"Big Johnnie said you were young. But you look ready to me," Baloney Boy said.

"Maybe I should just call Big Johnnie now," I threatened.

"What for? I'm just talking. I'm saying. I'mma wait for you. You let me know when you're ready, a'ight." He turned and walked away.

I dragged the heaviest bag on the cement, and kicked the light one like a soccer ball. Once I unlocked the steel doors, I just pushed the duffles down. I started to just lock up and head back to the train station. I thought to myself, *What if Momma comes tonight?*

Down below, I stood looking for a hiding place for the cigarettes. But there was no secure hiding place down here. *Where could I store the smokes?* I asked myself.

Opening the heavy duffle, I saw what I should've known already. Riot had already thought of everything. There was a heavy, thick linked chain and an extra heavy lock inside. I was glad she made it easy for me to lock the cigarettes away. I was insulted that she assumed that Momma was still smoking crack and untrustworthy. I was extra insulted that she thought Momma would steal from me, and the business I was doing to get the money I needed to save Momma.

When I returned to meet Riot, she was there but Revolution was not. She's great at using people, I thought to myself. She's controlling even what a person sees and doesn't see, and how long you get to see it for. She never allowed the pieces that she put together to get attached to one another. Yet, she liked for all of the pieces to be attached to her.

From living with Riot on lockdown, on the reservation, and on the road, I knew exactly what I wasn't seeing: the driver who drove her and her brother down here; the rented, borrowed, or stolen vehicle they rode in; the person whose identity she was using now; the hustle she had moving upstate. I also knew I had no idea exactly which day she had actually arrived down here to the city, on time for our meeting or even days beforehand. I knew I didn't know where in the city she was staying, or what exact day she would be leaving to head back upstate. And who knows what happened to Honey? I didn't know any answers, and I didn't see nothing that she didn't want me to see. I understood. Matter of fact, I might even respect it. Because of her secrets, I didn't have to feel guilty about mine. Still, we are partners and friends.

* * *

"What's your costume?" I asked Riot. Now she was dressed and standing on her own two feet, wearing summer sandals in the autumn coat wearing chill, in a long, funny colored, unfashionable printed fabric dress.

Because of her nice, slim, feminine figure, even though the dress was ugly, it fit her nicely.

"You're not supposed to ask me. If you ask me, it means my costume is no good," she said. I noticed her long earrings because she never wore jewelry when she and I were together. But I could see it was costume jewelry, which is only okay because it's Halloween. For me, I'd wear only genuine jewels—real gold and diamonds or nothing at all.

"Okay then, I won't ask," I said.

"I chose the most unpopular costume. Something no one wants to be for some reason. Hopefully you'll guess before we separate," she said.

"Aren't you cold?" I asked her. Her cornrows were beautiful but her face was reddish, I guessed from the cold air and her thin costume.

"No, I'm good. My costume is from a hot place," she said. "*I am hungry.* I was laid out on that table for half the day. Let's walk."

We began walking. "I heard about this parade down in the Village. I want to check it out. We can hop the train and eat down there," she said. I smiled. She was so relaxed and familiar in the area. It was like she was the city girl, not me.

"So you're a cat for Halloween. You're way better than cat woman." She laughed. "You're a dancing black cat." She pointed to my black ballerina tutu skirt. We both laughed. "And where's your tail?" she asked.

"I didn't want the boys chasing my tail," I said. "So I got rid of it."

"Oh that works," she said sarcastically. "Without the cat tail they'll never be able to see how pretty you are!" She laughed again.

"It's okay if they see and look and keep going, minding they business," I said. "But if they start sniffing or chasing my tail, that's something else!" We were heading down into the subway.

"How's Momma?" she asked, suddenly switching topics and feelings.

"Fine," I lied and she knew it.

"How's the people and the place where you are living?" she asked me.

"Good," I said one word.

"You been eating good?" she asked.

"So good, thanks to NanaAnna. How is she?" I asked, flipping positions.

"Perfect, you know more than anyone NanaAnna knows how to take care of herself. But I don't stay over there anymore. I'm not at NanaAnna's place," she said surprisingly.

The noisy train came screeching in as we stood on the crowded platform. Just then, I wasn't sure if her words were true. Maybe Riot was feeling the same as me, and just felt better with no one knowing for sure exactly where she was living and sleeping.

"Why? Did you and NanaAnna have an argument about something?" I asked.

"No way, you know that I worship her," Riot said and that sounded 100 percent true. "I just knew I was getting into some things that I didn't want to affect NanaAnna. So I bounced. Besides, I have identity. It's cool living as a nineteen-year-old with a driver's license, Social Security number, and everything that comes with that. Complete strangers call me *Ms.*, and they serve me like I'm an adult. I can work anywhere, represent myself, and when I talk, people listen without me having to threaten 'em." We laughed. "I got a passport. I can travel now, in and out of any airport going anywhere in the world," Riot said. I could tell she felt good about it.

"How's Honey?" I asked.

"Same," she answered with one word.

"About the business . . ." we both said at the same time. Then we smiled.

"I got the smokes, thanks," I said sincerely.

"You paid for them," she said. Twenty cigarettes per pack, ten packs per carton, fifty cartons, ten thousand cigarettes. That's a lot of paper.

I knew Riot wanted to know the details of my hustle even though I didn't know and she wouldn't tell me the details of hers. What was I supposed to tell her? I didn't want to tell her that I was the cigarette supplier for two crackheads, who I met at the homeless shelter where my mother used to stay in a bed beside 999 other homeless women. How could I? I wasn't ashamed. I just wasn't proud of it.

I sell the cartons to the crackheads cash on delivery. I don't listen to no mumbling, no begging, or no excuses. They had a built-in audience of buyers between the shelter and the blocks. Plenty of smokers couldn't afford a pack of cigarettes and at the same time couldn't resist. Swearing that their next cigarette was their last, they'd cough up, up to a dollar for one.

The crackhead tour guides who went searching for Momma with me that night worked hard. I told myself, even if they disappeared, I had my cash up front. Of course, I also knew that the shelter had more and more hungry and addicted women each day who would love to sell loosies on the low. When I delivered the cartons to them, I also used it as an opportunity to look for Momma.

"You're coming up," Riot said, calmly and quietly complimenting me. "Plus all of the cartons you already had," she added. I could see her mind moving around the calculations. Riot and I are both swift and sharp at counting. Numbers are way better than vocabulary words, I thought as Elisha suddenly ran through my mind.

"What are you smiling at?" Riot asked me.

"Nothing, how's our investment going?" Purposely, I kept it business.

"It's moving. Do you need money? Did you give Momma your money? Or did you spend it on those designer sneakers? She pointed to my Prada.

"What you know about these?" I asked her, leaning and admiring my kicks.

"When anything is expensive, everyone can just tell," Riot said.

"My money is straight. I'm just checking on our investment so I could know what to expect," I told her.

"I doubled it," she said casually. A huge eight, comma, zero, zero, zero flashed in my mind.

"But I had to reinvest some of that," Riot added. "But if you really need it, I could pay out your original four thousand," Riot offered.

"My two thousand," I corrected her. "We were fifty-fifty on four," I said. "You're the one working the money," I said, being honest about Riot's efforts. She smiled.

"I wish you would come back upstate with me," she said mixing emotion in our business. "Everyone who ever met you always remembers you. If I run into someone, they ask how you're doing."

"I gotta take care of Momma," I said. "Momma comes first." I wanted to be clear and Riot's eyes revealed that she got the message.

"Did you find a rehab for her? Otherwise you're gonna eat up all your profits," Riot said, trying to convince.

"Leave my fifty percent of our investment in," I said. "I wanna see it grow some more." I ignored the rehab talk.

"Okay, long as you know there is some risk involved," Riot warned.

"I trust you with our money," I said sincerely. Riot's eyes widened some.

"Trust is feelings and actions stretched out over time. Porsche, I loved when you said that to me," she said, seeming perfectly warm in the cold.

It seemed Riot preferred Manhattan over Brooklyn. Maybe it was because her first stop in Brooklyn was the Bed-Stuy projects. Maybe it was the furious fight I had with my cousin, or the encounter with Momma in the round cave. Whatever the case, it was midnight now. We were in lower Manhattan in the midst of some extra strange Halloween night parade. I was at ease in the mixture. There was so many things to pay attention to, no one was paying attention to me or us, especially the plenty of police patrolling.

Setting a date for our next meet up and re-up, Riot suggested, "Two months from tonight. I can flip the money good if I have sixty days just like this time." Soon as we were both bout to agree on it, we both realized that would be New Year's Eve. To avoid what we knew would be a police presence times one hundred, we switched it to January instead, and both looked like we thought that next year was a long way away.

"Let's take a picture together. Then let's take our photos apart," Riot suggested in front of one of the many money-making photographers milling in the midnight madness.

"Photos . . ." I repeated. "Should we?" I asked aloud but was really talking to myself.

"Yep, we should. It will just be one picture of a masked pretty kitty and one picture of an African white girl," Riot said. We laughed.

I rolled my black MAC lipstick over my lips to freshen up. I struck a dancer's pose under the photographer's powerful light and the glare of the street lamps. After the flash, I posed with Riot after she posed alone. She faced the camera without a mask or makeup. She held her head up, chin out and her blonde cornrows were glistening, as she wore what I now knew was her version of an African dress.

Chapter 35

Four hundred thirty-five days after I escaped lockdown, I picked up the cuffs and locked Momma's hands first and then her feet to an iron pipe connected to our steel radiator, which was cemented to the floor. She was kicking and cursing. Once she was locked, I stuffed a clean pair of gym socks in her mouth so no one would hear her yelling. It didn't matter. No one would hear her anyway. She came crawling into the underground after midnight, and Big Johnnie's store was closed. Still, I needed her to shut up. Through every episode of the crack house, her disappearances, her coming back wearing a hospital bracelet, her getting locked up for a few days, her reappearances, she used her "mother tone" against me, saying, "I'm the mother. You're the child." She would make me feel guilty for shit she did. Then she would make me feel guilty for pointing it out. She would promise me things, forget her promises, and call me a liar for reminding her of what they were. After a whole year, she still wouldn't talk straight to me, honestly. Everything was a joke or a scream or denial.

Out of all those days, 435 to be exact, she had spent only twenty-one nights with me, and, not really with me. I mean we were in the same room. I could see her, but I couldn't feel her or feel anything coming from her. She had me thinking crazy thoughts, like maybe I was adopted and that's why it was easy for her to treat me this way. On the coldest nights and the biggest holidays, I thought of dying, just fucking killing myself. I didn't because I wasn't sure how many days it would take her to come and discover my body. Maybe I would be dust by then and she would just sweep me under the bed or dump me in the trash, or worse, just leave me there.

"You're gonna listen to me now, Momma," I said, looking directly into her bulging eyes. "I promised to take care of you. So far it's only been you stopping me from caring for you," I said.

It seemed like Momma had something to say, but her teeth, tongue, and lips were just mashing down on the cotton socks. The few sounds that escaped were like notes from a harmonica.

"I wanna take you to see Poppa. He's locked down but he's not dead, thankfully . . . ," I said softly. "Remember when I bought you the bus ticket for a visitation to go up north with the other ladies? You know I wanted to ride up with you and see Poppa. You know I couldn't. You knew why. I took you to the bus stop myself where all of the ladies and families gathered to ride upstate. *You ditched me.* I don't know where you disappeared to so fast. I blew the whole afternoon looking for you, Momma," I explained. I wanted her to understand what had pushed me to this moment.

"I know you wanna see Poppa. I even know you wanna look good like you normally do, so Poppa can smile at you like he always did."

Momma's tears came spilling out. I had been crying already, so now at least we were feeling the same way. Before, it seemed like she wasn't feeling too much at all.

"Check these out, Momma." I showed her the Gucci heels that me and Elisha picked out together. I had told him how stylish Momma is, and that she needed an outfit to attend a special event. We had fun on Fifth Avenue in Manhattan that Friday. After I said that me and Momma wore the same dress size, but not shoes, Elisha told me, "Try on the dresses before you buy one."

I performed a fashion show for him, while the Gucci store salesperson grew more and more aggravated because we were unaccompanied kids. It's crazy how people think young and broke go together. It doesn't. At twelve years young I pulled out my money pile and hypnotized them. Used to seeing those plastic gold, platinum, or black credit cards, I knew my cash excited them and made them act right. These were the first fashions I spent *my* hard-earned money on. Since it was for Momma to go see Poppa, I knew it was worth it. Also, I thought Momma wouldn't visit Poppa, although her heart wanted to, unless she could do it like the caked-up Lana would do it.

Momma was squirming. I thought she wanted to say something

nice about the heels. But maybe she would say something mean? I rushed to pull the dress out from its cloth hanger bag. I held it against my body to show her, and pulled the heels near my feet to show her how perfectly the outfit goes together. After I knew that she could see that it was top shelf, I removed the socks from her mouth.

"Porsche, *that dress is gorgeous*," Momma said. "And, if you don't take these fucking cuffs . . ." I pushed the socks back in.

"So here's what we have to do, Momma," I said, like a girl putting together a grocery list. "We have to get you clean. Clean on the outside and inside. I'll be right here with you. Once you get clean, me and you could do almost anything. Momma, I have twenty thousand dollars."

Momma stopped squirming and resisting. I had her full attention now. "My money is not in here. I hid it, so you wouldn't be tempted. Once you get clean, we are gonna take care of everything we should've tooken care of a year ago," I promised her. It was the truth.

"Momma, can we work together?" I asked her, pulling the socks out.

"You lost your fucking mind," she shouted. I pushed the socks back in.

I picked up a piece of pink chalk so I could write on the small blackboard I purchased on Mr. Sharp's advice.

"Organize your thoughts, young Santiaga" Mr. Sharp once said to me. "After you organize your thoughts, organize your plans. Knock 'em out in steps, one by one," he said. "You have to have the discipline to get a plan done."

Mr. Sharp owned several businesses, but didn't own a computer. He said, "I don't trust 'em, don't need 'em." That worked out well for me because he needed someone to file and organize his papers. He said, "I used to keep all debts, numbers, and payments in my head. After age forty, a man who used to remember begins to forget. A tailor can never be comfortable with loose threads or sloppy stitches."

Now he needed someone to go down his residents list and match the rent checks received with the list. He needed someone to send out late payment notices. He needed someone to check over the building superintendent's work. For example, if a window had been reported broken, or a spill occurred, how long did it take the superintendent to respond, reply, and repair the situations? I became "Sharp's Runner." I would run right across the street and check things out. I only worked Mondays through Thursdays, three to six. Three hours a day was more than enough time to get Sharp's papers and errands in order.

Sharp said, "When a business owner gets older, he gotta figure out how to make his money work for him, instead of him working for his money." He told me I was his second set of eyes, hands, and feet. He paid me sixty dollars a day, not for any reason except cause he wanted to. From age eleven till twelve I was making $240 a week from Sharp, $130 per week from Big Johnnie. My sandwich money was separate from the weekly $130, and that little business was blowing up to be big. I had started a line of spicy sandwiches, using the spices that I learned about and cooked with. I'd label the Saran Wrap when it was spicy. I tested it out, and Big Johnnie kept ordering me to make more and more. I liked that people on the block didn't know who was making the sandwiches, except for the Baloney Boy who saw me in the first place. I made my meter money from all the businesses on my block, and cigarette money pushed my profits up like crazy.

I made a truce with the superintendent in Mr. Sharp's building that fattened my pockets some more.

"I don't want to see you get into any uncomfortable situation," I told him. "So, if I see a spill, broken glass, piss, or globs of dirty chewing gum, whatever, I'll clean it up for a fee. Then I'll assure Mr. Sharp that everything's good over here." I had only one hand on my hip when I told him.

"How much?" he asked.

"Five dollars each time I cover for you," I told him.

"Damn, that's too high," he said.

"It's a lot," I explained, "but on days when you be out and don't get back on time, when you really supposed to be working here at the building and on twenty-four-hour call, I'm making things convenient for you." I smiled sweetly. He agreed.

The superintendent was only one person out of the eighty-two apartments in the building who I earned money from for various services, even agreeing to walk one lady's two dogs at sunrise on week-days. I was awake anyway, just finishing up at Big Johnnie's.

I made a clay pot filled with chicken soup for a woman who I could hear coughing through her apartment door each day. She was so grateful once she got better she tried to give me some of her real jewelry. I wouldn't accept that cause I knew jewels were personal memories. I was waiting on my diamond set from Poppa. Until then, I wouldn't wear none. Since I rejected her jewelry, the lady tried to give me other stuff. I told her just pay me for those expensive organic ingredients and we even. She tried to get me to cook more food for her, but the cooking hustle would've tied up too much of my time. Time is money, and she couldn't afford me.

I emptied trash for seniors who didn't feel like it, supplied ciga-rettes, too, and received other perks and valuable gifts from people in the building who just seemed to like me, my work, and my manners.

After asking Mr. Sharp about the unmarked store on the block of businesses he owned, "the one filled with junk," I said.

"Those are antiques, not junk. I'm a collector," he confided.

"A collector?" I repeated. "Of what?" I asked.

"The most valuable things that the untrained eye either can't see or don't understand."

"If it's so valuable, why is the store always closed and empty?" I pushed.

"That's what I want people to think. I open it once a month for a night auction in the back room," he said.

"Auction?" I repeated.

"Yeah, that's when a small group of people who know the real worth of things come and bid big bucks for that 'junk' in my store." He laughed out two quick, cool sounds. "A pretty big player bought a music box from one of them auctions. He spent a small fortune get-ting one of my guys to get the box to play his favorite song instead of the tune it was already playing."

Then I knew why Mr. Sharp even bothered telling me about his private antique auction business. He was telling me a story about Poppa, without saying it was about Poppa. When Poppa gave Momma that music box that played an old Earth, Wind & Fire song, we all were amazed. Of course we had seen jewelry boxes before that played corny jingles. But, we had never seen a jewelry box that when you opened it up, played a badass song while a black ballerina spun round on one pretty black toe shoe!

Ignoring admitting out loud that Poppa was *my* poppa, I used Mr. Sharp's little story as an opportunity. "Your antique shop, let me clean it up for you, organize it, make it presentable. We'll hang a pretty curtain like the one you have here in The Golden Needle. Except, since we don't want everybody to know, we'll hang a black curtain."

"Whatever you want to do, my little moneymaking machine," Mr. Sharp said. But he was obviously the one with the real money pile, and he did an incredible job of not making it seem that way.

Mr. Sharp's lessons, plus my experience at hustling from being locked down, raked me in $1,100 a week on the average.

It was Elisha who taught me how to average numbers out and round 'em off. He didn't know about my hustles. He only saw me after school on Fridays. He taught me because he was nice like that, and besides, I had the habit of flipping through his books and asking questions so I could learn, catch up, keep up, compete, and outdistance the school kids.

I led Elisha to believe that I decided and registered at a junior high school in Manhattan because they specialized in fashion. It wasn't hard to convince him. I had original fly styles that Siri and I made up.

When I'd walk up to meet him at the market on Fridays, he would forever be surprised by my style, decorated denim, hand-designed T-shirts, all mixed in with the high fashions that Sharp got me in that one-day spree. Elisha was most amazed at a design I made in my hair out of one hundred red bobby pins. I wore my long ends loose at the bottom.

"You look Indian," Elisha said, touching the pins with his fingers.

"You mean Native?" I asked him.

"Not the dot Indian," he said. "Woo-woo, the ones with the feathers." He hopped around like he was doing a whacked-out Native dance. I hit him on his shoulder. "You're so ignorant, and you go to the best private school!"

"I'm just joking," he said, smiling.

When I was with Elisha for five or six hours only on Fridays was the only time I actually forgot about the hole in my heart.

My mind returned back to Momma. On the blackboard I wrote a list so she could keep track of time. Also I wanted her to see when she did good. I'd make the check mark to show our plan was really working. That's what I needed when I was locked up. I needed to know what I had to do to keep the authorities out my face. I needed to know in advance what the punishments were for things. I needed to be able to see an ending to hurt, even if it was way, way down the road.

1. Clean the drugs out of Momma's pretty body.
2. Keep the drugs out of Momma's pretty body.
3. Write letters to Poppa and Winter.
4. Find Mercedes and Lexus.
5. Get a new apartment with windows, a telephone, and computer.
6. Bring home Mercedes and Lexus.
7. Get Momma a new driver's license.
8. Buy Momma a new car.
9. Go see Poppa and Winter.

After I made the list, I felt panic reading it. I worried that the list was in the wrong order. Mercedes and Lexus should be at the top. No, writing Winter and Poppa was easiest. No, nothing could be done without healing Momma first. I knew that. I had erased and rearranged the list, until I decided that the order didn't matter. We would do it all as swiftly as possible, with healing Momma at the top.

Momma was sweating and shaking. I stayed calm. It didn't matter how bad it got, as long as she was here with me and unable to trick or abandon me again. Filling a large bowl with cool to warm water, I got a washcloth and began cleaning Momma's face first. Slowly, I wiped and sometimes scrubbed every inch of her skin, even the soles of her feet. Removing her filthy clothes with a scissor was easy. They were not clothes designed for Momma. They were not nearly good enough. I put 'em in the trash. I rubbed shea butter on Momma's cleaned, ashy, and bruised skin, everywhere. I cleaned my hands, and then put shea butter on Momma's chapped lips, same as lipstick. When I gave Momma some spring water to drink, she spit it back at me. I wrapped Momma in a blanket and put a new pair of socks in her mouth. "It's 3:00 a.m. I have to run up to Big Johnnie's to work," I said to her.

At Big Johnnie's you would expect that since I cleaned up each day, there might be nothing much to do besides make the sandwiches. Not true. It never failed that a full day of customers moving up and down each aisle led to many things being out of place. I imagined that he had three or four customers who came every day, didn't buy nothing, but went about touching every item purposely pushing it out of place. In my mind, one of 'em was a thief who sometimes would almost get away, but then lost confidence when he caught himself in a deadlock stare with Big Johnnie and his big and small guns.

Big Johnnie was licensed to carry weapons because he was a business owner. Or at least, that's what he once told me. In that same conversation, which was rare cause I hardly ever saw him, I told him he should get a lottery machine in his store. Then it would stay packed morning, noon, and night. He said that to get one of those machines, "the government wants to stick a microscope up my ass then shove a microphone down my throat. All of that and you only get a few cents on every ticket sold."

I said, "Not if you sell the winning ticket. Then, I bet you get a percentage!"

He smiled and said, "You're smarter than any of these knucklehead kids in this neighborhood." I ignored that comment and told him that I already had a winning number. "Oh really?" he said. "What is it, your birthdate?"

"No, it's just my lucky number but I'm not old enough to play it yet."

"There's all kinds of ways to play numbers, not only Lotto."

"Okay, you want to play it for me?" I asked him.

"Sure, why not. I'll play it and just subtract it from your pay."

"I know that, but will you pay me when I win?" I asked him.

"What kind of fella would I be to cheat a young girl who works so hard and cooks better than my ex-wife?" he asked. I told him my number: 1111. He promised to play it for me, put it in, and leave it in.

"Okay straight, box, and combinate it," I said. I didn't know what all that meant either, but I heard it enough before, so I said it to increase my luck.

When I returned downstairs, Momma had peed on the floor. I wasn't bothered by it. I had peed in many forbidden places when I was a captive. I cleaned it, changed her blanket, and gave her some water, still worried about her getting too dehydrated. She spitted it at me again and said she had to shit. I sat thinking for some seconds. Next I pulled out the heavy chain and lock I got from Riot and added it on so Momma could move around into the bathroom. The whites of Momma's eyes turned blood red with anger as she sat staring at the chain. "Sorry, Momma, I can't release you. I want to, but I can't."

Since she wouldn't drink water, I soaked a washcloth with spring water and put it in her mouth hoping that the moisture would ease down her throat. It was 6:06 a.m. now. So, Big Johnnie would be opening up his store. Momma's mouth had to be stuffed so she couldn't use her voice to alert anyone upstairs.

"Let's sleep now, Momma, for a little while." I sat down beside her in a way I wasn't able to since we had arrived here. Already I was enjoying her body warmth and leaning on her. Already I felt relaxed in ways that I never did when I was alone, or even when I was down here with Siri. Without dancing in Momma's empty closet until my body collapsed, without playing music that I loved, without R. Kelly singing me into sweet slumber, or Siri massaging and humming me into a reluctant rest, I slept in seconds, leaning comfortably on Momma. It was morning. Everyone else in the world may be awakening. However, in the space below the floor there were no windows. The sun never rose or set down here.

A foul smell snatched me from my dreams and nightmares. I awoke covered in chunks of mush. Momma had vomited on me. It was still slimy, leading me to believe that it had just happened.

"You crazy bitch. Whose daughter are you? Take these cuffs off me right now, or I'll start screaming. As much as I hate police, somebody better come pull your ass up out of here before I kill you," Momma said.

I didn't want to, but it was time for the duct tape. I taped Momma's mouth shut. I was teary-eyed. At least now she was sort of recognizing me as her daughter. At the same time she was threatening to kill me. I acted like I was searching for the keys to the cuffs, "Hold on, Momma, wait a minute, Momma," I said. Then, "Where did I put those cuff keys!" I came up behind her where she could not turn, move, or see, and it was done. Her mouth was sealed shut.

After cleaning Momma and cleaning the floor and packing up the dirty blankets and clothes and showering myself and dressing for the day, I realized I shouldn't leave Momma, but it was Friday. Time to meet up with Elisha, the only real joy in my young life.

Chapter 36

Siri said, "I'll go and meet Elisha for you." I stood thinking for some seconds. I started feeling maybe it was okay for her to go, maybe not. I love Siri. She has never left my side through prison, the reservation, my return to Brooklyn, and up until this moment.

"What will you wear?" I asked her.

"Give me something super pretty," she said.

"Why?" I asked her.

"I like to feel good sometimes, too," she said.

I listened to her and considered her words. Usually she is doing my hair and choosing my clothes and rubbing moisturizers on my skin and singing to me. I looked at the dresses I had not worn yet. They were dresses Mr. Sharp said "make ladies look like ladies, beautiful flowers." I chose one for Siri to wear.

"Okay, you can go. Please tell Elisha I'm really busy today. So, I can't make it."

"I'll tell him," she said softly.

"But Siri, take the shopping cart and this laundry bag with you pretty please, and wash these things for Momma. I really need them. And don't come home late!" I insisted.

"I'll do the laundry, but Momma doesn't like me. I know because you never even introduced us after all of this time," Siri said.

"She's not the real Momma, Siri, not until we get the drugs out of her. Then I'll introduce you to a lady you will love, who will also love you back."

"Okay." She giggled. "I won't be late or do anything wrong. Remember you like him. But I like you best of all, more than anyone."

Soon as Siri left, I thought about how I had given her the bag of laundry to mess up her meeting with Elisha a little bit. Maybe he would spend time wondering about the stinky smell in her bag instead of seeing how really pretty Siri is. Then, if he asked her out to any place new, she would have to say no, she couldn't go out with him, because she had to go to the Laundromat with her shopping cart and dirty things. This way, I would have let him know that Ivory didn't mean to leave him standing there waiting for me, which I had never done to him. I would have accomplished keeping him and Siri from going out on a real date. Third, I would have Momma's laundry all clean and folded, in case it got cold on this late October night.

Momma was looking at me strangely, like she was crazy or like she thought I was crazy. I Love You Momma, I gestured with my arms wide open. "I hope you're hungry. I'm gonna cook for you."

* * *

"What happened?" I asked Siri seven hours later. She came down the cement stairs, the cart wheels clanking at 10:00 p.m. She was hiding her smile, bursting with energy.

"I cleaned everything," she said. "I put detergent, this much . . ." She gestured with her fingers. "And I put fabric softener this much . . ." She gestured again. It seemed as though she had used more fabric softener than detergent. I walked to the cement stairs to meet her and pulled the cart the rest of the way. I opened the laundry bag, bent over it, smelled inside. It smelled pretty like lavender, and like the inside of the flower shop three doors down.

"Good job, Siri. How much did they charge for the machines and which Laundromat did you go to?" I asked her.

"I didn't go to the Laundromat. I didn't have to," Siri said.

"What do you mean?" I asked her sharply.

"I went to Elisha's apartment. He offered. He said, don't waste your money. We can wash it down the block at my house. He even pulled the cart for me."

"Oh no!" I said, throwing my hands up in the air.

"What's wrong?" Siri asked.

"I never go to Elisha's house," I told her.

"Why not? It's really close to the organic market. It's a really nice apartment, too. I met his mother."

"What did she say?" I asked Siri. I was at the beginning stages of getting red.

"She said that I was even prettier than I was the day she first met me in the market. She admired my dress and asked me to spin around so she could get a good look at it. She even liked my Joan and David heels. She asked me why I never came by for dinner when Elisha offered so many times. Then she turned to Elisha and said, 'You did invite her. Didn't you?' Elisha said, 'Many times . . .' She asked me about Momma and if I was going to keep her all to myself or bring her over to dinner to meet Elisha's family."

"What did you say?!" I asked, my voice growing a bit louder and losing patience.

"I said that we could set a dinner date and Momma would come, but it had to be a couple of weeks from now because Momma had the flu. I did good, right?" Siri asked me. I thought about it. I didn't want to be red at Siri. That was unfamiliar to me.

"You did good," I said, my voice softening some. "Momma will be okay in a couple of weeks. Right, Momma?" I turned and asked Momma. She rolled her eyes at me.

"Help me brew some tea for Momma," I told Siri.

"Okay I'll help, but why is Momma shaking like that?" Siri asked, looking frightened.

"She's okay. Big Johnnie is about to close for the night. We'll remove the tape, wash Momma's face, and give her this tea. This tea will make Momma's muscles relax. After she gets used to having the tea, we will feed her the chicken broth with the chopped garlic," I explained to Siri.

The truth was that I was using a "detoxification recipe" that I pieced together from my lessons with NannaAnna and from the small book section at the organic market. I had all kinds of ingredients, many of which were very difficult to locate. With Elisha's help, I found passion flower, kavakava root, skullcap, valerian root, licorice root, Siberian ginseng, and so much more. I also was using what NannaAnna had given me in her magical sack gift when we first met: shea butter, aloe vera leaf, lavender, and a special mix of sleeping tea that could put a person to sleep for a short or long period of time. Wrongly used, it could put a person to sleep permanently.

"Okay, I hope it works," Siri said.

"Me *too*. It will work, Siri," I said confidently. When I removed the duct tape, I ripped it off real fast so it wouldn't hurt Momma like it would if I peeled it off slowly. Momma gasped for air.

"Water," she said. I ran and got it, thrilled that now Momma was asking for water herself, instead of spitting it on me. I held the bottle to Momma's dry lips and helped her drink without choking. She drank it all. She cleared her throat.

"Who the fuck are you talking to?" Momma asked me.

"Huh?" I said, really not understanding.

"Who the fuck have you been talking to for the past hour?" Momma asked.

"Oh, sorry, Momma," I said. "She is Siri, my closest friend ever." I introduced Momma. Silly Siri curtsied. I laughed.

"Hello, Mrs. Momma," Siri said.

"Oh, my fucking god," Momma said angrily.

"Momma, Big Johnnie's is closed now. No matter how much noise you make, no one can hear you. All the shops are closed. Let's be friends at least at night. Talk nice to me, please. And be nice to my friend Siri."

I begged, sort of.

"Let's be friends at night!" Momma said. "Just how long does your crazy ass plan on keeping me locked up down here?"

I walked over to the blackboard and I pointed. "Momma, step one is for you to get clean. I will know when you are clean. You'll be nice to me like you always was before. You'll talk right and look right. You'll be eating right and drinking right. *Then* I can trust you," I said. Momma made a horrible face, stuck her tongue all the way out down below her chin. She began to scream and holler. It didn't matter. No one could hear her.

"Siri and I made this tea for you. It's important for you to drink it," I said.

"I don't want it. I'm not drinking that. I know what I wanna drink!" Momma said.

"Pinch her nose," Siri whispered, her lips pressed against my ear in secret-telling mode. I squeezed Momma's nose and held it. Her mouth dropped open automatically. I poured warm tea down her throat with one hand and held her head tilted back some with the other hand so she couldn't do anything but swallow. It went in. It went down. I was relieved. The valerian root tea did what nothing else could. It had Momma sleeping like an infant. I washed her with a damp washcloth sprinkled with Dr. Bronner's Peppermint Soap. I cleaned a deep-sleeping Momma from head to toe. Then I opened a tub of shea butter. It looked thick as wax, but in my hands it melted the same way butter does. I began spreading the shea butter on the soles of Momma's feet. Her feet had been swollen, bruised, ashy, and hard. I massaged her feet nicely to keep her heart from racing too fast. These are the gifts and lessons that NanaAnna gave to me. How could she know what a bitter fight I would have ahead of me?

After massaging Momma's feet, which changed her face from its irritable scowl to a look of deep peace, I washed my hands. Next, I massaged the shea butter everywhere on her body. I shaved her armpits and combed her hair. I chopped up raw garlic and dropped it inside two socks. I placed the socks on each of Momma's feet as she slept. I sprinkled small pieces of garlic all over her body, even her neck so she could inhale it. I placed a sheet over Momma first, then a blanket.

I flipped through the old songs I had collected for Momma. For me, part of getting Momma back, was getting Momma's stuff back. She had an incredible record collection. I remembered the colorful and unique album designs from back in Brooklyn. I even memorized some of the lyrics to songs she played over and over again. I collected the songs by memory, spending some evenings in the record shop singing a few lines of each record I recalled Momma playing and loving. The older shop owner would "name the tune" and then tell me who performed it. Then he would sell it to me. It seemed like the record shop owner took a liking to me playing this game with him. Slowly, I had already gathered more than fifty-two of her favorite songs.

I turned the music on soft and low. I was playing a song titled "Sukiyaki," performed by a group named A Taste of Honey. Momma would like this song if she only could remember herself.

* * *

Siri and I sat on the bed together.

"So, what was his apartment like?" I asked her.

"Very nice and really big. It takes up two floors," Siri said. "He's not rich like you thought he was, though."

"How do you know?" I asked. But I didn't really care that Elisha was not rich, not anymore. I had made a good amount of money on my own, and Elisha meant more to me than money, which meant he means a lot.

"Well, you thought he owned that brownstone. But there are four floors and two families living in the two apartments above his," Siri said.

"Maybe his family are owners and they make a pile of money from the renters upstairs," I guessed.

"Nope, his family is renting, too, and he goes to that rich private school on a scholarship because he's really freaking smart. He has an older brother named Azaziah and an older sister named Sheba and, of course, his mom and dad. Strange names, right?" Siri asked me.

"You met his dad?" I asked, surprised. Elisha never mentions him.

"Yep, but his dad didn't say nothing, just kept reading the newspaper like the house was empty, when we were all in there!" Siri said.

"And what did you two do while the laundry was washing and drying?" I asked. Siri giggled.

"Well, he kept saying my name, Siri, Siri, Siri!" she said, smiling.

"Why?" I asked.

"He seemed to think it was really funny that I insisted he call me Siri. Then he suddenly agreed."

"He asked me if I wanted to do a little play acting. I told him no, but we can sing," Siri explained.

"He got really excited and asked me if I needed music or if he should play his guitar. I told him I did not need music. He said let's go to my room. We were walking down the hall to his room. His mother said, 'Make sure you two keep that bedroom door open!' He agreed, but when we got inside his bedroom, he closed it at first."

"Why did he close it?" I asked Siri.

"I'm not sure but his room was nice. He has his own bathroom.

And, he had a a picture of you by his bed from last year when you were dressed up like an alley cat. I saw it. We should dress up in some different costumes again even if it's not the holiday," Siri suggested. "That was fun and you looked so nice, like you were a real cat in an exciting movie," she dramatized.

"Get back to Elisha . . ." I pushed.

"Well, he said that he couldn't believe that I was going to sing him a song for the first time in more than a year after we first met," Siri told me.

"And what did you say?" I asked Siri.

"I apologized to him," Siri said.

"For what?" I asked.

"I confessed that it was me, Siri, and not Ivory who pushed the shopping cart into him that day. I told him he shouldn't blame you for the way it happened," Siri explained. "Then Elisha asked me, 'Siri, why did you do it?' I told him, 'Because I knew that Ivory wanted to meet you and I wanted to make that happen real quick before you disappeared.'"

"What did he say?" I asked, my whole body shivering with curiosity.

"He didn't say anything else about it, but he looked like he understood. He asked me if I wanted to sing sitting down or standing up. I told him he could lie down and I could stand up. So he laid on his bed like this with his hands behind his head and his head on his pillow," Siri acted it out. "I stood next to his bed like this. I smoothed out the pretty dress you lent me, and got ready. Then Elisha jumped up really fast!"

"He asked if I minded if he recorded it so he could listen to it even when I wasn't there," Siri confessed. "He took me upstairs to his father's 'music room.' It was filled with everything music, albums, CDs, microphones on mic stands, and all kind of equipment."

"Did you let him record you?" I asked with disbelief.

"Just once. I only sang to him once. He was sitting in a leather chair that leans back. He had his feet up like this. He looked really comfortable. The room was so pretty and peaceful. It was super quiet. I thought of you, Porsche, and I sang, 'Lovin' You,' by Minnie Riperton. First I hummed the melody, then I sang the song," Siri explained.

I mashed my face in the pillow and muffled my scream. I couldn't believe what Siri had allowed. That song was one of Momma's favorites. I had just played it the night before. Siri was quick. I don't know how she memorized the words to that song so swiftly.

"And what happened?" I asked.

"Well, right afterwards, he stood up and touched my hand. He put my hand against his chest," Siri said.

I, Porsche L. Santiaga, threw myself to the floor. Siri looked at me lying there.

"Are you okay, Porsche?" she asked truly innocently.

"Then what happened?" I asked Siri in a loud whisper.

"Well, my hand was lying there like this." Siri put her hand on my breast. "Then Elisha said to me, 'Can you feel that?'"

"I answered him, 'Yes.'"

"Then Elisha asked me, 'What do you feel'?"

Then I told Elisha, "I feel your heart racing."

"Oh . . ." I dragged the sound out from my gut. "Then what?" I asked Siri.

"Then his mom came in without knocking and she said, 'Elisha, it's not like you to disobey me. Even though you are thirteen, you still have to respect what I say.' Then Elisha apologized to his mom and said he had the door closed only because he was recording. But by that time I moved my hand from his chest. We kept the music door open. We were in there listening to music. He knows all kinds of songs that I never ever heard of. He played a couple of songs that have nice-sounding instruments and no singers. Then he let me choose some songs. Right before we left to go fold Momma's laundry, he played a song and said it was for me."

"What song!" I yelled.

"'Adore,' by Prince.

I met his older sister and his older brother. Elisha is the baby. It seemed like the whole time, they were taking turns checking on us. They didn't have to check. I know you like him, and I like you Porsche," Siri promised.

Chapter 37

Three more days came and went of the same sweating, vomiting, shaking, pissing, shitting, washing, and feeding before Momma finally stopped cursing at me. On the fourth night, she called me gently by my full and right name, Porsche Luxurious Santiaga.

We ate together. She was tired of water, teas, and soups. She especially hated the organic vegetable juices. So I prepared wheat pasta in a thick, homemade tomato sauce. She wanted fried fish and fries. I told her I would bring some fresh fish back from work when I was done and clean and cook it for her as long as she ate it with a salad and piece of fruit. I promised I wouldn't duct tape her as long as she stayed calm during the daylight hours. I told her, "Momma, you got to move around, do a little exercise, so your blood can circulate. We can even dance together when you are feeling better."

Momma asked me politely that night, "When can I get out of these cuffs and chains?"

I said, "When we can trust one another again."

Dragging the box of unopened letters over to Momma, I said, "I know it's boring being trapped. If it's okay with you, Momma, and whenever you are ready, could you please open these letters so we can rescue Mercedes and Lexus from wherever they are?"

"Wherever they are, it's better than here, don't you think?" Momma said. "Do you think me, you, and the twins could live down here together? It's bad enough just you and me," she said. Momma's words were bitter, but at least she wasn't screaming no more.

"We can afford an apartment, Momma, I work. When you get better, you can work, too."

"You must think the twins are still babies. What year is this?" Momma asked.

"1998," I answered swiftly.

"Winter was born in '77. You were born in '86, and the twins were born in '89," Momma said. "So they're . . ." Momma calculated. I was so excited Momma's brain and memory was both working. Now, if we could only fix her broken heart and bring all of her natural feelings back.

"They're nine years old now," Momma said.

"No matter what age, Momma. They're ours and family should stay together," I said with my truest feelings.

"I guess in some dream world somewhere, 'family should stick together,'" Momma muttered. She shifted through the letters and chose one to open.

By the end of the week, she had all the papers opened, sorted, and read. She circled all of the numbers she needed to call, and names of people she needed to speak to, to get information on the twins. When she was fully recovered, I would uncuff and unchain her, and we would walk up those cement stairs together for the first time and into the sun.

I laid a pen and paper on the floor for Momma.

"Write Poppa," I requested softly. "I wrote his address for you in case you forgot."

"I know his address!" Momma said with attitude, revealing some traces of the meanness still in her. "You think he's a god or a king, don't you?" Momma asked me.

"He's my poppa," was all I answered.

"He's not only your poppa!" she snapped.

"I know. Winter is his favorite, and the twins were his babies, but I'm his daughter, too," I said, feeling bad for having to say that. Why couldn't she just treat me the same as my sister?

"Listen to what I'm telling you!" she said in her mother tone. "Your father has a son. He named him after himself, Ricky Santiaga Jr. Your father had another woman. Bitch thought she was better than me." Momma was looking angry-faced again.

"Where is he?" I asked. "Where is my brother?"

"Hell if I know. You might run into him on the streets. Somebody should've said something. Brothers and sisters not know-ing one another could be out there fucking each other!" Momma was mad.

I hoped by her saying all this, she was somehow squeezing out her hurt.

"I tell you one thing. Don't waste your time giving your whole heart to no man. A woman always loves him a thousand times more than he loves her."

I didn't say nothing, just let Momma's words swirl around my head and heart.

* * *

"Should I go again?" Siri asked me on Friday.

I was worn out from all of my jobs: Big Johnnie's, Mr. Sharp's, the meter duty, the cigarettes, and Momma! In fact, the other jobs were easy to me. Momma weighed a ton.

"Siri, do you like Elisha?" I asked her.

"I like you, Porsche," Siri said softly and sincerely like she always does.

"I know you like me. But do you also like Elisha?" I asked her, looking into her pretty eyes.

"He's nice. His skin is really nice. His hair is so nice. His teeth are so white. His body is . . ."

"Stop!" I interrupted her.

"But, Porsche, he's yours! The nicest thing about him is how he feels about you. He wants to take care of you," she said.

"Siri, no kissing, no touching or anything like that . . . ," I told her.

"We never did any of that with Elisha," Siri said.

"And we still shouldn't," I said firmly. "We can't give him our whole heart," I warned her.

"You can give him yours, Porsche. He loves you more than Momma loves you," Siri said, poking another hole in my already dam-aged heart. She saw my hurt expression and came to hug me.

"No touching, no kissing. I promise, I won't, but I think *you should*," Siri urged me.

By the time Siri returned, Momma still had not wrote one word on the page for Poppa.

"How about a letter to Winter?" I proposed. Momma looked blank. "Winter didn't do anything wrong to you," I said.

"How would you know?" Momma asked me.

"What then? What did Winter do wrong?" I demanded to know. I was in tears and angry at my tears.

"She was laughing at me," Momma said.

"Huh?" I asked.

"Winter didn't do anything wrong except she was laughing at me. I didn't see it at first. Looking back now, I see it, clearly. I'm sure," Momma said in her mother tone. "Winter had everything that come from me. I shared everything I had with her, gave her everything. She didn't share with me. When things turned fucked up, she laughed at me. She didn't save me."

"I did!" I told Momma anxiously. "And I will," I promised Momma again. She ignored me as though it wasn't possible for her to believe one word if it was sprinkled with love or trust, or if was coming from my tongue.

Maybe Winter knew that even if she gave you everything she had, you still wouldn't love her. Maybe Winter saw that after Poppa had a son with another lady, you were determined not to love none of us no more, I thought to myself.

Chapter 38

At 8 a.m. on the twenty-first day I removed the chains and cuffs, two hours after I finished working at Big Johnnie's. Momma had gained some weight back. In the dim light of the underground, her skin was glowing from the daily treatments I gave her. The shea butter had softened and healed her skin. The insides of the aloe vera leaf, which I smeared on the cuts I cleaned on the first night, had caused them not to scar. The whites of Momma's eyes were clear now. Even her hair, that I washed and braided many nights, looked a lot healthier.

Momma didn't run. She showered herself alone for the first time, and put on one of the dresses I had purchased for her recovery. In her new shoes and coat, which was really attractive, but not as badass as the Gucci outfit I got her, Momma looked familiar to me. We climbed the cement stairs together and pushed open the iron floor doors and walked into the sun. Momma threw her hands up to shield her eyes from the sun.

"Here Momma, use these." I handed her my sunglasses.

"It can't be!" Big Johnnie said when he saw Momma walking past the front door of his store. He was standing there, probably looking out for the deliveryman.

"You know it is!" Momma said, stopping for one second and striking a pose. I waved to Big Johnnie, linked arms with Momma and kept walking on to Esmeralda's.

"Make Auntie look nice!" I told Esmeralda after greeting her.

"Oh. It's nice to meet you," Esmeralda said in her thick accent.

She looked at Momma as though she might've seen her before.

Then she let it slide and serviced Momma nicely because she was with me.

* * *

"Perfecto!" Esmeralda said when she finished, spraying some spritz on Momma's hair. She pulled out her big handheld mirror so Momma could check herself out, all angles. Momma was touching her skin while looking in the mirror. She kept staring at me, then at herself as though maybe she wasn't sure. I walked over and paid Esmeralda. Momma's eyes watched the money leaving my hand. Additionally, I handed Esmeralda my bags of quarters after I pulled out a fistful.

"I'll be back, I have to take Auntie somewhere. If I'm late . . ."

"Okay, *mami*," Esmeralda said.

I dropped the quarters that I held in my hand in each of my customer's parking meters as we left.

* * *

"The twins have been adopted. There, that's it. It's finished," Momma said as she came outside of the office building where I was standing and waiting for her. Brooklyn Family Court and all of those marbled out buildings were all "official" type of places, so of course I didn't go inside.

"What do you mean, it's finished?" I asked, feeling panicked. "We can still see them, can't we?" I asked, as I followed Momma. She was walking really fast.

"Depends on how bad you want to see 'em!"

"What do you mean?" I pushed.

"The funny name person who adopted them said it's okay for the mother to make contact except *he lives in Africa!*" Momma said.

"Africa?" I repeated.

"Yeah, in the goddamn jungle!" Momma said. "Who the fuck would let a man take two little girls in the first place? Then of all places, out to the jungle?" Her eyes began bulging, all over again.

I didn't know what to say. I didn't have no idea about Africa, what country it was, where it was located, or how to go about getting there. I didn't think the jungle was a bad place unless they were in the jungle with a bad man. I shivered in the November cold air. My mind was moving in a dark direction. Pictures of myself waking up, a young girl in a strange place, checking in between my thighs, pushing a finger up into my pussy to see if I had been molested or raped flashed through my mind.

"What's his name?" I asked momma. "The man who adopted the twins?" I asked. Instead of saying a name, Momma pulled out a business card, flipped it around, and started spelling something.

"B-i-l-a-l-o-d-e, how that sound?" She had her hands on her hips asking me.

"Can I see?" I took the card.

"*Bilal Ode*," I repeated out loud first. Then it swirled in my mind repeating fifty-six times. I thought to myself, *I've heard that name before, but when and where?*

"Your father signed off on the adoption papers," Momma said. It was the only sentence she said as we rode the train together.

At 3:00 p.m. Momma and I were standing in front of the organic market as Elisha approached. He had a look on his face like he wasn't sure. I guess he was surprised to see me after being with Siri two Fridays in a row. And I was standing with a second person, which I had never done before.

"Elisha, this is Momma," I said before realizing that I should've said Auntie. Seeing him forced the truth out of me naturally. I was screaming at myself on the inside.

"Mrs.?" Elisha said, extending his hand.

"Santiaga!" Momma said a little boldly. I had not used that last name since my escape, only between me, Riot, and Siri.

"Nice to meet you, Ms. Santiaga," Elisha said calmly with excited confidence. "Should we take lunch together?" He directed his question to Momma.

"Dangerous," Momma said.

"Momma?" I asked.

"He's too handsome and got manners, too! *Hmph*, a handsome charmer," she said, like it was a big problem.

"Ladies tend to like me," Elisha said, smiling. I hit his shoulder so he could straighten up and act right. "What? It's true," he said seriously as we entered the market to the café sitting space.

"What would Ms. Santiaga like to have?" Elisha asked Momma.

"Coffee and something sweet," Momma said.

"Herbal tea and a raisin wheat muffin for Momma," I said. "No sugar!" I called behind him; I knew coffee and sugar were no good for Momma. It would start her back having intense cravings, and one thing would lead to another. A trail of caffeine, to a trail of sugar, to a trail of cocaine; the thought alone had my head hurting.

When Elisha returned with the market designer bag stuffed with lots of stuff, he placed the herbal tea and raisin bran muffin on the table first.

"That must be for Porsche cause that's not what I ordered," Momma said in her bossy mother tone. I put my hand over my forehead and dropped my head down. I had asked Momma a hundred times not to call me Porsche in front of anyone else, and to call me Ivory instead.

"You're right, Ms. Santiaga. I have your order right here." Elisha pulled out a hot coffee in a paper cup marked coffee and a hot cross bun drizzled with vanilla frosting and confectionary sugar.

"That's right," Momma said. "A man's supposed to give a woman what she wants." She pulled the cup over and bit into the sweet bun. Elisha sat down, shaking a carrot juice for himself and peeling the cap off.

"Porsche," he said to me. I didn't lift my eyes. I ignored. "Porsche," he called me again.

"Why aren't you answering him?" Momma said. "That's not polite." I looked at Momma, couldn't believe the game she was playing against me.

"Siri," Elisha said to me. "Siri!" I wouldn't lift my head. Why was he calling me her name?

"Ivory," Elisha said. I picked my head up and looked at him.

"How many names you got?" Momma asked.

"I like all of them," Elisha said, still looking my way.

"So, you like pretending," Momma asked, or accused.

"Of course, I'm a movie director. Porsche is gonna be a worldwide movie star," Elisha said without laughter and with unbreakable confidence.

"Oh, really," Momma said dryly. "It must be nice to be young."

"I'm serious," Elisha said. "Ivory is a great dancer. Siri is an amazing singer. I just met Porsche today," Elisha said, turning away from convincing Momma and back towards me.

"What can Porsche do?" he asked me.

"Oh, believe me! She can do way more than the other two!" Momma laughed.

"I see you prefer Porsche," Elisha said to Momma.

"She's the only one of them I know!" Momma said. "It's the name her father gave her. And Porsche *is the dancer.* You better believe that if you don't believe nothing else. I don't know what Ivory does," Momma said.

"She cries a lot," Elisha said, without a smile.

I felt naked and panicked beneath the weight of Momma's words. Elisha had always tried to make me happy after seeing some seconds of my sorrows. Back when I was eleven, he gave me the Godivas. Every time he saw me since then, he always brought me something tiny and sweet. He'd enjoy me till my tears appeared, then he'd give me something I never had before, some slices of mango, butterscotch, kiwi, some balls of tamarind, sherbert, or sorbet. Once, he even fed me a teaspoon of honey that made my lips squeeze in and my tongue dance.

"Elisha, we gotta go, sorry," I interrupted.

"Hold up, wait a minute," Elisha said, stopping me.

"I want to buy you something first," Elisha said.

"I'm not hungry," I said, wrapping up the muffin and then taking hold of the paper teacup.

"It's not food," Elisha said, looking into me, to calm me some.

"That's okay," I said to him. "Momma, can you step out, please?" I asked. She had trapped me in the booth.

Momma turned on me. She went full blast with her mother tone, "When a man says he wants to buy you something, *you let him buy you something.*"

* * *

At an AT&T counter in Albee Square Mall in Brooklyn, Elisha brought me a new Motorola Startac cell phone for $395 as Momma watched his thirteen-years-young man hands count out the cash and pay. He handed me the new box and said, "Now I have your number."

"That's what I'm talking about." Momma had an outburst. "Take it!" she said too loudly and striking a bizarre pose.

"It's cool, Ivory, this money is from my movie camera savings fund. I have to save ten thousand dollars to buy the camera to finish my first film. You are my muse."

"Muse?" me and Momma both said.

"My inspiration," he said. "You're worth much more than any cell phone." I took the phone from his hands. "Charge it and keep it on," Elisha said.

Even though I could afford any cell phone available and every cell phone on that counter, I didn't have ID, didn't know a Social Security number and name I could have used without telling on myself, much less an address. I saw that Elisha used his family plan, his address and details, and just paid for my cell phone unit himself. The gesture had my heart, with the two holes in it, thumping.

"My mother invited you for dinner, Mrs. Santiaga. Even Porsche's father is invited if you want to have him come," Elisha said, his parting words. Momma was just staring off into the distance after the "Poppa invite."

* * *

"So that's the boy who you like?" Momma asked me. "I'm glad you have someone. You're too focused on me. Yeah, that's one you will marry. I'm a hundred percent dead on," she said. "That's how I was, too," she continued, speaking about her young self. "I was with your father from fourteen to thirty-two. That's when they came and stole him away from me, saddest night of my life. Now I'm thirty-six. Even though he ain't here, I'm still his *only wife*. I had four of his children. No other bitch could claim that."

"Momma, are you ready to go see Poppa? You're right. You are his *only wife*. That's why you should never give up on him." I was trying to build Momma's confidence.

"I'm as ready as I'm ever gonna be. It's now or never," she said.

"We'll get up tomorrow early enough to catch the prison bus. I'll pack you a lunch, go with you to the bus stop, buy you a ticket, and watch you get on. I'll stay there until the bus doors close and the bus pulls off. I'll stand there watching till I can't see the bus no more. Then I'll be there at the end of the night to meet you even before your bus is scheduled to return so we can go home together." Momma hugged me.

"Don't care too much, Porsche. Every person you meet will use it against you." I was excited in those seconds, I couldn't concentrate on friends or enemies or suspicions. I was wrapped up in Momma's hug.

* * *

My new cell phone rang for the first time around 10 p.m. that same Friday night. "Hello," I answered. There was a pause, an exhale, then . . .

"Damn, I wasn't sure what to call you," Elisha said.

"You know me and I know you," I told him.

"Where are you?" he asked.

"Outside walking," I said.

"With who?" he asked.

"Momma," I said.

"Oh . . . ," he said. "I'm feeling a little cheated," he said.

"How come?" I asked.

"You owe me a do-over on our date today," he said.

I was silent.

"How about tomorrow?" Elisha asked.

"Okay," I said.

"I knew you missed me, too," he said without laughing.

"I do," I said, before I could stop myself from saying the truth.

"I have an audition early morning so let's meet around noon. Is that cool?" he asked.

"Yes," I answered. "But how come you always have an audition if you're going to be a movie director, not an actor?"

"Acting jobs pay good money," Elisha said confidently. "That's how I was able to buy the majority of the movie equipment that I own now. I'm saving up for the camera. It's my one last big thing." He sounded excited.

"After the auditions, do you ever get the job?" I asked him.

"I see I'm gonna have to buy you a television next," he said. "If you had one you would know *I get the jobs*."

"Oh, sorry. I don't have time for the television. How much do you have so far in your $10,000 camera fund," I asked curiously.

"I had $2,800. After today, I have $2,400. But that's not for you to worry about," he said.

"I'm not, you'll do it. I can tell," I told him.

"Alright, tomorrow then," he said. "Noon?"

"Wait . . . ," I said. "Let's change our meeting till 5:00 p.m. I forgot I have to work."

"You didn't tell me you had a job. Where?" he asked.

"I'm the meter maid," I told him. He laughed some.

"A twelve-year-old meter maid?" he said.

"A thirteen-year-old movie director?" I said.

"I'll be fourteen next month on December 14," he said, showing off. "Besides, you once told me you were a witch and had me traveling all around Brooklyn with you to buy herbs and brews for one of your spells! Remember that?" he asked. He was messing with me. I was just playing about the witch thing cause I didn't want to tell him the truth; that I was gathering herbs and natural remedies to get Momma off of crack. Back then, when Elisha checked out my list of "weird stuff," provided by NanaAnna by way of Riot, I had to say something. So I told him I was a witch about to cast a powerful spell. He didn't mind, though. At least he acted like he didn't mind and even enjoyed my tale and the witch hunt adventure of gathering "the potion ingredients."

"Alright then," Elisha said after our words were paused, "Five p.m. It'll be the first time I seen you on a Saturday."

"Thank you for the cell phone . . . ," I said softly.

"Tomorrow," he said. We hung up.

Momma was staring at me as I was speaking to Elisha. Afterwards she only made a sound, "*Umm hmm.*"

Chapter 39

When we reached the iron doors to the underground, Momma stopped instead of lifting it so we could climb down the cement stairs.

"I'll open it," I said. Momma wouldn't move out of the way.

"What's wrong?" I asked.

"I don't want to go down there no more," Momma said.

"It's just for the weekend. We can go get the apartment on Monday. I have the money ready. I promise. I even have the place. You sign everything. I'll pay for it," I explained, feeling suddenly nervous. I did have the place. I just needed Momma to go meet with Mr. Sharp so she could take care of the parts that only someone over eighteen could take care of. If Momma would show up, sign everything, every single day after that, I would do the work, pay the rent, and make her happy.

"If I go down there, you gotta get rid of those fucking cuffs and that heavy chain. If you ever do some shit like that to me again, I'll break your neck," Momma threatened.

Momma's anger was slowly mounting. We had a successful day, had gathered important information, accomplished some things, sat down together for a nice meal in a restaurant. Upon ending up back here, she turned tense.

"I only did that to help you get clean. It was the only way to beat that drug without the hospitals. I hate the hospitals. I told you before, Momma. And look at you now, so pretty."

"And what about you?" Momma asked.

"Huh?"

"Everybody got they own thing. I got mine. You got yours."

"What?" I seriously didn't understand what Momma was getting at.

"I get rid of my friend Mr. Crack. You get rid of your friend Siri," she said, mean-faced.

"That's not the same thing," I said. "The crack ruins you, makes you act strange," I said.

"Siri makes you act strange, standing around talking all day to somebody who ain't even there. You even got that handsome boy acting like she's real. If I gotta get rid of Mr. Crack, you gotta get rid of Siri," Momma said.

I knew Momma was just bugging out at the moment. There is no person named Mr. Crack. There is a girl and a closest friend of mine named Siri. I began perspiring in the November cold standing on a slab of iron on the cold cement floor. Siri had been with me in the underground when Momma was nowhere to be found. She was with me on lockdown and at the bottom. Siri loves me and that I knew for certain. I couldn't say the same thing about Momma. I couldn't say for sure that she loved me. I couldn't feel it. This was only day one of her being better, by not cursing me out, spitting on me, threatening me, ignoring me, or abandoning me.

"Don't worry, I'll hide," Siri said. She was peeking around the corner so Momma couldn't see her.

"I promise I won't lock you up anymore, Momma. I'll send Siri away so you don't have to see her. Just please let's stay together. After you see Poppa tomorrow, you'll be so happy. You can ask him about the twins and Mr. Bilal Ode. Monday morning first thing, we'll go get the new apartment." I said that part softly and sadly, but I didn't know why. Probably it was because I knew Momma didn't believe me, or believe in me.

"We'll see . . . ," Momma said. We stepped off the iron, opened the door and we went down.

"We'll sleep in the bed together, okay, Momma?" I asked after we were in our pajamas. Momma rolled her eyes, but laid down first. I threw my arms around her waist and one leg over her body as she slept. I couldn't chain her anymore, but at least I would feel it if she tried to run away while I slept.

But I couldn't sleep. I just laid with my eyes opened and my body locked around Momma. Even at 3:00 a.m. I didn't leave to work at Big Johnnie's. I wasn't required to work Saturday and Sunday mornings for him, but usually I did anyway and there was always work to do. At 5:00 a.m. I woke Momma. "Time to get ready for Poppa," I said softly to her.

In Manhattan, on Columbus Circle, at 6:30 a.m., Momma was as pretty to me as the sky. She wasn't perfect, but even the sky has some lines, streaks, and explosions in it.

The ticket man moved down the lines, rows of women, some teens and kids. Most had packed lunches for the long ride. A few women had done the same as Momma, worn jeans and kicks for comfort and carried nicer clothes in a dress bag or carryon to change into before meeting their husbands, fathers, brothers, or sons. Momma was wearing my Gucci sneakers, the second pair from Mr. Sharp, which I had only worn once or twice. "That's twenty-six dollars each," the ticket seller said.

"Just one, please," I said, handing the man the cash bills. I turned and passed the ticket to Momma. The ticket man moved on. I called him back to attention.

"This is the ticket to get to Niagra Correctional Facility, right?" I asked.

"Yes," he said.

"You go straight there, right?" I asked.

"With a couple of stops," he said, moving on with his ticket business.

"No stops!" I had an outburst. I needed the bus to go straight to the prison. What if it stopped somewhere and Momma got off? Would she do that? What if she did? She'd go looking for Mr. Crack in some strange place that I didn't know, or no one I knew, knew. I felt myself begin to panic.

"What are you yelling for? So what if it makes stops!" Momma said.

I thought to myself, maybe she's happy it makes stops. Maybe Momma's putting together her plan to abandon me. As my temperature raised up, the lady standing behind me said, "You can take the dark blue express van over there. It's a straight ride, double the price."

"C'mon, Momma," I said, picking up her bag and grabbing her hand.

"This ticket is good enough. You already paid for it, and I need some pocket money!" she said.

"Okay, I'll sell it!" I said about the twenty-six-dollar bus ticket she held in her hand.

"Let's go before it fills up." I pulled Momma along.

Over at the express van I purchased a fifty-two dollar ticket. Right before I paid, I checked, "You are driving straight to Niagra Correctional Facility, right?"

"That's right, this is the express, you get what you pay for!" the driver confirmed.

I walked Momma onto the minibus and didn't get off until she had her things packed away and her seat secured.

"Are you okay, Momma?" I asked.

"I know how to ride a bus! What about what I told you?" she said. There was no need for me to pretend. I knew she was asking again for some "pocket money." I had it, of course, but didn't want her to have anything she could cop with. I wanted her to ride up and back with only her round-trip ticket, to be certain that she would return to me.

"Are you okay?" a woman in the seat behind Momma asked me.

"She's fine!" Momma said in her "mind your fucking business tone." Then Momma looked at me and said, "I'll get off." She was threatening me. I knew she meant it. I handed her a twenty-dollar bill.

"For emergencies, Momma, okay?"

"Okay, Shorty. You're holding us up!" The bus driver pointed to the sign EXPRESS. "We make it up there first."

I walked down the aisle, my thighs trembling, even my fingers shaking. I stepped down two steps and stood on the curb watching as they left.

Planning to sell my ticket and looking for a potential customer, I knew I would have to knock a couple of dollars off the price to move it, unless the slow bus was sold out. If it was sold out already, I could sell my ticket for ten dollars more than I paid for it.

"You selling that?" A woman who looked just as uneasy as me asked as I stood there holding it.

"No," was the word my ears overheard my mouth saying. My feet had their own meeting and were moving up the stairs into the slow bus to Poppa's prison. My nerves tangled like the wires inside of a heavy phone cable; I plopped down into a seat.

I gotta follow Momma, make sure she's okay, I thought.

"What if we get captured? A prison is one of those official places we're not supposed to go, and we don't even have ID," Siri said. She was sitting beside me now. I felt bad that she had to hide from Momma.

"*I have to go*, Siri. We'll reach there after Momma, but at least we'll be in the same area where she is, and we can all come back together."

* * *

When scenes of the city were no more, it was the same as going from Earth to Neptune, I imagined. As farms and farm animals, land and more land, winter-brown grass and naked trees appeared in front of us, I began to feel even more uneasy. It felt like a trip back to a place where I never wanted to return. It didn't feel familiar like the green orchards of NanaAnna's where everything blossomed and clear water streams flowed freely.

We were headed to a place where men are stacked in steel cages with iron bars, with no one to look at except themselves, with no love, and cold floors, no privacy, and no promises, with no furniture, and no future.

As I counted cows and horses I wondered what men who lived like Poppa would feel and act like. I wondered what they would do day to day inside of there, and how different it might be from what they would have done if they were not in there at all. I guessed a heated hate would grow in their hearts like it grew in me when I was trapped. It would be hatred so heavy they couldn't stand up straight. All of their backs would curve towards the floors like animals. They wouldn't be cows or horses, though. They would become beasts like the little girls I dormed with. They couldn't do nothing but attack each other. The biggest beasty-est ones are the guards, though. The head beast is the warden who drags her long hairy tail down the hallways behind her and has the nerve to manicure her claws. Her eyes were made of fire and her mouth was nothing but a hole where deadly stink-filled gasses escaped, the type of gasses that should only be kept in an ass.

"Wake up, wake up . . ." Someone was shaking my shoulders.

"Have some water. Were you having some kind of nightmare? Where's your mother?" The woman was pressing her face between the slight space between two bus seats.

"She's in the back," I lied. "I'm okay. No, thank you, I have water," I lied again.

It didn't matter what I told her. I have money. That should fix anything. Seats that were empty when we first left Columbus Circle in Manhattan were now filled.

"Last stop before Niagra Correctional Facility," the man-voice announced.

* * *

In a crowded waiting room, busloads of women, some teens and kids and babies waited to be "processed." There were signs everywhere reading DO NOT LEAVE YOUR CHILDREN UNDER 18 UNATTENDED. Me and Siri sat next to two women who had kids, to act like we're part of their bunch. Momma wasn't in here. She must have already been processed and visiting with Poppa. I'd wait out here. *Being "processed" is the official part*, I told myself.

After more than an hour it seemed like none of the women and children who approached the area to be searched and processed were coming back out here. The crowd where we were was shrinking.

"They're going out some other door," Siri said. "After they meet their husbands they're exiting elsewhere. What if you missed Momma?" Siri asked me. I felt panicked. My butt muscles and my jaw muscles tightened and my fingers were becoming stiff.

* * *

"Every week there's at least one," the guard standing over me said. "Now, you're too young to be alone, and too old to be lost. What's your excuse?"

I shrugged my shoulders. My tongue was dry like beef jerky or pork rinds that they used to sell in the corner store back in Brooklyn when I was seven.

"Let me see some ID," the guard said.

"I don't have none," I said truthfully.

"Who did you come up here to see?" she asked me.

"I don't know. My aunt came up here to see someone. She made me sit and wait alone."

"What's your aunt's name?"

"Everybody calls her Lucy," I said swiftly.

"Lucy what?" the guard asked. I thought of the last name I heard the most ever.

"Lucy Jackson, but I think that's her other name," I said.

"Other name?" the guard asked.

"Before or after she got married again," I said.

"Forget all that. What's your name?"

"Ivory," I said.

"Come with me, Ivory," the guard said.

The guard walked me to the counter where more guards were standing behind a thick closed-in glass. She unclipped a tag hanging on her guard shirt and placed it against the glass. The heavy door clicked, then opened. Two guards looked over the high countertop and down at me.

"You got another one?" one of the guards said.

A drop of pee squeezed out of me. I felt it spread in my panties. I stood behind the guard as she removed her gun and checked it at the counter.

"Headed for the other side," she said to the other guards. I felt bricks on my head as I tried to figure if "the other side" was a good or evil place?

"Teach her mother a lesson. How many times do we have to tell them we're correction officers, not babysitters."

"You know I will," the guard said.

Small drops of pee kept falling and sliding a crooked path down my leg inside of my jeans then drying around my ankles.

"This is not a place where you should ever want to be," the guard said as we walked and walked down a slim corridor where there was nothing but officers and workers. I could not see even one prisoner or one cell. That would've been something, to get a glimpse of Poppa.

But this must've been the guard's secret passageway, I thought. Again she placed her pass on a thick glass window. A heavy door clicked.

"Lucy Jackson!" she announced to a room filled with women and some kids packing, putting on coats and jackets, boots and sneakers, and pocketbooks. If I were Lucy Jackson, I wouldn't have answered the guard either. She called out that name like, "Come get your ass whooping!"

"Lucy Jackson," the guard's voice boomed again. Sweat rushed out of my pores and spread onto my face until I was nothing but sweat and piss.

"Last call for Lucy Jackson! Ladies check around and see if you lost any of your kids!" The guard was criticizing them all.

"Oh!" a lady said. "She's on the bus with me."

"We rode up together." From her voice I could hear she was the lady who was seated behind me, who woke me out of my nightmare. I walked over to her and held her hand.

"I'll take her. Her mother's probably on the bus going crazy looking for us," the woman said.

The guard looked at us both suspiciously.

"It ain't like none of y'all would be asking for no extra kids, so go ahead," the C.O. said sarcastically. When we exited my remaining pee blasted out.

"You can let go now," the woman who got me out of there said. "I don't know what kind of trouble you're in, but I wouldn't wish that place on my worse enemy," she said, and walked away.

"I'm looking for the express bus," I said to another woman walking beside us. She didn't even look at me, just kept walking and looked at her watch.

"It's gone. It leaves a half hour before the big ones pull out."

My heart dropped into my socks. I tried to take deep breaths and blow air out to calm my panic.

As I looked back through the barbed wire fences at the cement castles and the guards on the rooftops weighed down with weapons to kill, I struggled to climb the bus stairs.

"How long till we get back to New York City?" I asked the driver.

"Seven hours including all stops, same as coming up, going back."

* * *

A stray dog on the midnight Brooklyn streets followed me from the subway stairs toward the underground. I didn't hate him. I didn't love him either. He kept trying to smell me. He wasn't growling or foaming or looking like he wanted to attack. I stopped and stood still. He pushed his black nose into my private space and sniffed, sniffed, sniffed.

"I know. I stink," I said to him. He started wagging his tail like he thought we could be friends. Once I realized he wasn't a threat, I started walking faster to get back to Momma.

* * *

Momma left me one thing, the Motorola Startac cell phone from Elisha. Her Gucci dress and heels, all of the new clothes I purchased for her, the dopest shit Mr. Sharp bought for me; my kicks, shoes, and Gucci backpack, the chain, lock, and cuffs were all gone. Even the gold earrings that Poppa bought for me and placed on the tip-top of my money tree were missing.

"It's okay. We were growing out of some of those clothes anyway," Siri said to me. "It will be fun to go shopping for new stuff." I guess Siri didn't know that I missed Momma more than any item. I was being mugged by grief and slowly drowning in pain. All I saw was black before I collapsed on the cement stairs.

Chapter 40

Seven days before my fourteenth birthday, I had now served more time with Momma than my time served in prison. Still, I wasn't sure which sentence was worse. I didn't know whether to celebrate or slash my throat. In fact, I know less now than I knew when I was eight, nine, and ten in juvy. At least in there, I had the pride and certainty of being a Santiaga, the deep and true love and intense loyalty to family. Back then I let that love fight for me *and win*. I risked everything for that love, definitely my freedom and even my life.

Now it was too hard for me to figure, understand, or accept what was happening with me. No one else seemed to know or say anything about it. No one asked or cared enough about me, except Elisha. Other people cared, but not enough. In fact everyone who knew me knew so little about me, even less than I knew about myself.

On the block where I lived beneath the ground, and everywhere I went as myself, people said I was beautiful, gorgeous, attractive, the bomb, the shit, the brick house, the ten, the dime, the baddest, the best, the top and the bottom bitch. They used words like *mysterious, elegant, exotic, sensual, sensuous, young, firm, soft, sweet, powerful*; I heard them all on a regular. None of those words moved me even a millimeter.

I had never spread these pretty dancer's thighs for anyone. The more I ignored, the more I said no, the more I resisted, the more interested they were. Problem was, I wasn't interested at all. I was the pretty girl with five holes in my heart. The holes were so deep and so painful, I couldn't give love to anyone. I felt even if I gave in and gave my whole heart to Elisha, all he would be getting is Swiss cheese.

Plus, I was afraid to love him. Momma said, "Never give your whole heart to any man. You'll end up loving him ten thousand more times than he'll ever love you." Everything Momma ever said mattered the world to me, even the meanest, most evilest words Momma said counted a lot.

I did make one decision: I was leaving the underground, the space beneath the floor with no windows and no sunlight. I would leave in a body bag or I would walk out on my own. Either way, I would be gone. Fear flew away one dark night screaming and kicking, while locked in the beak of a black raven; the fear of me not being in a space where Momma might return. That's it, plain and simple.

That's what I mean about my life. It didn't make sense. I have $50,000 dollars in a heavy locked safe in the wall space at Mr. Sharp's place of business. I had a hundred thousand chances to leave the underground, but I couldn't and wouldn't. I was always waiting on Momma. There was also the little detail of my being both a juvenile and a fugitive, no ID, no Social Security number, no working papers, no rights. So Big Johnnie's underground space was the hideout, where the longer I stayed, the more money I hustled up and earned.

Big Johnnie was like an uncle to me now, Mr. Sharp like a father. He even said he would put me in the charm school, and when I reached sixteen, I could debut in the debutante's ball. He wanted to escort me in the place of Poppa. My neighbors and the local business owners were like distant relatives raising me, feeding me, keeping my secrets, not asking too much.

I made money like a money machine. Everyone said I was so smart, useful, hard-working, well mannered. I even hit the number 1111, and got my five-thousand-dollar jackpot. Riot had paid me back my four thousand dollar investment plus four thousand in earnings from flipping it. The eight thousand—she labeled the eight thousand a "buyout." She said it wasn't an end to our friendship, "just an end of our deal." She had something major to do, and she had to do it alone.

People said I was lucky. All I could do was smirk at that. "Lucky."

Elisha's mom said I had wings like an angel that only special eyes could see. She said she saw them the first day she met me in the aisle at the organic market. I guess so. I sure couldn't see my wings.

I didn't know why there was no substitute for Momma, Poppa,

Winter, Mercedes, and Lexus. I don't know why the people who looked out for me the most couldn't fill up even one of the five holes in my heart.

I came close with Elisha. Really close, really, really, really close.

Of course, what happened between Elisha and me all happened in scenes, like in any great film that has never been made yet. And, of course, everything in his life started with two words: *my mother*. Everything in my life started the same way: *my momma*.

SCENE 1

Age twelve, my momma stole everything except the cell phone Elisha bought for me. She even took my two heavy duffle bags, the chain, and the lock. I guess she needed them to carry my belongings out and to keep others from stealing them from her. Of course my momma could not steal my $20,000 that I had earned up until that point, to get our new apartment and take care of her. My money was stashed in Mr. Sharp's safe even back then.

Completely crushed for three weeks, I worked all my jobs, but wouldn't talk to Elisha. I felt too ashamed and bruised. When I finally called him, he wouldn't take my call. I went looking for him. I was twelve. He was about to turn fourteen.

Outside his brownstone I rang four doorbells for four separate apartments, which made a bunch of different faces pop out the windows, including his.

"I'm in the middle of a production," he said coldly. I knew he was angry that I had stood him up and ignored him.

"It's cold out, but I'll wait," I said.

"So do that then," he responded.

Outside I was hopping around in the December freeze blowing cold air out like cigarette smoke, waiting for him to either come out or let me in.

An hour later the front door opened. A girl our age came walking out and him after her. She cut her eyes at me. I just watched her. He saw us two staring at one another and said, "Ivory, this is Audrey. Audrey, this is Ivory."

"You're leaving, right," I said to Audrey, no greetings. Why even front? She left.

"You wanna come in, or you want me to come out?" Elisha asked in an even tone, with no excitement or feeling in it.

"I'm froze," was all I said. He widened the door to let me in.

"Your mother?" I asked, looking around at his pretty brownstone place.

"Not back from work yet," he said. "Everybody's out. Step into my room." I walked behind him.

"Look at my hands." I showed him my frozen fingers and red palms. He came up close, grabbed both of my hands and pulled them underneath his shirt, then moved them underneath his armpits. His skin was warm like a bakery oven. My heart went crazy. All of my muscles began to move in a way that I could feel them, even between my thighs. I felt blood rushing about and even my then little titties, especially the nipples, seemed to swell. My panties got wet. I was warming up rapidly. I fidgeted, afraid that I might pee. I was overwhelmed and embarrassed.

"You know what I hate?" he asked me, breaking our soft silence, us still standing close together, him still heating up my body. "I hate when I show a girl my true emotion, and then she starts acting fucked up because of it. It would be better if she would show me her true feeling, too," he said.

"Who are you talking about? That girl who just left here?" I asked.

"See what I mean?" he said calmly with a straight face. "You know it's all about *you*. You know how I feel about *you*," he said.

What could I do? That's what I said to myself. I felt Elisha did not know how extreme my love runs. If I told him my true feeling, what could happen next? I would be in the corner of his bedroom in his bed, lying next to him like I never had. His touch would make it impossible for me to ever leave him alone. I would move in. No, I just would never leave in the first place. I wouldn't even go back to collect my things. I wouldn't need no food, nothing. I wouldn't need nothing but him. I would be that girl who Momma talked about. I would love him a hundred thousand times more than he could ever love me. On the strength of just him holding my hands underneath his shirt and tucked beneath his armpits, that first touch and powerful feeling, he was stuck with my love forever, and what if it drowned him, and I was left broken and useless like my momma?

"You're not gonna say nothing?" he asked me.

"Please can you touch my face?" I asked him. He placed his hands on both sides of my face. His fingertips grazed my neck. A wave of feeling shot through my body. I stepped in even closer.

"Elisha," I heard a female voice say. He stepped back. "You didn't hear me come in?" she asked. "Come here, let me speak to you for a minute."

"Ivory, you can sit on my bed," he said to me as he walked out. I stayed standing.

"Look at you," I heard her saying, but I couldn't see them. "This is getting real serious. Does Mom know how you are in love with this young girl and got her in your room when no one else is home?"

"Sheba, be easy. We weren't doing nothing," I heard Elisha saying.

"You're not doing nothing now that I'm here," she said.

SCENE 2

Tuesday, December 14, on Elisha's fourteenth birthday I wanted to celebrate with him. But Siri and I discussed how we both needed to stay away from him. "You'll lose control," Siri warned me. "And that's okay if you want to surrender to him. But don't act like you can be around him without breaking your rules, 'No touching, no kissing, no giving your whole heart to him.'" It was extreme like that. I couldn't tame my feelings, or balance them out so I planned to stay away. Today I would drop off a birthday cake and gift to him and leave.

"Why are you looking your prettiest if you don't want to encourage him?" Siri asked me, as I picked up the shopping bag to leave to find Elsiha.

I went by his high school at 2:30 and waited for him to come out. He did, surrounded by friends, laughing and joking. I stayed to the side and waited. As they talked shit, and moved around to stay warm, eventually the boys all gave each other a pound and went their separate ways. Elisha was still standing there, with that girl Audrey. I walked across their path so he would see me. He did.

"Porsche!" He called out and began coming over, leaving Audrey behind. She caught on and rushed over also. He was staring at me. I was staring back at him and wouldn't even give the girl a glance.

"Tell her to leave," I said.

"Audrey, I'll catch you later," he told her. I began walking toward his brownstone and he followed without hesitation.

"You stay away, then show up to tease me, right? Is it a game?" he asked.

"Definitely not," I told him. "I'm trying to keep a nice young girl out of trouble," I said.

"This young man is no trouble," he said. "It's my birthday. You have to at least give me something that I ask for."

"Something like what?" I stopped walking and turned towards him.

"Something like, let's be tight like how we were before. Stop playing and let's talk and meet up every day. I mean once a week, Fridays at three like before. I think I messed up when I gave you the phone. You talked to me one time over that phone and that's it. My man said, 'You gotta treat girls like prostitutes, *then* they'll love you.'"

"That's crazy," I said.

"He's old school. That was some Slick Rick shit." He separated himself from his friend's words of advice.

"Elisha, I want to ask you for something, and I want to give you something."

"Ask whatever you want," he said, always confident.

"The truth is, I can't not love you." We were walking.

"Can't not? You do or you don't?" he asked. His eyebrows were raised and he stopped walking.

"I can't not. It means, I love you and it is impossible for me not to love you." His closed lips spread into a bright smile.

"But I'm not a regular girl. I have a lot of things going on all the time. My life is crazy. A lot of the time I'm sad, really sad, and sometimes I'm angry and don't wanna talk, can't talk. Sometimes I disappear for a little while. Sometimes I disappear for a long time. None of it has anything to do with you," I said.

"Don't you think I know that?" he said, serious-faced.

"I'm twelve. You're fourteen. Happy Birthday, Elisha! Let's me

and you meet up on my thirteenth birthday, July 26. Then we can start
up again from there."

"Sounds crazy. What's a man supposed to do until then? Eight
long months?" he asked me, looking sincerely hurt. When I didn't answer, he also saw my seriousness. He hugged me in the ice-cold wind.
I liked that feeling too much, him standing taller than me and his
arms were strong. He held me tightly so I would feel that he meant it.

I handed him the shopping bag with the homemade carrot cake
that I made for him with care. On top of the cake container was my
gift-wrapped birthday gift for him.

"Don't open it until I leave."

"Then don't give it to me yet. I'm walking you home," he said,
confident and determined. I knew there was no space for me to argue
that he shouldn't.

"You never danced for me," he said as we walked.

"You don't want to see that," I told him.

"Yes I do!" he said, becoming excited.

"Then you'll be so in love you'll probably come and kidnap me and
hold me hostage till I'm old enough."

"Old enough for what?" he said calmly and knowingly.

"Old enough to do what we want to do," I said.

"You said you love me, so don't you go loving no one else," Elisha
said with a calm but serious face. He grabbed my hand and held it.
My heart thumped.

Walking and wrapped in silence, it was settling into our hearts
that we had to separate. Both of us probably wondered if we would
love each other more or less or not at all by my thirteenth birthday.

"Don't open it in the street," I told him. "Open my gift in your
room, alone."

SCENE 3

On Saturday, July 25, at midnight, I heard a thump on the iron floor
door. I froze with fear. Last time a knock came like that, Momma
had fallen out and it was hard as hell for me to lift the iron lid with
her body lying on the top of it. I ran to the cement stairs and pushed

gently on the door. She was definitely not lying on it again. Why wasn't she coming in? "Momma," I said, softly lifting the lid. When she didn't answer or come in, I lifted my head out a little bit more to look.

"It's July 26," he said calmly. I couldn't see him. It was Elisha. I dropped the lid in a swift hurry. The steel slammed. My heart pounded. I ran down the stairs and then I ran back up, then down again. How did he find me?

I was so excited, nervous, surprised, angry, embarrassed, ashamed, attracted, I couldn't think in complete or orderly thoughts. I stood staring at the iron floor door. He didn't knock again or say anything else. Then slowly, I walked back up the cement stairs. I pushed it open, stuck only my hand out and waved him in. I ran down the steps and turned off the lights, but I don't know why I did.

The floor door opened.

"Elisha," I said softly.

"Turn on the lights," he said.

"Find me."

"Say something. Keep talking," he said.

Siri was so happy for me, she began humming beautifully.

Elisha wasn't talking at all, but I could hear him breathing.

Strong hands landed on my breasts, which were full now, no longer only swollen nipples. He felt around some, a light touch, his fingertips ending up at my nipples. He squeezed them, then pulled me into his embrace.

My nightgown was thin. Not until my naked body heated up like a tea kettle, did a thought speed through my mind that I should've gotten dressed. It disappeared as quick as it came.

Elisha was stroking my face. It felt so fucking good and so foreign and so powerful my pussy began pounding and pounding until it erupted. I was so wet between my legs I was embarrassed, but the good feeling was still racing around my body so strongly it didn't matter. His fingers were on my two lips and he parted them. I felt his lips over mine, and my mouth opened easily. He slid in his tongue and my legs trembled. It was my first kiss on my thirteenth birthday, underneath the floor where it was hot, in the dark with no windows. He didn't need to say that he still loved me or missed me or wanted to get up in me. His tongue and his body was saying it all. The sensation of my nightgown silk rubbing on my silky skin made me feel like I was in a complete loss of control. Could I die like this? It felt like something so good that after that there would be no reason to live. All I could hear was our breathing, tongues moving, lips sucking; then, him taking off his shirt and lifting my nightgown over my hips. Suddenly he grabbed my pussy hairs all at once like someone who was snatching a head of lettuce from the earth. Even the pull felt good. I fell to the floor. I didn't have to tell him nothing, he was right beside me in less than half a second. He was feeling my whole body, my bare skin hot enough to fry an egg.

"Elisha," I said.

"*Sshh,*" he said. A finger went in me, and my insides bursted like sparklers, firecrackers, and M80s on the fourth.

"Elisha," I said softly again.

"Stop frontin' and give in to me," he said. I heard his zipper opening and crawled away. I felt like if he found me, I would give him everything I ever had including my mind, body, and money. I'd have his babies and be following him anywhere and do whatever he said. I was so open, my heart and my legs and my mind and my everything! "What the fuck," I said to myself. "I'm worse than a slave."

"Okay. Don't hide from me. I won't hunt you down," he said.

"If I touch you some, do we have to go all the way?" I asked him.

"Do you want to touch me?" he asked.

"I do, all over," I told him. I crawled back over and sat on his lap. I felt his hair and his face, his neck and his shoulders, his chest and his arms. When I reached down and touched his hardness, I got too excited. He started kissing on me. I found myself moaning and singing.

"How can you touch me like that and not go all the way?" he asked me.

"I can't," I said.

"You can't?" he repeated. He made my body shake some more for the fourth time. Then he stopped.

"Turn the light on. I want to see you." I pulled myself up from the floor searching in the dark for a switch or the long string. My whole body was wet. My hair and gown soaked the cloth hugging my nipples and my hips, my nipples poking through powerfully. "You're so beautiful," he said. "I missed you like crazy. Don't ask me to leave you alone no more."

Watching Poppa from a distance for my first eight years of my young life taught me that we all have to hustle. Lina taught me that speaking nice and using manners wins friends, connections, and opens doors. Riot showed me to always seize and invest in the right opportunities even when the best opportunities meant using people.

Mr. Sharp once admitted that he had done a bid when he was young. When his time was served, no one would give him a chance or a job. He taught me, "Working a job will get you started but no matter how long you work a job, it will never make you rich." The people who want stacks have to think smart, own their own businesses, choose the right products, or sell excellent services, and have the ability to negotiate their way around every obstacle. I definitely listened.

"Santiaga," he said, "you're gonna make it big in this world because you are a natural negotiator. Since you're a beautiful young woman, you got the 'edge' over any smart man. Never sell your body. The first time you do, your value decreases immediately and keeps on decreasing until you're worthless. Don't let these men play with you. Use your mind to think, your talk to negotiate. Your beauty is just bait. Make them pay, but never let 'em touch it. Those are the secrets of life."

SCENE 4

Elisha and I were both young businesspeople. We were both used to working, negotiating, saving, investing, selling, and purchasing. That same night, on my thirteenth birthday, we tried to "manage" our love.

"It's 1:30 in the morning," I told him.

"My parents are at a convention in Washington, DC," he said.

"Oh," I said, not knowing nothing about a "convention," but understanding that Elisha was out late cause no one was making him stay home.

"I'm staying with you," he said. "I'm not moving."

"You want me to have your baby now?" I asked him.

"Do you want to have my baby?" he asked me.

"The truth?" I said softly. "I want to give you anything you want. No, I want to give you everything I have. I feel like my heart is gonna burst out my chest. But, Elisha, down here where I live, *morning never comes*. There are no windows and there is no sunshine."

"I see that," was all he said. "So what does that mean to you?" he asked calmly. He was caressing me, pressed against my back, both of us naked.

"You know how the sun reminds us of the reality? Down here is different. You and I could just stay down here and love each other until we die. But if there was a window, you would see the sunlight and remember your mother, remember your school, and your friends, remember that you're a movie director, remember your life."

"So?" he asked.

"So I'm saying. I want you to do it to me. I want to do it with you, but do we want a baby, now? Maybe we should accomplish something first," I said. I could feel him smiling, but he was still stroking my skin. We were lying on my bed trying really, really hard to manage.

"Alright, so after I make my first film and it's big, big, big, you'll give me some pussy?" he teased, touching me there. "I'll buy you a house with great big windows and plenty of sunshine. You'll be my wife and have my babies?" Elisha said it like he was on the set directing the movie scenes exactly how he saw them in his mind, and how he wanted them to go. His strong hand was lying over my pussy bush. My whole body was so ignited it was threatening to overrule my mind and everything my mouth was saying.

"How long before you think our love will disappear?" I asked him.

"Love never disappears," he said calmly. "It's impossible. If it disappears it was never love," he said.

Hot tears boiled and spilled from my eyes like water shooting up from the earth. He was sucking my nipples now and stroking my hips with his hands. I couldn't stop crying cause Elisha was the sun. I only wanted to revolve around him. I wasn't used to it though, this incredible feeling.

Elisha's light was cutting through my extreme darkness, and exposing something that my heart with five holes in it could not bear. Momma, Poppa, and Winter didn't really love me. They had all disappeared. When shit got fucked up, they didn't fight back hard enough. They didn't come get me. They didn't send no one for me. They didn't check on me. They didn't come see about me. Worse than that, they let their loving feelings disappear.

"I know. You had me suffer for eight months." Elisha said speaking of our separation. "Love didn't leave me," he said. "It was walking with me the whole time, just getting stronger and stronger." We were tonguing again. The heat was even in our mouths. I held his hardness in my hand. He placed his hand over mine and moved it up and down. I kept holding it, massaging it, jerking it until hot sticky fluid spilled all over my fingers.

"We can work it out," Elisha said. "There's a whole bunch of ways we can move. *Let's just make moves together.*" I was thirteen. He would soon be fifteen. My heart agreed. My tongue agreed. My mind agreed. I fucking agreed.

*   *   *

So what could be wrong? I was asking myself seven days before my fourteenth birthday. My thoughts had all turned dark. It was like I was being pulled beneath the ground beneath the underground. I was already underground. Could I actually be pulled down any further, any lower? Was there a last floor to the ground, a lowest level, a place where, no matter what, a person couldn't fall or be pulled or dragged any lower?

Naked, I was seated in the closet, collapsed after dancing, seven days before my fourteenth birthday, one night after seeing Momma, bruised and broken, *again.*

Elisha was too true and too right. Love does not disappear. Love never leaves. Even when someone you love does not love you, and does not return the love, the love you carry for them is still on. It's right there. Like Elisha said, it's walking right beside you night and day, day and night. It never goes away. Elisha's love has shown me who loves me and who never truly did. Problem was I loved them, my family. Since love never leaves, it was like every day I had five invisible people walking beside me, nonstop.

Somebody has to go, I thought to myself. Siri said, "Not Elisha, he loves us."

"It's me. I have to go."

Chapter 41

"Gentlemen are always discreet." Mr. Sharp had used this expression more than once in his back-office business conversations.

One day when I was helping Elisha study for his vocabulary exam, I asked him, "What does discreet mean?"

Elisha said, "Calm and cool, like nothing's happening even though it really is happening."

"Use it in a sentence." I pushed Elisha. He had to be able to use all of his vocab study words in a proper sentence anyway.

"Let me see . . ." He was thinking.

"My father flips through the pages of his naked girly magazine, while discreetly pretending to read the newspaper." We laughed. I understood.

Mr. Sharp's discreetness was elegant to me. He knew Poppa, Momma, and me. He never mixed or shared or exposed any of our secrets to the others. He never mentioned to me if he had seen Momma recently. If he did see her, he never mentioned what condition she was in. He never let on that he knew she lived in the ground beneath the store floor, one store in a string of stores, which *he* owned. He never revealed that he was aware that Momma was any different than how she appeared in the pretty photo that he had framed and given to me. He never used words like *crackhead, addiction, filthy, regretful, shameful, embarrassing*, in reference to Momma. Mr. Sharp never said if it was him who struck a deal with Big Johnnie to allow Momma to live in the underground for free, or if it was Johnnie who had some agreement with Momma himself.

Mr. Sharp only said that, even though he was just his tailor, he loved Poppa like a brother. He never said that he knew Poppa was doing life, and for what reasons he was locked up. Mr. Sharp never said if he had ever visited Poppa at the prison, or if he had written or received Poppa's letters. Had Poppa known that Sharp gave me a job, paid me well, put out a word of protection on the streets that no one should fuck with the attractive, ambitious little meter maid, personal assistant, errand girl, cigarette hustler? Sharp's word had kept away all the young hustlers and hotheads in the area who started sweating me as soon as hit thirteen. I don't know if Poppa knew. Mr. Sharp was so discreet he didn't say.

Mr. Sharp didn't ask me for ID, Social Security numbers, working papers, nothing. When I flashed him a sign, he'd drop a question or a topic that he knew I didn't want to discuss. He never said I was too young to think, work, earn, or be responsible, or asked me what happened or why.

It must've been shocking, a fourteen-years-young naked girl found half dead on his property. He never mentioned how I got to the hospital or why I was registered under the name Ivory Sharp. He never searched for approval, credit, or a financial reimbursement for his time and trouble posing as my biological father in the hospital or anywhere it needed to be done. That's why Sharp was an elegant discreet gentleman to me. So discreet in fact, he never uttered the phrase *attempted suicide* to me. In the end he was the bridge that held three Santiagas together.

Chapter 42

When Mr. Sharp called my cell phone, which Elisha had upgraded to a BlackBerry, I knew something was wrong. I was sixteen. It was the first and only call I had received from Sharp on my mobile. From age eleven through fourteen, all of our business had been face-to-face, in his office shop, based on spoken words and agreements. Our bond grew stronger each time one of us did exactly what we said we were going to do, exactly when we said we were gonna do it, and at the standard we expected of each other.

Now, having been away from him for two years, and him being used to receiving a call from me from a phone number or phone card that he couldn't trace back, and only on Sunday's, his voicemail to my BlackBerry was clearly an urgent call.

"Mr. Sharp," I said, returning his call.

"Ivory," he said.

"Yes?" I said.

"Where are you?" he asked.

"What's wrong?" I asked.

"Lana . . ." He said Momma's name. A cold wave moved through my body.

"I'm coming," I said and hung up.

I took a Lufthansa flight using a passport that identified me as Onatah Rivers. The same one I had been using for the past year. I ate nothing on the flight. I was a dancer with butterflies dancing in my belly. I felt so nervous, I kept having the feeling that I had to pee and poop. I would walk directly to the bathroom, lock myself in, and nothing would come out of me. After four or five times, I stopped falling for the trick my body was playing on me.

* * *

Face to face with Mr. Sharp, words weren't necessary. His facial expression told the story of Momma's death. His look, I know, was 99 percent pain that he felt *for me*.

"Do you want me to take you to the hospital where she is?" he asked.

"No," I said softly, sweetly, and sorrowfully. I knew he meant, where her dead, naked, cold body, and what remained of it is . . . being refrigerated.

"You should sit down then," Sharp said. "Here's the situation. I've made all of the arrangements. The wake will be at the Johnson's Funeral Home on Eastern Parkway, but it won't happen for at least ten days. Your father is processing through the red tape to be able to attend the funeral and it looks like it's gonna happen."

* * *

Shopping alone in Neiman Marcus for Momma's final outfit, I was shaking. With the wake set to occur in twenty-four hours, and the undertaker waiting for my fashion choices so he could dress Momma's dead body, my brain drew a black blank. My own mind was afraid to show me any images of Momma after 1994, when Momma was a stunner and the priceless crown jewel in Poppa's crown. It was as though my memory of Momma hooked and dragged down by crack was temporarily erased. The team-in-my-head were working feverishly to decorate and redecorate. They were spraying perfume on everything, covering up the stench, and removing the stains. They were converting Momma into an angel, who could never do and never did anything wrong.

Maybe that's how I ended up at the register with a white dress designed by Gianni Versace in his heyday, and the stilettos Momma definitely would've worn with it.

I paid in cash without blinking an eye, losing one breath, or even reviewing the receipt. I'm sixteen, and I'm made of money. I have it bulging out of my Birkin bag, falling out the sky over my head, and leaving a trail wherever I walked. Like Midas, every business venture I ever took on, doubled, tripled, quadrupled, quintupled, and turned to gold. My stacks of money was easy, getting my mind right was complicated. Fixing my heart was fucking impossible.

It's crazy. No, I should say, it's *ironic*. Elisha taught me that word. Momma had died on my sixteenth birthday. It had taken Mr. Sharp a couple days to make contact. Why that day? What was Momma saying to me? From now on, on my birthday, when I'm supposed to be happy and celebrating my life, I will be remembering Momma's death.

* * *

Undertakers look at dead people all day. For them, that's a normal life. When Momma's undertaker looked at the outfit I selected, he handed it right back to me and then excused himself, calling Mr. Sharp on his back-office phone, as I overheard the conversation.

"The young lady has purchased a white minidress for the Santiago corpse," he began saying to Sharp.

In my state of mind, I knew Mr. Sharp would take care of everything. I wanted to speak to him, but I couldn't. I couldn't assemble one sentence to say out loud, much less a string of sensible sentences. It was as if I was trapped in the corner of my mind screaming, while soft music played. It was not the kind of music I was used to or that I danced to.

There were no drums, no drum machine, no guitar, acoustic or electric, no bass, trumpet, violin, or sax, or even piano. The music I heard was the tingle of someone tapping the triangle, while another played only the xylophone. And that's it, no other instruments.

When my cell phone rang I just stared at it. I didn't pick up. It was an interruption to my music. When I returned to my hotel room, the hotel phone was blinking red with recorded messages unheard. Suddenly it began ringing loudly, too loudly to ignore. I picked it up but couldn't remember how to form my mouth to say hello.

"It's me," Mr. Sharp said. "There's a gentleman here to see you, a Mr. Bilal Ode. He's out in my reception area. Before you hang up, listen. I've seen this man before. He used to come with your father for fittings. Silent man, never said one word besides the greetings. I just thought you should know that, before you send him away without hearing him out."

Bilal Ode, Bilal Ode, Bilal Ode, Bilal Ode, a chorus began singing the name over and over again, opera style, until my tears boiled up and spilled. The African man who adopted my baby girls, the twins, and moved them to a place Momma called, "the African Jungle," I thought to myself.

"Are you listening?" Mr. Sharp asked me calmly. I hung up.

I didn't call down for them to bring the Benz around from valet parking. I couldn't speak. Downstairs I handed the parking attendant a valet ticket and a ten-dollar bill.

I got in and was driving to meet Bilal Ode at Mr. Sharp's.

"He left his card," Mr. Sharp said when I arrived. "He's staying at the Palace, a hotel in Manhattan. He said he needed to meet up with you. I can drive you over. You would do better with a driver at times like this." Mr. Sharp took over.

Chapter 43

The Palace Hotel's presidential suite took extra security clearances to access. Suited men began speaking into microscopic microphones pinned to their lapels, each with listening devices lodged in one ear. I was used to security escorts, VIP arrangements, and elite living. I let all the "officials" speak to Mr. Sharp. I was nothing but a pretty mute.

A security-styled man, suited differently from the security who were already escorting us, opened the door to Mr. Bilal Ode's suite. After both security teams once-overed, and exchanged a few words with each other, we were cleared to enter.

In a spacious area decorated with expensive old furniture, a tall dark man stood looking down on some papers, with his back to me. He turned around. My eyes trained in on him. His eyes searched me, then locked into mine.

"Hot sauce," my lips murmured. I remembered that feeling from when I was seven. A rush of heat raced around my body waking up every internal organ and thickening my blood.

"Midnight," was all I said, in an airy whisper, before I collapsed onto the floor.

It wasn't his diamond cufflinks, each princess cut placed precisely in a square surrounded in pure dark gold. Or the fact that carefully customed cufflinks send an electric current through the body of any woman who loves high-quality, manly, masculine men. It wasn't his Gucci gators or his Armani suit. It wasn't his white monogrammed dress shirt, so cleaned and pressed so perfectly it glistened, or his Yachtmaster Rolex or hundred-dollar dress socks.

It was his countenance. Elisha taught me that word, too. It was his complete composure. At sixteen, I am a woman who is highly regarded as erotic and exotic, a mesmerizing, hypnotic dancer, to be seen and amazed by, but never, ever touched. It was more than unusual. It was rare and difficult to be in the presence of a man so arousing that I'm forced to feel like I'm cheating on my own man, when I'm actually doing nothing at all. No, it wasn't rare. It had never happened to me before.

How could Midnight be so rough and manly, while tailored and manicured and prettier than me? On top of it all, so fucking cool and calm as though he was completely unaware of his power. His unconceited stance moved me. His victorious presence, after everything and everyone else had crumbled, insulted and enticed me. Was he laughing at the Santiagas? Or was it something else? What about Winter? What would she do? Fuck him or slap him? Maybe both.

When I woke my eyes were still closed. I was in the laying-down position. Then my eyes opened halfway. I was lying down on my side on a plush divan, covered with a silk paisley sheet. My instinct was to drag my hands up my thighs and push my finger into my pussy hole, then to smell it to see if anyone had messed with me while I was knocked out. As I did, my eyes fully opened now, landed on three Arabian-type females. They were the kind that would hang out with a dude named Ali Baba, and his forty thieves. They were the wrapped-up foreign ladies, with sex and longing in their shapely eyes. The ones who flew on magic carpets, had pretty belly buttons, and decorated feet.

What the fuck? What was happening to me now? *Porsche L. Santiaga*, I reminded myself. *Porsche L. Santiaga*, I thought again just to be sure that's who I am and that I was awake.

"Miss Porsche," one of the Arabian-type ladies said softly and respectfully to me.

"*Hmm,*" I thought. She knows *my real name*! For the past two years I had used at least twelve different names, none of them the real one, which Poppa had given me. I must be dreaming. Suddenly, I began laughing and laughing and was not able to stop myself.

"Miss Porsche Santiaga, are you feeling okay?" the Arabian lady asked me again.

I drew in a deep breath. Her and my eyes locked, and I simply nodded yes.

"I'm Sulima, director of protocol. She is Dr. Fatima Ali, and beside her is Rhakia Azziz. We were directed to ensure that you are feeling well, and to provide you with medical assistance if needed. We are also here to prepare you for your meeting with Aleema and Hasna."

"Who?" I said, finally speaking.

"Your sisters," she answered calmly.

"My sisters, Aleema and Hasna?" I repeated. "I have three sisters, Winter, Mercedes, and Lexus," I said aloud, more for myself than for them.

"The latter two," the director of protocol said.

"The latter two?" I repeated.

"I guess this is where we should start. As you know, they were both adopted into a new family. They are completely aware of that fact. However, they were also adopted into a new way of life. They are called Aleema and Hasna and of course they have maintained the name of their father as well." She looked at me as if to ask if I understood what she had said so far.

"To eliminate confusing the twin girls, who are thirteen and impressionable . . . ," she said.

"Where's Midnight?" I raised my voice a little louder than the therapeutic tone that the softspoken woman was using. "Where's Midnight?" I asked again.

The three Arabian chicks looked back and forth at one another, as if they suddenly didn't understand me.

"Bilal Ode!" I shouted.

"Yes, the men are engaged in a meeting in another room. Surely we woman can handle at least this much, can't we?" the lady doing all the talking said.

"Where are my sisters?" I want to see them. If not, I'll be leaving," I told them. I was sitting up right now and getting red was getting me clear.

The three women walked into the corner of the room and had a meeting with themselves. It sounded like a melody of whispers. I was looking at my Cartier watch, giving them sixty seconds, starting right now, to get their shit together and get my sisters out here.

"We will bring them in for you to meet them. We will also stay. As long as nothing inappropriate occurs, everything else should be fine. Can we offer you some water, tea, juice, coffee?" she said, too politely.

"Water would be best," the woman doctor said.

"No, thank you. I'll wait for my sisters," I told them.

After a particularly rhythmic knock by the director of protocol on one of the doors inside of our suite, Mercedes and Lexus entered from an apparently connected hotel room.

My tears betrayed me the second I got a glimpse. Their strut was graceful. They looked like two Winters, with slim pretty caramel faces and praline eyes. Their noses were slim and straight and their chins dimpled. Their smiles revealed perfect teeth. They were innocent smiles. They were the smiles of two perfumed and pampered rich girls who were now leaving childhood, curves of femininity rushing in to define things clearly. Four pretty hands without one single scar between them. Twenty manicured medium-length beautiful nails with only clear polish and that seemed more than enough. There was no uneasiness, awkwardness, fear, or sorrow in these pretty things. Definitely they were not the faces of girls who had just lost their Momma, or who had searched for their Momma for eight long years only to discover she was cold and dead and gone, forever.

Furthermore, these were girls who had never been sent to the bottom with chained ankles and wrists, had never been sprayed with ice-cold water and sent to sleep in a dorm with thirty-three crazy little strangers. These were girls who had never stood or crawled or laid down in lumpy or watery shit or barked like dogs or mooed like cows. Nope, Midnight had saved them with Poppa's written permission. Poppa saved them, but not me and no one saved Momma.

Their eyes darted towards the Arabian woman.

"Why is she crying?" Lexus asked her.

"She is sad because your *umi* has returned to Allah," the Arabian one said.

"I have three *umis*," Lexus said. The Arabian lady put her finger over her lips as if to say, *Don't tell Porsche our personal business.* Meanwhile, I'm like, what the fuck does *umi* mean? What were they discussing? Mercedes came over to me and gave me a hug.

"I remember you, Porsche," she said and embraced me.

I started bawling like a baby, her feminine scent mixing with my own. To be recognized and hugged was too much, enough to last me for the next five years. Now Lexus was hugging Mercedes, who was hugging me.

"Where do you live?" I asked them while I could ask them. I never wanted to lose track of them again.

An Arabian lady interrupted and spoke a foreign language to my twins. Their embrace loosened and the twins turned and faced her with full attention and respect. Then the twins began speaking a foreign language back to her as well. Instead of them saying where they lived, the director of protocol said, "You will be given all of the necessary information in your meeting with their guardian."

"When's that?" I shot back, my red feeling returning.

"He was prepared for you before your fainting episode. Now he's in several meetings," she said gently and politely, but I could feel the stab tucked in it.

"Baba always has meetings," Mercedes said to me calmly.

"So when then?" I asked the director.

"I'm sure he will reach out to you directly if you provide us with your information," she said, but I didn't like that it sounded like she was just guessing or making up her response.

I searched through my Birkin bag for pen and paper. I wrote my cell phone number and Mr. Sharp's numbers down twice. I handed one paper to Mercedes and one to the lady who requested it.

"No matter where you go in the world, please stay in touch with me, Porsche, your big sister. Please never forget me, okay?" I said.

Mercedes said, "I like your handbag, it's really nice."

"Do you want to have it?" I handed it to her until her little fingers were gripping it tightly.

"The shoes are pretty, too!" Lexus said. Finally she said something to me. I removed my shoes so she could try them. But she wouldn't. Instead she left them right where I left them.

"We don't wear heels yet," Lexus said.

"Your hair is nice. You just got it done, right?" Mercedes asked.

"You are definitely a Santiaga!" I said to her, laughing lightly.

"Let me see your hair?" I asked her to remove her headscarf. She took it off. Her hair was long, pretty, and well kept, like my own.

The director of protocol began speaking in a foreign tongue again. I hated that shit.

"Speak English! Speak English so I can be apart of this conversation with my family," I said, not yelling yet.

"Sorry to agitate you, Miss Porsche. I tried to converse with you concerning these matters in the first place."

"It's okay. We're all girls so I removed my hijab," Mercedes said to the protocol lady.

"Hijab!?" I repeated.

"We are Muslims. Our religion is Islam, and we do not remove our hijab in the presence of any man who we could potentially marry," Mercedes said.

"Muslims? Do you like that?" I asked. "Do you even understand what that means?" I definitely did not know what it meant or involved. More than that, I didn't want my twins to be anything that separated me any further from them.

"It's what is best for us, and we love our family and all of the women in our family are the same. We hope to live like them," Mercedes said.

"We have four sisters and five brothers," Lexus said. "And three mothers," she added.

"Four sisters?" I asked. "Including me?" I said.

"Oh, we meant in our house where we live," Lexus said.

"Plus you makes five sisters," Mercedes said graciously.

"Plus Winter . . . ," I said. Their eyes were wandering with uncertainty.

"Okay, six sisters," Lexus corrected herself.

"What about Momma?" I said, desperately.

"She is no more," Mercedes said.

"She is no more," Lexus repeated. Both of them were without a trace of one tear. My body shook with sorrow.

We shared a meal, Mercedes, Lexus, me, and the three Arabian women. I couldn't seem to squeeze them out of the package. Midnight's meetings never ended.

I was politely dismissed by the director of protocol. She told me that I would receive a call. She said the twins would not attend Momma's wake tomorrow because it wasn't how they believed it should be handled. She said they would both attend the burial because their biological father had requested it and their "guardian" had made the agreement and exceptions.

"What about their address? You said you would give it to me."

"Pardon me," she said, went into her purse and pulled out a card. I looked at it first just to check it. It was the business card for Mr. Bilal Ode, barber, with a Silver Spring, Maryland, address and the same cell phone number Mr. Sharp had recited to me for Midnight.

A lot of things didn't seem right. But who was I to start shaking down anybody else about their true identity, whereabouts, and occupation?

Out in front of the Palace Hotel, Mr. Sharp was in my Benz seated behind the wheel. He saw me before I saw him, pulled up, and off we sped.

Chapter 44

Wake, they call it, but the dead is in a permanent sleep. When I was much younger, if I overheard any talk of the dead or even saw a dead person in a movie or on television, I believed that there was a possibility that the doctors were wrong and the person would wake up suddenly and find themselves permanently trapped in a box without air to breathe, pressed deep into the dirt. Death was equal to horror for me back then.

Now staring down at Momma's remains, I was certain that she was never going to "wake" again. Wearing a black dress that Mr. Sharp made for her, and designer shoes, a short-length stylish wig, and a string of pearls that I had no idea about, Momma was dead for sure, because she did not look anything like a memory or photo of herself. And she didn't leap up to complain about the outfit she had been laid to rest in. Since my mind would not move beyond 1994, Momma's corpse appeared to be a complete stranger. Since the people inside me had worked feverishly hard to convert Momma into an angel in my mind, she couldn't be the crackhead in the box with the bullet wound in her face. She couldn't be the lady pile of deflated flesh that looked much cheaper than the conservative but expensive clothes she wore now.

Still my tears were spilling onto her face, as my heart knew for sure that Momma was "no more." Crouched over the opened coffin with my head in the box and my back to the empty seats in the room, I was wretched. *Wretched,* a word I learned from Elisha's book of synonyms when I was searching for new ways of describing my family sorrows: wretched, miserable, unfortunate, sorrowful, pitiful, contemptible, and downright melancholy.

The night before the wake I had not slept, not even for three seconds. Nothing could calm me. Due to the lessons of loving Momma, I hated drugs, wouldn't take an aspirin, a sleeping pill, an upper, a downer, a drink of any alcohol, a puff, a snort, an injection, a tab of ecstasy, or even something prescribed. *I was so cozy with pain.* We go so way back, that when it shows up, I let it fully fuck me head on, till it almost breaks me. Then I fight back. Eventually, I recover. There's no formula for a recovery date. It could be hours, days, weeks, months, even as long as a year.

"Momma, remember you said one day I would be a great dancer and that people would pay me millions to move my hips?" I cried into the coffin. "Well, you were right. Don't worry; I'm no stripper or stuck-up ballerina. I'm a showgirl in fancy expensive places, on the main stage, facing audiences of hundreds and thousands. Nope, I'm not a 'showgirl,' Momma. As you would say, 'I'm the motherfucking show stopper!' It's true.

"A hair hustler who lived in a tree house, and played a meanass drum in the wilderness underneath a full moon, got a gig in a casino owned by some Natives. He was so confident in my dancing, Momma, that he produced a show featuring his drumming and my dancing.

"I am the finale, Momma, the headliner. No one tells me what to wear. After my first performance, and a second sold-out show, I caught a big budget for costumes and styles, anything I wanted. I've been a beautiful bird, an exotic zebra, an alluring leopard, a black lion, even a lady cobra. Months later, I was given an orchestra. At rehearsals I'd sit and tell them, I want the sound of thunder, lightning, or a light rain. I want the French horns to make the 'sound of fog,' and the saxophone to make the feeling of love. I want the tuba to fill the air with fear, or the violin to send the scents of sweetness. I want the bass to arouse me, then the guitar to make me cum. I want the piano to calm me down. I want the xylophone to feel like moonlight and the trumpet to call out the sun.

"No matter how unique my requests are, they listened to me. They would perform their music, to be hypnotized by my hips and movements. The Natives think of me as a Native telling their story through dance. But it's just me, Momma, Porsche, dancing away my sorrows." I laughed a low laugh that came from somewhere in my gut.

"I know, Momma, what you wanna know? How much did it pay exactly and what the fuck am I complaining about when a rich bitch should be happy? The least it ever paid me was $2,500 a show. The most it ever paid me was $100,000, a weekend night performance. How often did I work? Every night for more than a year. My contract ended weeks ago. They offered me even more money per show to stay on. I wanted to refuse, but I was saving up that paper to buy back our Long Island palace for you, Momma. I wanted to be so caked up I could buy it in cash, and still have enough money left over to chill for a few years. I figured if you got your house and a new badass Benz, even flyer than the one Poppa got for you, you'd be ready to heal and hold your head up high. So, I gobbled up the extra dough and trained an understudy. She never got a chance to perform in my place. I was always ready, on time when the curtain lifted. Besides, everyone knew the audiences were on their feet *for me*.

"When my body began moving and expressing, I was dancing away my emotions, memories, and my strongest unfulfilled desires. I began dancing at first in one Native casino. Then I caught a cross-country Native casino tour. It became so popular that a rich European promoter booked our tour to France and England and Germany, as well as places I never heard of before, like Belgium and Poland. You should see those Europeans, especially the Germans, cheer for a young black girl moving her hips to some drumming so powerful it put me into a trance.

"When I got more comfortable on stage than in real life, I added on a hip-hop set. I never knew hip-hop would cause such fever world-wide. But it did, as I moved inside of those driving beats.

"What am I complaining about? I'm so angry, Momma, so angry. I promised to get back all of the things that were taken from you, but I didn't deliver to you in time. I let you down, and it hurts, Momma."

I remained crouched there in the coffin for five hours. Mr. Sharp tried to move me, but I was "inconsolable."

Me and Momma talked bad about our relatives who didn't even

fucking show up on Momma's death day. Aunt Laurie, and all her sisters and brothers, their children, nephews and nieces, cousins to me, none of 'em came through.

Siri didn't come, but she and I had already discussed that. Momma didn't like Siri, didn't like Riot. Both of them were the two women who loved me the most. And if I had invited Riot to the wake, she might've fooled Momma. She looked so different. When she had told me back when I was thirteen and she was seventeen that she was working on something big, I pictured her holding up an armored truck packed with millions just for the fun of it. I thought maybe she would swipe a huge diamond from a secured vault, just to showcase the mastery of her mind. Instead, she used the profits from her hustle to change her face and prints.

"Not for vanity, like some stupid fucking robot," Riot said, but for her survival, her hidden identity. She said she wasn't ever gonna get knocked and locked down again. She'd kill her captors before she ever let them take her. I could dig it.

"Now Riot's an owner of a management company, Momma. She does deals, big deals, and she plays hard. Her brother Revolution got an army that protects her, her money, investments, and clients. She manages me, Momma. I gladly pay her that fifteen percent to suck all of the stress, drama, and filth out of my life as a young, famous-anonymous dance phenomenon. She talks the business. I simply dance, shop, and chill. See how the tables turn, Momma, when you love hard, push hard, and fight and hold on to the very end? Now Riot works for me. Imagine that."

I wish Momma had liked Siri. Siri would have hummed a beautiful song for Momma's send-off. Instead, Momma laid there surrounded by silence thicker than cake, my random interruptions, and my tears.

By early evening Big Johnnie, Esmeralda, Bernard the Butcher, even the flower lady showed up. Even though they believed Momma was only my aunty, they had grief in their eyes. After all, they believed that I already lost my mother first and now my aunt who raised me after my mother's death. They were grieving for me. Who was grieving for Momma?

Mr. Sharp had a photo collage of Momma at the wake. He

promised to keep it for me. The piano lady he paid looked bored and frustrated. The undertaker showed up and said, "If you want to say a few words, you should say them now. I'm sorry to say time is almost up for this ceremony."

Moments later, I pulled my head out of Momma's mahogany coffin, turned to face the almost empty room, and spoke my heart.

"Momma was an angel. No one loved her more than me. No one ever will."

Chapter 45

Wired and without rest, I jumped up and down on the mattress in my hotel room. It was now the morning of Momma's burial. I felt a peculiar rush of energy. Siri and I showered. As I moisturized my skin, seated before the mirror, I looked in and saw behind me Momma's rejected death clothes, Gianni Versace and the stilettos.

"I'm gonna wear those," I told Siri.

"A white minidress to a burial!" Siri said, "No one would do that."

"Momma would!" I said. "Today is Momma's last day and I'm gonna represent her how I know she would want to be seen."

* * *

Mr. Sharp was in my hotel lobby. "I'm going to drive myself," I told him.

"It's not a good day to drive yourself," he warned me calmly.

I flashed him our secret sign and left.

Heads of hotel workers and businessmen were turning as I walked. They loved to see my hips sway. I ignored every eye, every word overheard. I jumped in my Benz soon as the valet brought it around. I was "Lana the stunner." Pushing an eleven-day, brand-new whip worth one hundred thousand dollars more than the red Benz Poppa had bought Momma, that Momma never got to drive or enjoy. I pumped up the music and said out loud, "C'mon Momma, let's go out in style!"

* * *

Mr. Sharp's throwback Benz was in the distance behind me, far off enough, but not so far that he wasn't captured in my rearview mirror.

Switching lanes and radio stations, I was searching for a song Lana
would like to play and hear. I was hoping she felt comfortable in this
outfit I wore for her. Maneuvering around the traffic with the notorious New York rough riders, rough drivers crowd, it was hard to think
straight and drive straight, but a Benz floats and glides over New
York potholes and around the cones, obstacles, and trash on the roads
and highways. Besides, a Benz was Momma's favorite ride and only
choice. That's why I copped it.

I looked to my passenger side when I heard Siri humming. She
wasn't sitting there. Was I tripping? Nope. She wasn't. Her voice
was coming through the radio and sounding incredible on my Bose
speaker system. "What song is she singing?" I asked.

Momma wanted me to switch stations or just cut it off. I couldn't.
It was a love song so sweet it stirred my insides and moved me to tears.
Siri was singing and someone was strumming that guitar so magically
the strings sent a vibration between my thighs. It was two guitars, one
electric, one acoustic, so arousing.

The radio DJ announced, "That song is moving up the charts and
heating up the countdown. It's the title track from a new film debut-
ing this weekend. The song track is 'Elisha,' and the movie is called
A Love Supreme. Highly anticipated! New York City, we're taking
your calls."

My thoughts were suspended. I rolled off the wrong exit ramp
and pulled over on a curb beneath a tree.

"You're caller number seven," the radio DJ said.

"Y'all should have *him* in the studio!" the caller said.

"Who?" the DJ asked.

"Elisha Immanuel!" the caller shouted and some girl was screaming in the background of her call. "He shot the film in Brooklyn, and
everybody wanna see it. He's a crazy cutie!" she said.

"Caller, gives us your name," the radio DJ asked.

"It's Takia from Brownsville!" she screamed.

"Guess what? We have Elisha Immanuel in the studio with us this
morning. Say hello!"

"Oh, shit!" the girl screamed and dropped the phone.

"Whassup Takia, it's Elisha. Hope you bring all of Brownsville
out this Friday. Everybody check out my new movie, *A Love Supreme*,

when it opens this weekend!" There was applause. "Brooklyn don't wait! New York don't wait! BX don't wait! Queens don't wait! ... Money-making Manhattan don't wait!" Elisha was pumping it up.

"Have you been getting this kind of reaction as you're promoting your first independent film around the country? Do you hear the excitement of the caller!" the radio DJ asked Elisha.

"Girls tend to like me," Elisha said calmly and laughed some.

"But fellas, take it easy. I got mine, won't grab yours," he said confidently.

"That's whassup," the DJ responded.

"We're in the studio with seventeen-year-old Elisha Immanuel, upcoming, independent, talented, young black man, and film director. There's talk about Sony Pictures and other big movie houses trying to sign you to a big seven-figure deal even before your first film debuts this weekend. Is that right?"

"True, but I'm feeling this independent route real strong. I've used the opportunity to boost a group of smaller businesses and Return Address Entertainment is taking a chance in this industry, that we can produce big box office hits without the Hollywood machine behind us. Our motto is, 'Show the people what they want to see.'"

"You've been touring the country, pumping up and promoting this film big time. So if all hoods show up strong in theaters across the country this weekend, you're like 'ching ching.' Your pockets gonna fatten like crazy! Talk to us about why you named your company Return Address Entertainment."

"Well, see there's this girl I love . . . ," Elisha said.

Then the studio audience and DJ started cheering him on.

"Whoa, whoa, whoa," the radio DJ suddenly said, interrupting him. "You're about to break a lot of hearts . . . ," the DJ said.

"A man should be able to say when he loves someone, right?" Elisha asked. Things turned silent.

"There's a girl I love, she travels all around the world. She sends me postcards and sweet letters and gifts, but there's never a return address," Elisha said.

"Sounds deep. Why do you think she does that?"

"She's afraid to let me love her. But she made me a deal. She said after I make my first film, she would let me wife her. She probably can't hear me right now, but if you listening, meet me in your wedding dress on Friday at three at our spot."

The DJ hit the applause button again and there was nothing but clapping on top of the moving beats. A song by Jagged Edge, "Let's Get Married," played, leading into commercials.

"That was Elisha Immanuel, y'all, one of Brooklyn's Finest. You also heard him playing guitar on the title track, named after himself, 'Elisha.' He's a hell of a promoter, marketer, and director, and a huge hit with the ladies, just another young black Brooklyn millionaire."

My heart with the five holes in it was swelling. I think it dropped into my lap. Parked beneath a tree, I didn't know the feeling of a nervous breakdown, but my nerves were pulsating, my whole body shaking. I was Porsche. I was Lana. I was Siri. I was Ivory. I was Onatah. I was splitting into little puzzle pieces that I couldn't put back together.

Elisha was doing that to me, again. He was loving me in a way I had longed to be loved by others in my family, with passion, loyalty, strength, and with battle in his blood.

Oh no! Elisha's love was highlighting the bitter, tasteless, and poisonous love I got from F A M I L Y. His love was turning Momma the angel back into Momma the crackhead. His love was turning Poppa the king into Poppa the fuckup. His love was turning Winter into the conceited, selfish bitch that never came to get me while she was free and balling, the same big sister who laughed at and never saved Momma. Elisha's love was turning Lexus and Mercedes into the little rich girls who forgot their roots and lost their feelings for their momma who birthed them. I fucking loved Elisha so much, that I couldn't love them no more.

I caught a migraine headache, felt temporarily blind, and was weeping all over.

* * *

Plowing into the graveyard, I jammed the brake so suddenly my floating Benz jerked. I took a deep breath in and blew out.

This is the day I bury them all, I thought to myself.

Finally, looking through my windshield, I saw armed full-geared-up police guards in the firing position. I froze.

"That's right, fucking kill me! Why not! I'm so sick of being a fugitive." I wiped away my tears in the mirror and slid on my Chanel sunglasses. When I finally pushed open my door, Busta Rhymes was wilding on the mic the way only he do. My Dolce & Gabbana stilettos were sinking into the moist earth. I grabbed my Birkin bag. "You're in a movie scene, Porsche, like when you were helping Elisha with his auditions. Except *you're the star now*. You were betrayed by all of these people. Don't let them see you hurt. Show them what they love more than they ever loved you, these fashions and styles, these whips, beautiful hips, and this fucking money."

Standing beside Winter, cause of everybody living she cared the least about me, I didn't have to say too many lines to her. I delivered each one without a sprinkle of love or affection in it. The same way she would've if it was the other way around. Winter was defeated. It was all in her eyes. Poppa was still sweating Winter, as normal. Poppa cried over Momma.

"Too late!" I mumbled to myself. Mercedes and Lexus stayed stuck on Midnight and to themselves. The armed guards crowded their cuffed prisoners, Poppa, and Winter.

As the closed coffin was lowered into the ground I kicked dirt over it with my stilettos. My heart cracked some more. I kicked some more. I was burying Momma and Poppa and Winter, all at the same time.

* * *

They were all gone back to their balls and chains and cells. I sat in the graveyard soil in Momma's white death dress and cried until my heart could feel free.

Chapter 46

Riding in the backseat of my blacked-out, black Mercedes Benz 600, I was watching Midnight through my rearview mirror. He was chauffeuring me, as he had chauffeured Ricky Santiaga many times in the past. His beautiful black silhouette was all I could see at the moment.

As I was exiting the graveyard gates, he had eased off of the brick pillar and walked calmly in front of my vehicle, sure that I would stop my car before running him down.

He walked to the driver side and opened my door, saying nothing. I tossed my left leg out first, turned my body and stood up. He followed me around to the passenger side backseat, saying nothing. I could feel the heat from his body. He opened the door for me. I entered and sat comfortably. He was, after all, the only man who came for me when I was locked down. He was the man who saved my twins, when I myself failed to save them. Not to forget, that he was the first man to ever rescue me and my sisters after my mother was shot in her face back when I was seven. He had covered up the incident to protect my young heart and ears, telling us only that my momma had an accident and would recover soon. For three or four days, he was our only protection. I remember, remembered, and was remembering.

I was thinking about how to think about him. Is he the hero or the villain? Or is he so clever, seductive, and disarming, that he was both? How did he become the main player? Why did he seem so paid? How come he was the last man standing in what was described as a one hundred-million-dollar empire? Should I allow myself to react naturally to his hypermasculinity as any woman would? Or should I squash that feeling and interact with him as my sister's step-father, which strangely, would make him a father figure to me also?

He changed the radio station, which accelerated my feelings. Now Maxwell was singing: The volume was low, which made it sweet and arousing. Suddenly I began thinking about how as I traveled through the United States and toured through Europe, restraining myself was simple. At home now, the closer I get to Elisha, the more open and sexual my feelings and thoughts become. Private, sensitive, and personal parts of myself that had been paralyzed by grief were awakening.

Now my eyes were back onto my regal driver.

Midnight had to be about twenty-nine years young, not too much over that, if any. Not even double my age, I guessed. Could I seriously shift myself and view him as a father? Maybe I should test him.

As a dancer, I had encountered many men who tried to get at me, despite the difficulty of the task. I had two big bodyguards outside of my dressing room and at all rehearsals and performances. One was a huge Samoan, the other a bonafide well-fed, overgrown black man. I was well hidden and secured, a minor in the "major leagues," so to speak. I was working in casinos where liquor I wasn't even old enough to look at was served around the clock. Most importantly, I didn't want none of those men to be successful in getting at me, not even for only a lustful close-up or stare, an autograph or "accidental" touch, or a private dance or a photograph or even a conversation. I was, and am, a sixteen-year-old virgin who had laid down naked body to body, who had been touched up passionately, caressed, kissed, and even sucked and licked by only one man, Elisha Immanuel, and my heart, mind, and body belonged exclusively to him. I could cum, and many lonely nights I did, just recalling the sensation and feeling and touch of Elisha. I could imagine so deeply it would be as though he was breathing in my ear, tongue swirling in my mouth, fingers pressing on my pleasure button. I could cum simply anticipating the night when he would finally push into me with full hardness and intent and a love that made my nerves tingle and then erupt.

Being that I was sure of my man, and our love, it was nothing but pure sport watching other men go crazy over me. I'd sit at my dressing room vanity table opening up their cards and gifts, looking over their fruit baskets, candies, and bouquets of flowers sent over directly. I'd

even receive jewels that I swiftly sent back, including a 10-karat diamond wedding ring from a prince from a country named Qatar, that
I never even heard of and doubt existed. Jewels were always intimate
to me, only to be accepted from blood or from someone I loved who
wanted to become my king.

I had rejected NBA jerseys from off of the backs of NBA players who had a thing for gambling, who happened upon my show. I
tossed VIP tickets in the trash from celebrities who wanted to mix it
up with me.

I could look at any of these men eye to eye and measure the intensity of their desire without experiencing any feelings of my own. I'd
be laughing on the inside, once I knew for sure that they had already
been informed, quietly and repeatedly, that I was underage. I knew
and I could tell that they didn't care. There would be this glint in their
eye that spoke to me, "C'mon, little girl, how much for me to fuck you
one good time?"

Mr. Sharp had prepared me well. "Your beauty is bait. Don't let
'em touch. As soon as you do, your value decreases immediately." So
I didn't.

Would Midnight look at me with that glint in his eye? How good
is he? Could he see me as his daughter? I wanted to know that for
starters, so I could move beyond the whole man-woman thing, to the
business at hand.

He looked back, finally. Didn't move his neck an inch. He was
using the rearview mirror I was using to watch him, to watch me. He
had an unusual gaze, hard to read. It wasn't the usual look I got from
men who looked into my unusually colored eyes, fell in, and drowned.
His eyes returned to the road.

"Where are we going?" I broke the silence between us.

"First stop is to get you into some clothes. You and I have some
unfinished situations. Should I buy you something new, or would you
like to give me your address?"

I rolled my eyes and turned my head, looking out of my window.

"Buy me something new," I said. I don't know why.

Parked on Fifth Avenue in Manhattan, he exited the car and
locked me inside with the windows slightly dashed. I didn't resist, just
sat calmly thinking. Why did he wait for me at the graveyard? Where

did he send the twins and his entourage? Why did he feel the need to drive with me in my car, and alone?

Forty-two minutes later, he opened the opposite back door. He put the purchases, which were hanging on hangers in the hanger cases on the hook and set a shopping bag on the floor.

Parked along a tree-lined sidewalk at Central Park East, Midnight got out saying he'd wait while I got dressed.

"Why not the presidential suite?" I asked him.

"Checked out this morning," he said.

"How do you know if these clothes will fit me?" I asked.

"They'll fit. I looked at you first. Everybody can see you," he said calmly. Behind tinted windows, I pulled off the white minidress and stilettos.

Unzipping the hanger bag, I found a pistachio-colored silk dress by Fendi. It was soft, feminine, and very pretty. Midnight liked women to be feminine and men to be men, I thought to myself. Then I also saw the pants. Checking the labels and tags, I could see the two pieces were not made as a set, although to the artistic eye they could work and blend nicely. It only took me half a second to decide that he wanted me in a dress and pants, covered like the Arabian chicks.

The outfit was high-quality and it worked. The designer pants hugged my hips perfectly. I wondered how could he know? So many clothes don't give way for the beauty of hips. I wouldn't say so, but I was impressed, even more so when I opened the Jimmy Choo shoebox.

I knew I looked good, clean, and rich. I also knew that none of this was what mattered most.

"What's next?" I asked him, my voice calling out to him through his slightly dashed driver-side backseat window.

"Do you have a cell phone?" he asked.

"Yes," I replied. He nodded his head to say that I should leave it in the car. I removed my cell phone and also had laid my handbag on the floor hidden beneath the shopping bag. He came around, opened the back door for me and extended his hand to help me out. We walked together beneath the blue sky and afternoon sun against the beauty of Central Park.

"Sit down," he said, pointing out a bench with his nod.

"Can we walk towards the carousel?" I asked him. He nodded.

"Are you okay?" he asked me, walking.

"I'm good . . . enough," I said, forcing a smile then dropping my head a bit.

"I regret that it had to be the passing of your mother that finally brought us together," he said, sounding sincere.

"It was a long journey with Momma and me," I said. "Nothing was sudden. When I got that call, I felt sorrow, but I wasn't shocked." Then silence fell between us, but nature still sang its song.

"I have some questions for you and some information," he said, facing forward instead of looking into my eyes. "My questions, your answers and the information we share is only for me and you. If you ever repeat it, you're on your own. I won't confirm it," he said.

"Then why are you asking and why are you telling?"

"I'm asking for my own satisfaction. I'm telling, for your satisfaction, safety, and for your freedom," he said. Then he added, "If you don't want to answer my questions and you don't want to know the information, tell me now." He stopped walking. "I'll take you back to your car. We'll go our separate ways and there will be no reason for me to return or to search for you, or to look back any further." I looked at his handsome profile. Each of his words were spoken with 100 percent certainty. He must feel good about himself. Unlike most of us, he didn't entertain, or make space for even a speck of self-doubt.

Standing at six-two, I took his words as a threat. He has my twins, so of course me and him needed to stay in touch. I had not "buried" the twins. They never abandoned me. They are innocent in all of this. I knew it would take some time to heal their feelings towards me, their big sister. I wanted to make it happen though, naturally.

"It's closed," I said, pointing to the carousel.

A hundred-dollar bill, crisp and clean as though he had made it himself, eased from beneath his gold money clip, exchanged hands, and the carousel began to spin.

"Lift me up, please," I asked him sweetly. "I'll feel better if you let me ride. Besides, you paid for it." I smiled. He placed both hands on my waist and lifted me onto the painted horse, which would normally bore me if Midnight were not the one beside me. He seated me sideways and ladylike. Out of some type of respect, I didn't throw one leg around the other side of the horse like I would've if I were back on the reservation. Midnight leaned against a still horse, facing me, as my horse moved up and down.

"Okay, ask me." I smiled. "If it's about me, I'll tell you honestly. If it's about anyone else, I won't."

"Why have you agreed?" he asked strangely.

"For my own satisfaction, for my safety, and my freedom," I said, using his words on him. Some carnival music interrupted us. I rode round and round, up then down as he stood, still guarding over me.

"Thank you so much. I feel much calmer. Please help me down," I said. He did.

Beneath a wide oak whose branches hovered over a small curved bridge that looked like it belonged in a fairy tale, we were paused in heavy conversation. We each held a bottle of water, which he purchased for us.

"This world is confusing, isn't it?" he said, leaning on the railing thoughtfully.

"Yes." I definitely agreed.

"And no one is who they say they are, are they?" he asked, but it also sounded like a confession.

"True," I agreed.

"And that includes you and I . . . ," he said with certainty.

"Yes." I exposed myself.

"And there are more liars than truth tellers, right or wrong," he stated.

"Right."

"Still, some people are good, and others are evil," he said.

"More evil than good," I said sincerely.

"I've been looking for you for eight years. If you were hiding, you did an incredible job. Your father asked me to find you and give you a good life. For three years, I was searching for you for him. For the following five years up until now, I've been searching for you out of a certain amount pride and disbelief," he said. He paused, then he admitted to me, "You were the only person who I ever searched for, but never found."

"I'm right here. You got me," I said, trying to lighten it up some.

"I know you must've been somewhere feeling a deep sense of

anger, the kind that strangles you so tightly that you feel prevented from doing anything else." He had my full seriousness now. He was describing my exact feelings.

"Anything else like what?" I asked him. I wanted to feel more from him.

"The most important things; like being free, being able to say the truth out loud when you feel like it, loving someone, getting married, having children, feeling safe, having peace of mind and heart. The things everybody should have, true?" he asked, turning towards me, but I knew he was sure, and that it wasn't a question.

"Yes," I said, and I meant it.

"It's an anger so thorough and complete that it turns into obsession so strong that you can't move on to anything else," he said. I wondered, how could he possibly know?

"Yes," I agreed.

"That anger pushes you to do things, and to say things that no one within your reach in your world can ever understand," he said.

"Yes!" I screamed out into the trees. I pictured Momma when I had her cuffed, and how she never understood that I was angry about what was happening with her, but everything I did to her, I did it for love. "Yes," I said again more calmly. He didn't react, instead stayed smoothed out like the coolest man in the world.

"The less they understand, the deeper the anger runs within you. Then it appears to everyone else to be insanity," Midnight said calmly.

"Yes." I thought of Momma cursing me, threatening to kill me. I thought of the warden, the guards, my teachers. My angriest tears boiled up warming my hot cheeks and spilling down my face.

"Then there is your need to have someone who is regarded as sane, respectable, and important, to admit to you that you have been seriously wronged," he said. I gasped.

"The more the sane and professional adults deny that you have been wronged, and that their system is wrong, and that your instincts and reactions were normal in light of the wrongs that they did to you, but won't admit to, the deeper your anger moves in, separating you from everyone else."

"Yes," I said almost silently. The taste of my tears was on my tongue.

"Where is St. Katherine's Group Home?" he asked, and I was humbled.

"22-15 Suphtin Blvd. in Queens."

"How long were you there?"

"Two months."

"Who is Lucy Jackson?"

"Foster care lady."

"How long were you with her?"

"Three days."

"Why did you leave?"

"Her husband was a pervert. He tried to show me something nasty," I said, trembling.

"Who is Evelyn Sandstone?"

"Foster care parent."

"How long were you there?"

"Five days."

"Why did you leave?"

"Her son was an abuser. He tied me to a chair in his room when no one was looking."

"Who is Bernice Wilkins?"

"Foster care parent."

"How long was you with her?"

"Four days."

"Why did you leave?"

"She was a drunk who wouldn't feed us."

Who is Mrs. Griswaldi?"

"Caseworker."

"What happened with her?"

"I stabbed her with a pencil. She got paralyzed."

"Were you convicted?"

"Yes."

"Sentenced?"

"Yes."

"How long?"

"Eight years."

"Where?"

"New York State Juvenile Prison for Violent Girls, Upstate New York."

"How long were you there?"

"Two years, 297 days," I said, and I could even give him the count on the hours, minutes, and seconds.

"What happened on July 20, 1996?"

"I left the NYS Juvenile Prison for Violent Girls."

"Where did you go?"

"I escaped."

"Where did you go?" he asked again. I didn't answer. I remained silent.

"What happened on July 20, 1996?" he asked again.

"I escaped and been on my own since then," I told him. It didn't matter how many times he asked that question. Pressed or tortured, I would never reveal NanaAnna. A promise is a promise.

He stayed silent for a while. He was so still. But I could see his mind moving. I appreciated the energy and feeling and concern he was showing me simply by concentrating so hard and trying to decipher my roller-coaster life. He had been searching for me for eight years! So many other people seemed so comfortable not knowing anything about what was happening to me.

"Who is Edith Kates?" he asked surprisingly and suddenly. Of course I remembered her.

"*New York Daily News* reporter," I said.

"Why is she looking for you?" he asked.

"I wrote her a letter," I said.

"When?"

"March 1996."

"About what?" he pushed.

"About a nasty news article that she wrote about my father."

"What is the Kennedy-Claus facility?" He asked

"Don't know," I said.

"Have you ever been there?" he asked.

"Never."

"Has anyone ever mentioned the place to you? Do you know anyone else who went there? Think about it before you answer," he said.

"Never, I'm one hundred percent," I said.

"Has anybody hurt you?"

"Only my feelings," I said.

"Are you sure? Did anyone put their hands on you?" he pressed.

"No, I mean I been cuffed and trapped. But no one violated me like that, just messed with my head. They do that to everybody on lockdown," I said.

I could see his jaw flinch. I liked this exact feeling. It was like if I had said someone had hurt me, and said their name, that person would suddenly lose their life. That was rare energy. That was extremely arousing to me.

"Where did you get that car?" he asked.

"I bought it."

"How?"

"With money I earned."

"Doing what?"

"Performing."

"Performing what? Performing what?" he repeated calmly, but still I felt the pressure of his presence.

"Entertainment, no sex, no touching, no nudity. That's what you wanted to know, right?" I said it too spicy.

"Do you have a driver's license?"

"No. I have a permit."

"Under what name?"

"Nobody is who they say they are. Not you and not me," I reminded him.

"When did you first meet Mr. Sharp?"

"September 1996," I said swiftly. Midnight's mind was merging what he thought he knew, comparing it to what I was telling him and counting it all up. I understood. But no one could count better than me. I had a heap of practice. He stayed quiet for too long. So I asked him.

"What about the information you were supposed to tell me? The information that's between you and me, that you won't confirm if I repeat it?"

He looked at me, into my eyes and at my hands and feet. It felt like he was examining me, looking into me, but I knew it wasn't in a dirty way. I can tell the difference. I know that dirty look and the feeling it brings.

"There is no warrant for your arrest. There is no reason for you to hide your identity. The juvenile prison has no record of your escape. You are on record as having been transferred to the Kennedy-Claus Hospital for Criminally Insane Juveniles on July 20, 1996, and released after effective treatment and time served on July 19, 2001, one month ago," Midnight said.

Now my mind was moving. Were the authorities saying that I was crazy and that nothing I say is true? Were they saying that all of the things that happened in my life from the time that I got locked up and for eight whole years, were all false? Were they saying there was no Riot, Lina, Hamesha, Lil' Man, Tiny, Jinjah, Rose Marie, Camille, Ting-Tong, Shana, and no Diamond Needles? Were they saying I didn't escape? There was no NanaAnna, no reservation, no drummer in the tree house, and no Onatah, her family, no casino and *No Elisha!* I began to sweat some. I could feel panic easing in, threatening a takeover.

Midnight pulled a folded clean handkerchief from his pocket, poured some of his water on it, and began to wipe my perspiration with the cool water.

"Under what name?" I asked Midnight softly, while shaking some. "Who are they saying went crazy?"

"Porsche L. Santiaga," he said almost silently.

"Why did they say they sent me to the insane hospital?"

"Violent uncontrollable repeated outbreaks, schizophrenia paranoia, psychotic treatment," he said as though he had read it off a file that he had studied for a long time. No wonder he had the three Arabian women supervise me when I went to see the twins. The authorities had told him I was a nut job. Did he think I would hurt them? My body began to tremble some: I tried to stop it, but my hands were shaking.

"Who did they say they released me to?" I asked, shaking and trembling.

"Your mother, Lana Santiaga," he said.

The anger that Midnight had just talked about began to raise up from my feet and was moving with the strength of a hurricane and

speed of a tornado. Tears were boiling up, flooding over from my insides. My anger was crippling me. Midnight took my hand and pulled
opened each stiffening finger. He was massaging my palm, same as
Riot or NanaAnna would do.

"I searched for you. I knew something illegal, inappropriate, and
unacceptable was happening to you. The state would not allow visits
to the Kennedy-Claus facility. A judge and the state denied each
of my requests. I knew they had to be wrong. They're powerful, the
authorities, the government. You were just a young girl," he said. "It
was smart that you wrote that letter to the *New York Daily News*. They
weren't expecting that. It might have saved your life. Strange things
happen to people in prison, especially the ones who no one is checking up on or looking for."

I breathed in deeply. Then I exhaled slowly. It hurt to struggle so
hard to get to a place, then have someone, anyone, say that I never
struggled, and that they simply released me when they wanted to.
That it was them who handed me over to Momma, one week before
her death. Now Momma was no longer here to prove that they were
liars.

"Don't think too much about it. There is the truth. Then there
is the lie. The government has an endless budget to manufacture as
many lies as they would like. They use one lie to cover up their last lie
and to set up for their next lie. Each of us could spend a lifetime trying to reverse the mud, stains, and false accusations that governments
manufacture daily. Or, we could just go on living the truth as we know
and understand it."

I was beginning to feel some relief. Midnight, the only man who
came for me, believed me. He didn't believe them. He didn't side with
the officials.

He didn't believe the doctors. He didn't believe the judge.

"Why do you believe me and not them?" I asked. "They have a
track record of lying. Can the state ever admit that they were out
maneuvered by a little girl when she was ten?"

"I took a good look at you. What I was seeing and what they were
saying was two different things. I've been around the world a few
times. I looked into many faces. I'm suspicious of anyone who doesn't

allow a person to see a prisoner face to face. Or a government that won't allow the voice of the accused to be heard openly, or a court that won't weigh the thoughts and testimony of at least two sides or however many sides there are," he said. I took a deep breath and exhaled big. I shook my fingers, and twisted my little waist some.

"Use this circumstance to your advantage. They said your time is served. It's better than the life of a fugitive where you can never relax being who you really are and were born to be."

"I have some questions. What about Momma? You said Poppa told you to save me and to give me a good life. Why didn't Poppa save Momma?"

"No human could save her. She gave her life to the drugs. Drugs are mind-altering substances. They alter the mind of the user, most of the time permanently," he said, sure that all users were hopeless, it seemed.

"Aren't those the same drugs you and Poppa were selling?"

"No comment," Midnight said, without smiling, gloating, or denying.

"Well, how do you earn your money now?" I asked him. "How does a barber afford the presidential suite?" I pushed.

"I don't hustle. I don't deal drugs. That's what you really want to know, right?" he threw that back at me. "The barbershop is just one small business that I own. There are many more," he said. "All legit," he added swiftly.

"What about my sisters?"

"You've seen their faces yourself, and heard their voices. What did you think about what you saw? I'm sure your own eyes don't lie to you."

"Where do they live?" I asked, avoiding telling him that he was right. They both looked safe, healthy, happy, and wealthy.

"All around the world," he said, also avoiding my direct question.

"Why don't you give them back to me? We're blood-related family. They're my sisters."

"You're a juvenile."

"So when I'm eighteen I can take them? I'll be an adult, legal, and you say I'm not a fugitive," I reminded him.

"If they want to return to you, I might allow it. But under some conditions. First, how you're living and if your life and home is better for them than their current place in the world. Two, if they want to live with you. Three, if you can provide, including their continuing education. Oh, and if you allow them to maintain a relationship with their adopted family. My wives love them. My wives raised them, and all of my children love them."

"How about you? You're so cool in this confused world," I said, maybe with too much emotion and attitude.

"I love them also. They are your father's daughters. If it wasn't for love, I wouldn't be here right now," he said comfortably. I like a man who can be masculine and comfortable when discussing love, like Elisha.

"Can I hug you?" I asked him, feeling emotional and grateful towards him.

"Nah, that wouldn't be right," he said, again with a smoothness that made me attracted and angry to be attracted.

"Why not?"

"Because you're a unrelated, unmarried woman," he said. I guess that was a line out of his "Muslim manual."

"I thought you said I was a young girl, a juvenile, a minor," I reminded him.

"That's what the law says. My eyes see something else," he said.

"What about Winter?" I asked him.

"What about her?" he asked without changing a tone or his face. He was unmoved.

"Did you ever love her?" I asked.

"No."

"Why not?"

"She's not the kind of woman I would love," he said.

"What about me?" I asked in too quick of a hurry.

"What about you?" he said calmly.

"Am I the kind of woman you could love?"

"It doesn't matter," he dismissed me.

"That's not an answer."

"You are Elisha Immanuel's woman. He is a good man, strong, solid, and capable."

"How do you know that?" I said softly, feeling like I had all of the wind and breath kicked out of my body. Suddenly I was feeling naked in an unsexy way.

"I told you. I've been searching for you since '94. When Sharp entered the picture, I found a whole new set of people who were connected and searching for you. Right now, Mr. Sharp is waiting for you. He was at the graveyard gate parked. I sent him back. Elisha has been searching for you for so long, that if you delay, he will become someone else's husband," Midnight warned, and his warning was burning in my breast, cutting through my heart, and churning in my belly.

"I just wanted to know if you were decent and if you thought that I am decent. I needed to know that, to hear that from you. That's why I asked you that question: What about me?" I said, trying to erase my guilt.

"I'm not here to judge you. As a man, I'm as decent as a man could be. I know I have a soul. I know I have to answer to the MAKER of my soul, above all else. I can see that you are a beautiful woman, clearly. I feel like you're decent and that your soul is good," he said. "InshaAllah, my instincts are right." He seemed to be thinking still. "Just be smart. Don't compare yourself to others as a standard. Ask yourself if you are living right and true. And wear some damn clothes," he said calmly. "Don't show the world the same that you should only show your husband."

"I'm not married yet," I said. I don't know why.

"I know. You're also not stupid. So you'll marry soon."

"So you like Elisha!" I said, turning excited.

"I like him. Your father likes him. He went to see him a few days ago."

"Elisha and Poppa." That was so hard for me to imagine or believe. Elisha had gone all the way up by Canada to meet my father.

"Yes."

"But how?"

"I know you think you did all of your living on your own. Some young heads think that way. Your father, Ricky Santiaga, protected you as much as any incarcerated father could protect his daughter. You might not realize that yet. Think about it: your father must have given you certain things that ultimately saved your life when you were in a tight spot." He looked at me to see if I was considering his words. I thought of my money tree.

"Between you and I, my father was a political prisoner. He was away from my life for many years. I fought hard the whole way through his absence. But the whole time *I knew* it was my father who made me a man, who gave me the foundation and the lessons in life that made me a fighter who could win, a strong fighter," Midnight said. "Mr. Sharp connected back to your father recently. But it was because of your father, Ricky Santiaga, and his reputation that made Mr. Sharp protect you. Mr. Sharp made it safe for you to be a young girl who didn't get swallowed by the streets. Mr. Sharp was the first one to pick up on Elisha. Sharp's man brought Elisha to Sharp for hanging round the back alley where you lived. Sharp had a sitdown with Elisha."

I didn't say nothing. Midnight was in the process of blowing my mind.

"After I hooked up with Sharp, I picked up Elisha. We didn't have the same kind of sitdown that he and Sharp had or like me and you are having. I tested him, roughed 'im up a little, to make sure he could hold his own. That's what men are supposed to do," Midnight said solemnly.

"That's good. Elisha loves a test," I said casually then smiled, letting Midnight know Elisha is damn sure strong. Yet and still, in my heart, I knew Elisha wasn't no killa. He walked with too much love for that.

Midnight had that energy like he had deleted a few men who deserved it. Like he eliminated them with a swiftness, without even a speck of doubt or hesitation.

"Now, you, Porsche, are Elisha's job. Make him work for you." Midnight smiled, his first smile, a million-dollar smile that is permanently pressed into my memory. I jumped on him, leaned against him, gave him a tight hug and a kiss on his cheek.

"Sorry," I told him afterward, pulling back. "I'm subjected to violent outbursts," I confessed. We both laughed.

Chapter 47

Four days later, in the back room of Sharp's Golden Needle shop, the immaculate carpeted place where both Ricky and Lana Santiaga had once stood at the top of their game, I was sliding into my red debutante's ball gown, designed by Mr. Sharp. It wasn't short. It wasn't long. The elegance of it was in both the fabric and design; the shoulder straps; the criss-crossing back out; the tapered waist; and the way it hugged my breast and stitched out my small waist and exploded in layers at my hips. It was "an eye catcher," as Mr. Sharp put it. "A traffic stopper and a shockwave." Once I was in it, I felt like a Spanish dancer, the ones who held castanets in their hands and made music with their fingertips combined with the click of their high heels. Then I imagined I was a female matador, wearing a dress so red that instead of one bull, it inspired a whole herd to charge and chase me.

Enticed by the feminine sleek satin heels that matched the dress and criss-crossed on my ankles, I still chose to wear a brand-new pair of red high-top Converses, which nearly gave Sharp a cardiac episode.

"I'm walking twenty-eight blocks to the organic market, Mr. Sharp, not on the New York or Paris runway!" He shook his head the way older people who love the young ones shake their head. "Drop 'em in your handbag, just in case," he said. I opened the red Epi Leather. He dropped them in.

With my skin glistening, my manicure and pedicure perfectly designed in an overpriced, by-appointment-only exclusive Manhattan salon and my hair freshly done by Esmeralda herself, I began walking down Sharp's block, past Sharp's building and down twenty-eight more blocks. My excitement mounted with each step. I loved that when I walked out of Elisha's life for a while, he didn't suspect me, like I was out hoeing or anything like that. "You said you love me, so don't go loving no one else," he had told me when I was twelve, and that meant the world to me. It made me hot when he had first said it. It kept me hot, on many cold lonely nights on the roads far away from Brooklyn.

The sun was bright and high. The air was thick and warm. I was feeling a thousand pounds lighter than I had in eight years. The Brooklyn summer sidewalks were swelling with people. None of them were wearing debutante gowns. I was wearing one, and several sets of eyes were massaging me—the men, the boys, and even the women. I was almost there, but couldn't see my way clear to the organic market.

Surrounded by three hundred people, Elisha finally saw me. As I pushed through them, he moved towards me. The people were cheering for him, I realized. However, it seemed that Elisha could only see me. Serious-faced till we reached one another, he grabbed me up and hugged me so tight and squeezed me so hard! Over his strong shoulder I saw cameras snapping our photos. He must've seen cameras, too, and him knowing that I didn't want my photos taken, grabbed my hand and bolted, pulling me through the crowd. Now we were running, and the crowd began chasing us. Elisha was leading, my feet were running and my heart was racing. The Eyewitness News van was chasing us with their television cameras. I couldn't fucking believe it. I looked back at the crowd and instead of getting smaller and farther away, it was increasing in size and getting closer as we ran. My body was excited. I didn't have time to think. I was just feeling the rush and the thrill of fleeing.

Traffic was jamming as people spilled into the streets. Drivers stepped out of their cars to try and see and understand what was happening. Shop owners were leaning out their doors, some of 'em calling out Elisha's name with enthusiastic familiarity. I began laughing. What was going on?

"Elisha, where are we running to?" I asked him, as we kept moving.

"I don't know," he said. "Long as we running together."

* * *

In a schoolyard in Brooklyn, Elisha's old school, at 7:00 p.m., one thousand people, many of them teens like Elisha and me, were sitting on the cement facing a huge outdoor movie screen, which Elisha had arranged. Excitement filled the air. Vendors with popcorn machines, hot sugared almonds, sliced fruits, ICEEs, ice pops 'n creams, and other treats outlined the yard and their businesses were bubbling. Kids and parents were racing back to squeeze in next to where their families were seated.

Elisha had still not let go of my hand from when he first grabbed it hours ago. We were seated in the center of the crowd, like regular viewers. Elisha had one arm and one leg tossed around me. It felt good. The movie soundtrack began and hundreds of more people gathered outside of the schoolyard fences to watch Elisha's first film, *A Love Supreme*.

The soundtrack was awesome. It had emotion and as a dancer and lover of music, I knew that only the best musicians could make music that made crowds of people all catch the same deep feeling at the same time from the same song. It was nice to see a sea of strangers, yet familiar faces, in a Brooklyn neighborhood all grooving together, bodies rocking in syncopation.

When the movie began I saw the familiar face of the female star. It was Audrey. My insides tangled a bit. I was thinking more clearly now. I had left her alone with my man for way too long, stupidly. How dark my mind must've been. So dark, I couldn't consider her, or any other girl or put the possibility of losing him in the first position. Maybe there would be love scenes. Maybe the two of them had rehearsed those scenes over and over again, the way I had laid with Elisha, reciting lines and quizzing him for tests and learning and loving him. Maybe in the making of the film, while I was Momma's little moneymaker, dancing out my sorrows and my madness, miles and miles away, Audrey had squeezed into his heart. I knew that didn't mean that I wasn't in his heart. But maybe it meant I was and she was, too.

That thought triggered the feelings that began to unfreeze my heart, which I had locked up and made ice cold at Momma's burial. I wrapped my arms around Elisha's waist. I could feel him, taller, wider, stronger than the strong he already was. While I was away, he had evolved from boy to man, and as both boy and a man he had always been so beautiful to me. As he felt me clinging to him, he held me even tighter.

In some moments, I recognized faces of Elisha's friends in the film, faces I had seen him talking or walking or working with in our summer together, which began passionately on my birthday when I turned thirteen. It was a close and thick love between us that continued till seven days before I turned fourteen. That was when Momma showed up to the underground, bruised and broken.

Elisha was down there with me, beneath the floor of Big Johnnie's store. It was only the second time we had been down there alone. I had told him that we shouldn't be down there together, because down there nothing would stop him from making love to me, especially not me or him. Down there, we would do things that felt so good that we wouldn't end up doing anything else but that, which would disappoint both of our well-loved mothers.

I knew Elisha was a great man, and I didn't want to be the reason he got stuck, causing him to lose focus, lose the confidence of his parents, especially his mother who loved and adored him tremendously. Elisha's dreams were in color and were larger than many young men could ever imagine. He believed in them, more importantly, he believed he could accomplish them easily. I didn't want to be the cause for his dreams to die. So we did that year together outdoors, in our market and in parks and schools, restaurants, and studios. Together we stood on the Brooklyn Promenade smelling the stinky water and acting out scenes while glancing at the incredible sky. We walked over the Brooklyn Bridge into lower Manhattan. We shopped in the most unique and most odd stores and window-shopped in the most expensive places. Occasionally we mixed with Elisha's friends, but the majority of times he kept me to himself, which is what we both preferred. Porsche was in love with him. Siri was in love with him. Ivory was in love with him, deeply.

Seven nights before my fourteenth birthday, he strummed a song for me beneath a weeping willow in Brooklyn's Fort Greene Park. It was one of those summer evenings where the night temperature was as hot as the day. The song he played was his version of Al Green's song, titled "Simply Beautiful." His fingers moving on those strings, love in every stroke, the music floating in the open air, sounding more better than in a closed-in room. It was a moaning kind of song moving mostly on feelings, much more than lyrics. Elisha had me so open that night that I wanted him to make love to me. Both my heart and my body couldn't wait or resist or avoid anymore. I didn't tell him with words.

When he walked me home, I was touching him in the back alley right outside of the metal door in the floor. So he was touching me back and we were against the brick wall unable to manage our passion any further. "Stay with me?" my lips said softly, and my eyes begged him.

"You know I want to," he said, his heart pounding crushed against my pounding heart. "But you know what that means," he added.

"I know," was all I said as I continued kissing his mouth. He took my hand. His fingers were so warm. He lifted the metal door. We walked down the cement stairs, our fingers locked together. He placed his badass red guitar, which he carried in a ruggedass brown leather case up against the wall downstairs in the dark. As he did, I removed my blouse and then my bra.

He began sucking my neck. My skin was all-fever-hot, hot enough to be hospitalized. I felt my nipples brushing against him, which sent a crazy sensation through me. I put my hands beneath his tee shirt and eased it up, both of us pulling it over his head together. We were tonguing now. I was unfastening his belt, my hands feeling all over his butt. My fingers were pushing then pulling down his shorts, his long and thick so solid now it was pushing against my belly, separating our bodies. I touched it, held it, and moved my hands up, caressing and feeling. Easily he eased me out of my skirt, the sensation of his fingers brushing against my tiny panties shot-put more fire on my fire. He lifted me up some. My feet were on top of his feet as he walked us over to the bed. I sat down, my back to the wall. As soon as I spread my thighs and he was over me, a thump came to the metal floor door. It was a familiar and painful noise to me so my legs closed and tightened. Elisha pulled my body back towards him like he didn't hear nothing. He was full on separating my thighs, pushing my knees apart, coming for me like crazy. His lips were over my lips, his tongue making love to mine. His finger was touching my moistness, stroking my insides. My mixed feelings, extreme worry and extreme pleasure went so wild my legs relaxed again and opened to welcome him in.

Momma opened the floor door and tripped down the steps.

It wasn't the fact that I was naked or that Elisha was erect and just about to push into me, or that his basketball shorts that he wore beneath his jeans were wrapped around only one of his ankles before he swiftly jumped back and pulled them up. It wasn't the fact that now Momma knew I was about to have sex or that Momma had interrupted us from an incredibly deep and true feeling and what would have been an unforgettable first time.

It was that Elisha saw Momma high, bruised, and broken. That crushed me. Now he had seen Momma in her lowest condition, and I knew there was no way to snatch that image back from Elisha's careful movie director eyes. I knew nothing could erase it. No amount of explanations could clean it up. There was no way for me to ever lift her up again. Maybe he wouldn't even understand why I loved her so much or worked so many jobs or spilled so many tears and had so many sad nights because of Momma. Maybe now he would regard Momma as trash, filth, a waste of life, flesh, and time. And those thoughts were too much for me to bear. Suddenly I felt like I weighed three thousand pounds in that moment. I was so heavy my shoulders were no longer able to hold me up. My body collapsed, leaving Elisha, Momma, and Siri alone.

* * *

My eyes shifted from the inside of my mind back to the movie screen. I could now see what Elisha the movie director had done. He made a film, using all of the businesses and businesspeople and friends and kids and families in Brooklyn as the beautiful background.

I looked around at the swelling crowds. Elisha's love, it seems, was contagious. It wasn't too long before I realized while watching the film, that this was the story of our love, mine and his. Our love was stretched across a huge screen for everyone to see, feel, and perhaps even envy. Our love was being acted out in front of the whole borough of Brooklyn, or perhaps before the whole world. He was sharing it with them, while concealing my identity for us, thankfully.

Tears boiled up in my eyes when the scene shifted and the main male lead was revealed. I was so relieved that it was not Elisha playing himself, but another actor who Elisha chose to portray him. My worries were being carried away on the wings of butterflies. I squeezed him tighter, our fingers interlocked, moist and warm.

I'm not too sure if I was really watching the film and listening and paying close attention like a ticket buyer in a regular movie theater at a world premier would watch and listen and follow the story. I was watching two films, the one on the screen and the one in my mind.

When the image of the space below Big Johnnie's floor came into view on the big screen in Elisha's film, I gasped. My body jerked. Elisha felt it. He stroked my hair under the Brooklyn moon as we sat body to body with tens of hundreds of people. Silently, I cried, my body shaking.

His love doesn't disappear. It walks with him, as he said, getting stronger and stronger. It was only me who kept disappearing, not wanting to cheat Elisha with my Swiss-cheese heart. Not wanting Elisha's love to highlight my loveless family. Meanwhile, while I was away, Elisha was loving me by memory, music, and making film, and by meeting the people who were connected to me in some way, including now, Sharp, Poppa, Midnight, and even Big Johnnie.

I'm better now. I repeated that sentence eleven times on the inside of me. No more searching for love that's right here, a love I can feel, a love I could breathe in, shower in or swim in, a stream of love that's always flowing, the only mutual love I shared.

"Momma, I'm giving Elisha my whole heart. Even if I love him one hundred thousand times more than he loves me," I spoke aloud, facing the night sky.

Elisha heard me. He wiped my tears with his fingers and gave me a warm kiss. His tongue made my insides move some.

My feelings were becoming too intimate for a sixteen-year-young girl seated in a crowd. It had been too long since I had been wrapped in his tornado of love. I wanted to lean back and have him touch me up, my back against the warm cement, as though no one was there surrounding us. I wanted his hand to travel up the inside of my red dress and stroke me some. I wanted him to squeeze my nipples or at least suck them. But everyone was there, it seemed. So, burning hot, I exhaled.

"I'll give you what you want," he whispered in my ear. "I waited two years. You wait a few hours. Your man ain't slow no more." Even his lips pressed against my lobe got me crazy. I felt I couldn't sit still.

*   *   *

Mobbed by applause, admiration, autograph seekers, press, staff, and security, Elisha kept his right arm locked around my waist and the other wrapped around my wrist.

Under night lights, the cheering crowd created a corridor for Elisha and his people to walk through and into the waiting limo that was flanked by black Crown Victorias and Suburbans. He held the limo door open for me. I got in, sat in the corner. He sat beside me, our fingers interlocked once again.

The limo door was opened a few times by people working for Elisha, I guessed. Each time he said to each of them, "Jump in the car behind this one." They could tell and I could see he wanted to ride with me alone.

"Elisha," I said. He didn't answer me. He leaned forward and grabbed a bottle of water and handed it to me.

"Don't talk, don't leave. Can you do that for me?"

"Okay . . . ," I said softly, opening the water and handing it to him to drink first.

On the Brooklyn Bridge memories of me and him moved through my mind. When I glanced at Elisha, he was looking away from me and out through the window. I could see his jaw flex. I wondered what he was thinking. He made me like this, by always pointing people out and asking me what I thought they had on their mind. Now I sat silently thinking only about him.

Minutes later, I said, "I have an answer to your questions." He looked at me, saying nothing.

"You were the first man to touch my body. No man has touched me since you touched me last. You were my first kiss, my first love, and you are the only man in the world who I love. I'm a little crazy and I know it."

He leaned in, pressed his lips against my lips, pushed in his tongue. His passion came pouring out without words, and his hands were touching me up, moving up my bare legs, and caressing my thighs like I wanted him to do.

Chapter 48

We entered New York University that same night after viewing his film. It was my first time ever being in a college. In a pretty auditorium, every seat was packed. As soon as the thousand faces turned back and spotted Elisha walking in from the rear flanked by his entourage, they jumped to their feet in loud applause. I wanted to slip and hide in the back row. He wouldn't let go. He sat me in the chair reserved for him, facing the audience, and stood behind the chair with his hands on my shoulders.

Elisha's parents, sister, and brother were all seated in the front row. His mother locked eyes with me. I felt her searching me, not in a bad way. I guess she was searching me for truth. Her stare was stern. I thought to myself, maybe now she can no longer see my wings.

Audrey, the new young film star, was seated beside Elisha's mother. She couldn't hide her true feeling from me, even if she hid it from others. The costars and Elisha's staff were seated across the entire second row.

"I'm Azaziah Immanuel. I'm a film student here at New York University and president of the student government for the upcoming school year. Tonight's guest is my brother, Elisha Immanuel. You all have just viewed his first film, *A Love Supreme*, along with college students across the country. I'm proud of my young brother, although his accomplishments are an embarrassment to me..." The crowd broke out in laughter. "Elisha Immanuel has completed in his senior year in high school what I haven't even started in my senior year of film school. Hopefully when he takes your questions, he'll give me some credit for helping him out!" The audience laughed, applauded, and then fell silent in anticipation of Elisha.

"First, I want to thank the Creator, then my father, Jamin Immanuel, and my mother, Elon Immanuel. Yes, my big brother Azaziah was a big help to me, so please show him some love so me and him don't have to fight." They laughed. "And I can't forget my sister, Sheba. She's always watching over me cause my mother makes her do it." They laughed some more. She's a certified public accountant and a graduate student at Barnard, in English Literature. That's my family. "Now I'll take your questions," he said, humbly.

"Hi Elisha, I'm Hannah. I just want to say your film was awesome! The cinematography was beautiful and executed so well. How were you able to direct a film with an African American cast and story, and not duplicate the stereotypes that are commonly perpetuated about our communities when it comes to film?"

"Honesty," Elisha answered her with one word. The crowd applauded thunderously. "If we remove the fear from our lives and our work, we can get to the good parts. If we're trapped in our fears and doubts, nothing but the same old things will come out. As a man, I'm not afraid to love, to show love, write love, direct it, and to put love on film. In every frame, whether it was a sad scene or a joyful one, I was giving the audience my heart." Elisha's smile lit up the huge space and moved the crowd. The energy in the room was swirling around him and moving through the atmosphere.

"Hi, Elisha, my name is Adam Silverstein. I hope I'm not perpetuating a stereotype tonight, but I'd like to ask about money." The crowd laughed. I didn't know why. He continued, "How were you able to finance the making of this incredible film? I could see that you used two cameras. Film students understand how expensive that is."

"You're the guy who wants my secret recipe," Elisha said. The crowd laughed. "There really is not a secret but there is a formula. I interacted with a group of people, businesses, and communities that welcomed me and invested in my ideas. I reached out to each investor personally, and gave them a chance to be a part of the process. I think community businesses want to see the youth, especially the young men of the neighborhood, doing something productive, building up instead of doing nothing or tearing things down. Simply put, I gave the businesses an opportunity to show that young black men are not the enemies, and that if a young black guy is making moves, they are willing to move with him, and push him and themselves forward," Elisha said. "It helped that my mom is an attorney and my sister is an accountant. They gave the project the business structure it needed. My brother Azaziah organized it so that my film debuted on three hundred college campuses across America. He saved me from having to depend only on ticket sales at the mainstream movie houses. My father works for UPS. He gave me the example I needed of how a man has to persevere and stay on course and sacrifice to secure his future, no matter how great the challenge becomes."

"Elisha, I'm Imani, I'm a sophomore here at NYU and I'm a serious student but I need to know, and I know I'm speaking for at least a hundred women here, are you single, and would you date an older woman? I'm nineteen!" Everyone went wild.

"It's Friday night. I'm single till Monday morning. On Monday morning, I'll go to City Hall and marry the girl I love." A low roar moved across the room. I couldn't miss the surprised, anxious, angry, and even twisted looks that moved across faces. Still, some were smiling.

"I'm single," Azaziah called out from the side wall where he was leaning and watching the audience.

"Why? Why marry so young?" a female student stood and asked.

"I need her. When I marry her, she's mine. That's what I need. A man's heart really can't take the woman he loves just coming and going. He wants her right by his side."

"Yo, Elisha, don't make these women go crazy. You making it hard on the brothers," a male student said. Everyone laughed at his statement, even Elisha.

"We gotta man up. It's time for that. Brother, don't you agree?"

The girls leaped out of their seats and began jumping up and down cheering for Elisha.

"Enough of your patriarchal sexist tirade," a female student said. Some of the crowd booed her. Others showed her support. I didn't know what she was talking about. "Where is your fiancé and what does she think? Can we hear her voice?" the female student demanded.

Elisha stared me over to where he was now standing. Slowly,

I stood, feeling shy. *Speaking and dancing are not the same thing*, I thought to myself. *You are not a fugitive*, I told myself eleven times. In the satin heels that Mr. Sharp gave me, which I had slipped into inside of the limo, I walked slowly towards Elisha. The male students all stood up and applauded for some reason.

"What do you have to say?" the same female who first asked about me said. The room went silent as though it was empty, but it was filled.

"I wanna do whatever Elisha wants to do. I wanna go wherever Elisha wants to go. I wanna give him everything he wants and everything I have. I'll be his wife and have his babies."

Elisha's father stood up from his seat with amazement in his eyes and admiration for his youngest son.

We left New York University in a complete uproar.

* * *

"Keep your bedroom door open, Elisha," his mother said after welcoming me into their home and commenting on my "lovely red dress." As she watched her son rush me away and down the hall hand in hand, she called behind him. "Even though you're seventeen, keep it open," she reminded him. So he did.

He was leaning up against his desk in his bedroom. I was seated on his bed. The beautiful silk and linen red taffeta layers of fabric were spreading around me. My high-tops and heels were set on the wooden floor. I was brushing my feet with my hands, admiring the way my manicure and pedicure designs matched up nicely.

"Even your feet are pretty . . . ," Elisha said.

"Are they?" I teased.

"Almost as pretty as your face," he said. We laughed some. "That dress is crazy," he said. "You're not supposed to look better than the stars on the screen or the stars in the sky on opening night." He smiled. I felt the normally confident Elisha was nervous and that was so sexy to me.

"Your movie . . ." I began to say.

"I don't want to talk about the film," he said.

"Oh," I said softly.

"Your mother," Elisha began saying.

"I don't want to talk about Momma," I answered softly.

He handed me a tiny box of Godiva chocolates, same as he did when we first met.

"I'm not hungry. I'm not sad tonight either," I told him, smiling.

"Open it anyway," he said calmly as he leaned on his desk, his arms folded across his chest.

I opened the chocolates, but there were no chocolates inside. Instead, there were three diamond rings all shining. I looked up to Elisha.

"One for Porsche, one for Ivory, one for Siri. I'm confident about at least two of you," he said, smiling. "I'll take either one of you or all three."

"Who do you love the most?" I asked.

"Whoever you are sitting right there in that red dress," he said. "If you tell me you're not either one of them three, I'll dump them all, and take *you* no matter what name you come up with."

"So is it me or the dress?" I teased. "If I take off the dress and give it to someone else, will you marry her instead, because she is wearing the red dress?"

"Take off the dress, let's see what I do," he said. I stood up. Elisha closed his bedroom door and turned the lock. He dragged the chair from his desk and tilted it underneath the doorknob.

"Elisha!" his mom called him. He was unbuttoning his shirt.

I switched the lights off and moved from the bed.

"Let's take a shower in the dark," I said.

"Elisha." His mom was right outside his bedroom now. I knew she wanted to talk. But we were through talking for the night.

"Elon, leave your son alone. He's a man now." Elisha's father's voice had spoken. It was the first time I ever heard it, and he was saying the right thing.

Dark, and in the cool shower, he washed me and I stood directly in the downpour. His hand moving the scented soap over my skin felt good to me. He scrubbed my pussy hairs the same as if it was the hair on my head. His hands wrapped around and cleaned my back, slid down and breezed through my crack. He was washing my thighs now and my legs were trembling.

"Your skin is on fire," he said. "Let me rinse you." He spun me around slowly, holding my shoulders so I wouldn't slip.

"Let me wash you," I said, taking the soap and caressing his upper body with suds. With soapy water I gripped the base of his hardness and washed him, moving up and down until it was clean and my palm was filled with warm sperm.

"You're cheating," I told him. He smiled, a little breath escaping from both our lips. "Let me rinse you," I said.

Both of us clean, hot and boiling with longing, we skipped the towels. Laying on the wood floor of his bedroom, covered in droplets of water, Elisha stroked my pussy hairs. "I like your bush," he said.

"You just like me," I said. He split it open and ate it like it was the inside of a Sunkist orange. When he sucked my sweetness there, a sound came forth from me that I wasn't controlling.

"*Sshh . . . ,*" he said. He was licking my nipples, sucking my neck. I threw my leg over him. On top, I wanted to please him.

"Be easy." He sat up. He placed both hands on my waist, picked me up and placed me over his hardness.

"Come down easy," he said. As I bounced down slow, he pushed up strong. He kept pushing until he was welcomed inside. He pushed some more so intensely that he hit the bottom and an incredible feeling vibrated through my body and a sound came out from my lips. The more he moved me and the more I moved, the more incredible it felt. The friction was his thick and hard pushing, pressing, plunging into a tightened, but moist soft space. Movement was my thing and my body was letting him feel that rhythmic flow of my hips. He hit the bottom again. I had bounced down, he had pushed up hard. Warm juice sprayed into me and oozed back down. Then even my rainfall came and my body trembled.

With him laying on the bottom, holding me steady by my butt as I laid on top, we were facing the window.

"See the window? See the moonlight?" He smiled. "In a few hours, you'll see the sun," he promised.

"You are my sun. I love you, Elisha."

"I know. I could always feel it," he said calmly. "And besides, girls tend to like me."

Chapter 49

After a night of intense feelings and tender kisses and arousing tongues touching, I still awakened with my pussy pounding. I squeezed my thighs together tightly trying to soothe it or slow it down. Elisha was asleep. He looked like he was deep in it and like he surely needed it. I resisted a so-strong urge to mess with him so that he would mess with me. Instead, I touched myself then pulled back my fingers. "So this is the scent of him inside of me with a little bit of blood mixed in it," I thought. I slid down and out of his single bed.

Both naked, our clothes were everywhere. As I tiptoed into his bathroom, I said to myself, "The red dress should only be worn once. That's the beauty, power, and influence of it." After showering, I wrapped myself in a big blue bath towel he had. I eased the chair from beneath his door and unlocked then turned the knob. The house was completely quiet.

Tiptoeing down the hall, I stopped in front of Sheba's door and tapped lightly with my fingernails. I couldn't hear her moving. Figuring she was still sleeping I turned to go back. Her door opened. I looked and her face appeared.

"Sheba, can I borrow an outfit?" I asked her. She opened her door some more. Then I stepped inside. She closed it behind me.

"You really are something," she said.

"What do you mean?" I asked her.

"So bold. You come in here and fuck my brother, sleep over, and walk through the halls naked."

"Elisha fucked me," I said. "It was our first time and it was really so nice. My feelings are still going crazy on the inside," I said to her.

Her mouth was dropped opened. I didn't know why. I was being honest with her.

"I'm not naked. I'm wearing the towel."

"I heard you, through the walls," she said.

"So then you must understand," I said. "Don't you have a boy-friend?" I asked her.

"*Umm*, yes . . . ," she said.

"So you definitely understand. I've been in love with your brother since I was eleven. Now I'm sixteen. We both really tried to man-age. How is it for you and your man? You two must be managing better than Elisha and me cause you don't have any babies, right?" I asked her.

"There is something called birth control," she said with soft sarcasm.

"I know, but I don't like medcine or doctors."

"So you two didn't use nothing!" she asked.

"No, and it felt so good."

Sheba threw her hands up.

"Where have you been all of this time, and what did you do to my brother Elisha?"

"I was working. And what happened to your brother?"

"You know what happened. You put some kind of spell on him that made him love you too much without you even being here. What did you write in your letters to him?" Sheba asked.

I knew she was referring to the letters I wrote to Elisha every other day for two years. The day after my disappearance from Brook-lyn, I wrote and mailed the first one to him from upstate New York along with my diary, which I dug up from the ground at NanaAnna's. Even though I had scratched out everybody's name except my own; he would still get to know and feel my true story. I had written to Elisha for many reasons, because I wanted him to know for sure that my leaving was not because I didn't love him. I gave him my diary because I trusted him and wanted him to know me, really know me—what I had lived through and why my moods swing so hard. I wanted him to understand that I needed time to separate from him, but not forever. I needed help with those holes in my heart.

"Why didn't you just ask Elisha what I wrote?"

"So clever, you enchanting one," Sheba said.

I didn't know what *enchanting* meant but I marked it in my mind to ask Elisha later.

"Elisha kept your letters in a trunk locked in his closet, every time he received one, he'd go in his room, close the door, and not come out. None of us knew what you were telling him. Whatever it was, it must've been so magical that it changed him," she said.

"In a bad way?" I asked.

"No, in a different way," she said, avoiding filling me in.

"Sheba, I have my own clothes of course, but not here. Can I just borrow a pair of jeans and a tee so I can run to the organic market? I want to make breakfast," I said.

"So now you're gonna cook in my mother's kitchen?" Sheba asked.

"I'll cook for your mom and for you, too."

* * *

Wearing Sheba's jeans and a Barnard T-shirt, Sheba's socks and my red high-top Converses, I prepared a fresh, should-be-delicious, all-organic ingredients (including all seasonings) meal. I grilled fish, with onions and hot peppers. I made salad and vegetable soup. As Elisha would say, "to give options" I made pancakes with maple syrup and organic strawberries. I didn't have the time to soak and boil down beans to go with the pancakes. I compromised and served a side of turkey bacon. Inside of separate, decorated dishes, nicely placed on the long Immanuel table, pecans, raisins, sliced bananas, cheese, and olives.

Oshadagea Oronyatekha, the healer, was the closest to a true mother to me. Or maybe I should say she was the closest to a true mother feeling. She had taught me well when I was ten, by teaching me how to teach myself. When I returned to her alone at age fourteen, exhausted and distraught, she welcomed me back in, thankfully.

"Food is natural medicine; if you want to heal, you must first heal with food." She taught me that healthy foods could even change people's attitudes and personalities and soften, then open, their hearts. I was trying to soften and open Elisha's family's hearts to me. I knew that trust is feelings and actions stretched out over time. I also knew that with his family, because I had suddenly disappeared, I was just getting started again.

Poppa Jamin was the first awake. He followed the scent directly to the table.

"Good Morning . . . Poppa," I said to him softly. Sheba shot him a look. He nodded, pulled out a chair at the head of the table, and then sat down. I watched his eyes surveying. He was a big man. When I asked Sheba what was his favorite food, she said fish. "He especially likes porgies, cause he catches them when he goes fishing from time to time." Sheba was difficult, but helpful.

"Good morning," I said when Mother Elon came in, wrapped in a pretty robe.

"She cooked it, I watched her," was all Sheba said. Her eyes widening some.

"Are you proud that she cooked and you watched instead of helping her?" Poppa Jamin asked his daughter. "Sit down," Poppa said to his wife. "It smells good," he commented.

Azaziah showed up willing, eager, and excited. "Man it's been a long time since we had a homemade spread like this . . ." He sat down ready to get to it.

"Go and wake up your brother, tell him to come down here," the father said.

Azaziah got up. "And we all gonna eat at one time!" Azaziah commented as he left.

No one's smile was brighter than Elisha's, but he wasn't the one I needed to convince. His heart was already open to me.

"You stayed asleep so long, we slipped out and went to the market. She cooked all of this. Weren't you worried she might disappear again?" Sheba asked.

"No," Elisha said confidently. "She accepted my wedding ring and I loved her right last night. If she left me after that, it would mean that I love her, but she isn't the right one for me." With all eyes on my three diamond rings, I kept my head down and spilled a few tears. I had felt the warmth and the warning in Elisha's words. A warning to me, a warning to them, a warning to us, not to take his love for granted. I understood.

Momma Elon said some words over the food. As they cautiously began eating, I peeked and thought I saw their hearts softening.

* * *

"Elisha, I gotta get my clothes . . ." I said, returning back to his bedroom after learning how to use their dishwasher, and choosing to wash the dishes by hand instead.

"You good?" he asked.

"I'm good," was all I said. His eyes were staring into me, beyond my body and into my feelings. "You left your bed sheet in the hallway," I told him, also noticing now that his mattress was bare.

"I know," was all he said.

"Let me wash it for you." I turned to go and get it.

"Just leave it there. Are you on your period?" he asked me strangely.

"No." I smiled. "How come you asked me that?" Instinctively, I pulled the tee and placed my nose inside and inhaled. He smiled at me for being insecure.

"Let's go. Thanks for cooking our breakfast. No one could front on that."

* * *

I was stupidly prepared to ride the bus or catch the train, but Elisha's driver pulled around in a Crown Vic. He opened the door for me. I got in.

"Where are we headed?"

"The Four Seasons Hotel in the city."

"We'll get your things and check out of there," he said.

"Okay," I agreed.

"You look pretty," he said.

"In Sheba's clothes!" I asked.

"In anything," he said. "What room are you in?"

"Suite 1111; I requested that room, that number. When I first checked in, they said that suite wasn't ready. I sat in the lobby three hours waiting for it."

"That's crazy," he said.

"Elisha, you don't ride the bus no more?" I asked him.

"Of course, but these drivers are on call and as directed all week because of the film premier. They'll drive us down to DC tonight," he said casually.

"Washington, DC?"

"Yeah, I gotta gig at Howard University. Sheba graduated from there. Some students will watch the flick after dinner tonight, and me and my band will play at their afterparty."

"You gotta whole band now?" I asked him.

"You know I gotta play my music. But I'm not taking you to the party," he said like it wasn't nothing. I didn't say anything, but I felt a little sad that I wasn't invited.

"I'm taking Siri. Maybe she'll sing something if I strum the strings right."

"It's up to her," I said. "Elisha, when we get to the hotel can you give me fifteen minutes to clean my room before you come in?"

"Definitely not," he said. "You know me. I wanna see how you was living."

* * *

"My man!" the valet said when the driver opended our car door and Elisha stepped out. Then the fellas that usually sweat me every morning, watching my hips sway, were now sweating Elisha.

"I checked your flick last night on Church and Flatbush, at the Kenmore."

"How was it?" Elisha said.

"Place was packed. You got the whole Brooklyn behind you."

"Elisha, I'll be back." I took the opportunity to run through the hotel doors and straight to the elevator. I was gonna try and fix up my room.

Upstairs, as I fumbled through my red Epi Leather bag looking for my wallet, which contained my room key. I broke a little sweat in the air-conditioned corridor. My bag was red, my wallet is red, my Converses are red, and the red DO NOT DISTURB sign was glaring just as I left it days ago. I found the key.

Dropping everything, I ran to the back bedroom and gathered up my Victoria's Secrets, which I had in every color, flung everywhere. I pulled out my empty Louis luggage, opened it, and began assembling my lingerie inside. In the bathroom I began collecting all of my carefully selected personal items. I never used the ones the hotels all around the world supplied. As I rushed around I caught a glimpse of myself in the mirror.

"Why are you panicking now?" I asked myself aloud. But I didn't know the answer. I put all of the lotions, oils, and creams in my leather waterproof case, and put the case inside of my saddlebag. A thought shot through my mind. I ran to the vault. I typed in 0726, my birthdate, and the vault door swung open. The program for Momma's wake was the first thing I saw. My eyes moved over Momma's photo. I stood stuck for some seconds.

"C'mon," Siri said. Then I collected the remaining stack of papers from the vault, including my passport, which listed me as Onatah Rivers, my driver's permit that listed me as Penelope Sharp, my vehicle registration and insurance papers, which listed Mr. Sharp's name and Penelope's. My release and discharge papers from Kennedy-Claus Hospital, my New York State identification card, and my Social Security card, all brand new, all listing me as Porsche Santiaga. I also had my Lufthansa Airline ticket stubs, postcards, flyers and advertisement cards written in foreign languages, inviting guests to see my solo dance performances. I had one envelope containing the last letter that I had written to Elisha, but never mailed after receiving the news of Momma's death. I pulled it all out, then realized I left the handbag I carried today back in the living room. I wanted to run and get it, but decided I better breathe before I collapsed in the closet where I was standing, next to the vault. I inhaled, exhaled, inhaled, exhaled, inhaled, and exhaled.

Siri said, "You're panicking because this is the part where Elisha mixes with all the other parts of our lives. But, Porsche, you should know by now, Elisha loves us. Everything is okay. It's better than okay. It's good. It's perfect," she said and her voice was sweet and calming.

When I stepped out of the closet, Elisha was standing there in my bedroom, where I had been staying for three weeks now.

"I'll get you a house cleaner," Elisha said, smiling. "What kind of hurricane happened in here?" he joked.

"I asked you to give me fifteen minutes," I said.

"You needed fifteen hours," he said calmy.

"Don't call housekeeping, please. I don't want them touching my stuff."

"They already told me you're stuck up," Elisha said, teasing.

"I'm not!" I said.

"They said you don't talk to anybody, you always keep your Do Not Disturb sign on. You make them leave your room service food outside your door, but you don't eat it anyway. They said you don't get no visitors, but you talk to yourself when you're walking through the lobby."

I just looked at Elisha, my hands clutching my papers.

"I like that," Elisha said.

"Like what?" I asked.

"What would I have done if they said something different about you? Probably gotten into a brawl and got sued. You know people want to get knocked out by a celebrity. Every punch is worth at least ten thousand dollars."

Finally, I smiled. I like the idea of Elisha knocking somebody out to defend me.

"That's not all. My man the valet said you push a mean rimmed-out, black 600 Benz with custom-made red leather interior and an AMG kit. The guy started to tell me how much it cost. I told him I know exactly how much it cost . . ."

"It's Momma's car . . . ," I said softly.

"But you bought it," he said seriously.

"True," I confirmed.

"What you got in your hands?" he asked.

"Personal papers," I said.

"Let me see 'em," he said.

"Why, are you the police?" I asked.

"No, I'm your man. Give in to me."

* * *

After we talked frighteningly honestly, seated on the floor in the hotel bedroom for a couple of hours, our emotions were stirring. Telling all the truths I could tell was like vomiting, without the stinky stench and mess. As I sorted out each truth for Elisha, it was the same as me sorting out each truth for myself. He wiped my tears with his fingers. In a room piled high with brand-new shoes and kicks, designer dresses and handbags, shoe boxes and shopping bags, we sat on the floor next to my scattered documents, which I nervously shared with him.

He kissed me; my heart started speeding. We were touching and tonguing.

"Elisha . . ."

"What, woman? You talk a lot."

"This morning when I woke up, my pussy was pounding. I never felt that same kind of strong feeling before. It was so powerful, even though you were asleep and not even touching me. It made me feel crazy." He kissed me again.

"It's just gonna keep getting stronger and stronger," he said, squeezing my nipples.

"I think I like you too much," I said softly. He raised Sheba's T-shirt over my head.

"You're supposed to," he said, unsnapping the clasp of my bra too easily. My full breasts popped out, the nipples rising right before both of our eyes.

"I might be a little scared," I said honestly as he pulled Sheba's jeans down from around my hips.

"Scared of what?" he said as he stroked my pussy through the thin panty. I began breathing heavy. I didn't give an answer to his question. "You can't front on that," he said, his lips pressed against my left ear as he pushed inside of me. Both naked all over again, I felt myself falling and cumming, falling further and cumming more. I was drowning and afraid of the overwhelming feeling and my complete loss of control. But it was a feeling I wouldn't trade for any other feeling in the world.

* * *

"Feathers, sequins, masks, glasses, hats, what is all this?" Elisha asked. We were finishing the last bit of packing, emptying the living room closets where my show outfits hung, nicely packed inside of dress bags, while the accessories were piled on a top shelf.

"Costumes," I told him.

"Costumes," he repeated, unzipping one hanger bag, revealing a dress a crafty Native made for me from sterling silver and turquoise. "That's an incredible design. You wore this?"

"On stage," I said.

"It must've been heavy," he said. "And it's see-through. You wore something underneath the dress, right?" he asked. I couldn't lie to him.

"I didn't, but the turquoise parts cover all of my private spaces. I can show you," I said. He stood staring, maybe imagining.

"I told you I'm a dancer," I said so quietly, without an ounce of brag in it. "Not a fucking stripper or a stuck-up ballerina, and no one touches me," I explained softly again, but I had already shared that world with him in many of my letters. He just never saw it up close and in person like how he was seeing my costumes up close now. After now knowing my body more than he ever did before, and after just pulling himself from between my thighs and peeling himself off of my curves. I could see that he was also in deep. "Put it on and show me your dance," he said.

"Nope, you don't wanna see it," I said softly. I realized I had just offered to show him. But something suddenly told me that I shouldn't.

"No, you don't want to show me," he said.

* * *

In the limo just us two, followed by a caravan of hired cars and trucks, we were rolling to DC, a three-hour trip from New York, in a fast ride.

"Elisha, what does *enchanting* mean?" I asked.

"Let me see." He was thinking.

"Having a magical influence over one or more people," he defined as I sat thinking about what Sheba was saying to me this morning.

"Use it in a sentence," I requested.

"Her pull on her man was so strong, people thought he was enchanted."

"I understand," I said.

"How about *patriarchy*, what does that mean?"

"It means the man, husband, father, brother, or sons are the bosses of the house, or the men are the bosses of the hood, the state, the country. What he says rules," Elisha carefully explained.

"Use it in a sentence," I asked him.

"If a house and the community are set up right, there will always be a patriarchy," he said. We laughed.

"So if a woman has enchanted her man, is he still the patriarch?" I asked.

"Yep," was all he said.

"Prove it!" I said. He paused at first, delighted by the test.

"A true patriarch doesn't have to keep saying *I'm the boss. I'm the boss*. He lets the women talk and cry cause that what they do. If he loves his women and his daughters too much, even an enchanting one, it doesn't take away from his power or position. He protects and provides for his women, handles the business, and makes them moan!" We laughed. "And gives them babies, so they can have something to focus on instead of getting themselves into trouble."

"So why was the girl yelling about patriarchy at NYU the other night."

"She's out of order." We laughed again. "Someone needs to tell her that the Earth—that's you—revolves around the sun. That's me."

Chapter 50

Since being locked up, I never had seen so many girls in one place. But these girls were not prisoners. They were relaxed and free. They were pretty, of every shade of skin, and type and style of hair. They walked confidently. We were "on the campus of Howard University," Sheba said.

"When I went to school here, there were seventeen female students to every one male student," Sheba said. "Talk about competition!" She was guiding us around. It was me and the girls from Elisha's staff and film, which of course included Audrey.

"Usually out here on the yard, on a Saturday night like tonight, the fraternities and sororities would be stepping. It's really a fun and amazing thing to see."

"Stepping?" I asked. "Is that dance?"

"You could definitely call it a kind of dance," she said, which made me curious.

"Sheba, did you dance?" I asked.

"You have to be a member to step," she said. "And yes, I stepped. I'm a Delta."

"A Delta?" I asked.

"Delta Sigma Theta; it's a sisterhood, a sorority," she explained.

"How do you have any sisterhood with seventeen women to every one man?" Audrey asked. "Sounds like a fucking fight."

* * *

Shoulder to shoulder in a packed college hall, Elisha had a thousand women, and one hundred seventy men, mesmerized by his rendition of a Carlos Santana joint. Showing off, he played two guitars in one performance, the acoustic and the electric. It didn't hurt that he was tall and handsome and that whatever he did and wherever he went everyone could see him shining. On his guitar he was more than good. His fingers were comfortable and swift. His strumming moved many hearts, especially mine. As he stood in the darkened hall beneath the glowing spotlight, him and his band, I asked myself, *Are you ready to handle this man who every girl of every type seems to desire?* I even was asking myself, what had I done to win his heart so solidly?

"What made you come back?" a voice to the left asked me. I looked over my shoulder. It was Audrey.

"My momma died. So, I had to come back to Brooklyn."

"I wish she would of lived," Audrey said, and I felt myself getting red real quick. I saw myself slapping the shit out of her. I saw the old Porsche stabbing her in her side or punching her dead in her face, but I didn't. I didn't like the slick shit she was saying, she wished Momma would of lived. I wish Momma would of lived, too, but I knew that's not what she meant. And what if I beat Audrey's ass and then had to explain to Elisha or anyone that I beat her because she wished my mother would've lived? The twist of her tongue and words would've made me seem crazy. Instead, I turned to her and forced up a smile.

"Thanks for letting Elisha practice on you," I said. "I could tell by the way he made love to me last night and this morning that he practiced on some bitch till I got home."

"Fuck you, Ivory!" she said. I smiled again.

"That's the thing about being an understudy. Everyone feels cheated when the understudy performs. Everyone wants the real thing," I told her calmly.

She pushed me. I pushed her back. She fell against Sheba. I went in my black Gucci bag, my fingers deciding on my box cutter or my bag of Back the Fuck Up, which I always carried. Luckily for her, Sheba held her still. Sheba straightened Audrey out and walked her away from me. When I looked up, Elisha was watching me. I don't know what his eyes were saying right then. So we just stared at one another as he strummed out the finale of his session. I didn't take my eyes off of him. He didn't take his eyes off of me. Maybe that's what he wanted. Maybe he was hypnotizing me. I was willing.

When he disappeared from the stage, the next group appeared. The crowd got a little restless while they set up. I felt a mixture of emotions. I felt the feeling you feel when you got beef with a next girl on lockup, and everyone's moving in population. You must keep your eyes moving and watch all hands and mouths, too. It was so easy for another girl to just stick you and keep walking. You wouldn't even know what happened until you saw your own blood bleeding. Then I also felt too pretty to get low like a prisoner. I was wearing the dress that Elisha chose from my wardrobe, a black Christian Dior. I was standing high on my Giuseppe Zanotti heels. I didn't want to fight, but then again I never did—but I would if I had to.

An emcee introduced what he was calling a go-go band. He wilded up the crowd and said, "This is how DC do it!" I got excited seeing all of the drums, really excited. They started tapping em. The music wiped away everything else. The drumming that began just grabbed me. What was it? Why did it sound so good? Why wasn't this music familiar to me? The beats jerked my joints and my body. My hips began to move and bounce. The beats wouldn't allow the body to flow. The way they were being banged out, the body had to shake. My hands and arms began dancing. My shoulders and breasts began vibrating, my butt and my thighs bounced. I bent my right leg and bounced it up in the air. I could make my thighs shake and inch open to the beat. Even my calves were excited. I felt so aroused, it was crazy. I couldn't fight the drum when a drummer touched it up right, and I never wanted to.

A body pressed me from behind and an arm went around my waist. I bounced on that body backwards, and took my hips all the way down to the floor and back up again. When I turned rhythmically, not losing one second or one beat, I saw what I knew. It was Elisha. I pressed in on him close, still making my whole body shake against his. When he danced with me, them DC girls caught the fever, but not all of 'em could catch those sexual magnetic beats with each groove of their bodies. The ones who could, the ones who obviously grew up hearing that go-go, pulled up on Elisha. He was dancing with me. I was dancing with him. They were dancing with us, showing him just how wild and open they could get. The dense crowd surrounded us, watching. The band was playing to us, and the crowd was chanting like crazy. The temperature in the room was rising so hot, even the walls were sweating. The only way I could stop was when Elisha carried me out of there. He did, leaving the go-go girls shaking and bouncing back there. I didn't fight him of course. I just wrapped my arms around his neck and tried to slow down my pulsating body and racing heart. I would've kept going till the lights came on or to the last tap of the drum.

* * *

"Celebrity rule: we always arrive on the set after the party starts. We always leave the set before the party ends," Elisha said. We were all gathered in the reserved roped-off area of the parking lot where our vehicles were parked. Elisha had his right arm around my neck, my body in front of his body, which was pressed against my back. He was speaking to his team; many were faces that were not with him at NYU. Azaziah, Sheba, and Audrey walked up and joined in a minute late.

"She is my wife," Elisha announced. "For the men, look at her once so you know. Then don't look at her no more." They laughed some. Elisha didn't laugh. "For the ladies, treat her good. She's wearing my rings."

* * *

"You must've fucked her. That's why she's mad," I said with heated words, spoken softly.

"You have been gone two years. I never once accused you," he said. "And you're wrong. If I would've fucked Audrey, she wouldn't be mad. She wouldn't say or do nothing. She'd just wait for me to fuck her again." That was the convo and the feeling on our way home Saturday night, or Sunday morning round 2:00 a.m.

* * *

His mother was standing over us. A dream, I figured, cause I was naked-naked, lying beneath Elisha who was definitely naked. We were glued together by our now-dried fluids. His strong sleeping body pressing me deep into the mattress. Through the fog of my sleepy mind and eyes, I became aware that my pussy was still pounding, again. What a strong feeling our lovemaking had heaped on top of the deep feelings we already had for one another. And an argument, no a disagreement, didn't cause us not to love. It pushed us further, further inside of each other. I wrapped my arms around him, caressing.

"Ivory," his mother said. But she wasn't really there. What would she be doing in Elisha's room while he and I were sleeping in a so-intimate way?

"Ivory," she said again. "Get dressed and come out to the reading room. Don't keep me waiting long. I'm on my way to the service."

I gasped, for real. I gasped again. "Momma Elon . . . ," I said, tucked beneath her son, but she was already on her way out the bedroom door.

* * *

Monday morning Elisha married me. Momma Elon thought it was "all too fast." She believed that we should have a big religious wedding. "Why not wait four months until you turn eighteen, Elisha?" his mother had asked him. Elisha confided in me that Momma Elon said, "Sixteen is the legal marrying age for women, but *you* still need my signature," she had warned Elisha.

"Pop will sign for me. He has already agreed to it," Elisha told his mom. "He might not have mentioned it to you yet, but me and him talked it through thoroughly. He knows I will handle it. He knows it's what I need," Elisha had told her. "But I don't want to do it that way. I want you to see my heart and understand and give in to me," he said to his mother.

When Momma Elon summoned me to their family reading room on the second floor to speak woman to woman, I felt nervous. It's peculiar how it makes a girl feel in the presence of the mother of the man who has been feeling all over her body. Especially, when a girl knows that his mother knows for sure, and that it's happening right under her nose and beneath her roof.

"Ivory, do you know the saddest thing in the world that a mother could ever feel?" she asked me. I was fresh out the shower, the three-to-five-minute kind of shower, and the only kind that could've awakened me that Sunday morning.

"Not exactly," I said, pulling at the hem of the skirt I had thrown on. My thighs were pressed closed and tight, my calves one over the other, embarrassed and tense.

"It's when a mother loses her son or daughter."

"Loses," I repeated.

"Loses him in any way, to the world, to senseless violence, to racism, to illness, or insanity. It's when a mother's child passes away at any age, and leaves this earth before she does," she said sadly and serious-faced. I understood the words she was saying, but truthfully, I didn't get it.

"The second saddest thing for a mother is watching her son or daughter suffer, especially when there's nothing the mother can do to fix it. Like when I was seeing my son heartbroken," she said. I felt the accusation. Now I got it.

"Good mothers raise their sons and daughters well, with continuous prayers that other mothers will do the same. This way, when my good son meets another mother's daughter, he will know to treat her with the utmost respect and to love her well. If the young lady has also been raised well, she will do the same towards my son. She will treat my son with respect. Mothers know that once a girl who our good son loves takes root in his heart, we can no longer protect him from the hurt of heartbreak."

"Mrs. Immanuel, I respect and admire you, and I like you a lot. I know that you like me, too, although I am not sure how come. I know that Elisha is your good son and that he is way better than me. But I do love him strong and true. I don't think I can say that I was raised well. But I am sincere. My mother was a good mother, but sometimes even that has a time limit. My mother passed away three weeks ago. It was a pain so great in me and it still is. I'm so grateful to Elisha because he is healing me from my hurt." Her faced softened some when she heard of Momma's death. I was lightened to see that she had feelings enough to consider Momma. That made me like her some more.

"I know you saw how Elisha and I were this morning. I apologize for you seeing us. We didn't mean to show that to you. We were stupid and sloppy for doing it that way. Truthfully when we finally saw one another starting on Friday afternoon, we both have been so happy. Friday night was our first time ever loving one another in that way," I confessed.

"Elisha wanted me to see the two of you in that way. He showed me the blood on his sheets for that very reason. He was creating a preponderance of evidence in your defense. My son is very much like myself. When he wants something, he wants it. He fights until he gets it. But he has never fought with me, until this. Since there is no talking to him about you, I'll talk to you. Nothing is more important to me than my family. So you and I need to get on the same page," she said.

I thought I saw her turning from Momma Elon into a prosecutor. I wanted to keep her in momma-mode. I didn't think I could handle the prosecutor. So I said the things that I thought were the answers to all of the questions and thoughts that she might have for or about me. I wanted to say it, before she asked, which would've been too much pressure for me.

"My father is a famous hustler doing life in prison. My sister is doing fifteen. Somehow, my two youngest sisters and I are all okay. I'm glad you invited me up to speak to you, because I didn't want you to think that I deal in duplicity. I know you make good money and you might think that I came back here for Elisha's money. But Mrs. Immanuel, I returned to Brooklyn for my momma's funeral. Before that, I had been in Germany. I came to find Elisha because I love him and he loves me. I don't need his money at all, but I think it's so dope that he knows how to make it, and that he made a movie like he always said he would."

"Would you sign a paper saying what you just said about not wanting his money?"

"If you want me to, sure I'll sign it. Even if Elisha didn't make a movie, I would still love him like crazy. You introduced me to your son when I was eleven."

Smiling, she said to me, "I have two handsome good sons, so this house has been filled with plenty of pretty faces looking for the both of them. I chose you for Elisha because, when I first looked at you, I saw that your heart was good and somehow your soul was glowing. After I chose you for Elisha, his heart chose you for himself.

"You and I should always work together. Even separate from our men, you and I have to have some harmony. I am accustomed to having a very close, happy family, although I can't get any of them to go to temple with me."

"Temple?" I repeated.

"We are Hebrew," she said. "See, there are so many things that I should talk to you about. It's nice to see that you are humble and willing."

"I promise to make your son happy. I won't disappear. If I'm alive, I'll be right beside him. I can cook and I clean. I work really hard. I can't promise you anything about temple or religion. I don't even know what *Hebrew* means. What I know is, I am already happier than I've ever been," I said softly. "And I agree to the first and the second marriage ceremony. And I won't break Elisha's heart on purpose ever," I swore. "And Momma Elon, you don't know this yet, but my promise is as good as gold." I smiled sincerely.

I wanted to be a good daughter-in-law to her, truly. I had every reason to love her. She was everything I ever wanted from my momma. She loved Elisha the way I wanted Momma to love me. I also thought that just maybe, at our second private wedding ceremony, in her church or temple or whatever, I would get to invite Midnight, Lexus, Mercedes, Riot, and maybe even NanaAnna somehow. I would send invites to Onatah's whole family. They would definitely show up, including her brother, my drummer, and his wife. Maybe as a wedding gift, Riot would bring Lina to me and allow two of her puzzle pieces to attach themselves to one another for a change. I fantasized about having the Diamond Needles as my bridesmaids, all eleven of them, including Siri, of course.

Lastly, but really importantly, there is the elegant Mr. Sharp, Big Johnnie, Esmerelda, and my whole who-over-forty crew. Mr. Sharp would outfit the entire event and place some of our photos on his wall at The Golden Needle.

"Ivory!" Elisha's mom seemed to have raised her voice. "You day-dream, don't you?" she asked me.

"Sometimes," I admitted.

"Do you have any idea whose car that is parked in my garage?"

"It's mine," I told her.

Chapter 51

As we left City Hall—Elisha, Momma Elon, Poppa Jamin, Azaziah, Sheba, Mr. Sharp, and myself—we were met on the steps by at least fifty reporters, who were joined by a swelling mob of fans. I can't say I was surprised. I saw the excited looks of the women working behind the counter when we first arrived, and believed I saw the girl who phoned in the fact that Elisha Immanuel was in the building getting "hitched."

"Elisha! Have you seen this?" a reporter asked, holding up the *New York Daily News* headline, which read, *Elisha Gets the Gold!*

"Nah, I was focused on getting the girl first!" he said, smiling. He was still holding my hand. I was standing hidden behind him.

"Who is she?" A reporter called out.

"My wife!" Elisha shouted back, causing the reporters to laugh.

"Is there a 'pre-nup'?" a reporter asked.

"For what? I'm gonna love her forever!" Elisha answered. The cameras were steady clicking. "It's all hers anyway," he stated boldly to my disbelief. I wouldn't dare look back to see the expression on the faces of his family, our family, Momma Elon in particular. Although, I understood that feeling Elisha was expressing, of wanting to give the one you love everything you have and being more happy to see them have it than to have it to yourself.

Maybe Elisha was feeling now what I was feeling on the cold winter evening when he placed my hands underneath his warm underarms. I felt the love swelling in me. I wanted to give him everything I had and anything he wanted. That feeling grew so strong, that on Elisha's fourteenth birthday, I withdrew my twenty-thousand dollars cash from Mr. Sharp's safe. It was the same money that I had worked my ass off to earn and save for Momma's apartment. I placed it neatly inside of a pretty box stuffed with pretty tissue paper, and decorated with a pretty red ribbon. I gave it to Elisha along with a carrot cake I made from scratch with love for him. Both of these were my gifts to him. I wanted him to have his movie camera, and realize his dream. My dream about Momma and us getting a new apartment together was looking impossible back then. Momma didn't want to live with me, it seemed.

Filled with love for Elisha, and sorrow for Momma after she removed all of my things, clothing and belongings, except the cell phone Elisha had given me, I handed the gifts to him in the cold wind and asked him not to open them until he got home and was alone in his bedroom. It was twenty-thousand dollars cash, plus almost a hundred dollars for the organic ingredients for me to make the home-made carrot cake and then place it inside of a quality cake container. I never missed or regretted the money.

"Thirty-five million on your opening weekend! What do you have to say to that?" a reporter shouted.

"Show the people what they wanna see," Elisha answered.

"What do they want to see?" a woman shouted.

"*A Love Supreme*," Elisha smiled and promoted. People applauded.

* * *

Elisha agreed to convene in a nearby hotel for a roundtable for the high-visibility press, which included the *New York Times*, the *Wall Street Journal*, *New York Daily News*, Associated Press, the *Amsterdam News*, *Newsday*, as well as *The Source* and *Vibe* magazine.

"Thirty-five million . . ." Elisha whispered to his mother as we entered the room where the press were gathered. "Did you see the headlines?" he asked her, leaning her way.

"I saw a write-up with that kind of prediction early yesterday morning in the *Wall Street Journal*," she whispered back.

I offered to step to the side. Elisha, holding my hand, pulled me closer to his side and held me there.

The Associated Press reported asked, "Elisha Immanuel, can you please confirm that your film is an independent film, made without the backing of any major movie house?"

"Confirmed," was all Elisha said, which caused the crowd to laugh.

An older man from the *New York Times* asked the next question, "Elisha, why is the film titled *A Love Supreme?*"

"It's a salute to my father. He's a retired musician, a sacrifice he made for our family. Instead of pursuing an uncertain music career, he labored and earned and paid my mother's way through law school and raised a family. He always enjoys listening to all kinds of music, including John Coltrane, who had a track titled "A Love Supreme." My father has been married to my mother for twenty-five years. He worked at UPS for twenty years. His life is like a jazz instrumental. Besides, the title of a successful film should welcome in the whole family, grandparents and all, each generation," Elisha explained.

"Was the film based on a true story?" the *Vibe* magazine reporter asked.

"How did it feel?" Elisha turned the question on him. There was nervous laughter. "If it felt real it was," Elisha said solemnly.

"About the movie soundtrack," *The Source* reporter asked, "you have two cuts moving up the charts and heating up the top radio countdowns in every major urban area, and moving with a bullet on Billboard Top 100. Will you pursue a music career in addition to film directing? And when will you showcase a live performance from Siri of her remake of 'Loving You' retitled 'Elisha.'"

I fidgeted. They were talking about my girl, Siri. Elisha gripped my hand more tighter. He was letting me know to trust him. I do trust him, more than anyone else.

"Siri is a shy Brooklyn girl I know who sings from her soul beautifully. She doesn't want to be in show business, but she agreed to sing that song only for me. That's why it's retitled 'Elisha.' I knew the whole world would want to hear her voice. So I recorded it. We're gonna let it rock. If it hits number one maybe she'll change her mind by popular demand," he said.

"How does your new wife feel about the new artisit Siri singing so passionately to her husband?" a woman from *Newsday* asked. Everyone laughed.

"My wife has known me since I was twelve. She knows girls tend to like me," Elisha smiled brilliantly. The cameras were flashing.

The *Newsday* reporter followed up. "Where did you and your wife meet? Why such a young marriage? You are reported as being a seventeen-year-old high school senior," she asked.

"We met in an organic market in Brooklyn. I love her more than anything. She's my motivation. And a man should get what he wants and make it his own."

"A thirty-five-million-dollar opening weekend; how will such a young man manage all of that money?" the *Wall Street Journal* reporter asked.

"Oh, I'll manage." Elisha smiled again, bringing the group to laughter.

"Who is you attorney of record?" the *Wall Street Journal* asked.

"My mother," Elisha said.

"Who is your management?" they followed up.

"My mother." Everyone laughed. "I think I can finally afford to pay her fees. When I get back in September, I'll retire her from Wall Street."

"What's next? You got the gold, the girl, and the fans obviously adore you," the *Amsterdam News* reporter asked.

"Honeymoon in Dubai," Elisha said.

"Sounds like a film title!" the *New York Times* reporter blurted out.

* * *

"Dubai?" I asked Elisha when we were alone. He pulled up a world map on his computer. "I'll show you where it is." He pointed. "You traveled over here, that's Europe. We're going over here. We'll meet your sisters and family out there," he said. "That's why I chose it for us. I thought it would make you happy."

When Elisha and I had our intimate discussion seated on the floor in my hotel room Saturday afternoon, I told him that I still loved my twins, but that I had buried my true feelings for Poppa and

Winter at the same time as I had buried Momma. Elisha said a one-word response: "No."

"What do you mean *no*?" I asked him.

"No, you can never 'bury them.' They are your family *no matter what*. And, if you can bury them, that means that one day you could bury me. You loved them before, so love them now. Love them always. Real love never disappears."

AFTERSTORY

Siri cried uncontrollably. Hers were silent, soft, warm tears.

"Porsche," she whispered. She was standing in the corner of our bedroom in her yellow sheer nightie and gold slippers. "You are only loving Elisha and little Elisha. You are forgetting about me." Because Siri cried, I cried, too, even though my life now is 93 percent peace and pure happiness.

"Woman," Elisha said. That's what he calls me when he doesn't know what to call me. We were lying in our huge bed beneath our Egyptian cotton sheets, next to our wide wall-length window. The moonlight was incandescent, causing Elisha's beautiful dark brown skin to glow even more than it did naturally.

Incandescent, a word Elisha taught me, among hundreds of words he had taught me, but this one I learned on the first night we moved in here. It is our new house, which he had promised me when I was thirteen, "a house with great big windows." And since Elisha already came from a house filled with love, he saw no reason to actually separate from it. His wealth and popularity made many doors open to him. That, coupled with a large number of people making an exodus out of downtown Manhattan and Brooklyn, made it possible for him to buy the brownstone he grew up in, as well as two more on the opposite side of his backyard, one to the left, and the other to the right of it. The three buildings represented his commitment to remain strong and loyal to his neighborhood, the people and the businesses that knew and supported him, and to those facing trying times. The three brownstones, plus renovations and extensions, made up the Immanuels' East Coast estate.

Our newly born baby, nearly six months young, Elisha Jr., began fidgeting in his sleep, the same way his small body always reacts when he suddenly hears his father's voice after not hearing it for some hours. I placed one finger over my lips so Siri could see it and try and be quiet. I wanted Elisha Jr. to sleep some more while I sorted out my thoughts and feelings.

Elisha pulled my body close to his. He placed his fingers on my face. Elisha is so comfortable with my tears. He had even told me that he fell in love with me "because of the honesty" of my tears on our first date. I still don't know the secret of why a woman's sincere tears move men.

Now he was gently wiping my tears away with his tongue. Then he began kissing me. My body gave in to him as it always does.

He was moving over me now, both of us enjoying the intense sexual feeling that takes over when both of us are trying to bump, grind, and love each other quietly as another person (Elisha Jr.) lays on the same bed, and still another (Siri) stood watching, closely.

It felt so good, our movement, and the passionate way that Elisha expressed his love to me. He was deep inside of me now and deeper inside of the feeling. I am already pregnant with our second, and the sensitivity of the recently impregnated womb intensified the pleasure of each touch, push, and movement. Now I was breaking my own rule to keep quiet. I was moaning, unable to hold in the sound of what our thrusting was making me feel. There was no one living in the next room or up close enough for me to hold back the sounds of our love. There was no reason for Elisha to place his thick fingers over my mouth and whisper *sshh*. My husband isn't a moaner, but his heavy breathing and way of coming for me and working up a slight sweat fucking thrilled me. I was excited by the way my hips moving excited him, the way he gripped on to the headboard or mattress mashing me even more made me come harder and I shook some. We were both moist and warm now. Elisha kissed my ear and rolled off. Like a magnet, my body turned towards his back and clung to him. I pushed my hands through his arms, my fingers resting on his abs.

"Elisha," I whispered, kissing down his spine. I began caressing the back of his legs. "Elisha, we gotta get going," I said.

"That's why you were crying," he said. I knew it wasn't a question.

He knows me too well. He knew that I was shaken up because today is the day that he'll drive me to upstate New York, to one of the many, many prisons, to visit Winter Santiaga, my big sister, for my first time.

Elisha owns his own business and sets his own work schedule. Even though he is his own boss, he is also, as he explained to me, "the product." Therefore, he is most often very busy, and in high demand. He could've ordered his driver to drive me, and his security to accompany me; however, he handles all matters involving his wife, personally and privately, attentively and compassionately.

"You say you want me to get up, but you're still touching me, which means we both wanna stay right here in these sheets," Elisha said as he turned to face me.

Soon as he started sucking on my breast, Elisha Jr. burst out of his sleep in protest. Elisha Jr. seemed to believe that my breast belonged only to him. Now our son was suckling from my right nipple, and my husband's lips were locked around my left nipple. It felt good, and confusing. My son's suckling makes me feel loved and needed in a really pure way. It was as though he was pulling life out of my breast and becoming more alive because of me. I felt a love for my son and from my son that seeped deep down in my bones and even circulated in my blood. My husband sucking on me was so erotic and exciting it made my pussy muscles contract wildly, which aroused me like crazy.

Seventeen years young, I'm a wife and a mother. This whole feeling, of having a loving husband, father to our son, made me wonder why every woman wouldn't want this exact life? Quietly, I decided that every woman does want the same feeling, things, and life, but most don't have the confidence to pull it off, didn't know how to make it happen, couldn't "seal the deal," so to speak. I do know for sure that love is completely different than business. Many women don't know how to be sweet, don't know how to love and be loved, don't know how or who to allow to love them. Don't know how to inspire their men to become great men. I almost fell into this same category. I am so happy that Elisha always had the type of love I admire, needed, and respect, "that fighting love," the kind that doesn't give up or give in, especially when a man can feel that his girl loves him, too, but just needs a little help and a little push to pull herself together, then merge.

Elisha and I began playing a rhythm on Elisha Jr.'s back to get him to burp. Our hand song made us both sleepy-smile. Another thought came to me while holding our son. *How could any mother not be in complete love with her children, the way I am?* Then inside of one second, my 93 percent peace and true happiness shattered into pieces as I thought of my momma. Why didn't she love me? Why didn't, couldn't she love me enough? I knew now that drugs were mind-changing substances. Thinking about it further, I realized that more than altering a persons mind, drugs had the power to change and erase a person's heart.

"Is Siri around?" Elisha asked me.

"She sure is," I told him honestly.

"Tell her to get under these sheets. I wanna touch her," Elisha played.

"Turn around, she's already in. She's lying on the other side of you. But why touch her while you have me here?" I asked him. Then I put Elisha Jr. in the rocker next to our bed.

"Siri is more freaky!" he said.

"Siri, is that true?" I asked her.

"I just do whatever I feel, Porsche. You said I could spend some time with Elisha. But lately you've been hiding from me and keeping Elisha all to yourself. Only you have been having it all." I was facing both Elisha and Siri. Then she placed her pretty hand on Elisha's strong arm from behind him.

"She's saying that I'm greedy, Elisha," I said. He laughed.

"You are," he said, placing his fingers a little ways inside me. "I feel it pounding still," he said, as his smile lit up the night.

"What does Siri do to you that makes you ask for her when I'm loving you?" I asked.

"She sucks me here." He moved my fingers to his chest. "She sucks me here." He moved my fingers to his thickness. It was rock hard, again. "And she sucks my toes!" he said.

"Get out of here!" I said, cracking up. "She does not!" I told him.

"I do," Siri said softly. "And I like it a lot. And Elisha likes it too much."

"She says she does!" I told Elisha. But there was no way I believed it.

"I told you. She's sweeter than you. I know you two are best friends, but you should compete with her a little, since you are here most of the time and she only comes around every now and then." Of course I knew Elisha had a deep and special feeling for Siri. I understand, because I have a deep and special feeling for Siri, too. She's soft and warm, pretty, calm, and wild at the same time. She is a comfort and she always allowed Elisha whatever pleasures he could imagine. Sometimes those two went further than Elisha and I would go. Like, the photos she allowed Elisha to click of her naked and oiled body, sitting on the sound board in his studio, wearing nothing but Elisha's expensive, colorful guitar strap. He shot the photo from behind her. Her beautiful back, small waist and seductive spine pointing a path to her pretty butt cheeks. Her legs were cocked open. And in the other shots, she was naked and in pretty poses, which suggested she was making love to Elisha's guitar. I had told Siri she could sing for my man, the rest of the things that she did in his studio, those two got into all on their own.

But I, Porsche L. Santiaga, am the dancer, the movement specialist. I don't suck toes, but I do amazing things with my body, which keeps my husband constantly craving me. I was already stroking him. Soon as I began, he stopped talking.

"I hope Siri does all that sucking after a hot shower," I whispered.

"*Uh huh . . . ,*" he said quietly. "So let's get in the shower, the three of us." We did.

* * *

Nervous, my fingers were twitching slightly. Only Siri could see me shaking as we sat side by side on my divan facing the mirror. Elisha and I had separate bathrooms that were more like exclusive salons, and separate dressings rooms as well.

Moments after our erotic encounter in his shower that shot water from overhead, mid-waist, and up from the floor, I was seated in my pretty camisole and panties. It's funny in a sad way. When I am next to Elisha, I am so good. When he is not right next to me, I am not as good, but not bad either. When I tried to explain my feelings of love for him to him, all I could say is, "You are everything." He asked me if

I got that from an old song by the Stylistics. I told him I didn't. These were just the best words to describe my true feeling.

His mom wanted me to "know God," but so far I only knew Elisha. She asked me if I had something I was grateful for. I told her I'm grateful for Elisha. If I close my eyes, I see him. When he's not there, I imagine him. When I'm with him, I'm so open and joyful that I could easily explode. When I feel myself getting or going down no matter where he is, he catches me. He never allows me to sink too low. He never goes too far from me or leaves me behind. He protects me, not just my body, but my feelings and my thoughts. He gave me the best things ever, his heart and our son. He also gave me back my twins by marrying me and building us a home that was so well constructed, safe, and credible that it made me "good enough" for Midnight to allow Mercedes and Lexus to come spend some weeks with us. With Elisha I feel powerful; without him I feel vulnerable. Alone, I could earn, fight and survive. With Elisha, I could live, love, and have peace. He had tended to my heart and filled up the five holes, which no one else in the world was able to do. I wasn't sure if this was one one of the things I needed to fix, but I was sure that I didn't want to fix this feeling.

"Do you know the meaning of Elisha's name?" Momma Elon had once asked me. "Elisha, in Hebrew means, 'God is salvation.' Azaziah means 'strength.' Sheba means 'oath.' My name means 'oak tree,' and my husband Jamin's name means 'right hand.'" I was remembering her words. "We have these names for a reason," she said, trying to ease and pull me up to her standard.

"What about going to school? You're so young and you need a quality education," Momma Elon had asked.

"Everyone going to school is trying to study so that they can get the things that I already have," I told her softly and respectfully and sincerely.

"What about a job? It would give you the feeling of accomplishment and success," Momma Elon pushed.

"I couldn't accept a salary job at this point, Momma Elon. I can still earn in entertainment in one night, what it takes so many workers and even executives a year of full-time work to earn," I said. She made a thoughtful face, like she wanted to fight the point but knew what I was saying was true.

"That's the way it is, Momma Elon, and I didn't set it up to work that way." You must understand me, right? I said it, and I meant it. Being Elisha's wife and Elisha Jr.'s mother is what I have and what I wanted most. It's what Elisha Sr. wanted also.

I understood what Momma Elon was getting at, that when you have a talented mind or body, you should want to keep it alert and active, by working on things and getting things done, so you could feel good about yourself. The truth was, I had more than enough to think about and do. As Mr. Sharp taught me, I was making my money work for me. Sharp and I stayed "father-daughter close." Through him I was still flipping and investing the money I had earned before marriage. It's just that now I do it for sport. Before, I did for survival, and mostly I did it for my momma.

There were also my special things, like my new organic garden. I had to work hard to keep it nice, especially when the seasons changed. It made me feel so good when I cooked meals for our whole family with vegetables, fruits, and herbs that I planted, watered, and grew.

* * *

My thoughts were tangled about whether or not I should wear my seven diamond bangles. These were sparkling jewels, the cleanest, clearest gems I had ever seen. Elisha had purchased them in Dubai on our honeymoon. He pushed and placed each one of them on my right wrist. They were so pretty it was impossible for them not to raise jealousy in the bosom of any girl—the ones with jewels, the same way as the ones without.

I didn't want to raise jealousy in the heart of my big sister, Winter, I thought to myself. But I did want her to fully look at me and see me in the right way. I wanted her to feel that I had done well in life even though I was the forgotten, invisible middle sister. I wanted her to see me and really believe in her heart that I was good enough, even by her incredibly high standards that she measured fashion, friendship, popularity, and beauty when she was young and free. I wanted her to look at me with her sixteen-years-young eyes, not the older incarcer-

ated ones. I wanted her to choose me, to begin to write me some letters from prison, and anticipate my replies. I wanted her to think that
I was cool and to yearn to chill with me the same way I always wanted
to be holding her hand and following her around, believing that she
was a queen above all other girls when I was eight. Back then when
I was deep asleep, I even dreamt of chilling with Winter, without her
trying to get away from me.

"Put 'em on," Elisha said, stepping up behind me. "Dress up for
me," he urged. As I saw the reflection of his smile spreading, my mind
switched towards pleasing him.

In a mean tailored black-wool Burberry dress and black tights,
rocking my seven diamond bangles and matching diamond earrings,
I slipped into my black Burberry three-quarter-length leather with
the fur lining to repel the freeze. I picked up my black Epi Leather
wallet, dropped it into my black Epi Leather bag, and stood staring
for a minute, choosing between my black Manolo Blahniks or my
Fendi riding boots. I chose the heels for Elisha. I took the boots along
so I wouldn't bust my ass if snow began to fall. I pumped my Paloma
Picasso perfume twice and walked out into the corridor, down the
marble stairs, and into the foyer.

In the foyer, I pressed the intercom button and said, "Morning,
Momma Elon. Elisha is coming across with Elisha Jr. I pumped
enough breast milk and everything else you'll need is in the baby
bag."

"Ivory, breathe and don't worry, not even a little bit," she said in
her 4 a.m. sleepy voice.

"I'll try," I said. "We'll see you tonight." I signed off.

She knew Ivory was not my real name. She was the type who
holds on tight to an idea, things, and even more so to the people she
loves, really tight. So, since I first introduced myself to her as Ivory,
she held on to it. I didn't mind. Elisha's mom had so many good
things about her, it was easy to overlook our small differences and
disagreements. She was patient with me, very patient. In all things
personal she was sweet, sensitive, and supportive. It was only in con-
ducting business that she was cold. In business mode she was cold and
calm and composed even as she attacked. She was never a prosecutor
in her real life, but give her some friction and she could flip into one

like you never seen or heard. When it came to money, *she was mean,* a smart and swift shark. I wasn't mad at her for that. She kept the money train moving and oversaw Elisha's biggest deals and dealings. She combed through his contracts with a fine-toothed comb, marking pages up with her red pen and deleting whole clauses that she said didn't belong. She became known for putting together unprecedented deals, with perk packages so sweet they were worth almost as much as the check they had to cut just to be in business with the Immanuels.

Elon Immanuel, Esquire got Elisha endorsements as though he was a top-rated professional athlete. But, he wasn't an athlete. He was the super young, super charming, super smart, nineteen-year-old movie director.

Looking at the umbrella choices, rain hats, and accessories, I wondered if I should wear my black leather Gucci gloves. I held my hands up, checking out my manicure, each fingernail half black, half white and precisely drawn without error. "Too pretty to cover up," Siri said softly. I pulled down the Gucci gloves and dropped them into my bag just in case.

Elisha was some minutes late. I knew he was saying a prayer, which he had said was completely new for him. Momma Elon was incredibly grateful that her son prayed now. She thought it was because of me. It wasn't. I believed it was because during our three-week honeymoon in Dubai, he saw so many powerful, monied men bend their knees in prayer that he felt moved.

"Over here, the good guys and the bad guys, the poor and the rich all bow down." Elisha had observed with his careful director's eyes and it moved him. He told me that before our trip, he looked at temple as a place for women, and the bending of knees and lowering of the head as a sign of weakness in men. When we reached home safely, Poppa Jamin, Azaziah, and Elisha all surprised us by praying together one night. We women left them uninterrupted. I took it like I took anything with Elisha. He was full of surprises and unembarrassed about his love, when he loved, whether it was his God or wife or his family, who he confidently brought along with us on our honeymoon. The night of the Immanuel men's first prayer together became the start of their nightly prayers together.

I turned to look back at our beautiful home; two of our Brooklyn brownstones were connected by a bridge that Elisha designed. In our spacious backyard, which stretched over three lots, was a tree house, not something thrown together, but a badass tree house imbedded way up in the trees. It was like a private place for me, and only those who I invited. Yet I never invited anyone accept Riot and Elisha.

"I was so jealous of that fucking Indian in the tree house," Elisha had once said to me. I wanted to correct him and say, "Not Indian, 'Native,' " but I knew better.

"Why? He wasn't my man," I softly told Elisha.

"I don't care. Just the fact that he knew you, took care of you when you fell, and *you danced* for him made me crazy. He told you to grow up and come back to him and you did."

"I didn't!" I said, truthfully. "By the time I was fourteen, he was married. I didn't go back for him or because of him anyway. *You know that.* I wasn't never in love with him. I was in love with his drum and the beat."

"When you feel like running, run into our backyard. There's plenty of room. You want to live in the trees, live in your tree house that Elisha built for you!" He smiled, but he was still fuming like it all happened yesterday! "When you wanna dance, dance in your studio. The one Elisha built for you. Move your hips for me, only for me, please." I felt him so sincere. As I had promised, I wanted to do whatever he wanted and to go wherever he went, so I moved these hips only for him and for myself when I'm alone. Maybe one day I would direct a dance studio for young beautiful angry girls like I used to be. A dance academy at juvy would probably change everything and everybody for the better, I imagined, even the warden, although I knew that there is nothing like living free alongside your family.

Poppa Jamin, Elisha's father, never said too much. I could see in his eyes that he understood why his son was "enthralled with his enchanting young wife." That's what Sheba called me, *enchanting.* Momma Elon thought I was "peculiar," a daughter-in-law who was "strangely emotional." A daughter-in-law whose moods "swing like a pendulum." A daughter-in-law "who daydreams for hours and retreats into silence at times and cries and climbs and hides in a tall tree, where the birds live." Despite her careful and continuous critique, Momma Elon and I had made our peace. Now we lived comfortably in the day-to-day details of being the two women who loved Elisha the most; the two women who Elisha kept at his side by choice. What sealed our bond, really sealed it, was one of my rare panic attacks that occurred during our post-honeymoon travels. We were on a seriously tight schedule. All of us had accompanied Elisha on a college tour, which wrapped up at Harvard in Massachusetts. After Harvard, we were scheduled to fly into Los Angeles, California, for a round of business talks with some executives that Momma Elon described as "Hollywood's top brass."

I had been feeling sick for the past few days of the tour. Momma Elon wanted me to see a doctor. Each day, I refused. She said she was pretty certain that I was pregnant. I agreed with her, but still refused. She said I was being "ridiculous," and that if I "were in fact pregnant," I would have to see a doctor quite often. "Is there a physician who you are more comfortable with?" she questioned and pressed. "None," I replied, as I sat feeling red and placing the word "ridiculous" onto a list of words that I hate and feel offended by. We both went to bed angry at one another. Before sunrise, I was sicker than I had been all week. I told Elisha I couldn't fly for seven hours to California feeling the way I felt. When Elisha told his mom he was canceling our flights, she was so frustrated. The volume of her stern voice was propelled by the bedside speakerphone, "Of course she feels sick! She's with child! Let her drink a ginger ale from the minibar. The feeling will pass. This is important business and Elisha you know what that means. Our itinerary is tight. If we push back one thing it will delay and change everything else. And, there's the serious matter of your going back to school. You've already missed too many days."

"She's my wife and I love her," I heard Elisha say. "We fly together or not at all," he added. Then there was silence between them, mother and son. The plane we were all scheduled to take from Boston's Logan International Airport to Los Angeles, California, crashed into the World Trade Center and exploded that same morning. Me, Elisha, Poppa Jamin, and Momma Elon all watched the flat screen in the living room of his parent's executive suite, in complete shock and horror. It was my first time seeing Momma Elon's tears as she watched those who she was sure were some of her coworkers, being driven out in all directions by heated clouds of fire and smoke, many faces and bodies covered in ash. All business came to a standstill, as lives became more important than money for the whole country, for once.

After the Immanuels had returned to Brooklyn safely, and a few weeks after Elisha had donated money to the firefighters who graciously strived to contain the uncontainable, Momma Elon said to me, "That must be the reason why I saw your wings the first day I saw you in the organic market. There are not even words in the English language that I can use to express how grateful I am that you felt too uneasy to fly and that Elisha felt too uneasy to fly without you."

Eight and a half months later, Elisha Jr. was born without doctors, and against Momma Elon's "better medical judgment." But she yielded to her "enchanting daughter-in-law," because of the "precarious circumstances." Instead, Elisha Jr. was born at home, without the epidural drugs. There was only Oshadagea Oronyatekha, aka Nana-Anna, the only "healer" I would allow, and her two accompanying midwives. I didn't let them poke our son up with needles, unknown innoculations, diseases, or any strangeness. I knew too well how it feels to be too small to protest against being drugged. When I was young, because I was young no one would listen to me, or hear me when I said I don't want medicine or doctors. Still, our son was so healthy and happy, a peaceful baby boy who became the Immanuel family's "love charm." Everyone was so taken with our son that even Elisha's grandparents moved into our estate. Sheba and her man decided to marry. Her man was so drawn to our baby that Sheba finally saw the light. She then realized that she didn't need another degree to have a baby and begin her family. Privately, I had mentioned to her during one of our polite but brutally honest exchanges, that if she wouldn't give her good man what he wanted, the next woman would! After all, Sheba is my sister now. Why shouldn't I share with her some of the true things I learned, thankfully, right before it was almost too late.

Our son made Azaziah catch feelings and become more serious. He admired his younger brother even more once he became a husband and then a father. Instead of juggling and playing with a bunch of willing silly girls, Azaziah began to narrow down his group of women, in search of a true love and a woman he could respect and be comfortable enough to marry. As a family we were all super close, but never overcrowded. In our spacious surroundings, we could all stay together and still enjoy one another.

All of the alarms were shut off and then reset as we rode in reverse out of the long driveway and up to the iron gate. The remote caused it to open. I looked back at the gold plaque that was embossed with our family name IMMANUEL. We were leaving in Elisha's hunter-green Range Rover, the house where we all lived, loved, and worked together. Although we traveled often, this was my favorite place to be.

* * *

"Winter," I said as I walked in and saw her. I hesitated, unsure if we were allowed to embrace. I glanced around. Other than the fact that there were at least twenty sets of eyes staring at me instead of their loved ones who they came to visit, I counted ten guards, twenty tables where each inmate sat with a maximum of three visitors. Elisha had stayed back at the guest registration building. I wanted to come in alone because Winter and I are separated sisters with so many un-spoken words and unexpressed feelings and probably even secrets between us. I thought bringing my husband would change something about the honesty between me and her. Winter and I are so separated, in fact, that we have now spent more time apart than we ever had liv-ing together back on our Bedford-Stuyvesant, Brooklyn, block and in our Long Island mansion. I knew we would even remain separated for six more years if Winter was required to serve out her full fifteen year sentence.

I saw someone else in here touching an inmate. So before sitting, I went and embraced my sister, my arms collapsing around her. Her body felt a bit stiff and restrained and had no particular scent, causing me to recall that "captured feeling" that makes a prisoner's muscles tighten so tensely that even peeing was hard work. Finally I released her, pulled back, and walked quietly to my chair on the opposite side of her visitation table.

Not looking me in my eyes, she stared at my manicure and said, "I heard you brought Elisha Immanuel up here with you." I didn't answer back because I was thrown off a bit, never thought that these would be the first words that we would exchange after over a nine-year stretch of being apart from one another, minus Momma's sorrowful burial.

"My husband . . . ," I said softly.

"Yeah, him," Winter said stern and swiftly, as though she were quick and I was slow.

"Who hurt you?" I asked, regarding the thin scar that ran down the side of my pretty sister's pretty face.

"It's nothing," she said. But I knew it was something. I could see that it was an old scar that she had come to accept without choice. I also knew that Riot knew an overseas surgeon who could lift that scar right off like it was never there in the first place. I told myself when my sister gets out, if she doesn't mind doctors like I do, I'll have it removed so she could feel good enough to look each person in their eyes when they were speaking to her, especially the ones she knew loved her most, her family.

"A couple of pictures with Elisha Immanuel would go over big in here," she said. "I mean business-wise," she added in a way as though she wanted to say she wasn't a fan. She was just a businesswoman grabbing an opportunity and exploiting a celebrity.

"I put money on your books before I walked over here. You can live easy with that for at least a year or two. Get whatever you need, whatever you want," I said. She didn't respond. She didn't have to say *thank you* to me. That's not why I came up here and not why I gave it to her. I gave it because I understood what it is like to be in her position. I love her and wanted to help before she thought there was no good in the world, which is easy to think when you're locked down in and up.

"Have you visited Poppa?" She broke the silence between us.

"Not yet, but I will," I said. I didn't tell her that Elisha had been to see Poppa a few times and had stacked money on his books without being noisy about it. I also didn't mention that Elisha was thinking about directing a film about our father, the infamous Ricky Santiaga. Elisha thought the true story of a real Brooklyn hustler could best be told realistically by someone on the inside:

"A Ricky Santiaga joint could be bigger than all the flicks from that genre. Maybe we flip it around and tell it from the perspective of the hustler's daughter," Elisha suggested. "It wouldn't be all about guns, drugs, and betrayals, although that would definitely be a small part of it. It would be about a father, a brotherhood, and a network of families who set up, built, and ran an economy in a Brooklyn hood that nobody in power gave a fuck about," Elisha had once explained to me.

"But look how it ended," I had said to Elisha, thinking and speaking as the "hustler's daughter," or at least as one of them.

He and I had often talked in detail about stories, true and made-up ones. Together we read screenplays, wrote our own screenplay, and even watched films lying on our backs in our family film room. When we disagreed too much, it would end with a popcorn fight. We'd have fun making up while plucking kernels out of the plush carpet. Elisha, like his mom, would never give up on convincing someone, especially me, about his point.

"That's why I'll juxtapose Ricky Santiaga to another Brooklyn man. The two stories would give the audience some options before they draw any conclusions," he pushed.

"Juxtapose!" I repeated. "Now you talking slick, Elisha," I complained.

"*Juxtapose*, it means to place two things, two stories, two people side by side, to compare," he explained and defined.

"Oh," I said softly. I was thinking. In the back of my mind, I was admiring this married high school graduate who got accepted to Harvard, Howard, Stanford, Columbia, and NYU universities. I was told you had to be brilliant to do all that. All I knew was they accepted him. He rejected them, at least by delaying his decision for a year and privately letting me know that it was all up to me, and that they needed him more than he needed them at the moment. Each of the colleges were in talks to get him to donate a wing, building, or fund, especially the schools that his family members had attended and previously graduated.

"So what did you come up here for?" Winter interrupted my thoughts. "It's been nine years. You're my first visitor, besides some nosy-ass reporter, but she definitely doesn't count."

"I came to see you," I said.

"For what?" she pushed. I didn't know what kind of answer she was searching for. All I could give her was my true feelings.

"So you could see me, too. We're family. It's not alright for me to have while you . . . I'm saying, we don't have Momma anymore. You're our big sister, so it's like you're the momma now."

"I'm not nobody's momma," she said straight-faced, giving me a cold feeling.

"I am, I have a son," I said softly. "Should I show you his photo?" I asked.

"Later, show me before you go," she said. "And you should have been put money on Poppa's books," she added.

"Elisha did. He even visits Poppa," I revealed.

"That's what I'm talking about," she said a little excited.

"Poppa must've told you. I know he writes you a lot of letters," I added.

"He might have mentioned it," she said casually, as though it was a small fact that could easily have been forgotten.

"You know we have a brother?" I said suddenly.

"No we don't," Winter said confidently.

"Yes, we do," I said softly in almost a whisper. I wanted to talk about it, not challenge her.

"Our family is only the ones who grew up on the same block, same building, in the same apartment and lived in the same house together," Winter said.

Now I was quiet again. I knew what Winter didn't know, that Ricky Santiaga Jr. has the same handsome face of our father, same hair, same eyes, and even the same jawline. The morning after Momma's burial, Midnight had taken me to get my Social Security card and New York State identification, and to handle all of the paperwork that gave me back my true identity. He had even given me a copy of my release papers issued from the Kennedy-Claus nuthouse where the authorities lied and claimed I served out my time. After spending the whole day together, and even enjoying a dinner, he took me to meet a lady who looked like a lady our father would be attracted to. Her name was Dulce Tristemente, and Ricky Santiaga Jr. was her son and the son of our father. It was one of those things that didn't need to be questioned, denied, or tested. Blood recognizes blood. Would Winter be angry that I had feelings for the handsome young brother who handled himself like he was twelve instead of eight years old?

Was it wrong for me to give him my phone number and invite him to remain in touch if he didn't mind? Was it okay that I took his photo and even carried it in my wallet?

"His mother is a real bitch," Winter said, getting red. "She was supposed to hand over some money that Poppa had set aside for me. She fronted. She's first on my payback list."

Just then, Winter looked like Momma to me. My mind juxtaposed the two of them, Momma and Winter. The memory brought tears to my eyes.

"What you crying for? This is not a crying place. In here if you gotta do that, you gotta do it in the dark where nobody can see." She was serious.

"Okay, maybe the bitch is not first on my payback list, but she's definitely on it," Winter said. "There's a few snitches and a few bitches that gotta get tagged back. I'm waiting for the day the real motherfuckers get released from all these upstate cells and put a spark to the phony motherfuckers that stepped into our spots when we got knocked and did a fucking horrible bootleg job of pretending to be us."

"You don't need a list. I'll be here on your release day. You'll have me and everything you need," I promised her softly and sincerely. A smile spread across Winter's face. Her smile caused me to smile some. I was relieved that finally I had said something right that moved my sister to feel good and to feel connected to me, her full blood relation.

"I had a dream that Midnight was waiting for me early morning on my release day. He pushed a blacked-out black Bentley, had it parked sideways in front of the prisoner release door. He was looking so rich and strong the C.O. got tight that I had something to go home to. I was hyped cause I knew he would run back and tell everyone how I'm living now. In the dream, when I got in his ride, all of the girls up here, I could hear them screaming and cheering for me through those thin little wired windows. Midnight took me straight to Fifth Avenue, bought me everything I chose. That dream was crazy!" She smiled some more. Her face was still lovely, caramel-kissed, and slim. Her chin dimpled.

My heart sank some. I guess my offer to pick her up and take care of her for the rest of our lives wasn't popping enough. I don't push a Bentley. Elisha doesn't either. Momma Elon does.

"Have you seen him lately?" Winter asked, snapping me back to reality.

"Seen who?" I stalled, but I knew.

"Midnight!" she said, excited.

There were about one hundred true things that I could've said about him and a few other topics, but I didn't want to. I wanted Winter to keep her dreams and her fantasies. I never wanted for my sister to be discovered hanging from a ceiling, her sheets twisted and wrapped around her neck. I didn't want her depressed, dead, and dangling until some authority cut her down, erased her from the count, then threw her body in a pine box in an unmarked grave in an anonymous graveyard. I didn't want it to happen, and I never wanted to receive that call.

So there would be a whole bunch of true things that I wouldn't lie about, but I also wouldn't say. I would never tell Winter that Midnight is not thinking about her at all, and wouldn't've considered her even if she were not locked up. I wouldn't tell her that even if she flashed through Midnight's mind like lightning, she would be just as swiftly forgotten. I couldn't tell her that Midnight is rich, international, so fucking handsome and cool and that with the passing of time he only gets better. I wouldn't tell her that Elisha went cruising on Midnight's yacht. I definitely wouldn't tell her that Midnight has a badass battalion of wives, each of them so beautiful, smart, talented, and sweet that they would make any girl or woman who was just as pretty looking as them, and not normally "the jealous type," feel green and a little insecure, causing her to step up her game, seriously.

In fact, when I asked Elisha if he felt jealous that Midnight had three wives, he said, "I have three wives, too—Porsche, Ivory, and Siri." Then he pointed out the three diamond rings on my finger and my wedding band. "That's eleven karats total, your favorite number," he said. Then I loved him even more.

Maybe Winter would see me as a traitor for falling in love with one of Midnight's wives as she galloped at top speed on an Arabian horse across the desert like a beautiful mirage. She rode more better than any Native I had come to know and love. She let me ride freely. As I mounted the horse, I imagined I'd race her. Then she mounted her horse after making sure I was fine on mine. Then she left me in her wind and dust.

Uh un, I wouldn't tell Winter none of that.

"What about that wife he showed up with at the graveyard?" Winter asked. I felt a ways about her speaking so easily and casually about Momma's burial day as though anybody else mattered or could be the focus of that sad morning. "Did they break up yet?" she poked. "Wait till I get back. I'm gonna grab her spot. That's my spot anyway," Winter said. I laughed nervously. I could see that for Winter, time was standing still. She was frozen and everyone living on the outside was moving forward and had passed her as they lived into their future.

"Hey, what about Buster? At the graveyard that's who you said was your man. I know he hustles, right? He copped you that big body Benz. When did you meet Elisha? Did you choose him cause he had more money? What did Buster do when you dumped his ass? Did he threaten to murder Elisha? Did Buster get at him? Did they fight?" she asked, leaning forward with great interest to my response.

"Buster?" I repeated unknowingly. Then I was racing back through my mind and through doors that I had slammed closed and locked shut, I thought, forever. Placing myself back in the graveyard where Momma was, my heart cracking, my body aching, I remembered. Busta Rhymes was rhyming when I pulled up into the graveyard. His voice was jumping out of my Bose speakers. That was why I called his name when my big sister asked me about my one hundred fifty thousand dollar Benz. Winter didn't know how close I was to having a complete nervous breakdown on the day of Momma's burial. That, plus my anger at her and Poppa. I could've said or done anything on that day at the graveyard. I wasn't even fearing the armed officers who took aim at me when I pulled up. Somewhere in my mind, I had let go enough not to care if they killed me and tossed me in the box with Momma. Somewhere, and somehow, I hoped maybe they would.

"It was always only Elisha," was all I said. "My son's name is Elisha Jr.," I murmured, and really I was speaking to myself now. I was missing my baby and the warm feelings that he gave me. My breasts were swollen, hard and brimming with breast milk. I imagined

Elisha Jr. crying out for me. He's a peaceful baby to the whole family, a kind of living love charm. But at night he's only peaceful if he sees me. If I am not holding him, him staring into my eyes, lips locked around my nipple, one hand squeezing the other nipple, drawing breast milk like his life depended on it, he would go off. He would be crying a wordless screaming song, that I knew meant, "I want my momma. Where is my momma?" I understood. For fourteen years, I felt the same exact way about my momma, and sang the same exact song, differently. Elisha Sr. needed me. Elisha Jr. needed me. I needed them just as much, but probably way more. Because of them, I could feel a deeper love inside.

"I heard you had a fight on the block in Bed-Stuy, nearly blinded a bitch," Winter said.

"Our cousin," I said.

"I know she deserved it. I watched how her family flip-flopped on Santiaga the second he got locked."

"That fight was six years ago," I said, still used to counting up everything. "Who told you about it?" I asked.

"Porsche, the whole hood is up in here. Minus the niggas, of course! They serve their time elsewhere. Even my girl Natalie is in here. I know you remember her!"

"Yeah."

"There's nothing that goes on in the Bed-Stuy hood that we don't hear about, nothing," Winter said proudly.

"Oh," I said. I couldn't muster up the feeling to care or see the value of keeping up with the aftermath of Poppa's empire and reign over Bed-Stuy. Back then, Winter and I both saw, loved, and enjoyed the beauty, the families, the money, the cars, clothes, and jewels. But unlike Winter, I had made it back onto the Bed-Stuy blocks, and up into the crack buildings and houses. I saw the ugly. I saw it clearly.

"Winter, is there anything that you want that you can't get that I could give you?" I asked.

"Not really." She reacted too fast to have considered it. Just then a teenaged girl walked up to our table. The guard signaled her to return to her visit table. Winter signaled the guard as though their roles were reversed. "I got her. That's only two at my spot," she called out.

"You're Porsche Immanuel, right?" The thirteen or fourteen years young girl asked. I knew she already knew. Everybody knew. When Elisha married me, it made headlines even in places where neither of us had ever stepped foot. Two weeks after our City Hall vows, *Vibe* magazine placed Elisha on the cover with bold print running over his chest. "Young, Independent, Rich, and Married," the headline read. When the more than a million readers flipped those pages, in every flick of Elisha I was there, his hand holding my hand so tightly, or me partially hidden behind his back, hugging him, or his arm around my shoulders or neck, or me looking sweet on him not knowing that I was being photographed and in an outdoor moment that I instinctively and stupidly thought was private. Then there was also the photo spread of him in the *Rolling Stone* magazine.

"Yes," I answered her.

"Can I get an autograph? And can we take a photo together?"

"Not right now. I'm visiting my sister. I never get to see her," I said, not wanting to hurt her feelings. Her young feelings were hurt anyway. I'm always uncomfortable about giving my autograph. Even as a dancer, onstage I wanted to amaze people with my movements. After the show, I wanted to be left alone and I made that happen. I'd stay tucked away in the privacy of my guarded dressing room. Now I was completely uncomfortable signing an autograph in front of my big sister. As she walked back to her table, her whole family was looking my way like I was the villain. I felt disgusted inside. Why were strangers always showing more interest in me than my own blood relations showed me?

"Do you miss me, Winter? Did you ever miss me?" I asked her. "Do you miss Momma? You must miss Momma! How come you haven't asked about the twins? Did you know they're so smart and pretty, look just like you, and can speak a bunch of different languages?" I shot the questions out of a dangerous mixture, love, passion, anger, and disgust, and maybe even a pinch of hate.

"What's the sense in asking about them? Whether they doing good or bad, right now I can't do shit about it. I asked you about Midnight. You don't seem to want to give up any info. Do you want me to beg you? You know that's not my style," she said calmly but I could feel the razors in it. I stood up.

"I'll get Midnight to pick you up on your release day. That's something I can do for you," I said. I was in the beginning stages of getting full-blown red.

"It's good you're leaving, cause I was getting bored anyway," Winter said.

"I was going to the ladies' room, not leaving," I said truthfully. But did I need to admit that I need to squeeze milk out of my breast to feel comfortable enough to stay here longer?

"Well, you might as well keep on going from there. Now I see why these visits are fucking ridiculous anyway."

"Ridiculous," I repeated. My body began trembling beneath my Burberry.

Winter obviously didn't know what it took for me to come up here, facing my fears and reentering a prison place, being searched, patted up and down, even my fingertips being drug-tested to see if I had handled any drugs in the past twenty-four hours. She must've not known how many hours Elisha drove to get here, us leaving our house at 4:30 in the morning. She couldn't have known how hard it was for both of Elisha Jr.'s parents to leave our newborn at the same time. She must not have known how I protected Elisha Jr. from coming into a prison space where even babies are searched, Pampers opened, and infant clothes lifted and shuffled around. She don't know how shaken I was leaving my husband in the prison visitation registration receiving building surrounded by C.O.s who admired him and left their posts to gather around him to get autographs or to hand him demos or to discuss screenplays or book manuscripts they were thinking about or working on.

"You're right. She doesn't know," Siri said. "How could she know? And, Porsche, why do you always get upset at someone who doesn't know any better?"

* * *

I felt like dancing. Not in my pretty dance studio that Elisha had built on our family property. I felt like dancing naked inside of a small closet with no windows and very little air until I collapsed. Instead I came out of my coat and then my heels. I rolled down my tights. Standing barefooted outdoors on the cold cement, I hiked up my Burberry dress and stepped into Elisha's Rover. I laid my coat, tights, and Blahniks on his backseat, then turned and placed my feet up on the dash, my toes pressed against the passenger window. He just watched me.

I loved that he didn't ask me one question about the visit, and for a whole hour we rode in silence, first narrated by the sounds of Coltrane's "In a Sentimental Mood," followed by a group of cuts from Poppa Jamin's jazz favorites handed down to his youngest son.

"Juxtaposed to who?" I asked Elisha without warning seventy minutes later. He smiled then lowered the volume on the music. "That's easy . . . ," he said. He still loved tests.

"That Midnight cat," he said. "I couldn't get him to say nothing about anything or to even speak about the whole drug-dealing era. He's the type who you gotta watch. A great movie director/writer could make millions off of a real life character like him," Elisha said, always excited about film. "Ricky Santiaga, the man who built an empire, a man who everybody knew. A name that rings bells in the hood, sounds alarms in the police precincts, and raises respect in the prison system. Ricky Santiaga juxtaposed to his right hand, the silent man who nobody knows. Somehow, the right hand ends up with an empire and an army. He does big business seemingly, minus the drugs. He even raises Santiaga's youngest daughters. In the end, he remains best of friends with Santiaga, still carries out the duties of a retired right-hand man, which suggests there was no betrayal between them. Now that's juxtaposition at its finest." Elisha schemed. I smiled at him.

"Maybe the story gets told by two sisters, juxtaposed to one another. Both daughters of the same hustler, one is speaking from her cell, the other from her clandestine treehouse, a secluded location."

"Clandestine," I repeated softly. I'd ask him about that word later. "I hope you know your man pays attention," he said. "I know," I said, smiling now.

The CD switched. Now Elisha was playing a new song that Siri recorded for him. All of her songs were only for Elisha. She would only sing them to him. But, he would bring them to the world to feel. Siri didn't mind, as long as she didn't have to show up. She sang to him because it made him feel good. It made him happy. It made him love her even more.

"Porsche, some people in the press think you married me for my money," he said. "Even some of my friends and coworkers had their doubts about you and us. None of them realized, *I married you for your money!*" he said it like it was a fact. I slapped his shoulder. I knew that was Elisha the actor speaking now. The guy who I first met when he was twelve. The actor was still a part of him even though he prefers directing so I just listened to him as he began setting up the scene. He was about to rescue me and I loved that.

"Seriously, you fucking inspire me like crazy, like how you put your pretty feet up here. Your painted toenails and pretty dancer's legs inspired me to get through the first hour of this ride home." He was flirting with me.

"I'm sure you see a lot of pretty girls everywhere you go, Elisha. And they see you, too!"

"What did you tell me when you were eleven?" he asked me. "You said none of 'em are like you, none of them are the same thing." He asked and answered the question himself.

"True, but that's not because of being pretty. That's because of what I've been through in my life in a short amount of time," I said.

"I know. Everything you went through was rough while you were going through it. But, when you look back on it, every true story, every day, month, and year of your life, and all of your feelings, is pure gold. That's why *I married you for your money*! I don't need to hire any writers or researchers. I'll never run out of stories. My first film was about you. Probably my next ten films will be about you.

I could go to dinner with a thousand women one by one. Business or no business, I'm just checking my Rolly waiting for them to finish up so I can get home to my wife." He laughed. I laughed, too. I loved the way he could cure me without any drugs, doctors, or hospitals. I fucking loved that about him.

"I know no matter what girl I see, she won't be prettier than you, can't cook as good as you do. She wouldn't love as deeply as you do, or feel as good as you feel to me. She wouldn't care for my family as sincerely or have survived and fought as hard as you did. She wouldn't have earned her own first million on her own, then walked down the Brooklyn block stealing the show in her red Converses and red ball gown. She wouldn't have ever lived on an Indian reservation, and shopped at an expensive Brooklyn organic market even on the same day she was wearing dirty skips and a dingy white tee shirt. She wouldn't have showed up weeks later, Gucci'd up and designer down to her fingernails. No girl would've been able to get me to follow her lead through Brooklyn to any strange places I never took a look at before to find strange ingredients and things I never heard of before she came along. She wouldn't have dropped twenty thousand dollars in a box and handed it to me with a homemade carrot cake like it was no big deal. Then disappear for eight months, return, and never ask about the cash. She wouldn't have crashed into me with her cart so boldly, or got me so open in an underground space, and then disappeared for two more years so I couldn't forget her and didn't want to and had to work so hard to not lose my fucking mind. And I wouldn't and couldn't have loved anyone else half as much as I love you."

My happy tears were spilling now. He was healing me. "What other woman would have a best friend like Siri, who's a little bit sweeter and softer than her? Would she let Siri sing me a song that makes my blood boil and allow me to make love to her, too? Porsche, *no one is more fun than you.*"

He wiped my tears. "Another woman could have her BA, BS, master's, or her Ph.D. and still couldn't figure out how to be a little moneymaker like my wife was even before I married her. She would have the degrees. But you're the real genius. Your life, all seventeen years of it, that you shed so many tears over, is your riches. *The Adventures of Porsche Santiaga* is worth a billion or at least one hundred thousand bricks of pure gold."

Acknowledgments

To the MAKER of all souls, I give my deepest gratitude, loyalty, appreciation, and submission.

No one else is worthy of worship.

You Can Get in Touch
with Sister Souljah:

E-mail: souljahworkshard@gmail.com

Mailing address: Sister Souljah
Souljah Story Inc.
208 East 51st Street, 2270
New York, New York 10022

Turn the page

to enjoy an excerpt

from Sister Souljah's novel

LIFE AFTER DEATH:

Winter Santiaga is back.

After a nasty breakup of any couple, the war begins. I knew bitches who keyed their ex's ride, or punctured his tires, or banged in his rims with a hammer. I knew bitches who beat the new bitch's ass who their man had replaced them with. Or even choked her, stabbed her, shot her, or mercked her. I knew even live-er bitches who, instead of killing his new bitch, killed him. I knew bitches who ran up his credit cards, crashed his car, cut up his clothes, pawned his jewels, and even burnt down his house. But when a man and woman used to be lovers, living together, working together, eating together, showering and fucking together, and one betrays the other, betrayal makes the matter more meaner than murder. 'Cause you can just kill someone if you want to, no matter who you are. No matter where they hide. They bound to resurface eventually. Let down their guard eventually, and that's precisely when they can get got. But ex-lovers, where one betrayed the other, sold him or her out, flipped on 'em, or was way-worser, like working as an undercover police, spying and telling on her or his lover, murder ain't good enough get back. A betrayed nigga or bitch wants to be the one who delivers the hurt, witnesses the pain and the torture and the downfall of the lover who is the traitor.

I know. Bullet was the main one who betrayed me. He's at the top of my payback list. He was my nigga for many months before I got arrested. Yeah, he was a hustler. I fucking loved that. His fuck game was strong. I loved that too. Once he and I first hooked up,

I never fucked around with no other nigga but him. I'm a loyal bitch. Loyalty runs through the Santiaga blood. But he never fully acknowledged my loyalty to him. He never gave his loyalty to me. It wasn't about me thinking, expecting, or believing that he was out fucking some random bitches while we was together. He didn't cause me to feel or think that he was. It was that he . . . I don't know. He loved me with his mind and body but never gave me his heart. He treated me like a suspect who was bound to turn on him or turn him in. I wasn't. I'm the one bitch that wouldn't . . . ever. Santiagas are born snitch-free.

Bullet put our Manhattan condo in my name, and he made every purchase for both of us in my name. Back then, at the time, I thought that meant he loved me. Of course I did, he provided. In turn, I covered for him. Held his coke, concealed his weapons, and carried his cash here and there quietly whenever he told me to. I was trying to earn my way up and also into his heart. I thought we should be on some Bonnie-and-Clyde shit. But fuck Bonnie and Clyde. We should have been on some Winter-and-Bullet shit, handling our business, styling while stacking our chips, eating and fucking, chilling and staying together.

Turned out he put everything in my name not for love or for providing for a top bitch and daughter of legendary hustler and entrepreneur Ricky Santiaga. Instead Bullet was on some Brooklyn scheming. He made it so that if everything or anything went wrong, he could drop all the legalities and blame onto me without losing any street credibility because it wasn't like he actually snitched on me. He simply left a paper trail and documentation all in my name that told the fictitious story of me being the hustler and him being blameless, unarrestable, and scot-free. On the day of my arrest that led to my conviction as a drug dealer sentenced to serve fifteen years on a mandatory minimum, which at the time I had never even heard of, my nigga Bullet had a car rented in my name. In the rental car was me and the product. I was 'bout to ride round trip to Virginia on a run with him, a big and necessary business move.

Simone, who for some reason can't get the fuck out of my mind or life or death story, saw me sitting there on our Brooklyn block in the rental waiting on Bullet. I didn't see her, though. Simone had bullshit beef with me that she swore was real. So soon as she saw me that day, it was on. Bitch threw a brick through the rental window. Bitch dragged me out the car swinging. We thumped. My nigga Bullet saw the rah-rah from a distance. He started rushing over. He fired one shot in the air to cause the commotion to break. Seeing him boosted my confidence, but the gunshot distracted me from keeping my eyes on her. Simone took advantage and sliced my face. Bullet held my bleeding face in his hands. He sat me back in the rental car. He tossed the gun beneath the seat. He walked around to the driver's side. I was relieved that he had rescued me.

But the furious fight and the gunshot drew out the cops. They cops swooped in, and Bullet, instead of jumping into the rental car and speeding away, walked off calmly as though he never intended to get in the car with me at all. I was arrested in the rental car that was in my name, with the weight stuffed inside teddy bears, and the weapon tossed beneath the seat. They cuffed and jailed and grilled and investigated me. They asked me for names or just one big name. I gave them nothing. I rejected their bullshit tricks and game. The name is Santiaga, royalty not snitches. I wasn't mad at Bullet for being a hustler, obviously. I wasn't mad at him for renting me the condo or even for taking me on his big business run to Virginia. I was down for him. I wanted to go. I didn't like being left out of the business or the action. It's that that nigga Bullet didn't come for me. He didn't add a dime to my legal defense. He didn't send one of his men to make sure I had all that I needed. He didn't put one cent on my commissary. He didn't write me one letter, slip me one kite from his peoples on lock. He didn't check for me, and to me, that meant he never loved me. That's why he's on my payback list. He betrayed me. I never betrayed him, not even once.

So I understand this little sixteen-year-young-looking one, oddly named Ubs, who is tight and at war with her ex. He seemed more my age than hers. But I know that once a bitch blossoms, gets curves and titties and hungry between the thighs, whether she's twelve, thirteen, or sixteen, whether or not the law says she's a minor, she is bound to hunt and chase down a man she chooses for herself. A young sexy bitch, I know, can make it impossible for even an older guy to resist her powers, no matter who he is. He could be handsome or ugly, paid or broke, married or single, hustler or preacher, politician or teacher, doctor or lawyer, or even a goddamn judge. I accept that. As long as it's not the other way around, some old guy hunting, chasing, and cornering her young ass. Fucking and raping are never ever the same thing. He says she betrayed him. He says she's the police. She seemed too young to be anybody's police. And in the I guess seconds I had seen her, she didn't seem like a cop. But I ain't from down here. I don't know how shit goes 'round here. Everything is unexpected. It's like I'm stuck in the world of the unseen and unknown and can't control or predict the action.

But now I am not alone down here. Of course I choose him. He chose me in the first place. He was the greatest sex I ever had. The wildest feeling I ever felt. He was the only man who ever caused me to let go of Midnight, who *never fucked me at all*. I like a man who *gives a bitch what she wants*. A man who *doesn't make a bitch feel lonely*. Wife number five! Oh hell no. That would never, ever be me.

My new nigga is my forever nigga, from now until the real lights-out. Even though he only fucked me once on the same night we met, I was able to exist inside of that fucking memory. And unlike Bullet, who left me because I was cut and bleeding and would obviously wear a scar, and who set me up to take the fall, or didn't set me up but reacted only to secure himself, my forever nigga is different.